WEIGHT
OF THE WORLDS

D. B. GREENHALGH

A NOVEL

WEIGHT OF THE WORLDS

BOOK 1

D. B. GREENHALGH

For Atlas and Ajax,
Whose names I borrowed so that they may
one day read of heroes like themselves.

Atlas, pre-eminent in mighty strength, who holds the vault of heaven on his back, and moans

— AESCHYLUS, *PROMETHEUS BOUND*

CHAPTER 1

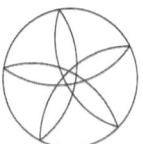

ATLAS GILGAMESH STERLING had only just turned fourteen years old when he was abducted from his bed by strangers from a strange land.

His parents, of course, became desperate with fear and worry. The instant they realized he was missing, they called the police.

Nearly a dozen police cars were soon parked along the street where Atlas and his family lived—the same street where Atlas had first learned to ride a bike, climb trees, and throw a baseball. It was a good street, a safe street, where nothing very bad had ever happened before. Therefore, the police men and women were sympathetic, helpful, and optimistic.

"He's sure to turn up any minute now," one said.

Another said, "My sons used to take naps in strange places from time to time. Once, I found the middle one napping in the bathtub. He even had his pillow and blanket with him. Have you checked the bathtub?"

"He's fourteen," said Atlas's mother. "He hasn't napped in the bathtub for years."

However, just to be sure, Atlas's parents had already checked the bathtubs, and the closets, and the treehouse in the backyard that Atlas had once filled with old computer monitors and other techno-junk in order to turn it into a space station. On clear nights, Atlas used to spend the night in the treehouse and watch the stars through a telescope given to him by his grandparents.

Atlas regularly enjoyed quiet alone time, and it wasn't uncommon to search the whole house before finding him in a secluded corner, buried in a book or his thoughts. It had been several years since anyone had found him in a closet or bathtub, though Atlas did still spend the night in the treehouse, occasionally.

"Has your son had a bad experience at school recently?" asked another policewoman.

"What do you mean?" asked Atlas's father.

"Has he been bullied? Did he do poorly on an exam? Does he have a crush? Maybe he's pining for her."

"Pining for her?" asked Atlas's mother.

"Yes, pining," said the policewoman. "One of my boys spent two days and nights outside a girl's house, watching and waiting for her to come out. He didn't eat or sleep the whole time. Turned out she was on vacation with her family."

"Turned out he was a creeper," Atlas's mother said under her breath.

"What?" said the policewoman.

"No," Atlas's father said quickly. "Our son isn't bothered by bullies. And he tells us about all his exams, good or bad."

"And if he had a crush on someone, he certainly wouldn't *stalk* the girl," said Atlas's mother.

"I didn't say he was stalking her," said the policewoman. "I said *pining*. When boys get to a certain age, they don't think clearly. They can be irresponsible and awkward when they pine." She frowned when she saw the annoyed look on Atlas's mother's face. "I'm just saying…it's something to consider."

Atlas's father put a hand on his wife's shoulder, partly to calm her down, and partly to hold her back. "We're pretty sure he's not camped outside a girl's house," he said.

"Well, I'm sure he'll turn up soon, then." The policewoman smiled weakly and returned to her colleagues who had begun organizing the neighbors into small groups tasked with searching the surrounding streets and woods.

Atlas's father wrapped his arms around his wife and squeezed her shoulders. She shook her head and wiped a tear away. Atlas's father clenched his jaw. *They don't understand Atlas*, he thought. *They don't understand he's not like most kids. It was kind of those police men and women to offer some hope, I guess. And I can't blame them for suggesting where Atlas might be. They're doing their best.*

The detective who took their statement, however, was not so encouraging.

He arrived later than the others, in an unmarked car. After speaking briefly with a few officers whose search parties hadn't yielded any clues, he approached Atlas's parents. He listened intently to their version of the events preceding Atlas's disappearance, but scowled and chewed on his pen when they mentioned Atlas's recent birthday. "Unfortunately, you'll most likely never see your son again," he said.

"Why the hell would you say something like that?" snapped Atlas's father. He hugged his wife again, this time to hold himself back.

"Because it's the truth," the detective said matter-of-factly. "No point in lying to you, or giving you false hope."

"I want your badge number. I'm filing a complaint," cried Atlas's mother.

"It's written on the top of the report. I'll leave a copy with you," said the detective. He circled his badge number on the report. "But, you have to understand. In cases like this one, recovering your son is impossible."

"It's not impossible!" yelled Atlas's father, getting louder. "Missing children are found all the time. Maybe not everyday, but it happens often enough."

"First name, Mr. Sterling?"

"What? Pete...uh...Peter."

"Thanks," said the detective. "Of course, children are found. And when they are, it's the best feeling for us. Makes you remember why you love being a law enforcement officer." He traced the cross of the T's in Pete's full name six times. "But, in this case, it's just been too long."

"Forty-eight hours!" Atlas's mother said. "It's forty-eight hours, isn't it? Isn't that how long you have before it's *been too long*? Our son's been missing less than three."

"And your name, Mrs. Sterling?"

"Filomena. But, I go by Mena."

"Either is fine, thanks." The detective scribbled Mena because it had fewer letters.

"And my last name is Morandi," said Mena. "M-O-R-A-N-D-I."

"Oh," said the detective. He scratched out where he had written Sterling. "And you're the boy's *biological* mother?"

"Of course I am!"

"And you're married? The two of you? To each other?"

"Yes," said Pete.

"I didn't take my husband's last name when we got married," said Mena.

"Oh. Okay," said the detective. "Takes all kinds to make a world, I guess."

"What's that supposed to mean?" Mena snarled.

"Nothing," said the detective. He coughed. "In most cases, yes. The first forty-eight hours is the most crucial recovery period." He looked up from his clipboard. "Not in this case. Not in cases like *this*."

"What makes Atlas so different?" asked Pete. He frowned, wondering if the detective was purposely being obtuse, or just lacked empathy.

"The origin of the kidnappers." The detective pronounced this O-rEE-gin. He resumed filling out his report.

"What do you mean?" Mena asked.

"And who says origin like that?" added Pete.

"I do. A lot lately." The detective scribbled in his report. "Mostly in cases like this."

"You say *cases like this* again and you'll wish you hadn't," Pete said.

The detective looked Pete up and down twice, then snorted nervously and rubbed his finger under his nose three times.

"You see, your son isn't the only young teen to have gone missing recently. In fact, he's the fifth in the month since I got involved."

"The fifth?" said Pete.

"Yep," said the detective. "And I know there have been ten more cases investigated by others in the county."

"So there's a serial kidnapper in the area? Why isn't this all over the news?" Mena asked in disbelief. Her patience had just about run out.

"At first, due to the children's age, we assumed they were runaways. It's not uncommon for young teens to run away," said the detective. "Most come back on their own after a few hours... day or two at most. Not these. Some have been missing for nearly two months. Eventually, we established they were kidnappings. However, due to the circumstances, we felt it was best to keep it out of the press."

"Don't you think we had a right to know that our children were at risk?" Pete slammed the fleshy part of his fist against the wall of the house. The stucco cracked and a small chip fell to the ground.

"We determined that releasing the information to the public would only cause a dangerous panic." The detective looked up at Pete again. "But if it makes you feel better, nothing you could have done would have stopped the kidnappers."

"How can you know that?" asked Mena. She spoke quietly now, almost in a whisper.

"It's because of the orig...um, because of where the kidnappers are from." The detective stuck his pen in the corner of his mouth and chewed on it for a second. "You see, these kidnappers aren't the type we normally see."

"I didn't realize there were *normal* types of kidnappers!" said Pete.

"These kidnappers came from very far away and they seem to be targeting specific children."

"But we're nobodies," cried Mena. "Average, middle-class nobodies. We don't have money for a ransom. Why would they target us?"

"They didn't target you. They targeted your son." The detective rattled his pen against his teeth. "And fourteen other fourteen-year-olds. All of them born on the same day, in the same hospital. That's a lot for a hospital that size. Did you realize that?"

"I mean, it seemed busy, but it's a hospital...how would we know?" asked Pete. His ears rang. They seemed as if they didn't belong to him.

"Very unusual." The detective scribbled in his report. "That's how we know they're connected."

"Why would kidnappers target children with the same birthday?" Pete stepped closer to the detective and stared down at him. "If you knew they were targeting these children, it should have been easy to figure out which others might be at risk. Why didn't you do anything about it?"

"I have done a lot, actually." The detective leaned away from Pete, but didn't cede his ground. "For your information, I'm the one who discovered they were born on the same day. And...I'm the one who figured out where the kidnappers came from."

"But you didn't warn us!" Mena said. She suddenly grabbed the detective's hand and bit him on the forearm.

The detective stumbled backwards and clutched his injured arm. "Ow! Dammit!" He probed the bite marks with his finger. "You bit me! You can't bite law enforcement."

"I'll bite you again!" said Mena.

"Or I will," said Pete, stepping in front of Mena. "I'll draw blood unless you tell us this instant everything you know about the kidnappers."

"I can't," said the detective. "It's for the public good."

Mena side-stepped Pete. She narrowed her eyes.

The detective retreated a little. "Okay. Okay! I'll tell you." He tapped his pen across the top of his clipboard. "But you have to keep it to yourself. For the safety and peace of mind of the public." He continued under his breath, "Not that anyone would believe you, anyway."

"What was that?" Pete asked.

"Nothing," said the detective.

"*Where* are the kidnappers from?" Mena menaced.

"From space."

"What?" said Pete.

"From space."

"The kidnappers are from *space*?" said Mena.

"That's what I said." The detective chewed on his pen again. "Well, not space, exactly, I guess. I suppose they'd have to be from some planet or other, not space itself, although they must have travelled *through* space to get here, so I guess it's correct enough to say that they came from space."

"Are you crazy?" Mena said.

"It's the only explanation that makes sense, given the evidence." The detective tapped his pen rapidly on his clipboard.

"What evidence?" asked Pete.

"Well, first off, there were no windows broken or doors kicked down in any of the houses where children have gone missing. In fact, there were no signs of forced entry whatsoever. The kidnappers didn't leave fingerprints or trace DNA. There have been no ransom letters, even though two of the children come from wealthy families—*extremely* wealthy families. Considering all those factors, it's pretty obvious who took the children, really."

"That's your evidence the kidnappers are from space?" Mena regretted biting the detective, worrying his peculiar stupidity might be contagious. "That's not evidence. It's a lack of evidence."

"Well, yeah...now that I think about it. Most of those sound pretty insignificant on their own, but when you consider them as a whole…" Once more, the detective resumed his report. "And you have to admit that the spaceship videos are pretty definitive."

"What? Spaceship videos?" Pete snatched the report away and scanned it for any mention of a spaceship, or anything else to prove the detective was the most inept and improperly employed public servant in the state. Pete was definitely going to file a complaint.

The detective calmly retrieved his clipboard. "The surveillance videos, of course. Security videos from two of the wealthier families' homes clearly show several non-human persons exiting a spacecraft, entering the houses, and returning to their ship with the children apparently sedated. Then the ship takes off in a flash of light. It's the same in both of the videos. Did I not mention the videos before?"

"No, you didn't!" Mena cried. *This is a bad dream,* she thought. *A terrible, horrible, very bad dream.*

"I know it's a lot to take in. But at least you understand why I said there's nothing we can do. As a species, humans can't yet travel to distant planets, and even if we could, there's no way of knowing to which planet the children have been taken. On top of that, there's also the problem of relativistic space travel."

"What?"

"Relativistic space travel. You may have heard it called *near-light speed.*" The detective stuck his pen behind his right ear, then immediately pulled it back out. "Einstein's relativity says that as an object—such as the spaceship that abducted your son—travels away from another object at speeds approaching the speed of light, time appears to slow down for the object traveling at near-light speed. It's called time dilation."

"I understand how time dilation works," Mena sneered. "I've read a book before too. And I've heard it explained better." She looked at the bite marks on the detective's arm and gritted her teeth. "Why would you even mention that? First, you tell us an absurd story about our son being kidnapped by aliens, and then you make things worse by implying that even if Atlas were to return, we'd be too old, or dead, for it to matter!"

"It's important you understand the facts," said the detective. "You need to understand that your son is gone, almost certainly for good. It's not a pleasant fact, but that's how it is. You have my condolences." He scribbled a few more notes in his report. "Now please, you must keep everything I've told you to yourself. We need to keep the rest of the population calm."

Pete squeezed Mena's shoulders again. His knees felt as if they were about to give out. "You can't expect us to keep silent on this."

"I'm afraid you must," said the detective. "Or you'll be detained indefinitely. Then you'll lose your daughter also." He gestured with his pen at the police officers returning from their searches. "None of these officers have clearance to hear what I've just told you."

"Heartless bastard!" screamed Pete. He fell to the ground and sobbed.

"You can show us these videos?" Mena said, as she helped her husband back to his feet.

"I shouldn't, but I can," said the detective, eyeing Mena cautiously. He signed his name at the bottom of the report. "At the station. Once you sign an NDA. It's for national security, you understand."

"Let's go, please," Pete said. "Now. I need to see it for myself."

"Of course you do."

"Kidnappers from space," Mena mumbled. "My baby's been taken to space."

"Please keep it down," said the detective. "There's nothing more we can do." He tore out one of the carbon pages and handed it to Pete. "Now, here's your copy of my report. It doesn't say anything about the spaceship, of course. Can't have anything on the public record about that." He chewed on his pen and grinned dutifully. "Remember, my badge number is in the top left corner."

CHAPTER 2

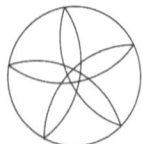

ATLAS AWOKE JUST in time to see the Earth fading into the black of space through the porthole above him. No sooner did he realize what he was looking at than it was gone. Nothing but a faint dot of bluish light remained where the Earth had been.

It hit him all at once. His stomach became a black hole, endlessly collapsing on itself. His heart evaporated and his lungs froze. "Mom," Atlas finally whispered. "Dad." A tear escaped his eye, but he quickly wiped it away. Crying wouldn't get him back home. He began to count backwards from one hundred by threes. It was something he did when things were hard.

"That is not real," a voice behind him said.

Atlas sat up and turned towards where he thought the voice had come from, but could see nothing, only darkness. "What?" Atlas said, almost inaudibly. *Don't show fear,* he thought. "What?" he repeated, but only slightly louder.

"I am sorry, but I can not understand you when you talk so quietly," said the voice. It seemed to come from a different direction.

Atlas cleared his throat. "What? Who are you? Where are you?" Atlas curled himself into a corner of the bed. He took a deep breath and summoned his courage. "Answer me."

"One question at a time, please." The voice was firm and deep, but also pleasant and friendly. "Otherwise, neither of us will know which one I am trying to answer."

Atlas couldn't decide which question was the most important, or remember in which order he asked them. "The first one."

"Let us see…the first question you asked was 'What?' Am I to take that to mean that you did not hear what I first said to you or that you did not understand what I meant by it?"

"Both," said Atlas.

"I said, 'That is not real.'"

"What's not real?"

"More questions," the voice grumbled. "You should learn to wait to ask the next question until after you have received the answer from the last one. Sometimes the answers for many questions can be found in the answer of one."

"I apologize," said Atlas.

"No need. But apology accepted nonetheless," the voice said. "Now then, as I was saying…that is not real. The image you saw in the porthole—of your planet slipping away into the blackness of space—it is just a simulation they use to trick you."

"Trick me? How—?" Atlas stopped himself before he finished.

The voice chuckled. "Good. You are a quick learner. That will be to your advantage."

Atlas heard a thump, then the shuffling and dragging of something heavy and awkward across the floor, approaching him.

"See for yourself." The voice was much closer now, but not yet upon him. "Look closer."

Atlas looked up at the porthole, but refused to move away from the corner of the bed. Short, bright lines of light whisked by the porthole at incredible speed. "Stars," he said. "We're traveling at a very high—relativistic, or near-relativistic—speed."

"That is what they want you to think." The voice laughed. "But it is not true."

Oh no, Atlas's mind raced. *The last thing I want to deal with right now is some crazy conspiracy theorist—like Uncle David.* That's what they want you to think, *is something Uncle David says all the time, and also* They got everyone else fooled, but not me. *What did Mom and Dad say to do? Discretely shake your head and try not to aggravate him any further. Sometimes Mom bites him when he won't shut up.*

"Why isn't it true?" Atlas asked. His mouth was dry.

"I am afraid interstellar travel does not work like that, despite how your Earth movies like to portray it," the voice continued. "No, no. That porthole is not real either. On the other side of that wall is another wall and then another. The detention bays of these old Theban ships have impressive security features. There is no escaping. If there was, I would have escaped long ago."

Based on the sound of the slow and heavy movements, Atlas doubted the body belonging to the voice was in any kind of physical condition to escape.

"Beyond that last wall is a bathroom, if you can believe it. The *porthole* is nothing more than a simulation designed to make you believe you are traveling away from Earth at an exceedingly fast speed."

Atlas wanted to ask a million more questions, but he kept his mouth shut.

"Good. You did not interrupt with more questions," the voice said. It hadn't gotten any closer, and the shuffling and dragging had stopped. "The idea, I believe, is to help you figure out where you are and what is happening to you. Give you a frame of reference when you wake up in the dark. It seems cruel, but it is actually a nice thought, if you want my opinion."

"I don't. Seems like an awful thing to do to a person...tricking them into thinking they've been taken away from Earth." Atlas chewed the tip of his tongue and puckered his lips together like he always did when he thought someone was being unfair.

"But you *have* been taken away from Earth," the voice said. The dragging and shuffling began again, this time moving away from Atlas.

"But you said it wasn't real."

"It is not. As I said, interstellar travel does not work like that.

You are not being taken away from Earth. You have *already* been taken."

"Already been taken?" Atlas mumbled. He slumped down until he was lying on his back on the bed, his head turned towards the wall below the porthole that wasn't a porthole.

"I could not quite hear that." The voice waited a few seconds, but Atlas didn't repeat himself. "Well then, on to your second question…who am I? That is a good question, though its answer matters very little since I am a fellow prisoner, and one with considerably worse prospects than your own, so I can be of little help to you."

"But you have helped me already." Atlas needed to keep the conversation going if he wanted to avoid feeling sorry for himself. "Just like you said, you've answered several of my questions before I could even ask them."

"Have I? Good." The voice chuckled. "Considering how many questions you have already asked, I am pleased. I am glad to help in what little way I can. Surely—and do not take this the wrong way—but I assume you have many more questions?"

"Millions. But I'll try to only ask the most important, relevant ones." Atlas turned onto his side to face the voice, even though he couldn't see anything. "What's your name?"

"I thought you were going to wait for my answers to your other questions?"

"I did. You answered them both at the same time. You're a fellow prisoner and you can't escape, so you're in a cell. Probably a separate one from mine. Who and where you are, just like I asked."

The voice chuckled again. "You are a clever one. That is good news for you, I am sure. Most of the others have not been nearly as clever. Nor were they as seemingly unafraid as you."

The others? That was a question for later. "Your name?" Atlas asked.

"Ah, yes. My name is Tachonamewharuts Orsetulidex."

"Wow. That's quite a name."

"Is it? It is quite common where I come from. One of the top five most common surnames on my home world, and my forename was number seven on the list of top names for the solar cycle in which I was born. My friends call me Taco."

Atlas let out a hoot of laughter.

"What is so funny?"

"They call you Taco?"

"Yes, it is the common nickname for Tachonamewharuts. I do not see why that should be so funny."

"I'm sorry. It's just that taco is the name of a type of food on Earth."

"Well then, it will be easy for you to remember."

"Does this mean we're friends?" Atlas asked.

"Not yet. I do not know your name yet."

"I'm Atlas. Not short for anything. No nicknames. Just Atlas." He didn't share his last name. Just common sense. Stranger danger, identity theft, and all that.

"Well, Atlas Nodzhordoraneetheen, pleased to meet you."

"Pleased to meet you, Taco." Atlas couldn't help but giggle slightly as he said his new friend's name aloud. Then, as he thought about how strange it was to have a new friend that he had never seen, Atlas remembered his friends from home, and his mom and dad, and his dogs, and his teachers, and his grandparents and cousins, and even his sister, Maggie.

"Where are we? And why have I been taken away from my family?" Atlas tried to keep his voice from betraying the tears flowing down his cheeks. "I know that's two questions, but..."

"That is alright," Taco said. "Unfortunately, I am unable to answer either of those questions."

"Unable?"

"Sorry, my new friend. I do not know. Not for sure, anyway."

"But we're not traveling anywhere?"

"No. We have arrived, some time ago, in fact. Leaving and arriving are practically the same thing, after all."

Atlas wanted Taco to explain what that meant about leaving

and arriving being the same thing, but it wasn't the most pressing question. "Where have we arrived?"

"As I said, I do not know. But if they treat you like the others, this will be your delivery. You woke sooner than most of the children. The sedative they gave you must have worn off earlier than our captors expected."

"I have a fast metabolism," Atlas said. It was true. He ate more than anyone he knew and couldn't hardly gain a pound.

"They will come for you soon. And it will be the first and last time you see your new friend, Taco."

Now or never, Atlas thought. *Better ask, then.* "Others? What others? Children? I'm hardly a child."

The lights came on all at once. Atlas squinted as he looked from cell to cell but could see no trace of Taco, or any other prisoner.

Another voice spoke, this one metallic and harsh. "Please step to the back of your cell, face the wall, and kneel with your hands behind your head. This is for your own safety."

Atlas blinked repeatedly as he looked around the brightly lit detention bay. He saw no trace of the new voice's owner. Must have been an intercom. "Taco," Atlas whispered. "Where are you? You said I was going to see you?" Atlas strained his ears for a reply, but heard nothing. He risked calling out a little louder. "Taco! Where are you?" The lights forced him to squint.

The harsh voice spoke again. "Step to the back of the cell, face the wall, and kneel with your hands behind your head! We *will* use force, if you do not comply."

Atlas did as commanded. But, as the voice had said nothing about being quiet, he decided to risk full volume. "Taco? Where are you?" Atlas closed his eyes.

"I am here," said Taco. "In my cell. I have not moved. But please do not turn around. They will get very angry if you disobey their orders."

"I won't. But I was hoping to see you," said Atlas. "To put a face to your voice, even if only for the first and last time. So I can remember you."

"Why do you need to see my face to remember me? Can you not remember my voice, or our conversation?"

"I can, but it would be easier if I could tie your face to those memories. Humans work best that way."

"You should remember me well, then. You looked right at me."

"I did?"

"Yes."

"I'm sorry, but I didn't see you. Or anyone else, but it was very bright all the sudden and I couldn't see very well." Then, a thought occurred to Atlas. He had been looking for a fully grown, humanoid creature. But why should aliens be humanoid? Atlas tried to remember everything that he had seen throughout the detention bay, just in case he had accidentally failed to recognize what his new friend might look like. "Are you a box?"

"Excuse me?"

"I saw a box in the middle of the cell near mine. Are you a box? Was that you?"

"Certainly not. I was sitting right atop the box. Still am, in fact."

"I didn't see you," said Atlas. "Are you very small?"

"Of course not. I am quite large, actually," Taco replied. "Well, in comparison to yourself, at least."

"I didn't see you."

"Oh, I am sorry." Taco laughed. "Occasionally I forget to verify my visibility."

"What? You have to verify your visibility?"

"Yes. I am a Vitrian."

"A Vitrian?"

At the same time he wondered what a Vitrian might be, Atlas wondered whether or not the harsh, metallic voice was coming to retrieve him or just wanted to make him kneel facing the wall forever.

"Yes, our bodies can become invisible when we are nervous, or scared. Only those species whose eyes are sensitive to ultraviolet light can detect us when we go transparent."

"Unless species like mine use UV-sensitive goggles," said Atlas.

"You are correct." Taco said.

"Why are you nervous?"

"Excuse me?"

"You said you become invisible when you're nervous, or scared. You don't seem scared."

"No," said Taco. "I do not believe that I am." He paused for a few moments. "I suppose I might be nervous, though I do not yet know the reason. That can happen to us periodically. Our transparency mechanism is highly sensitive, and combined with an overactive subconscious, we occasionally spend the entire day transparent without realizing it. Although, I can usually become visible at will. Unless...well, that's interesting, it seems I may have a reason to be nervous. You are not an interstellar assassin, are you?"

Atlas waited for Taco to laugh, but he didn't. After another few awkward seconds Atlas replied, "No. Of course not. I'm only fourteen."

"I have met assassins half your age," Taco said gravely. "And I have killed every one of them."

"And I've assassinated people three times as invisible as you," Atlas said. It wasn't a complete lie. He'd butchered dozens of invisible pirates, bank robbers, and extraterrestrial ninjas—all imaginary, of course.

There was another moment of uncomfortable silence, then Taco burst into laughter. "Good. Good! You are clever and also bold. That will be to your advantage, Atlas."

"Thank you." Atlas questioned how being clever and bold could really help him when he was hundreds or thousands of light-years from everything he had ever known. His heart sunk again. He bit his lip until he was confident the pain was real. Atlas opened his eyes and found he didn't need to squint anymore. Also, it wasn't a bad dream. "Is anybody coming, do you think? Or will I have to stare at this wall forever?"

"They will be here soon. It takes a long time to undo all the locks and switches that keep us trapped in here."

"Well, since they're taking such a long while, would you mind if I asked you a personal question?"

"You may ask," said Taco. "But I reserve the right not to answer."

"How long have you been here?"

"In this cell?"

"Yes," said Atlas. "You said there were others like me. How long have you been here? How many others did you see? Were they all from Earth?"

"Well, my new friend, that is a lot of questions at once—"

A loud hiss interrupted Taco, and the sound of several sets of footsteps filled the room. Then, with a screech of metal, the door to Atlas's cell was opened. Two sets of arms grabbed Atlas and hoisted him to his feet, still facing the wall.

"Name?" demanded the metallic voice.

"What?"

"Your name! Now."

"Atlas."

"Surname!"

"Nunoyobiznes," Atlas said.

"Surname! Now! Do not test me, Philadelphian."

Philadelphian? *I've never lived in Philadelphia.* "Sterling," Atlas said.

"Birthdate!"

"Why does that matter to you? My birthdate is based off a solar calendar specific to my own solar system."

"Silence, you fool! We have brought you 9,000 light-years away from your planet in a fraction of a fraction of a second. Don't you think we could translate your primitive calendar to the Galactic Standard?"

"I'm sure you could, just as I'm sure you're capable of looking up my birthdate for yourself," Atlas said.

"Turn him around," barked the voice.

The persons holding him fast brusquely spun Atlas around. Before he could catch a glimpse of anyone, the back of a dark-gloved hand smashed across Atlas's left cheek.

CHAPTER 3

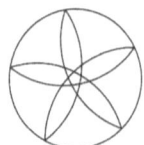

THE FORCE of the blow knocked Atlas free from the hands holding him. Stars flashed before his eyes and he fell backwards. He kicked wildly at the knee of his nearest captor, but missed, flopping hard onto his back instead. Atlas rolled onto his side, groaning and gasping for air.

The voice laughed. "Now, why would you try to kick poor Banka like that? What has she done to you? It was I who struck you."

A feminine hand reached down to help Atlas to his feet. Atlas took it and stood. A beautiful young woman stood before him. She had gray—almost purple—skin, black hair streaked with purple, and silver eyes that shined like stars. Letting go of his hand, she smiled. Atlas couldn't help but smile back.

"And yet, even after you have unjustly attacked her, Banka bears you no ill will, choosing instead to offer you her hand," said the voice.

Banka stepped to the side and Atlas saw the owner of the metallic voice for the first time. *Another woman,* Atlas thought. *Well, another female...probably. They are all females. All five of them. But, I could be wrong.*

"That is Banka's way. She forgives everything." The figure spoke through a black helmet, like a motorcycle helmet. In fact, her entire manner of dress could have easily been mistaken for motorcycle gear—black and shiny, almost leather-like—while Banka and the other three wore lighter-colored fabrics that conformed to their bodies neatly and complemented their unique skin tones.

"Forgiveness is but one of Banka's many virtues," the motorcyclist said. "She would never wish you harm. However, she is a member of *my* crew and I hold no such scruples. Out of respect for her, I do not retaliate against you. But if you should attempt to harm another of my crew again, you will very painfully regret it."

"You hit me first," Atlas said.

"You were being insolent. I am Pakhet, the captain of this vessel. You will show—"

"You kidnapped me!" Atlas interrupted. "You brought me 9,000 light-years away from my home against my will. I do *not* submit to your authority."

Pakhet stepped towards Atlas and raised a hand to strike him again.

"That is enough, Pakhet!" bellowed Taco.

"Quiet, Vitrian! Or you shall promptly have much greater concerns."

"You must deliver him in good health and condition. Otherwise, your contract will be forfeit," Taco said. "Not just for him, but for all the Philadelphians."

Atlas looked at Taco's cell but still couldn't see him. Wait, there! A shimmer, or something like it. More like a smudge. It moved.

"I can always get another boy," said Pakhet.

"Not like him. Not from the same region. Not with the same birthdate."

"Why should any of that matter?" asked Pakhet. "He's just a boy. Any one of a million could easily take his place?"

Taco laughed. The smudge that seemed to be him shook. "You speak as if you have kept me locked in here my entire, wretched life." The smudge moved higher. Taco had stood up. He really *was* tall. "I have travelled to parts of the Galaxy of which you have never even heard legend."

Atlas heard the familiar shuffling as Taco's smudge approached the bars between their cells. The shimmer-smudge became more opaque until it revealed a broad, purple face with pink tusks at the corners of its mouth and three white horns protruding from its bald head. A large scar on his cheek took the place of the smudge. The rest of Taco's body remained transparent from the top of his bare shoulders down.

Taco must be naked, Atlas thought. *How else would he be invisible? Gross.* He shivered.

The Vitrian pressed his face against the bars. "I admit I was not sure at first." He spoke forcefully but not loudly. "There are, as you well know, hundreds across the Galaxy willing to pay small fortunes for xenotypically rare slaves. You have transported so many over the past two months. But Atlas here makes fifteen children. And you got so upset when he would not tell you his birthdate. Fifteen Philadelphian children? All with the same birthdate? You think I do not know what you are doing? I have heard legends about the Fifteen Philadelphians in more languages and on more planets than you could visit in your lifetime. What do you think the Olympians will do to you, if you fail to deliver all fifteen in perfect health?"

"For someone who has seen so much, you know little about how Olympians treat their captives. What I might do would be but a tickle in comparison," Pakhet said. "I would never do business with an Olympian."

"The Titans, then," Taco said. "They are the only other civilization that takes those old legends seriously." He grinned. "Though perhaps not as vengeful as the Olympians, the Titans would also give you great cause to regret your failure to fulfill the contracted terms." Taco backed away from the bars, keeping his eyes on Pakhet. He lowered his voice, but it remained firm. "And do not think I am unfamiliar with the Theban myths. I know your interest in these children extends beyond a simple business transaction."

Pakhet did not reply. She stared at Taco for a moment—or at least, that's what Atlas assumed she was doing, since he couldn't see her face—then she turned back to Atlas.

"You will come with us. Do not pay much mind to what the old Vitrian has said. I do not fear the Titans and will deliver you to them in whatever condition you compel me. I suggest you cooperate."

Atlas nodded. Pakhet turned and left the cell without saying another word. Banka and the others positioned themselves around Atlas and led him out. As they were about to leave the detention bay, Atlas turned back towards Taco, but the Vitrian was invisible again and too far away for Atlas to see his smudge. And then, they were through the several doors of the detention bay, each door snapping shut with a series of pings and clicks as the locking mechanisms slipped into place.

"What did he do?" Atlas asked. No one replied. Atlas slowed his pace enough to allow Pakhet to get a few paces ahead of them. He spoke softly. "Taco. The Vitrian. What did he do? Why is he your prisoner?"

"Quiet, Philadelphian. You should mind your own business," said the Theban woman to his left. Her black hair was pulled back and tied into a tight knot on top of her head, like Banka's. Instead of purple stripes, her hair was streaked with red. Her skin was gray-red.

"Fine," said Atlas. "What's your name, then?"

"That is also not your business."

"But it is."

She turned to him and sneered, but didn't say anything. The Theban behind him prodded Atlas in the lower back with something and grunted. It was sharp enough to be unpleasant, but not enough to be painful.

Atlas quickened his pace slightly. "It is very much my business to know who my captors are. You might say it's the entirety of my business, in fact. There's not really much other business I can be about, now is there?"

"Your business is to quietly walk with us to the preparation room where you will be prepared for sale." The Theban prodded him again.

"Aren't you going to fatten me up first?" quipped Atlas. "It'll take a lot, I'm warning you. I have a fast metabolism."

"We don't want you fat," said the Theban to his right. Her skin was gray-green and her hair was lighter than the others—brown with green streaks—but she wore it tied into a knot on top of her head, same as the others.

"It was a joke," said Atlas. "Because you're selling me like I'm livestock. Get it?"

"You should learn to shut your mouth. The Titans have even less patience with the foolish than I do."

"At least feed me before you sell me. I wouldn't want to pass out from weakness in front of the buyers. That would be embarrassing for you—and me. You never get a second chance to make a first impression, right? Probably drive down the price as well. That'd be no good."

"You will be fed in the preparation room," said Banka.

"That's a relief. I'm starved."

"Finally!" said the gray-red woman. The group stopped in front of a plain metal door. She tapped a sequence of taps on the door itself, which promptly slid open. "Go in. Shave your head. Bathe. Change your clothes for the ones on the table. Place your old clothes in the disposal. You will eat once you have completed the other tasks."

"I'd rather not shave my head, if it's all the same to you," Atlas said. "I just got it how I like it."

She grabbed Atlas by the arm and pushed him into the room. "You will eat once you have completed the other tasks!" The door slid shut.

Atlas tried to replicate the finger-taps. The door remained shut. *Dammit.*

In the middle of the small room stood a table and a single chair. A change of clothing lay on the table. He touched the black material and lifted it to test the weight. It was remarkably light and soft, but otherwise plain. However, the clothing was way too big for him—at least two people too big.

On the far side of the room was a grated drain with a simple spigot directly above. No curtain or other privacy screen. At least there are no windows, Atlas thought.

To the left of the shower, a short shelf stuck out from the wall. On the shelf sat a small, cylindrical device. It reminded Atlas of an electric razor, but without the rotating blades. Atlas picked it up and touched it lightly to his arm. Instantly, all the hairs within an inch radius of the device disappeared.

"Well, I hope that's not permanent," he said aloud. "Oh well. It'll make a good story, anyway. 'Remember that one time I was kidnapped by aliens and accidentally deleted a two-inch circle of hair on my arm?'"

His stomach growled. Atlas looked around the room. No mirror. "I'll just have to be careful I don't accidentally erase my eyebrows or eyelashes." He held the cylinder to the top of his head and pressed down gently. There was no mess. Not a single hair fell from his head. It truly was like he had erased his hair.

Slowly and methodically, Atlas made one pass after another across his scalp until he was sure he'd deleted all of the hair on his head. "'Two-inch circle of arm hair? Atlas, you also deleted all the hair on your head!' they'll say. 'Oh yeah. I forgot about that.'"

Atlas took off his clothes and folded them neatly—like his mother taught him—and set them on the table next to the over-sized clothes. He searched the pockets of his jeans for some trinket he could keep as a reminder of home. Nothing. Not even pocket lint. And they'd removed his shoelaces too. If only his mom didn't cut out the tags as soon as they brought clothing home from the store. That'd be something small enough they probably wouldn't notice.

Disheartened, Atlas placed his clothes through what he

assumed was the aforementioned disposal. Immediately, the chute slid closed and became impossible to discern from the rest of the wall. Gone without a trace.

As Atlas stood naked under the spigot, waiting for the shower to begin, a single tear rolled down his cheek. A stream of warm water began to fall, washing the tear away and diluting it into oblivion. Atlas counted backwards from one hundred by threes.

The water had a mild, but pleasant smell, like a sea breeze. Atlas assumed it was infused with a disinfectant of some sort. He scowled. *Made me shave my head. Bathed me in disinfectant. They think I'm filthy.*

He closed his eyes and pictured his parents' faces. He thought about the time his family had visited the ocean and camped on the beach. Maggie was only seven. Dad had dropped the family camera in the ocean on their last day. All the photos from the trip were lost.

As the scented water poured down his face, Atlas created a snapshot in his mind and memorized every detail. He sat cross-legged in the sand, Maggie draping her arms over his shoulders and grinning enthusiastically with her tongue stuck out at the camera. Dad off-balance and falling backwards, pretending he didn't have enough time to get into place before the camera's timer was up. Mom with her face turned away from the camera, the light of the sunset catching her profile perfectly as she laughed at the family antics. Atlas wore the calmest, most contented smile.

Let them take everything from him, even his hair. No one could take that snapshot.

Only when the shower automatically turned off did Atlas realize there were no towels. He went to the table and picked through the new clothes, just in case he had overlooked the towel. Nope. However, the fabric seemed to constrict and contort as it came into contact with his wet hands, almost as if it was alive.

Intrigued, he picked up the oversized underwear and pulled them on. The clothing reacted with the water on Atlas's skin, shrinking to the perfect, comfortable size. The pants and long-sleeve shirt also began to transform as they lay on the table. *How the hell—? Wireless underwear? Why?*

Atlas finished dressing. His new clothing had form-fit to his body, but with no apparent change to the texture of the fabric. It struck him that his new garments were similar to what the Theban women wore, but darker.

For the next few minutes, Atlas walked, skipped, leapt, and danced around the room, testing the feel and fit of his clothes. Though tighter than he preferred, they allowed for a full range of motion without resistance and were so light and comfortable that it almost seemed as if he was naked. The shoes were thin, almost sock-like, but with a dynamic sole that seemed to adjust its rigidity to whatever surface he stood on. Atlas tested them on the limited surfaces in the room: floor, wall, drain, chair, and table.

Though only a few minutes had passed, the clothing was now completely dry.

"Prisoner I may be, but these clothes kick ass. Not even the richest man on Earth has magic underpants."

Mom was right, he thought. *It's the little things that get you through the big things.*

"I am glad you like them."

Atlas spun around to the door. Banka stood inside the room, the door closed behind her.

"How long have you been there? Did you…uh…see any of that?" Atlas stepped down from the tabletop.

"I saw everything. There are, of course, cameras in here."

Atlas flushed with embarrassment. "Including the shower?" He glanced around the room, but couldn't see any cameras.

"Don't worry," Banka said. "I won't tell anyone that you cried."

"That's not what….uh…Okay. Thanks."

"It is only natural that you would miss your family."

Of course I miss them, Atlas thought.

"Why couldn't I at least keep my clothes?"

"Please sit down and I'll bring you some food." Banka went to the shelf with the hair-deleter. She tapped a sequence on the wall and a tray slid out.

Atlas watched for a moment, then sat as directed. Steam rose from the tray. And then, the aroma reached his nostrils.

"Pizza!" As Banka brought the tray closer, Atlas stood, craning to see if his nose was playing tricks on him. Sure enough, there it was—a large pizza with pepperoni, jalapeños, and pineapple. "How did you know?"

"We know everything about you," Banka said. "We carefully research every target before we initiate retrieval procedures."

"I knew it." Gratified he had been right when he had challenged Pakhet about knowing his birthday, Atlas took a large bite of the first slice of pizza. It was exceptional, like Aldrighetti's Spaghetti Ghetto. The crust especially was exactly right.

"Where did you get this?" he asked.

"Your favorite restaurant."

"But it's so fresh."

"Yes. It very recently came out of the oven."

"How?"

"It doesn't matter, and anyway, it would take too long to explain."

Atlas chewed the crust of his second slice. He felt confused. Up until then, he'd been treated like a prisoner. Now they had gone to the trouble of feeding him his favorite food from his favorite restaurant. But why? *I hope this isn't some sort of last-meal ritual,* he thought. *Then why give me this high-tech, expensive-looking clothing? There is something more going on. I need more information.*

"I'm sorry I tried to kick you," Atlas said.

"I have forgiven you."

"Like Pakhet said."

"Yes. And now you must forgive her," said Banka. "She likes to threaten, but she would never damage merchandise. It would decrease our profits and ruin our reputation."

"I'm not merchandise. I am a person."

"I am sorry," Banka said. "Perhaps the translation made an

error. Or perhaps your language doesn't have the appropriate term."

"Like slave? Is that a better term?"

Banka recoiled in disgust. "Slave? You are not a slave!"

"Well, on my planet when you kidnap someone and sell them, that's slavery."

Banka frowned. She grabbed Atlas's hands and looked into his eyes. "We are not slavers. You are *not* for sale."

Atlas freed his hands. "That's not what whatever-her-name-is —the woman behind me—said."

"Sometimes the translator has issues finding the appropriate term with unfamiliar languages," Banka said.

"And just now you spoke about profits and reputation."

"We are fulfilling a contract. We were contracted to find you, to bring you here. We would never...could never...not after..." She looked down at the floor. "I see now, from your perspective, how it must look. But please believe me that we would never deliver anyone into slavery."

"And why should I believe you?"

"We were slaves once. All of us. On Olympus."

"All of you? Including Pakhet?"

"Especially Pakhet. She was held by an unusually terrible, sadistic man. He did horrible things, but she escaped, finally. And then, when she was free, she rescued all of the Thebans that would go with her."

"How many of you are there?"

"Never mind that," said Banka. "You must hurry and eat, or we will be late."

"Right. Wouldn't want to be late to my own auction."

Banka took his hands again. "We are taking you to the Academy, not to an auction. As I said, the translator must be having trouble with your language. Let's see, how else can I put it?" She dropped Atlas's hands and frowned. Then she smiled again. "We are recruiters."

"Recruiters?"

"Yes." Banka was clearly pleased with her word choice. "We were contracted to recruit fifteen children."

"I'm *not* a child," protested Atlas.

Banka smiled. "No. I suppose you're not."

"And if I'm not a slave, I'd like to return home."

"That is impossible," Banka replied. "You are to become a cadet. Like the others."

"A cadet?" Atlas frowned. "Can I resign my commission, or whatever?"

"Or apprentice," Banka continued. "If you combine those two words in your language, perhaps it might be a better approximation of the term."

"I don't want to become either of those," said Atlas. "I want to go home."

"You can't. It's far too dangerous." Banka cocked her head slightly. "The Academy is the safest place in the Galaxy for you right now."

Atlas sighed in exasperation. "So let's see, I'm going to become a cadet-apprentice hybrid on another planet 9,000 light-years from my home and you, my recruiters, are going to be paid for my involuntary conscription? Sounds like slavery to me."

Banka looked at her feet. "We are retrieval contractors. Be patient, young Philadelphian. When you get to the Academy, you will understand."

Atlas was tired of arguing over the definition of slavery, so he changed the subject. "I'm not from Philadelphia."

"But we brought you from Philadelphia." Banka looked puzzled.

"No, you did not. I live in a different city more than a thousand miles west of Philadelphia."

"Philadelphia is the name of a city?"

"Yes, and an important one in my country. It's where the country began. My family and I flew through it once, a few years ago, on a trip to visit my grandparents. But that doesn't make me from there. We didn't even leave the airport."

"Fascinating...but your planet? What do you call it?"

Could this all be a big mistake, Atlas wondered. *Have they recruited me from the wrong planet?*

"Earth. I live on Earth. I am an Earthling," Atlas said.

Banka appeared reassured. "To us, your planet is called Philadelphia. And it has held that name for thousands of Galactic Standard cycles." She paused a moment. "Of course, that's only the best approximation the translator can make of our term for your planet, and as we've seen, the whole and proper meaning of several things we've discussed can be misconstrued in translation."

"So you keep saying." Atlas started into his third slice of pizza.

"It will all become clear for you once you commence your studies at the Academy."

"The Academy?" Atlas asked with his mouth full. "That's another thing you keep saying that I hope the translator gets wrong. I'm abducted from my home and taken 9,000 light-years away from my family and then I'm forced to attend a snooty school? That's just my luck!"

CHAPTER 4

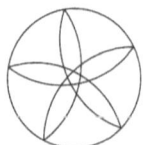

BANKA TOLD Atlas the names of the Thebans who would accompany him to the Titan Academy. They were the same women who had escorted him earlier. The gray-red woman who pushed him into the preparation room was Aura. The woman opposite her with the gray-green skin was Lanta. And Diana had prodded him in the back.

Atlas quietly finished the rest of his pizza. He offered some to Banka, but she declined, citing a severe allergy to Philadelphian yeast. *How did she know that? The other Philadelphians, I guess.*

Before long, Atlas was being marched through the ship corridors again with Banka and the other three surrounding him as before. Pakhet didn't join them, however, and this time Diana wasn't the only one carrying a weapon. Aura and Lanta carried metal bows slung across their backs, although neither carried arrows. *How curious,* Atlas thought. He deduced their bows must fire energy projectiles of some sort. *Anachronistic, but also innovative. Interesting.* Diana's spear presented more questions. It was far too blunt to pierce skin. *How did it work, then?* Banka wore something on one hand—a gauntlet of some sort. It appeared nearly useless—hardly more than a fashion statement.

"So, Pakhet's gone ahead to make sure the deal's not going to fall through, eh?" Atlas asked. "I hope they don't deduct my tuition from your fee, I'm more than happy to take out a student loan. You did all the hard work of kidnapping me, after all. It's only fair."

"You Philadelphians don't know how to keep your mouths shut," Diana said. "The Academy will teach you."

"That's not entirely accurate," said Banka. "Several of the Philadelphians were quiet. And remember, Diana, this is not a Theban Academy. The Titans are much more lenient when it comes to educational discipline."

"What good are our methods, if they don't marry them with our discipline?" Diana asked.

"There are many effective methods," said Banka. "The Galaxy is large."

"Ours are better, which is why the Titans needed us to teach them about trans-light travel," said Diana.

"The last one was very quiet," said Lanta. "I don't think I heard her say a word the entire time."

Aura laughed. "Don't forget the one who wet his pants. His endless chatter suddenly became perfect silence."

"It's only funny to you because you didn't walk through it," Diana said.

"No, it's even funnier because you *did*," Lanta said.

"That poor boy," said Banka, shaking her head. "Pakhet went too far. I scolded her quite harshly for it."

"It was a harmless joke," said Aura. "How could she know he would take it so seriously?"

"Pakhet threatened to sacrifice him and drink his blood if he couldn't be quiet," said Banka. "She took it too far."

"You're one to talk," said Aura.

"She was going to drink his blood?" Atlas asked. "Wow, what's wrong with her? She's sick."

"Nothing is wrong with her," said Diana. "She is the pinnacle of health."

"No, that's not what I mean. I meant she's got a screw loose or something. That's a pretty sadistic thing to do to a kid."

"Hold your tongue," said Aura. "Or I will hold it for you."

"And what's with the motorcycle helmet and leather clothing?" Atlas asked. "The rest of you don't dress like that. Why the helmet? What's she trying to hide?"

"Pakhet's wardrobe is none of your concern," said Diana. She prodded him with the spear. "Keep walking."

"Aw, lighten up," said Atlas. "I'm trying to engage in some banter. You know, let off some steam."

"Are you overheating, Philadelphian?" asked Banka. "Your clothing is designed to prevent that. Perhaps it is malfunctioning."

Malfunctioning?

"No, it's an expression. And please, my name is Atlas. I realize it's easier not to think of me as a person with a name, but I *am* a person and my name is Atlas. And I know you all know it."

"You give yourself too much credit, Philadelphian," said Aura.

"Or perhaps we do not give enough to ourselves," said Banka. "If we truly believe that what we are doing with these Philadelphians is different than what the Olympians did to us, we should call them by their proper names. We should treat them with kindness."

A bit late for that, seeing as I'm the last one, Atlas thought.

"They are weak," said Aura. "They need to toughen up if they're going to—"

"That is not our responsibility," said Banka.

"Pakhet believes it is," said Lanta.

"And she is wrong!" Banka snapped.

The group walked in silence.

"Banka is right," Diana finally said. "What have we accomplished except ensuring that the Philadelphians hate and distrust us? I spoke of discipline, but tell me, how does our behavior help them see us as anything other than bullies? We, who hang such lofty hopes…"

"Diana," said Banka.

"He heard what the Vitrian said," said Diana.

"Taco," said Atlas. "His name is Taco."

Atlas began to feel awkward, like when witnessing a friend get in trouble from their parents. Finally, the group reached the exit hatch of the ship. Banka began tapping a pattern.

"Wait," said Aura, stopping Banka. She turned to Atlas. "I am sorry for my behavior, Atlas." Her eyes were yellow, like lemons. "Could you please convey my apology to the other Philadelphians?"

"Uh, sure thing." Atlas didn't know what else to say.

"And mine as well, please?" said Lanta. "And my twin sister, Ata's. You've not met her, as it's her turn to serve on the bridge, but she would appreciate, I am sure, if you would also offer her apologies to the others."

"I will."

Diana put a hand on Atlas's shoulder. Unlike the other Thebans, her white hair was cut quite short and instead of streaks, dark blue spots were scattered throughout. "Perhaps it has been too long since we reflected on our own abduction, so many years ago. But please understand, the stakes are extremely high. Not only for the Titans, but for Thebans as well. So much depends on you Philadelphians, Atlas."

"That's enough, Diana." Banka placed her hands on Atlas's other shoulder. "It's not for us to discuss these matters."

"No," said Diana. She frowned and looked at Banka. "It is not."

"Come on, ladies," Atlas complained. "You can't set me up like that and then withhold the details."

"We've already said too much," said Aura.

"Let us go." Banka tapped the pattern onto the exit again. The hatch hissed and slid open. Two steps extended from underneath the opening.

Lanta touched Atlas on the arm. "It's important that you understand. We are here for your protection, Atlas. Please be careful to stay within our perimeter."

"Pakhet went ahead to scout our route," Diana said.

"If I'm so important to the Titans, why am I in danger?" Atlas asked.

"Not all on Titan are Titans," said Aura. "The Olympians have many spies."

"We must go now," Banka said. "We are nearly behind schedule." She stepped outside and turned to face Atlas. "Welcome to Titan."

Atlas walked out of the Theban ship and looked around. He frowned. "It's not quite what I was expecting."

"What do you mean?" asked Lanta.

Atlas shook his head. "I don't know, I guess I expected lanes and lanes of flying vehicles zipping overhead." He shrugged as he looked across an empty field. "And, you know, extraordinarily tall buildings."

"There are tall buildings in town," Aura said. "Some are even ten floors or more."

"That's not very tall," Atlas said. It was impossible to hide his disappointment. "I meant like two hundred floors tall."

"Ha!" Lanta laughed. "Why would you need a building so high? A whole town could live in one building."

"I don't know. That's how we imagine advanced civilizations in our movies," Atlas said. "They're all sprawling urban planets filled with breathtakingly tall buildings. This looks like we're surrounded by farmland."

"That's because we are," said Banka. "All towns on Titan are surrounded by farmland. How else would the citizens get fresh food?"

Atlas looked back at the Theban spaceship. It was somewhere between twenty and thirty feet tall and probably fifty meters in length, built out of a material that looked similar to stainless steel. It had no wings for atmospheric flight. *Vertical launch? Awesome.*

"At least your spaceship is pretty cool."

Aura smiled. "It doesn't travel through space. At least, not anymore."

"It is capable of orbiting a planet indefinitely," said Diana. "But it hasn't carried propulsion engines for generations."

Generations? Looks pretty good for being that old, Atlas thought. *But no propulsion.*

"Can it fly?" Atlas asked.

"I suppose it could hover, if we ever needed it to, but only a few meters off the ground," said Lanta.

Atlas thought about this as they crossed the concrete landing pad onto a paved road. "And this? This is what spaceports are like?"

"Yes and no," said Lanta. "It's really a space we lease from a local farmer. It used to be the foundation of a slaughterhouse, I believe."

Slaughterhouse? How charming.

"But there's no runway," Atlas grumbled. "Or launching pad. Or ticketing and baggage. I don't see a single building. Where are all the cosmopolitan aliens waiting for their flights to exotic planets?"

Atlas felt sincerely disappointed. For an advanced civilization, Titan sure was awfully rural. No mountain-high sky-scrapers. No endless streams of flying traffic overhead. There wasn't even a bustling spaceport filled with strange aliens from all corners of the galaxy.

"Spacecraft haven't needed runways for over a century and a half," said Aura.

"Not since trans-light travel was perfected," said Lanta. "Only an empty spot to land."

"You mean to park," Atlas said, beginning to understand what Taco meant by leaving and arriving being the same thing.

Banka nodded. "Yes, I guess that is an appropriate word. And it fits trans-light travel well. You're parked one place, then you're parked somewhere else thousands of light-years away." She seemed pleased.

"Don't ever say that in front of Ata. She takes trans-light travel very seriously." Diana grinned mischievously.

"That's because our great-great-grandfather invented it," Lanta told Atlas.

"*Sure* he did," said Diana.

Lanta glared indignantly at Diana. "He did."

Diana smirked, apparently pleased with herself for provoking Lanta.

"I'd never really thought about it much before, but you're right, Atlas," said Banka. "Trans-light does sound much less romantic compared to what interstellar travel used to be centuries ago—years-long voyages where your fellow travelers became close friends."

"Or lovers," said Aura.

Banka ignored her. "Nowadays, the longest part of the journey is entering your destination into the computer. Well, that's progress I suppose, trading nostalgia for efficiency."

Dissatisfaction washed over Atlas. He couldn't help but feel like he'd missed out on a proper interstellar kidnapping—one that would have taken years of traveling at relativistic speeds and which would have made it impossible to ever see his parents again due to time dilation. Sure, this particular alien abduction could potentially have a much happier ending in which he might someday be reunited with his family, but in a proper interstellar kidnapping, at least there would have been busy spaceports filled with hundreds of different alien species plotting wars, invasions, business takeovers, assassinations, vacations, and romantic trysts. This was kind of boring.

An old slaughterhouse in the middle of a farm?

"So, where is this Academy? Is someone going to pick us up? Do we at least get to ride in a hover vehicle?"

"We'll walk," said Banka. "It's not far."

"This way, Atlas." Lanta pointed towards the woods beyond the fields.

"And it's much safer to walk," said Diana. "We'll keep off the roads, for the most part."

"Except outside the Academy," said Aura.

"You must be especially careful when we reach that road," said Lanta. "Stay near us, and stay low."

"We must hurry." Banka looked towards the sun. "We'll lose the light if we don't get going."

Atlas spent the next fifteen minutes walking among the four Theban women, and pondering the many ways that being one of the first humans to visit another planet was proving so underwhelming. Even the woods they walked through had much in common with Earth forests. The trees looked a lot like Earth trees, and the undergrowth looked like Earth undergrowth. Atlas sneezed. *Great. And I still have hay fever*. The smell. That was one thing different. There was a faint, tickling smell to the air. It didn't seem to bother the women.

"Do you live here?" Atlas asked. "Where is your home?"

"Titan is not our home," said Aura. "Thebes is our home world."

"Tell me about Thebes," Atlas said. "Is it very much like Titan?"

No one answered.

"I was just wondering if there were any planets more exciting than Titan."

"You may one day wish for the calm of Titan," said Lanta.

"Lanta!" scolded Banka.

"Thebes was exceptionally beautiful," said Aura. "My grandmother used to tell me stories of all the places she and my grandfather visited. Canyons twenty kilometers deep, and mountains twice that high. Waterfalls where the water fell so far it was nothing but a fine mist by the time it reached the bottom. And it had five moons. That would have been something to see! So few inhabited planets have more than one, and almost never more than two. And there were so many forests that you could circumnavigate the planet and never step out from under the shade of the trees."

"That is an exaggeration," said Diana.

"Diana is the only one of us to have been born on Thebes," said Lanta.

"But she was very young when she was taken away," said Aura. "Barely more than a baby."

"True. But I still remember it. And it was breathtakingly beautiful. There weren't *quite* as many trees as in your story."

"What happened to it?" Atlas asked.

"The Olympians." Banka quickened her pace. "We must hurry."

"They destroyed your planet?"

"Might as well have. It's uninhabitable now," said Diana.

"That's why you Philadelphians are so important," said Lanta.

"Enough," said Banka. "That is not our place."

"I am sorry."

"I have already forgiven you."

"Why shouldn't it be our place?" said Diana. "The Titans wouldn't know anything, if not for us. We gave them trans-light. We told them about Philadelphia. We taught them about the—"

"Enough!" Banka commanded Diana. After a deep breath, Banka's eyes shone with an intense green light as she turned to Atlas.

"We were once a great civilization, or so we've been taught. And yet, we were defeated by the Olympians, a culture far less advanced than our own. They took our technology. They took our planet. They took many of our lives immediately and many more in slavery. Now, we are nothing." Banka's voice broke. "Nothing but vagabonds. The Titans took in what was left of our people, when no one else would. They shared their planet with us. We owe them much more than they owe us. Therefore, it is not our place to discuss these things with the Philadelphians."

Diana shook her head, but remained silent.

Atlas reflected on all this. "I am sorry about your planet."

Suddenly, Banka halted. She motioned to the others to get low and crept a few feet forward to crouch behind a boulder. Peeking above it, Banka scanned the surrounding woods. A hooting shriek sounded up ahead.

"It is alright." Smiling, Banka motioned them to stand up.

"What was that?" asked Atlas.

"A red wooly lizard call," said Diana. "It's Pakhet. She's come to meet us."

Sure enough, a few seconds later, Pakhet appeared from behind some trees. She carried a bow similar to the ones Aura and Lanta slung across their backs.

"Well met, Pakhet!" said Diana.

"Indeed," added Banka. "Though unexpected. Is something wrong?"

"Nothing is wrong." Pakhet's voice sounded as metallic as before, but less harsh. "But we must adjust our route. There is a public protest near the Academy. Many people have gathered. It's loud, but peaceful. The citizens must not see the Philadelphian."

"His name is Atlas," said Aura.

"And he deserves our respect and friendship," said Banka.

"What are they protesting?" Lanta asked.

"The where of the protest matters more than the why," Pakhet said. "Why not protest on the plaza?"

"That's suspicious," said Diana.

"We must now enter from the plaza," said Pakhet.

Banka frowned. "That's not ideal."

"Too many buildings," added Diana. "And very little cover. We'll be exposed."

"I didn't have time to scout the buildings. The crowd only gathered an hour ago," said Pakhet. She turned to Atlas. "Can you run, Philadelphian?"

"My name is Atlas. And yes, I can run."

"How fast? Most Philadelphians are quite slow, I have found."

"I am fast for my age. The fastest in my neighborhood."

"That will have to do." Pakhet turned to the others. "When we leave the woods, we will sprint to the Academy." She turned back to Atlas. "It's less than three hundred meters."

"Most of it in the open," said Aura.

"That's what I said," said Diana.

"You did?"

"Yes, I *did*."

"Sorry, I didn't hear."

"Is this really such a big deal?" asked Atlas. "Why not try again tomorrow? You take me home, I'll sleep in my own bed, and we try again tomorrow. You'll have to find some place to park your ship, though. My back yard's definitely not big enough."

"We cannot delay, if we are to fulfill the prophecy," said Banka.

"No," said Pakhet. "Our contacts confirm that Olympian spies have discovered that we identified the Fifteen. The Olympians do not know how many we have retrieved, but there will be more spies every day. They are under orders to disrupt the prophecy at any cost."

"You mean they'll kill me," said Atlas. It was a strange feeling, realizing that someone wanted him dead.

They don't know anything about me, or my opinion about any of this, he thought.

"So you understand." Pakhet pulled Banka aside and whispered something to her. Banka shook her head. Then, Pakhet turned back to the others. "I'll take point. Lanta, you are the shortest, so you will take the center with the Philadelphian. If he cannot keep up, you must carry him. Banka will take Lanta's position."

Ten minutes later, they reached the edge of the woods. Pakhet and Banka scanned the open area from behind the last few trees. A large fountain burst up from the middle of the plaza. Other than a few low benches around the fountain and some boulders and stones scattered on the ground, the whole area was empty. It was quiet, except for the dull roar of chanting from protesters several streets over. Pakhet nodded and everyone crept up to join her and Banka.

"See that building, Philadelphian?" Pakhet pointed to a large, high-walled structure with steel accents.

"The fortress?" asked Atlas.

"That's the Academy. They know we are coming, but this is not the entrance where they are expecting us, so I will have to open the gate." Pakhet touched the center of Atlas's forehead. "Probably nothing happens, but if you get separated from us, run there as fast as you can. Pay no attention to anything else. Do you understand, Philadelphian?"

"Yes."

"Okay." Pakhet stood up. "On my mark."

Lanta grabbed Atlas's hand and squeezed. "We will protect you," she whispered.

"Now!"

Atlas ran as fast as he could, though he wished Lanta would let go of his hand. Running without being able to pump both his arms was awkward. Still, he was pleased at how well he was able to keep up with the Thebans. Halfway to the Academy, however, his lungs began to burn, and his side began to cramp. He had never been able to keep his top speed for very long. It was embarrassing. No time for that now. He set his sight on the gate of the Academy, grit his teeth, and pushed through the pain.

Atlas slipped on a pebble. It was only the most minor of a disruption, but it slowed him a fraction behind Lanta. A loud buzz zipped in front of his face. Lanta fell, still clutching his hand, and pulled Atlas hard to the ground. His head struck a large flat stone and everything became fuzzy.

"Sniper!" Diana yelled. "Take cover!"

"The Philadelphian!" Pakhet called. "Get him behind something."

Atlas's head throbbed from the impact. He felt someone grab his legs and drag him backwards.

"Let go!"

Atlas realized he still clutched Lanta's hand.

"Let her go!"

He let go and was dragged several more feet. Then, he was lifted and set against something hard.

"Were you hit?"

Atlas opened his eyes. Diana's gray-blue face was only inches away. She and Aura crouched low in front of him. Everything buzzed. Their voices. Their faces. The air.

"Were you hit?"

"No," he panted. "I'm okay. My head…hit…something hard. Dizzy."

"I'll carry him," Diana said.

"Where are Pakhet and Banka?" Aura asked.

"Pakhet made it to the gate. I don't think she has an angle on the sniper," Diana said. "Banka is pinned down on the other side of the fountain. When I draw fire, you spot the sniper and give me what cover you can. Tell Banka. She'll take care of it. Then, you get Lanta."

"Understood."

"Ready, Atlas?"

"Um…yes."

"Let's go." Diana took a deep breath, scooped him up, and sprinted towards the Academy gate. She cut left and right as she ran, carving a random zig-zag pattern.

Atlas felt nauseous. He closed his eyes and tried not to vomit. Several times, the loud buzzing zipped near them. Diana kept running.

"Banka! North-east building! Ninth floor!" yelled Aura.

Atlas opened his eyes in time to see Banka peek over the fountain to spot the north-east building. She tapped a pattern on her gauntlet, smiled at Atlas, and disappeared.

THE OLYMPIAN SNIPER was still looking through his scope, his finger on the trigger of his rifle, when Banka appeared behind him. He was nearly twice her size, but Banka easily tore the weapon from his hands with one arm and threw the sniper against the wall with the other. With her gauntleted hand, Banka crushed the barrel and flung the rifle to the far side of the room.

The sniper stood and rushed at Banka. She effortlessly dodged his fists and kicked him squarely in the chest. He stumbled backwards towards the open window.

Recovering his balance, the Olympian lifted a stool and swung it at Banka. She blocked it with her bare arm, splintering the seat into a dozen pieces. The sniper followed with a quick kick to her stomach. Banka grimaced and staggered backwards a few steps, but didn't double over.

Fists raised, Banka stretched the grimace into a serene smile. "I've already forgiven you." She exhaled slowly and relaxed her shoulders. Then, she tapped a new pattern on her gauntlet and repelled the Olympian out the window.

THE ACADEMY GATE flung open as Diana and Atlas reached it. Pakhet took Atlas from Diana and carried him to a protected corner of the courtyard. Someone screamed and then was suddenly silent. Diana left to help with Lanta.

"Clear!" called Banka.

"It is just," whispered Pakhet. She set Atlas down in a small alcove and ran towards the Academy entrance. "Medic! We need a doctor!"

A tall young woman came out to meet her. They talked briefly, then the young woman ran back inside. Seconds later, she returned carrying a large bag.

Atlas watched it all. Everything buzzed. The edges of people and objects began to blur together. The adrenaline was subsiding, and the pain in his head was increasing. His side was covered in blood. *Was I hit? No. No pain there. Whose blood? Gray. Diana? But she...*

The edges of his vision blackened, and Atlas lost consciousness.

CHAPTER 5

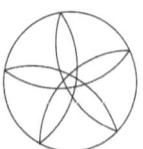

ATLAS AWOKE IN A SOFT BED. Too soft. Not his bed. He opened his eyes. The lights in the room came up gradually, allowing his eyes to adjust as the brightness increased. Not his bedroom.

It was a simple room. Nothing ornate or extravagant. Light gray walls with white accents. Neat and tasteful. He was wearing a loose, hospital gown-like garment.

Am I in a hospital? Why? Where is all the hospital equipment? What happened? His head felt foggy and muddled. He'd been kidnapped. Yes. He remembered that much. And Pakhet slapped him. But she wasn't so bad, after all. She and the other Thebans...

The door opened and a tall young woman entered. She was dressed much like the room, simply but tastefully in shades of white and gray. Even her hair was white.

"Hello," she said. "My name is Circe. How do you feel?" There was something familiar about her.

"Fine, I guess." Atlas couldn't decide if he'd seen her before.

"That is not a real answer."

"I don't understand."

"Exactly. When you say fine, that doesn't tell me anything. I can't understand how you are doing unless you tell me with specifics." Circe came closer. "So, how do you feel? Are you in pain?"

"I feel good. No pain. But I feel kind of strange, like it's cloudy in my head."

Is she a doctor? Atlas remembered seeing her before. Carrying a bag of medical supplies. Talking with Pakhet.

"That's a side-effect of the anesthesia. It should pass in a few more hours."

"Anesthesia?" Atlas felt around his body, looking for stitches or missing parts. Nothing on his stomach or back. *All limbs accounted for. Wait! Good. Still there. One...two...okay. All good.* "What did you do to me?"

"You had some swelling from the fall you took. We had to open you up to prevent permanent brain damage."

Atlas felt around his shaved head. No part of his scalp seemed to have been injured. No bandages or stitches. No swollen tissue or tenderness. "Where exactly did you open me up?"

"Your skull, of course. Where else could swelling lead to permanent brain damage?" She smiled with pride. "Our techniques are quite advanced. You wouldn't find a scar even if you knew where to look."

"Then I suppose I wouldn't be able to tell if you did something *else* to me, or removed something against my will."

Circe laughed. "They warned me you were a suspicious one."

"Well, let's see..." Atlas began. "I was kidnapped, taken 9,000 light-years away from my family—without even the courtesy of a proper, relativistic journey to destroy all hope of ever seeing them again—"

"You'd rather have no hope of seeing your family again?"

"Of course. And you would too, if you thought about it. In an ideal interstellar kidnapping, the effects of relativistic time dilation would eliminate the possibility of seeing my family again. I'd eventually move on and live my life without the constant fear of failing to get back to them looming over my head." Atlas sighed heavily. "Instead, thanks to the miracle of trans-light travel—however *that* works—I have to live with the possibility of one day, maybe, seeing my family again, which means my every thought and energy will be consumed with trying to get back home as quickly and in as few pieces as possible. That's a lot of pressure."

"You might think differently once the anesthesia—"

"Excuse the interruption, but you interrupted me first, so we're even." Atlas closed his right eye because it was easier to focus his clouded head with only one eye open. "As I was saying, I've been taken 9,000 light-years from home, I have to live my life terrified of never seeing my family and friends again, I've apparently had major brain surgery but don't even have a cool scar to show off, nothing—not even this hospital room—looks like it's supposed to, and some alien sniper tried to kill me. All because..." Atlas remembered how he had fallen and hit his head. "How is Lanta? You healed her, right? With your advanced techniques..."

Circe spoke gravely. "She didn't make it."

Tears welled in Atlas's eyes. "It's my fault. I stumbled. It should have been me."

"If it had been you, then all would be lost," a new, yet familiar, voice said.

Atlas looked toward the door. Gray-green skin. Brown and green hair. Lanta! He turned a spiteful look toward Circe. What was she? Doctor? Nurse? *What kind of a joke is that? Telling you that someone died taking a bullet that was meant for you when Lanta is actually standing in the doorway. What a horrible person!*

Lanta stepped into the room. "My sister well knew the risks involved, and the importance of keeping you safe."

Sister? *Twin sister,* he remembered. Understanding washed over Atlas. Tears streamed down his cheeks. "I'm so sorry, Ata," he finally managed to say.

"Lanta would be moved by your tears, but know she died peacefully when they told her that you were safe inside the Academy."

"I'll leave you two," said Circe. "I'll be back to check on you soon, Atlas."

"Thank you, Doctor Circe," said Ata.

"I am sorry about your sister," Dr. Circe said. "I did the best I could."

"I know. And I am grateful," Ata said. "Do not trouble yourself for Lanta's death. The coward Olympian who killed her has paid with his life, and those who sent him will soon pay their debt as well."

Dr. Circe nodded and left.

Atlas lay back on his pillow and stared at the ceiling. He left the tears on his cheeks and thought about the memories the wet streaks left behind. *I barely knew Lanta. But she died protecting me. She helped kidnap me. But she didn't deserve to die. The last thing she said to me:* We are here to protect you.

Ata pulled a chair next to Atlas's bed but didn't sit down.

"So, Banka killed him?"

"Yes," said Ata.

"Good. I wish I had seen it."

"Do not wish for such things, young Philadelphian. Death is all around us, lurking in the shadows and waiting to snap us up at any instant. Experience has taught me that those who seek death are often the most quickly and completely consumed by it. That is no way to live."

Atlas didn't understand but he repeated it three times in his head so he would be able to remember and ponder it later, when his head wasn't foggy.

"All would *not* have been lost," Atlas whispered.

"Sorry? I didn't hear that. Could you repeat it?"

"Never mind," Atlas said. "Just thinking out loud. Was Diana hit? I remember being covered in someone's blood."

"Yes. She was grazed across the chest, but she is fine," said Ata. "You were both very lucky. A few centimeters in any direction and one of you would be dead."

"I'm glad she's okay. I'd like to thank her."

"She and the others are preparing Lanta for her rites."

"Shouldn't you be there?"

"In our funerary rites, it is tradition that friends and colleagues prepare the body, not family."

"I am so sorry, Ata." Another round of tears ran down Atlas's cheeks. "If my sister...I don't know how..."

"I know what is at stake," said Ata. "Lanta knew. We all knew the risks when we accepted the contract from the Titans. But we also understood the importance. History will honor my sister for her sacrifice."

"I'm glad you believe that." Atlas's voice broke. "I don't understand why you do, but I'm glad you believe it."

"You will come to understand. All I ask is that you not forget Lanta's sacrifice."

"Never."

"This will not be the last time the Olympians attempt to kill you and the other Philadelphians," Ata said. "Pakhet wanted me to make sure you understand that. You must always be alert. The other Philadelphians will not likely listen to us. *You* must tell them. Make them understand."

"But we're just kids." It didn't make any sense. He was just a regular kid. Maybe the other fourteen were extraordinary, but not him. "Why do the Olympians want to kill us?"

"You are the Fifteen. And they fear you because of it," said Ata.

"We're only *the Fifteen* because you abducted me and fourteen others."

"You and the others were selected because you met all the criteria, as prophesied. Had we not retrieved you when we did, in a matter of months, weeks, or days, you would wake up in your bed with your throat slit, and an Olympian assassin standing over you."

Atlas sighed. "What is the prophecy? I never volunteered to fulfill any prophecy."

"I can't say any more," Ata said. "It's not my place. You will understand soon enough."

"Everyone keeps saying *that* too."

Atlas frowned. More than almost anything else, he hated when people told him *you'll understand when you're older*, or the *I'll tell you when you're older* variant. Invariably, they acted like they were trying to protect him, when most of the time they were protecting themselves from an awkward or difficult conversation.

"We say it, because it is true. Now, sleep and recover your strength. We will be gone before you wake, Philadelphian. Good luck." Ata moved to leave.

"Wait!" said Atlas. "Can you answer *one* question? I need to understand."

"There are many things that need to be understood, but it is not always that we get the opportunity to understand them."

"Please tell me, what did Taco do?" Atlas asked.

"Who?"

"The other prisoner from the detention bay. The Vitrian. Why did Pakhet imprison him?"

"That is not my business. Nor is it yours."

"Maybe not, but I need to know why you would consent to his imprisonment—why *all* of you would consent to it—after what you've been through."

"You mean our being slaves on Olympus?" Ata asked.

"Yes."

"Don't be fooled, young Philadelphian. The Vitrian is extremely dangerous, even old and maimed as he is."

"So he harmed one of you?" Atlas asked.

"No."

"He threatened to harm you?"

"No."

"Then what?"

"He is a war criminal." Ata said this firmly, but her eyes betrayed a lack of conviction.

"I don't believe that," said Atlas. Was it possible? No...maybe. How well could he know Taco after such a short conversation?

"His own people are the ones who accuse him," said Ata.

"Then why don't you hand him over to them? I'm sure there's a sizable bounty."

"We are not bounty hunters." Ata hesitated. "He has information, I suppose. Pakhet needs it, but the Vitrian will not give it to her."

"Information about what?"

"I do not know. But I trust Pakhet." Ata walked to the door.

"One last thing," Atlas said.

"You said *one* question," Ata said. "I answered one."

"Last one, I promise," Atlas said. "It's an easy one, I think."

"Go ahead," Ata smiled.

"Can you all...um...teleport like Banka did?" The question Atlas really wanted to ask was whether teleportation was safe for humans.

"Unfortunately, no," Ata said. "*Teleportation,* as you call it, is an ancient Theban technology that only those with a similar genetic background to Banka can survive. Even then, it takes a heavy toll. She mustn't engage it often."

"Thanks," Atlas nodded as he grappled with yet another disappointment. *So no teleportation either.* "I truly am very sorry about Lanta."

Ata smiled weakly. Her eyes betrayed deep grief. "Rest well, Atlas. You will need your strength. And good luck." The door slid closed behind her.

AN HOUR LATER, Atlas woke up again. Dr. Circe was pointing something metal point-blank at his head.

"Bang!" Dr. Circe said. "You're dead."

Atlas started. Fortunately, he wasn't wearing any pants. Unfortunately, he filled the bed pan. A rush of embarrassment coupled with the relief of emptying his bladder washed over him.

Dr. Circe laughed as she looked at the metal device's display and made a note of the readings.

Atlas scowled. *What a clown! How unprofessional! And tactless.*

"Just checking up on you," Dr. Circe said. "All is well. You should be able to join the others for dinner tonight."

But it was almost evening when I arrived, he thought. *How long have I been asleep? How late do they eat dinner?*

"I thought the Thebans were leaving?"

"They have left, as they said they would. I meant you should be able to join the other students."

The other students. "And they're all my age?" Atlas asked.

"Exactly. You all share the same birthday, in fact." Dr. Circe shined a light in his eyes and made some more notes. "What's the matter?"

"I don't do well with people my own age."

"Then you shall fit in," said Dr. Circe. "Most of them don't get on very well with each other."

Atlas changed the subject. "Are you a Titan?"

"I was born here," Dr. Circe said.

"That's not what I asked."

"Isn't it?" Dr. Circe smiled.

Atlas shook his head. She was impossible. "Where are my clothes?"

"They are in the drawer against the wall. They have been cleaned."

The blood. "Ata told me Diana is okay?"

"Yes. The bolt grazed her upper left breast, but will recover fully."

"I would have liked to thank Diana for saving my life."

"I saved your life, and you have not yet thanked me," said Dr. Circe. "I was beginning to think it was a Philadelphian custom not to express gratitude."

"Of course, I am grateful," said Atlas. "I apologize for not saying it sooner."

"No need to thank me. It is my duty." Dr. Circe finished her notes. "You appear to be fully recovered from both the procedure and the anesthesia, and therefore, you are free to leave the room anytime." She rolled him onto his side. "You're also free, of course, to use the restroom as you wish." She removed the full bed pan.

Atlas's face flushed. "Sorry about that. But you gave me one helluva start, waking me up with that scanner-gun thing pointed at my face."

Dr. Circe carried the bedpan into the bathroom and emptied it. "It was pretty funny." She clapped her palms together, then left the room.

The door opened again almost immediately. Dr. Circe poked her head in.

"You might also want to consider that some of us would be *grateful* for even a far-flung chance to see loved ones again." She closed the door again.

After a moment, Atlas stood up and was surprised to find that he wasn't dizzy. In fact, he didn't feel any different than before the incident. He felt around his head again, just in case he might be able to find some faint scar. Nothing. Strange. A perfectly smooth scalp. How convenient the Thebans made him shave his head. He was already getting used to being bald.

When he opened the drawer to retrieve his clothing, Atlas found a small, rectangular piece of glass tucked in with the clothes. It lit up when he touched it. A screen.

Patient's Record of Treatment
>   Patient: Atlas Gilgamesh Sterling, Philadelphian 15
>   Age: 14 Philadelphian solar cycles
>   Diagnosis: Cerebral edema due to acute head trauma
>   Treatment: See Video
>   Prognosis: Expected full recovery within 16 to 24 hours.

Sixteen to twenty-four hours. So, I've been here nearly a day already, Atlas thought.

Atlas tried to scroll around and find the video. The display didn't respond. He touched the word 'Video' and a recording began to play, of course. There was his head, and then a surgeon's hands holding a tool that simultaneously cut a chunk of scalp and skull out of his head without touching him. There was his brain. Atlas dry-heaved. He didn't watch the rest of the procedure.

Once his stomach settled, Atlas touched the part of his head where, according to the video, the hole had been cut in his skull, but still couldn't find a scar. Atlas pressed around the whole area and then again with more force. It wasn't sore, or soft, or remotely tender. *Now* that *is impressive technology. No flying cars, spaceports, or teleportation, but scarless brain surgery is pretty impressive.* But who would believe him without evidence? *Better hold onto this video.*

Atlas dressed in the clothes he had received on the Theban ship. There were no pockets, so he tucked the piece of glass in his waistband.

A few minutes later, he left the room and stepped out into a hallway. Lining each side of the corridor were identical doors, each bearing a metal plaque. The plaque across the hall read 'Philadelphian 14'. Atlas turned to the door he had exited. It read 'Philadelphian 15'. Written in English for their benefit, he guessed.

Turning back to the door across the hall, Atlas knocked.

"Just a sec," a voice said. Male, probably.

The door opened and a large, red, fuzzy-haired, human head popped out. "Howdy! So, you're Fifteen?"

"I'm Atlas. Yeah. I'm number fifteen, I guess."

"Great! We're all here, then. I suppose they'll have to finally get started with us now." He offered his hand to Atlas. His fingers were long and spindly, like the rest of him.

"I'm sorry, what's your name?" Atlas said. The boy was so tall that Atlas had to tilt his head to make eye contact.

"I apologize. I'm just excited. My name is Homer. Homer Borgnino. Number Nine."

"But the door says—"

"This isn't my room. It belongs to Pallas. I don't know her last name, yet. She's Number Fourteen, obviously." He stepped aside to reveal a girl with tight, dark curls sitting on the bed, facing them. "I'm just visiting. Pallas doesn't talk much, but she doesn't kick me out either." He turned to the girl. "Hey Pallas, this is Atlas. He's Fifteen. We're all here now, isn't that great?"

Pallas didn't answer. After Atlas waved to her, she tentatively waved back.

"Nice to meet you," Atlas said. Pallas looked at her hands, which she folded in her lap.

"Nice to meet you too, Atlas-Fifteen," Homer said. "That's how they refer to us. Name and number. It's kind of cool. Like we're robots. There aren't any robots around, though. Totally disappointing, right? All this cool technology they have, but no robots."

"No flying cars either," Atlas said. He was watching Pallas. She continued to stare at her hands.

"Exactly! Least not that I've seen."

"So there are girls here too?" Atlas said.

"Of course there are girls," said Homer. "This is an advanced civilization. Even their ancient prophecies treat girls and boys as equals."

"I didn't mean...I just hadn't thought about it, that's all." Lanta had mentioned a girl, Atlas remembered. Said she was quiet. *Poor Lanta.* He looked at Homer's red-fuzzed head and felt his own bald scalp. "She has hair."

"It's a wig," said Homer. "They let the girls wear them, if they want. Most don't after a few days. Pallas has only been here two days, though."

"Then why did...?" Atlas touched his scalp again. "What's the point...?"

A low, pleasant tone sounded three times in the hallway.

"Food time! Let's go," said Homer. "They have the best dinners here. All brought in directly from Earth. And they take requests. Just put in that you want tacos and the next day you get tacos from your favorite taco truck back home. It's great! I'm having fried chicken tonight. You'll probably get pizza or hamburgers. That's what they usually do for your first night."

Atlas was still watching Pallas and trying to take it all in. He had been told about the other Philadelphians—Earthlings—many times, but meeting them, especially one as enthusiastic as Homer, was disorienting for some reason. But why? *Until yesterday all I had ever known were Earthlings.* Why was it suddenly so strange to meet one? *At least Pallas provides a nice foil to Homer's overbearing eagerness*, he thought.

"I had pizza earlier for...uh...the last meal I ate." How long ago was that? His stomach growled.

"Hey, if you get it again, I'll trade you some chicken for a few slices?"

"Sure."

"You'll love it. Eddie's makes the best fried chicken ever. You ever been to Eddie's? It's on the north side of town, back home."

"No. I don't live near there," said Atlas.

"You're going to love it. Even if you don't get pizza, I'll give you a piece. Change your life."

"It's just chicken."

"You won't think that once you've tried it." Homer grinned confidently.

"If you say so." At first, Atlas had been interested in trying the chicken, but Homer was so enthusiastic about it, Atlas knew he'd be disappointed.

"Pallas, come on," Homer said. "It's dinner time."

"I know." Pallas stood up and walked towards the door. She looked at Atlas—really stared into his eyes—for an uncomfortable amount of time. She wouldn't let him look away. Then, Pallas took off the wig and tossed it to her bed. She fixed her gaze on Atlas again.

"You'll be picked as a squad leader," Pallas said. "If you want to survive, you'll make sure I'm on your squad."

CHAPTER 6

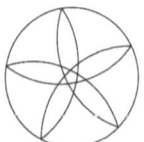

ATLAS FOLLOWED Homer and Pallas to the dining hall. Even though he had only known Pallas for a few minutes, suddenly seeing her without hair shocked him. Atlas wondered how long her hair had been before she'd been forced to delete it. Had it been dark and long with tiny curls like the wig? Had she deleted it compliantly, or had the Thebans done it forcibly?

Homer held the door for Atlas and Pallas. The other Earth students were already eating and didn't look up from their meals as Atlas and his new friends entered. The room was small, but bigger than it needed to be for so few students.

Atlas looked around the room. No one seemed to notice or care he was there. *Thought they'd at least be interested in the new kid,* he thought.

A few of the other students looked like they had a month or two of growth atop their heads. Pallas's hair was already starting to grow back, and Homer's red thatch had been growing for at least a few weeks. Atlas was glad to know his hair would grow back, but couldn't understand why they'd had to shave their heads in the first place. *Are the Titans terrified of lice? Surely their advanced medical science had developed less extreme treatments for parasites. Maybe not. How was it possible to perform scarless brain surgery but be incapable of removing simple hair parasites without shaving someone bald?*

Maybe the Titans preferred short hair. Dr. Circe had short hair, but not that short. However, it was unclear if the doctor was a Titan or not. She definitely wasn't Theban.

Then again, the Thebans had made the Fifteen shave their heads, not the Titans. Maybe that was a Theban thing? Diana had very short hair. But again, not that short. And the other Theban women all had long hair tied on top of their heads. Except maybe Pakhet, of course.

Atlas couldn't figure it out, and it bugged him. It didn't make sense. There had to be some reason. So many unanswered questions. *Why am I here? Why me? What is the prophecy? Why did the Olympians try to kill me? Why did Lanta have to die?*

Atlas shook his head. *And I'm fixating on hair.*

He recognized one of the boys in the dining hall. Oliver Ryan. One of the popular kids at his school.

Oliver sat by himself at a table on the far side of the room. Atlas left Homer and Pallas and walked up to Oliver.

"Hey Oliver," Atlas said. Oliver must not have heard, because he didn't look up. But it wasn't that noisy in the dining hall. "Ryan?" Still nothing. *Right, his friends call him O.* "Hey O!"

Oliver looked up. "Do I know you?"

"We go to the same school."

"Look around, buddy. Everyone here goes to the same school."

"I've never seen any of these people before," Atlas said. Then he realized what Oliver meant. "I mean, we went to the same school back on Earth."

"You new, eh? Thirteen or Fourteen?" Oliver asked. He seemed annoyed, like Atlas was bothering him.

"He's Fifteen, Mr. Ryan," Homer explained, coming up behind Atlas. "Sorry to interrupt your meal." Homer put his arm around Atlas's shoulders and tried to steer him away.

"Hold up," Oliver said as he stood. He was very large for his age, easily a head taller than most of the boys, though not quite as tall as Homer. Oliver was easily the more imposing figure. "We were having a conversation."

"Yes," squeaked Homer. "I'm sorry."

Oliver looked down at Atlas. "You went to Douglas? That's new. Most of these went to Hobbes or Washington Carver."

"I still go to Douglas," said Atlas. "Soon as we get home."

"We ain't going home." Oliver sat back down. "Better get used to the idea. Sooner the better. Cry it out, if you have to, but get used to it."

"Crying won't fix anything. And I refuse to get used to the idea. I'm getting home. Soon as I can."

Oliver slammed his fist on the table. Suddenly, two other boys and two girls surrounded Atlas and Homer.

"Please remove yourself from the vicinity of Mr. Ryan," said the girl closest to Atlas.

"Look, Penny," Homer began. "We're real sorry. He's Fifteen. He just got here. Ain't had time to learn about anything."

"I can speak for myself," said Atlas. "And I know well enough about what's going on. The Olympians tried to kill me right outside the gates. They got a friend of mine instead." He bit his lip. *Poor Lanta.*

"You brought a friend?" asked the other girl.

"Don't be stupid, Nerissa," said one of the other boys.

"I'm not stupid, Theo," Nerissa shot back.

"You're an ass," Penny snapped at Theo. She turned to Atlas. "What friend are you talking about?"

"Lanta. One of the Thebans," Atlas said.

"Who are the Thebans?" asked the other boy.

"The women that brought us here."

"The kidnappers?" said Nerissa. "One of them was your *friend*?"

"Not at first, of course. But eventually, yeah, she was my friend. She died protecting me." Atlas blinked three times to discourage the threatening tears.

"Friends? How long were you with them?" asked Homer. "Weren't they mean to you?"

"Quiet! We're asking the questions," said Penny. "How long were you with them?"

"Look, there's no reason to be rude," said Atlas. "He has every right to ask a question as you do."

"Except there are four of us, and only two of you," Theo said.

"So, what? You going to beat us up?" Atlas smirked and put a hand on Theo's arm. "We're all on the same team here."

Theo shook him off.

"We are *not* on the same team," said the other boy.

"We're all Earthlings or Philadelphians—whichever term you want to use. Hell, we're all from the same county, right?" Atlas looked around the room. All eyes were watching him. "They brought us here for a reason. We work together and we get home that much quicker."

"Enough!" Oliver slammed both his fists on the table and stood up again. "You don't get it, do you? You fool! The Olympians will kill us, no matter where we go. They will kill our families! They will destroy Earth, if we fail. The sooner the rest of you understand that and get out of *our* way, the sooner my friends and I save your asses!"

"What's his problem?" whispered Atlas, mostly to himself.

"Look what you did," Penny scolded him.

Nerissa put her arm around Oliver. "It's alright, O. We'll take care of them. You got other things to worry about. Just enjoy the rest of your dinner. Leave them to us."

"Time for you to leave," Theo said to Atlas. "Eugenio, you mind removing these two from the dining room?"

"No problem," said Eugenio. "Let's go." Eugenio grabbed Atlas and Homer by the back of their necks and pushed them towards the door.

"But we haven't eaten," squealed Homer. "And I ordered fried chicken."

"Don't worry, Mr. Ryan loves fried chicken," taunted Eugenio.

"Let go of me!" said Atlas. He struggled and twisted, but couldn't free himself from Eugenio's grip. The rest of the students in the dining hall watched as he and Homer were thrust towards the exit. One or two chuckled quietly. Several others looked down with shame when Atlas met their gaze.

"Wait," said Oliver. "Let them eat."

Eugenio stopped, but didn't let go of Atlas and Homer. Instead, he flung the boys around to face Oliver. "What?"

Pallas stood in front of Oliver, speaking quietly. Compared to him, she looked like a flea before a giant. Oliver waved Eugenio off.

"Aw, come on, O! I was having fun."

"Let them eat," Oliver said.

Eugenio pushed Atlas and Homer forward. "You heard Mr. Ryan. Go eat."

Homer walked quickly to the service area, retrieved his fried chicken, and found a seat as far from Oliver and his group as he could manage.

Atlas didn't move. Eugenio shrugged and returned to his table. Pallas and Oliver continued their conversation. Every once in a while, Oliver nodded. Nerissa approached him, but he waved her off. After another minute, Penny tried to approach, but Oliver turned her away as well. Finally, he sat back down at his table.

Atlas couldn't be sure, but it looked like Oliver scratched away a tear. Pallas remained standing in front of him, unmoved. Oliver nodded twice, and Pallas turned and walked to the service area for her food.

Penny, Theo, and the other two crowded around Oliver. At first, he didn't acknowledge them. Then he told a joke and laughed at it more than anyone. The rest of the students in the dining hall took their cue and returned to their food.

"What did you say to him?" Atlas whispered to Pallas. He retrieved his food—two fast-food cheeseburgers—and followed Pallas to a seat next to Homer.

"It was a private matter," she said.

Atlas thought quietly for a moment while he chewed his cheeseburgers. "You're right. And I don't need details. But whatever you said kept Homer and I from going hungry or getting beat up."

"Or both," Homer said between mouthfuls of chicken. "And we are very grateful." He smiled a big, open-mouthed, semi-chewed chicken smile and held up a styrofoam cup that came with his meal. "They even got me coleslaw."

"Yes, we are grateful," Atlas said. "But I would feel better if I knew at least a little about what you said that changed Oliver's mind."

"I asked nicely," Pallas said. "Why does it matter?"

"Yeah, why does it matter?" Homer said. "We got to keep our food and our faces."

Atlas frowned at Homer. "But at what cost?"

Pallas looked down at her food. There wasn't much to look at. Steamed carrots and broccoli next to a small, simply grilled chicken breast.

What restaurant serves that? Pallas must not have much of an imagination, Atlas decided.

"Look," Atlas began. "Oliver and I went to the same school, but I didn't know him well, and he apparently didn't know me at all. But, I know that someone like him doesn't just change his mind 'cause you *asked nicely*."

"You underestimate him," Pallas said.

"I don't," Homer said. He was beaming, ecstatically eating his chicken.

"He didn't send you away," said Pallas. "His goons did. He got upset, but he didn't send you away."

"Good point," grunted Homer through a mouthful of slaw.

"What was the deal?" Atlas said.

"I don't know what you mean," said Pallas.

"Yes, you do. What did you promise him? I need to know if you…"

"If I what?" Pallas raised her voice. She glared at Atlas. "Go on. If I what?"

"If you promised him something…to protect us." Now it was Atlas's turn to look at his food.

"How typical!" Pallas said. "I'm just a little woman, so of course the only thing I would have to offer is sex, right?"

Homer nearly choked. He coughed bits of chicken onto the table.

Atlas blushed. "That's not what I meant."

"Then what did you mean?"

"Just that I hope you didn't promise a favor—a non…uh… sexual favor—to get us out of trouble."

"That's almost as bad," Pallas said. She cut her chicken into tiny pieces before she put anything into her mouth.

"I'm sorry." Atlas didn't know why she thought any favor was almost as bad as her earlier accusation, but he'd stuck his foot in his mouth enough for one day. He quietly finished his cheeseburgers.

"So, what do you think you're going to order for dinner tomorrow?" Homer asked as he gnawed on his last drumstick. Bits of fried chicken dribbled down his chin. "You have to do it before you go to bed, otherwise you get the same goop they feed us for breakfast and lunch. I'll show you how when we get back to the rooms."

Atlas looked at Pallas but she wouldn't meet his gaze. "I don't know. Maybe fried chicken." He turned to Homer. "You made it look so appetizing."

Pallas laughed quietly and glanced at Atlas. The awkwardness broke. "I didn't promise anything," she said. "I presented my argument and he listened. I told you, you underestimate him. That's all I'll say."

Atlas nodded. "I'm sorry."

"I think I'm going to order tacos for tomorrow," Homer said. "*Tacos de cabeza*. Head tacos. It sounds gross, but it's not really, and they're pretty good. There's no brains in them. Those are *tacos de sesos*. Tacos de cabeza are made from the meat on the head of the cow. Cheeks, face, stuff like that…"

"That sounds worse than brains," Pallas said.

"Yuck," said Atlas.

"They're good! I'll let you try one."

"No thanks," said Atlas.

"Yuck," said Pallas.

Atlas and Pallas laughed.

"More for me," Homer said. "Y'all are missing out, though."

"I'll have to take your word for it and live with the consequences," Atlas said.

"Me too," said Pallas.

A different door Atlas hadn't noticed opened and the other students became silent. Oliver and his group stood up, as if at attention. Atlas turned to look. Three unusually tall males and an even taller female entered. The men were dressed in black, the woman in white, like Dr. Circe. She was much taller than Dr. Circe, however. And she wore her dark hair—black, almost blue—combed back and tied in parallel knots down the back of her head.

"Are those Titans?" Atlas asked.

"Yes," whispered Homer.

"They look like humans," Atlas said.

"Shh!" said a girl at the table next to them.

"They look like humans," Atlas whispered.

"But taller," Homer said.

"A lot taller," said Atlas.

"And I heard they have three lungs, three kidneys, two hearts, and the guys have four—" Homer looked at Pallas and didn't finish. His cheeks turned pinker than normal.

The Titan woman walked to the center of the room. All the students turned their seats to face her. Oliver and his group remained at attention. Penny stole a sideways glance at Oliver and smiled admiringly.

Someone has a crush, Atlas thought.

"I am sure you all know by now that the fifteenth Philadelphian has arrived," the Titan woman began. "I know there are rumors, so let me clear them up. One of the Theban women we contracted to retrieve you all was killed by an Olympian sniper during the transfer of Fifteen to this facility. Another of the women was also shot, but survived thanks to the skill of our own Dr. Circe."

Atlas bowed his head as he thought of poor Lanta who had taken a slug meant for him. And he thought of Ata, who was now without her twin sister. The other Philadelphians whispered among themselves.

"The sniper met his end at the hands of one of the deceased's colleagues," the woman continued. "Another three Olympian operatives have been captured and are being interrogated at another facility.

"We had hoped to retrieve you all without incident. Our intelligence said that we were at least six months ahead of the Olympians in identifying you. The most recent report indicated the Olympians had yet to discover your planet's coordinates."

She paused to look around the room.

"We've learned that the sniper and other agents have been here on Titan for nearly ten years as an embedded sleeper cell. They were activated when the Olympians learned how many of you we had already retrieved."

The Titan began to slowly pace as she spoke. "Let this be the first lesson you learn from me: the Olympians want you dead. They don't care that you're young. They will kill you all and anyone that tries to help you, given the chance." She paused to make sure they were all listening. "They will give you no mercy. They deserve none from you."

The Titan walked in a slow circle, carefully studying each of the students. Oliver and his group stood at attention and didn't make eye contact.

"We brought you here to protect you and prepare you to fight back," she said. Most of the others, Homer included, dropped their eyes when she met them. Pallas met her gaze unflinchingly, and studied the woman's face, her head cocked slightly. Atlas simply nodded.

"Out of necessity, it took some time to gather you all here." The Titan finished her circle, and stood again in the center of the room. "We had to be quite sure that we retrieved the right students. Additionally, we did not wish to draw too much attention by trying to retrieve you all at once. And finally, trustworthy retrieval contractors are...well, they are uncommon."

"Excuse me, ma'am," Atlas said.

Several in the room gasped audibly.

Theo stepped forward. "Quiet, Fifteen!" he barked.

"That's not necessary," said the woman. "Go ahead, young man."

"My name is Atlas. I'm number fifteen, they tell me. The woman who died was a friend of mine. Her name was Lanta. She died protecting me. But she would have just as readily died protecting any one of you. That was their job, and they were exceptionally good at it, obviously." Atlas looked around the room. "We're all alive."

Atlas could see Theo seething. The others in the room watched him with a mixture of disinterest and resentment. *Perhaps they think I'm chewing them out.* He reflexively shook his head.

"Anyway, the Thebans told me a bunch of times that I'd understand why I was taken from my home once I got here. Well, I've been here for more than a day now, and I still have no idea why we're here—why you brought us here."

"You are here to fulfill a prophecy," the Titan said.

I already knew that much, Atlas thought. He bit his lip.

The Titan spread her arms wide. "All of you are here to fulfill a prophecy." Her face was grave and intense. "And to stop the Olympians from destroying the Galaxy."

CHAPTER 7

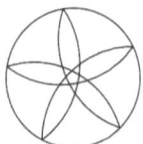

"Is that all?" asked the Titan woman.

"Not quite, ma'am," Atlas said. "I've two more questions. Well, actually, I have a million more, but only two I think you'll answer right now."

"Go ahead then."

"First, what's your name? And second, how long do you think this whole saving the galaxy thing is going to take? Baseball season starts in three weeks and my team has a real shot of winning it all this year. It'd be nice to be home in time for opening day."

Some of the Philadelphians laughed. Others looked from Atlas to the woman, and back again, terror in their faces. Theo glared at Atlas.

After an uncomfortable silence, the Titan also laughed. "Sorry, the translator had some trouble with *baseball*. I'm afraid you won't make it home in time for this season. Or next season." She became grim. "Truthfully, some of you may never make it back."

The room was silent and heavy again. This lady sure knew how to kill a joke, Atlas thought.

"As for your first question, it is more important that you understand *what* I am rather than *who* I am," the woman said. "I am your instructor, your trainer, your teacher, your coach. I am all of those things and more."

"So what do we call you?" Atlas asked. "Are you a commander, or captain, or something like that? Do we get to call you Sarge?"

A few more laughed this time.

"I am not in the military, so no. You may call me Nike."

"Like the shoes?" whispered Homer.

"Victory," said Atlas to himself. He nodded in understanding. "That's what we're supposed to think, right?" he asked Nike. "Probably not your real name, or even what your real name translates into, but you need us to look to you and think *victory*, so you picked a name that will translate to something significant from Philadelphian culture. Makes sense. If we lose, the galaxy goes boom, right?"

"You are clever, Atlas-Fifteen. But perhaps it would have been more so to keep that observation to yourself." She turned her attention to the others. "It is true that you must put that thought first in your minds. There can only be victory." Her gaze fell on Oliver and his friends. "If we fail, all is lost. Your families. Your friends. Your planet. All lost forever." She returned to Atlas. "I will prepare you to achieve victory, but we shall only finally accept it after immense personal sacrifice." She surveyed the students again. "And you begin to pay that price tomorrow morning. Get some rest. You will need it."

Nike left the dining hall. The three Titan men followed behind her.

"We better go," Homer said. He nodded towards Oliver. Theo and Eugenio glared at Atlas. They whispered to each other and menacingly drew a line across their throats.

Atlas decided he'd poked enough bears for the day. He stood and moved to gather his tray.

"I got it," Homer said. "You go ahead."

"Let's go," said Pallas. She stood and grabbed Atlas by the arm. "Move."

"What's the rush?" Atlas said. "I'm not afraid of them."

"Don't be an idiot," Pallas said as she dragged him towards the door. "You drew attention to yourself, in front of everybody. Theo and Eugenio don't like it when people draw attention to themselves, unless that person is Oliver." She pushed Atlas into the corridor.

"How would you know? You've only been here a few days more than me."

Pallas grabbed Atlas's hand and pulled him towards their rooms. "Oliver's cousin was my best friend as a kid."

"We're still practically kids."

"Some of you are," Pallas said. She became quiet, seemingly lost in thought. "Sybil died about two years ago." She paused for a second, then shook her head and continued hauling Atlas towards his room.

"I'm sorry," Atlas said.

"I've known Oliver for five years. Theo and Eugenio have been his friends since their mothers met each other in the hospital the day they—the day *we*—were born. I know them well enough." She grimaced.

"What about those girls with them?" Atlas asked.

"All I know is they went to school with Theo and Eugenio back on Earth," Pallas said as they arrived at Atlas's room. "You have to open it. It's coded to your biometrics." She tapped the door. Nothing happened. "See?"

Atlas touched the door and it opened. "Cool." He turned and smiled at Pallas.

Pallas pushed him inside. "Stay in here and don't come out until morning. Things will be calmer in the morning."

"Seriously, don't you think you're overreacting, just a little?"

"No." Pallas touched the side of the door frame and Atlas's door snapped shut.

"Well, good night," said Atlas. *Think she can hear me through the door?* "Good night, Pallas," he yelled. He pressed his head against the door to listen for a response. It slid open as soon as he touched it. "Oops."

Pallas stood there, glaring. "I said, don't come out!" She touched the side of the door again and it shut in Atlas's face.

"You going to stay out there all night?" he called. *What does she think Theo and Eugenio plan to do? Beat me to a pulp? Cut off a finger? A limb? Slit my throat for drawing attention to myself?*

"And I thought she didn't have much of an imagination." Atlas shook his head.

The whole thing was absurd. Everything that had happened the last few days was absurd. He felt a sudden wave of melancholy and decided the best thing to do was go to bed.

Atlas went to the drawer and looked for some pajamas. Nothing. In fact, aside from underwear, there wasn't any other clothing. One set of clothes? He pinched his shirt and sniffed it. *This is going to get funky.* Atlas remembered the glass rectangle tucked in his waistband. *No need to carry this around, I guess.* He pulled the glass out and tucked it underneath a pair of underwear. Then he peeled off his clothes and climbed into bed. The lights gradually dimmed until the room was nearly perfectly dark.

At first, Atlas thought he'd feel funny trying to sleep in what had been his hospital bed a few hours earlier. Within a few minutes, however, he was snoring.

NINE AND A HALF HOURS LATER, Atlas awoke to a persistent, but pleasant beeping. After unsuccessfully searching around the room for a few minutes, he realized the sound was coming from his drawer. Underneath his underwear, he found the glass rectangle, lit up like a county fair and beeping incessantly. His stomach growled. As he lifted the glass rectangle, the beeping stopped and the display changed to tell him that breakfast was in fifteen minutes.

As the lights in his room reached full brightness, Atlas held the glass up and squinted as he scrutinized it. "Where are the speakers?" The screen turned white. As far as he could tell, it was just a piece of glass. After another few minutes of turning the glass over and over in his hands, Atlas put it back in his underwear drawer.

The whole bathroom was covered in a white ceramic of some sort, but without grout lines or visible seams of any form. There was a shower, a separate bathtub, a heated, automatic-cleaning toilet (quite pleasant), a touch-free sink, and a medicine cabinet filled with new toothbrushes, toothpaste, mouthwash, deodorant, and over-the-counter pain medicine—all brands that could be found at any corner drugstore on Earth.

"That's curious," he said. *Why the medicine?*

Atlas stepped into the shower and warm water immediately streamed from four different directions. *Much nicer than that Theban shower.* A small dispenser in the wall squirted soap onto his hands when he placed them near it, which was neither novel nor impressive. However, the tiny squirt of soap lathered more than enough to wash his entire body. And it glowed slightly as it reacted with water. That concerned Atlas a bit, but it all washed away cleanly, and he didn't grow an extra arm. When he finished the shower, a gust of warm air blasted up from the shower floor and rapidly dried him off.

"I love this bathroom," Atlas said. Then he smiled wryly as he thought about all the amazing technology he had witnessed the last few days—his scarless surgery, trans-light travel, interstellar fast-food delivery (*Dammit! I forgot to order dinner for tonight!*), and the glass rectangle.

But the thing that excited him the most was the bathroom.

"It's the little things, after all."

He laughed again as he looked at his face in the mirror and felt his hand around his scalp. The faintest of stubble was beginning to grow. *Still don't know why they made us shave*, he thought.

Suddenly, the mirror lit up. Five minutes until breakfast, it read.

Better get a move on. Atlas put on some new underwear before he noticed that his clothes had been neatly folded and stacked. They lay on the floor where he had left them after undressing the night before. Atlas was certain he hadn't folded them.

Did housekeeping or someone come in while I was showering? Why wouldn't he or she put them in the drawer, or at least on the bed?

"Creepy."

"Three minutes until breakfast," a voice blared from the bathroom.

Atlas peeked back into the bathroom. The mirror flashed rapidly and repeated, "three minutes until breakfast," over and over.

"Alright! I'm hurrying," Atlas said as he pulled on his clothes.

"Two minutes until breakfast," the mirror said.

Atlas hurriedly brushed his teeth and hurried out the door. Pallas was waiting outside.

"Did you stay out here all night?" Atlas asked.

"Of course not. I wanted to talk to you before breakfast."

"Okay. We better hurry, or I'll never hear the end of it from my mirror," Atlas said as he started down the hall.

"What?"

"Never mind. You sleep well?"

"Not at all. I was thinking."

"I slept great."

"Good for you." Pallas stopped and grabbed Atlas by the shoulders. "I need to say this before we get in there, and you need to promise me you won't mention what I have to say to anyone else."

"Um...okay. What is it?" Atlas felt uncomfortable. Why was she talking to him? They barely knew each other.

"We can't trust them."

"Who? The Olympians?"

"No—well, I mean, of course we can't trust the Olympians. But I'm referring to the Titans. We can't trust them either."

"Why do you say that? If the Titans hadn't brought us here, the Olympians would just kill us on Earth."

"Yes, maybe. But that doesn't mean we can trust them."

"They saved our lives," Atlas said.

"So they say." Pallas frowned, clearly frustrated. "But why?"

"So we can fulfill the prophecy, of course. Whatever that means."

Pallas rolled her eyes. "According to Nike, it means stopping the Olympians from destroying the galaxy."

"I admit it sounds crazy," said Atlas. The whole thing was so absurd. Fifteen kids against an entire advanced civilization.

"I just don't buy it."

"Buy what?"

"That the Olympians will destroy the galaxy or that they even want to."

"They tried to kill me," said Atlas. He felt attacked and defensive. "They obviously consider us a threat, no matter how ridiculous it sounds."

"I'm not on their side," Pallas said. "It's just that Nike wants us to believe the whole galaxy is at stake, but I'm not convinced that's true."

"So what if it's not? I'm not going to let the Olympians win, whatever the stakes."

They killed Lanta. That makes them my enemy, Atlas thought.

"But that's my point," said Pallas. "What does victory look like? What does it mean when we win, other than that the Olympians lose? Why should we hand the victory over to the Titans? Can we trust them with whatever power that entails?"

"I don't know." Atlas's stomach grumbled. "Probably not. But for now, I'm going to pick the side that didn't kill my friend when they tried to kill me." Atlas could tell Pallas wasn't persuaded. He started again towards the dining hall.

"Just keep an open mind," Pallas pleaded with him. "The Titans will try to convince us to see and do things their way. When it comes down to it, their way might not be the right way. They have an angle just like the Olympians."

Atlas looked at Pallas. "Why are you telling me this?"

"I told you yesterday. You're going to be picked as a squad leader."

"You don't know that. You barely know me."

"There's no other choice," Pallas said. "Oliver will head one squad, of course. And Daphne another, probably—maybe. But there are no others besides you that could lead the third."

"How do you know there will be three squads?"

"Everyone knows that."

"Not me," said Atlas. "I've only been here a day and a half. And most of that first day I spent with my skull cut open." They arrived at the dining hall.

"Three squads of five. That's the plan. Alpha, Beta, and Gamma. That's all any of the others talk about. Oliver and his group will be Alpha—everyone agrees because they were the first five brought here, and they're very organized—but the others argue all day long about who will be Beta and Gamma."

That explains why Oliver told us to get out of their way, Atlas thought.

"No one knows for sure, of course. But that's what everyone believes." Pallas put her arm on Atlas's shoulder. "And I want you to be my squad leader, but I need to know you're not going to accept everything the Titans say at face value."

Atlas smiled. "You don't have to worry about that." He opened the door to the dining hall. "Now, let's eat."

The rest of the Philadelphians were already seated and eating. Pallas handed Atlas a tray with a bowl of mush that looked similar to oatmeal, except that it was green.

"What's this?" Atlas sniffed at it. It kind of smelled like oatmeal, but also a lot like dirt.

"Some local grain. It's terrible, but edible. It's supposedly one of the only things on the planet that humans can eat," Pallas grimaced. "It fills you up and gives you plenty of energy. That's the best thing anyone can say about it."

"Hey Pallas! Atlas!" Homer called from an otherwise empty table. "I saved you seats."

"Morning, Homer," said Atlas. "How'd you sleep?"

"Same as always. On my back." He grinned. "Sorry, that was my dad's joke."

"Sounds like a dad joke," Atlas said.

"How are you this morning, Pallas?"

"Well, thank you." Pallas focused grimly on her food.

"Pallas still isn't used to the green stuff yet," said Homer. "If you close your eyes as you swallow, it's not so bad. You do get used to it, sort of. Every breakfast and lunch, no matter what. No wonder they bring in whatever you want for dinner. They'd have a mutiny if they didn't. Plus, it really wakes you up. Like you drank a quart of coffee, but without the frequent trips to the pisser. Or the racing heartbeat."

Atlas closed his eyes and put a spoonful of the green oatmeal in his mouth. It was slightly bitter and also kind of sour. But the texture was nothing like oatmeal. More like raw egg yolks, or swallowing a loogie. He opened his eyes. They watered slightly.

Homer was grinning ear to ear. "Well, what did you think?"

"It's pretty bad." Atlas grimaced and shook his head. A rancid aftertaste lingered.

"Yes it is," said Pallas. She hadn't been able to work up the courage to eat any yet.

"Well, might as well get it over with," said Atlas. He picked up his bowl and tilted it to his lips. "Here goes." He bent his head back and half-poured, half slurped the entire bowl in twenty seconds. When Atlas finished, he gagged.

Homer laughed and Pallas smiled.

"Water," Atlas choked. "I need water."

"Here, have mine," Homer laughed and handed Atlas his glass. "That's a way to do it!"

Pallas lifted the bowl to her mouth, closed her eyes, pinched her nose with one hand, and gulped the food as fast as she could. "Yuck!" she said as she slammed down the bowl. "I think that was worse than eating it one spoon at a time. Is there any water left?"

"I'll get more," said Homer. He hurried over to the service area and brought back three glasses of water. "Here you go."

Pallas guzzled down two glasses. The two boys laughed heartily.

Their laughter was interrupted by Nike's entrance and the sudden silence it invoked. She was alone.

Atlas looked around the room. Oliver and his group, of course, stood at attention. Everyone else had frozen mid-conversation, mid-gesture, or mid-bite.

"It is time to begin," Nike said. "Please clear your tables and follow me. Quickly."

Oliver and his group broke attention and cleared their table. The others followed in silence. Atlas trailed behind Pallas and Homer.

"We'll start every morning with a five-mile run," said Nike. "Normally, we will run before breakfast, but today will be the exception. I set the pace. Keep up with the group or you will run twice that distance now and then again after lunch."

Some of the students groaned. Atlas almost cried. *Anything but long-distance running. I'd rather lose a finger.*

"Not a runner, eh?" whispered Homer.

"Not *long* distance," Atlas said. "I'm more of a sprinter."

"I've run two marathons," Homer beamed.

"What about you?" Atlas asked Pallas.

"This is going to suck," she said.

CHAPTER 8

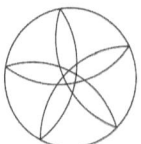

NEITHER ATLAS nor Pallas were able to keep the pace Nike set. The Academy running track was only four hundred meters around, which meant Atlas and Pallas had to run it forty times, and had another forty to look forward to after lunch. At least it was air-conditioned.

When they finally finished the fortieth lap, Atlas and Pallas collapsed onto the ground. "Why are we doing this?" Atlas huffed. "Why *did* we do this? What would they do if we refused? Just sat down right here and refused?"

"I...don't...know," Pallas heaved. "Probably...let us...starve."

"Or force-feed us a double ration of that green oatmeal," Atlas said.

"That...would be way worse."

Atlas groaned. "I'd rather run two-hundred miles."

"Me too," Pallas said. "Well, come on then. We'll be late for the first class." She stood up.

Atlas wrinkled his nose. "I don't want to call them classes."

"What would you call them?"

"I don't know." Atlas thought about it as the two walked to the dormitory. "Calling them classes makes it seem like this is just another normal day in my life back home. Wake up, have breakfast, and go to school." He began to count backwards from one hundred by threes in his head. "This is not normal. This is *not* our home!"

"I know that," Pallas said quietly. "I never said it was."

"I know. Sorry, I wasn't upset at you." Atlas sighed. "But I'd rather be home. I never asked to be the fulfillment of an ancient prophecy. It's not fair."

"Life's not fair." Pallas touched the door to her room. It opened and she stepped in. "It never has been and never will be," she said. The door closed.

"Well, that was melodramatic," Atlas said under his breath. He realized he'd been even more so.

Inside his room, Atlas stripped off his sweaty clothes and ran to the shower. The mirror was flashing yellow. The first class started in eight minutes.

Three minutes later, the shower shut off automatically. "The shower knows I'm late," Atlas muttered. "That's annoying, but also kinda' cool."

After a quick—almost *too* warm—blast of air dried him off, Atlas retrieved a fresh pair of underwear and turned to the clothes he had stripped off. Again, they were folded and stacked neatly in the same spot he had left them.

"What the hell?"

Atlas picked up the shirt between two fingers and held it out in front of him. It was dry. No sweat stains. He smelled it. Clean. At least, it smelled clean. *Are these new clothes? Who brought them in? How'd they know I was in the shower again?*

"So very creepy."

Atlas dropped the shirt back in the pile. It landed a crumpled mess. Then, as Atlas watched, the shirt began to move. A bump the size of a small animal moved around under the crumpled shirt.

With a startled yelp, Atlas kicked the shirt across the room. It hit the wall and slid down in a clump. Atlas picked up the pants and shook them vigorously. The last thing he wanted was an alien spider or small rodent climbing around inside his pants.

Nothing fell out. He cautiously put the pants on before retrieving the shirt.

There it was, laying against the wall, but now perfectly folded. He picked up the shirt and shook it. Nothing fell out.

"Nah, that can't be it." He tossed it in the air and let the shirt fall to the floor. Within seconds, the shirt began to move again, slowly bending, scrunching, stretching, and gathering until it was perfectly and neatly folded.

"Three minutes until class!" screeched the mirror.

Atlas picked up his shirt again and pulled it over his head. "Self-folding clothes—self-folding *and* self-fitting," he said. *Self-cleaning, maybe? Who thinks of that? I look like a burglar or dancer but these are the best clothes I've ever had.*

"Little things," he said.

There was a buzz at his door. Atlas touched it open and was met by Pallas and Homer.

"We need to hurry," Homer said.

"I said you could go ahead," Pallas told Homer.

"I don't mind." Homer grinned. "Now we can sit together, if there's room. Hurry up."

The three of them jogged to the Amphitheater. Pallas stopped Atlas outside the door. Homer went in without noticing.

"Remember, don't take everything they tell us at face value," Pallas said.

"I won't, Mom," Atlas said.

Pallas scowled.

"You're not going to kiss me in front of all my friends, are you, Mom?" Atlas said, though as soon as the words left his mouth, he regretted them.

Pallas pursed her lips tight. "Go on, make a joke of it. I'm right. You'll see." She turned and stormed into the room.

Atlas frowned as he watched Pallas go. Sometimes, when he opened his mouth...why couldn't he keep it shut? He followed Pallas inside.

"Atlas!" Homer whispered loudly, enthusiastically waving them over to the seats he was saving.

Pallas made Homer give her his seat and sit between her and the other saved seat. Atlas noted there were quite a few available seats in the room. He considered sitting in one of them.

The clock above the small stage ticked the hour and the doors behind the podium opened. The room became silent. Atlas hurried to the seat next to Homer and sat down.

"Just in time," whispered Homer. "What took you? I thought you were right with me."

"Not marathon runners, remember?"

A large, old man entered with a slow and methodical pace. He was enormous, clearly a Titan, and even with his aged frame hunched forward, he was easily more than eight feet tall. Like the other Titans, the old man wore simple clothing, though it was difficult to tell exactly if it was black, brown, gray, or blue.

The Titan carried an old, dusty book tucked under one arm. He steadied his gait with a cane that was a little too short to support him. As he walked, the book began to slip out from under his arm. He had to stop and readjust the book every few steps. Finally, he reached the podium, and with tremendous difficulty lifted the book high enough to set it on top.

He coughed six times without covering his mouth.

Advanced alien civilization or not, old men never think the rules of hygiene apply to them, thought Atlas.

Recovered from his coughing fit, the old man opened the book. The room immediately went dark.

This whole place is so melodramatic. Atlas turned to look around the darkened room. He could see nothing at all. No light crept in under the doors, or from any other source. There wasn't even an exit sign.

Turning back to the front, Atlas noticed light now emanating from the top of the podium. The old book was glowing. And then, an explosion of bright shapes and figures shot up out of the book and flew about the room.

Some of the students gasped and others clapped. Was this a circus? Or a magic show? At least it didn't feel like the boring school orientation assemblies he was used to on Earth.

The flying shapes slowed and settled into positions around the ceiling. Without warning, the seats tilted back so that the students could comfortably look up. Atlas hadn't noticed the domed ceiling before, but now, as the shapes and figures found their places, the resulting image overhead resembled an ancient star chart—complete with illustrated constellations, orbital paths, and ancient-looking script.

"Like a planetarium," said Homer.

Despite the old book being the only source of light, Atlas could now see around the room. The other students seemed entranced by the display. Many smiled with open mouths. Others craned their necks excitedly, turning so quickly that Atlas was sure they would wake up with stiff necks the next morning. Even Pallas appeared enchanted by the spell of the almost magical star chart.

Only Oliver remained stoic and, apparently, unmoved. Had Oliver always been so serious? No. The kids at school—back on Earth—used to think he was funny, almost a class clown, except he was always very respectful of teachers. *What happened to him? Does he know something the rest of us don't?*

The old man spoke, his face illuminated by the book. "Ninety-five generations past, the Titan civilization first ventured into space." The star chart zoomed into a narrow segment displaying a planet and its moons.

"Three moons," said Atlas. "Guess I didn't have time to notice them when I was running for my life." *How does that affect the tides?* he wondered. *Don't suppose they'll take us on a field trip to the beach? Not with Olympian assassins running around out there.*

"In accordance with the observed pattern in every advancing civilization we have since studied, our first steps into the great emptiness were likewise halting and tentative. Short orbital flights led to the exploration of our moons and eventually the planets within our solar system."

As the old man described the Titan space program, dotted arcs on the ceiling traced the paths of the various missions, zooming wider when it became necessary to show the exploratory missions to the fifteen planets within their system.

"The excitement of the era knew no bounds. For eight generations, space exploration filled the popular imagination, and the potential for discovery seemed as infinite as the Universe." Images of Titan spacecraft, astronauts, probes, and rovers flew across the ceiling. "And yet, the outcome of these explorations was decidedly less optimistic. None of the other planets in our solar system sustained life at any level, and the complex organisms necessary for the establishment of sustainable colonies could never survive in such harsh environments."

The old book projected the plans for multiple proposed colonies alongside the image of a corresponding planet. A large black dot appeared in the center of each plan before they faded away, leaving nothing but six barren, rotating planets.

"So melodramatic," Atlas whispered to Homer.

"What?" Homer said.

"Never mind."

"Enthusiasm for our space program waned. Constrained by the speed of light, further space exploration seemed pointless and wasteful. For several generations, the space program was abandoned altogether." The old man turned a page in the book. The dome filled with stars. "Eventually, we cast our gaze into the heavens once again with renewed wonder. This time, however, our goals were much grander and bolder." The stars on the ceiling zoomed into a small section of the sky. "We identified a system with multiple planets within the star's habitable zone and at least two of those planets appeared to have liquid water on the surface." A solar system with three highlighted planets filled the dome.

"Located less than eight light-years away, the possibility of making contact with intelligent life or colonizing other planets re-energized our entire civilization. First, we attempted to make contact, broadcasting high-powered communication bursts to the planets. When they went unanswered, we sent exploratory probes to the planets, all the while preparing spacecraft and astronauts to make the nearly twenty-year journey. The probes sent back astonishing images of a lush and flourishing ecosystem on the middle planet." The old man turned the page again. Images from the probes flashed across the dome. Peculiar animals, insects, and plants featured prominently. Also projected were breathtaking landscapes of snow-covered mountains rising above fertile rain forests; endless, blooming flatlands irrigated by innumerable winding rivers; and tens of thousands of islands peaking out of a crystal-green sea.

"It's a paradise," said Homer.

"Yes," Atlas said. He looked at Pallas. She nodded, her mouth slightly agape in astonishment.

"Most importantly, the probes sent back data confirming the environment could sustain our species." The old man turned a page again, revealing a large spacecraft orbiting Titan. Smaller vessels traveled to and from the large vessel, bringing supplies and people. "Initially, we sent only five hundred colonists along with enough food and livestock to sustain them for two generations—enough for the initial journey, a five-year exploratory expedition, and the return trip, if necessary. To our great delight, the first colony flourished. Their population quadrupled before the two-generation time frame had elapsed." Images of the early colonists and their settlements floated across the ceiling. Many included small children and babies. "The expedition proved so successful that over the next six generations, we sent over a million colonists to the new planet, which the original colonists had named Olympus."

Atlas felt a sudden icy pit in his stomach.

Pallas gasped quietly.

"So, the Titans and Olympians are related," Homer said. "That certainly makes things interesting."

The room lights slowly came up, the images on the dome faded, and the old book ceased glowing.

"Alas, further colonization was brought to an end by a vicious and bloody conflict amongst those of us who remained on Titan—a conflict that decimated our population and left large swaths of the planet all but uninhabitable."

"World war," Homer whispered.

"Sounds even worse," said Pallas.

"Out of the ashes of that conflict arose a dark and vile tyranny. For thirty-three generations, Titan was ruled by a despotic dynasty that nearly destroyed everything we had achieved scientifically, economically, socially, and culturally. Much of the knowledge we had previously attained was lost. Most egregiously, we had no contact with Olympus during that period."

"Why didn't the Olympians return during all that time to see what had happened?" Homer asked quietly.

"Who says they didn't?" said Pallas. "Would you have stayed?"

Atlas shook his head.

"Once better times finally returned to our planet, and we had begun to rebuild our communications capability, we attempted to contact the Olympian colonists, but received no response. We assumed them all lost."

Atlas fidgeted in his seat. "This is starting to get a bit long."

"Hush," said Pallas. "I'm trying to listen."

"Weren't you the one telling me not to take what the Titans say at face value?"

Pallas ignored his question.

"On top of all the other devastations we had endured, the loss of the Olympus colonies nearly broke our spirit. We decided against any further attempts at colonization or space exploration. Our civilization required significant reconstruction and further exploration of the cosmos would have been an unwise utilization of resources. For the next twenty-five generations, we rebuilt our society and restored our world to the best of our ability, anxiously seeking out any surviving scientific and cultural artifacts from before the Great War. Much of what we had once known, however, we had to rediscover."

Atlas yawned. He looked around the room. The old man should have kept his light show going. Several of the other students were beginning to nod off. Not Oliver or his group, though. Of course not.

"When we finally ventured into space again, we dispatched an archaeological expedition tasked with discovering the fate of the Olympus colonies. However, once the expedition craft entered the Olympus system, we lost contact with it and never heard from them again. A generation later, a strange spacecraft entered our orbit. They attacked without provocation, destroying an entire city before we could disable their ship."

"Bastards," said Homer. He glanced at Pallas. "Sorry, I don't usually swear."

"Don't worry about it," Pallas shrugged.

"When we boarded the enemy ship, we discovered it was piloted by Olympians, all of whom had committed suicide. Nearly 500,000 Titans were killed during the incursion, while only twenty-eight Olympians lost their lives."

Pallas tried to covertly wipe a tear from her eye.

"During the ensuing generations, we engaged in a desperate space and arms race, fighting innumerable battles out in the black emptiness between Titan and Olympus. The outcomes of most we did not learn until nearly a generation later. And yet, we continued building and sending heavily-armed spacecraft hurtling towards Olympus at fractionally relativistic speeds, hoping to intercept and destroy their next wave before it reached us."

The old Titan was beginning to depend more heavily on the support of the podium and his cane.

Atlas began to slouch deeper into his seat and experimented with closing his eyes for several seconds at a time. Wasn't that green oatmeal supposed to keep you awake? He wished for another light show.

"The war was destroying our economy and decimating our resources. And worse, we did not know if we were at all successful in repelling the Olympian invasion, or if we were merely delaying the inevitable." The old Titan again coughed without covering his mouth. "In a last, desperate effort, we positioned our most heavily-armed spacecraft fleet in a defensive perimeter around our system and waited. But the Olympian fleet never materialized. A generation later, we made contact for the first time with a new, sentient race. They appeared rather suddenly within our defensive perimeter, having been previously undetected. At first, we panicked, though our fears were quickly assuaged. The Thebans had arrived."

"Thebans!" Atlas sat up in his seat.

"Why are you so interested in them?" said Homer. "They were so mean."

"...been forced from their home world, which was decimated, they claimed, by the Olympians. Without a world to call their own, we accepted them as refugees. Many continue to live here to this day."

"They're my friends," Atlas said.

"Friends don't kidnap," said Homer.

"...brought with them an extraordinary technology, which they freely shared with us. The Olympians had also acquired it during their pillaging of the Theban home world, and the Thebans wished to help us protect their new home."

"They saved my life!" Atlas snapped. He thought of Lanta, her body lying motionless in the grass as Diana carried him to the protective walls of the Academy. "They saved yours too. The Olympians would have killed you back on Earth."

"...trans-light technology enabled us to better defend ourselves from the Olympians, but more importantly, it allowed us to travel to distant, inhabited systems, make contact with many other sentient species and to engage with them in cultural and material exchange."

"The one in the helmet. She...she made me pee *my pants*," Homer whispered behind his hand.

"That was you?"

"They told you about it?" Homer slumped back in his seat. His freckled cheeks turned bright red.

"I'm sorry about that," Atlas said. "They all felt bad about it. Wanted me to apologize to you for them."

"...Titan merchants first heard rumors about the Celestial Sphere."

"Really?" Homer asked. "They were sorry? Really?"

"Very sorry," Atlas said.

"Will you two shut up?" Pallas said. "We're finally getting to something important."

"At first, the Sphere seemed a silly superstition, but our new Theban friends also admitted knowledge of this legendary and powerful relic. After an extensive investigation across more than a hundred inhabited planets, we came to believe in the literal existence of the Celestial Sphere, although each culture we spoke with held slightly different beliefs about its purpose. Some believed it an object of creation, the source of all life in the Galaxy. Others believed it a regenerative force, a fountain of youth for stars and planets. Still others believed it endowed its possessor with the divine right and power to rule the Galaxy."

"This is getting silly," said Atlas.

"During this same period, trans-light travel made it possible for us to deploy spies on Olympus. We feared they would soon resume their attacks against us, and hoped to avail ourselves the luxury of advanced warning. What we learned instead was considerably worse. The Olympians had begun their own investigation into the Celestial Sphere."

"So, its okay for the Titans to research the ultimate power in the galaxy, but not for the Olympians?" scoffed Pallas.

"They believe it is a super-weapon of nearly unlimited

destructive capacity," continued the old Titan. "Although our investigations uncovered only a handful of other cultures which considered the Sphere a great weapon, it is clear the device is one of immense, unimaginable power. Weapon or not, we are certain the Olympians could find a way to weaponize the Celestial Sphere against us and any other system they choose."

"Afraid," said Pallas. "They're afraid."

"I think they're justified," said Homer.

"They have no proof," Pallas shot back.

"Despite our extensive research, we were unable to determine the exact nature of the Sphere. Nor could we narrow down its location. Nearly three generations of investigation passed without yielding any concrete answers. Our singular consolation was that the Olympians had made even less progress in their investigations than we had."

"So, it became less of an arms race, and more of an arms scavenger hunt," Atlas said.

"Winner destroys all," murmured Pallas.

"Only once it became clear that the limits of our scientific knowledge could not reveal the truth of the Sphere to us, did someone finally suggest we seek insight from the Oracles." The old Titan took a deep breath and folded his hands across the book.

A female in the audience huffed incredulously. Atlas couldn't see who it had been.

"For many generations—well before our first forays into space —the ancient Oracles directed our people in times of war or peace, famine or prosperity, and even indifference or love. No matter the concern, those who sought after and followed the counsel of the Oracles inevitably procured the solution to their dilemmas. After the Great Dark Age, some of us attempted to resurrect the ancient Oracular rites, but with only limited success. Many of the Ancients' more esoteric practices, it seemed, had been lost forever. The modern Oracles proved incapable of discovering the Celestial Sphere."

The Titan wrung his hands together, a look of profound

sadness and shame settling over him. He gripped the edges of the podium. "Most fortunately, the Ancients had recorded numerous divinations which had not been sought by any recorded patron. It was in one of these *unbidden* prophecies that we finally discovered the key to reaching the Celestial Sphere."

"The prophecy," Homer said. "Finally."

"In an ancient, underground monastery, we discovered a copy of a text we believed had perished in the Great War. Within it, we discovered the following passage:

"When heaven moves at light's behest,
And stars burn hot as the sun,
Then blood spills blood until
All stars bleed with fear.

"Holy are the words I speak.
Holy are my tears.
Holy are the oceans deep.
Holy are my warnings.

"Then look not thou inward
For salvation nor defense.
But in fifteen children trust
The preservation of the Great Circle.

"Holy are the words I speak.
Holy are my fears.
Holy are the mountains steep.
Holy are my seeing eyes."

The old man wiped his nose with the cuff of his sleeve.

"Shouldn't it rhyme?" asked Homer. "I thought it would rhyme."

"Maybe it rhymes in the original," said Atlas. "It is a translation, after all."

"Quiet, you two," said Pallas. "I'm trying to memorize it."
The old man cleared his throat and continued.

> *"When clouds the sun before your face*
> *And evil doth conspire,*
> *Then five will rise and overcome,*
> *Bringing down peace, justice, and vengeance.*
>
> *"Holy are the words I speak.*
> *Holy are your ears.*
> *Holy is the secret's keep.*
> *Holy, holy Philadelphians."*

"That's it?" Atlas said. "That's why we were kidnapped? It's so vague and imprecise. It could mean almost anything."

"Are you kidding?" said Homer. "That was *amazing.*"

The Titan closed the book. "Before the Thebans arrived, we had never heard of Philadelphia. When we presented the prophecy to their leaders, they told us about your planet. Using the criteria and dates encoded within the prophecy, we were able to locate you."

"Encoded dates?" Homer gasped. "Awesome!"

"However, the Olympians have kept spies on Titan for at least as long as we have had them on Olympus. They learned about the existence of the prophecy and were able to locate a more recent transcription of the ancient original within the archives they brought on the first colony ships."

"We can only hope their version has some errors in it," said Pallas.

"Our spies discovered the Olympians have also resurrected the ancient, oracular rites that are our shared heritage." The look of sadness and shame settled over the old Titan again. "For several generations, the Olympian Oracles have steadily been gaining influence and power within Olympian culture. Their

Prime, a man named Delphi, has prophesied that only *your* deaths will lead the Olympians to the Celestial Sphere."

The room became still and extraordinarily silent. Atlas thought again of poor Lanta. *Always,* he thought. *I will remember her every time I reflect on death.*

"As you know, they have already made an attempt on the life of one of you. They will try again," the old man said solemnly. "But do not worry. You are safe here within these walls."

"Don't make promises you can't keep," said Pallas under her breath.

"And within these walls, you will be trained to find and retrieve the Celestial Sphere, thereby protecting Titan, Philadelphia, and the entire Galaxy from the tyranny of the Olympians!" The Titan raised his fist with a dramatic flourish.

"So, who is this guy, anyway?" asked Atlas. "He didn't even introduce himself."

"No idea," said Homer. "I thought I'd missed it when I was distracted by the flying lights."

"I am Themis, sole descendant of the ancient Oracle Themis whose prophecy you have now heard and will soon fulfill," the old man said, as if he'd overheard. "Under the direction of the Titan High Government, I have assumed the position of Prime Director of this Academy. Your mission and training will occur under my supervision. Now, go and eat well. You will need the strength."

CHAPTER 9

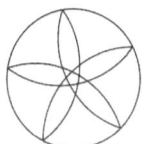

AFTER CHOKING down another bowl of the green stuff for lunch, Atlas and Pallas had to run another ten miles on the Academy track. One of the Titan men who had been with Nike the night before supervised their run. He didn't give his name when Atlas asked. Atlas shrugged and began his first lap.

When they finished the fortieth lap, Atlas flung himself to the ground. The Titan left without a word.

"I don't care if I die doing it, but I'm keeping up with Nike tomorrow," Pallas said after catching her breath. She sat up to face Atlas who remained lying on his back.

"Agreed," said Atlas. "The only thing worse than running five miles is running twenty."

"You'd think we could have figured that out without having to prove it."

"Yeah, that's pretty dense of us," said Atlas. "And somehow we're supposed to find the Celestial Sphere and save the galaxy?"

"Well, five of us anyway."

"What? You mean fifteen."

"No, five. The prophecy said only five would succeed."

"What about the other ten?"

Pallas turned to Atlas. "Probably better not to think about that."

"Yeah." Atlas furrowed his brow. "So, what happened to not taking what they said at face value?"

"I'm not. But they do tell a compelling story," Pallas said. She looked at the inside of her wrist. A rectangle of light shone from her skin. "We need to go. At least we won't need to shower."

Atlas sat up and looked closer. The light emanated from a glass like the one he had in his underwear drawer. "How'd you get it to stick to your arm?"

"It just does." She pulled the glass off, showed it to Atlas and then attached it to her wrist again. "Even sweaty." Pallas shook her hand in the air, but the glass remained firmly attached.

"You mind if we run by my room so I can get mine?"

"Sure. But we need to hurry." She stood up and grabbed Atlas by the arm, pulling him to his feet. "We're going to be late for Combat Training."

"Combat Training?"

"That's our next class." Pallas wrinkled her nose. "Sorry, but I don't know what else to call them."

"No worries," Atlas sighed. "That's what they are, after all. And anyway, it may not be normal school—at least compared to what we're used to—but this is our new normal. For at least two baseball seasons anyway. Might as well get used to it."

"Yeah," Pallas said. They walked a few steps in silence. "I still don't trust the Titans."

"That's fine. I don't think I do either. But can you imagine any school back on Earth offering a class called Combat Training?"

"No," Pallas laughed. "I can't imagine that." She became serious. "But our teachers on Earth also didn't expect us to save the galaxy."

"No," said Atlas. "Just Earth."

A few minutes later they had retrieved Atlas's glass and arrived at the Palaestra. As usual, the rest of the students were already there, mingled in clusters around the padded room.

"There you two are." Homer came barreling up to them. "You

have to be my partner, Atlas. I'm going to be murdered if I have to spar with any of the other boys."

"But you're so much taller than me."

"Yeah, but I'm weak. Like, so...so weak."

"We're fourteen years old," said Atlas. "Compared to Titans, we're all weak."

"That's why we're here," Pallas said. "To learn how not to be weak."

Homer looked at Pallas and smiled weakly, but his eyes were wide.

"The three of us will be partners," said Pallas. "There's fifteen of us. There has to be at least one group of three."

"Right." Homer was visibly relieved. He smiled again, this time sincerely.

Nike stood in the middle of the padded floor.

"Welcome to the Palaestra. I'm sure you've had more than enough speeches for the day, so we'll get started. If any of you need me to explain why you need combat training, see me after class and I'll explain what *the Olympians want to kill you* means."

Several of the students laughed. Atlas didn't think it was very funny. He thought about Lanta.

"If you haven't already found a partner, please find one and spread out across the floor." Nike paused while the students positioned themselves around the room. "We will not throw any punches today. However, when we are in this room, we do not *pull* punches, because the Olympians will not pull punches. You will hit hard. You will kick hard. You will be punched hard. And you will be kicked hard. You will get injured—some days more so than others."

Homer groaned.

"In your bathrooms, you will find medication to relieve pain and swelling, if you deem it necessary. However, I think you will find that the Amrisia mash you consume twice daily will provide sufficient relief."

"Is that the green stuff?" asked Homer.

"Such a pretty name for such a horrid substance," said Pallas.

"Now, we will begin with a simple defensive drill," continued Nike. "First, you will charge your partner. The partner will use your momentum against you like this." One of Nike's assistants charged her from close range. As he reached for her, Nike threw him over her body. He landed flat on his back with a thud and a groan. Nike stood up straight and faced the students. "Now, you try it."

Everyone chattered nervously. Homer groaned again.

"Excuse me," said a girl from the other side of the room.

"Yes?" answered Nike.

"My partner is too big." Her partner stood at least a foot taller. Nearly as large as Eugenio. "I realize that I won't have a choice when faced with a real enemy, but I really want to make sure that I learn this correctly. Once I can execute well against someone my size, then I'd feel more comfortable trying against someone as big as Ajax."

"What's your name?" asked Nike.

"My name is Arete. Most people call me Reedy."

"Number?"

"Twelve. Arete-*Twelve*," she huffed. "My apologies."

"Well Arete-Twelve, normally I would not let you exchange partners for the very reason you stated. However, since Ajax-Seven is so much taller and this is the first day, I will make an exception." Nike scanned around the room before settling her gaze in Atlas's direction. "You. Partner with Ajax-Seven. Arete-Twelve, take his spot."

Atlas assumed Nike was getting back at him for his comments the night before. "Yes, ma'am." He started towards Ajax. "Right away, Sarge," Atlas said under his breath.

"No, not *you*. You." Nike pointed at Homer.

Homer moaned and looked to Pallas for help.

"You'll be fine," she said.

Homer walked over to Ajax, who shook his hand vigorously and slapped him hard on the back.

"Hello, I am Arete. You can call me Reedy, if you want."

Reedy is a good nickname, thought Atlas. She was thin as a reed with a slight shrill in her voice, like a whistle. Her hair was quite short still, likely brown, maybe black.

"I'm Atlas. This is Pallas."

Reedy stretched out a hand, but Pallas just nodded. "Thank you for letting me join you. I really want to do well and I've never done anything like this before."

"Do you want to go first?" Atlas said.

"Maybe it would be better if the two of you went. Then I can watch you both a few times before trying it myself."

"Okay." Atlas turned to Pallas. "You want to charge or toss first?"

"You charge," Pallas said.

"Sure. I'll go slow this first time."

"No, don't pull punches. I'm not going to."

"If you say so," said Atlas. "I don't want to hurt you."

"Maybe it would be better to practice at a slower speed first?" Reedy said.

"No, just charge me," Pallas said, scowling at Reedy.

Atlas shook his head. Then he pivoted sharply and charged, hoping to catch Pallas off-guard. But Pallas was ready and threw Atlas over her back like he was a sack of feathers. He landed hard, the wind knocked out of him.

"Ow!" he said, once he recovered his breath.

"You threw him unnecessarily hard," Reedy said. "Although, I suppose he deserved it for trying to catch you unprepared."

"Your turn," snapped Pallas.

"Oh, I couldn't attack you like that."

"Why not?"

"Because you haven't done anything to harm me. Aggression is immoral. I won't attack."

"Are you serious?" asked Pallas.

"Of course."

"Fine, I'll attack you." Pallas took a few steps back and

prepared to charge. "Are you ready? I don't want to catch you *unprepared.*"

"I'm ready."

Pallas charged, but Reedy didn't move. Pallas crashed into her at full speed. Both girls fell to the floor with a hard thud.

"Sorry," said Reedy, picking herself off the ground. She offered a hand to Pallas. "I didn't want to do it wrong, so I didn't do anything."

Pallas rubbed the side of her head. "Doing nothing counts as doing it wrong."

Reedy retracted her hand. Her shoulders drooped. "Yes, I guess you're right."

Atlas reached out to touch Reedy, but pulled back before contact. "Hey, she didn't mean anything by it."

"Yes I did," said Pallas. "Now we're both injured. Because you were too—"

There was a loud commotion on the other side of the room. Most of the students gathered in a circle looking at something on the floor. Atlas and the two girls hurried over to see what had happened.

"Penelope-Two, please go get Dr. Circe," Nike said. "Quickly."

Penny looked at Nike hesitantly, and then at Oliver. He nodded and Penny turned and jogged towards the medical center.

Atlas pushed through the circle of onlookers. Nike stooped over someone sprawled across the mat. Ajax stood opposite Nike, nervously biting his finger nails.

"Oh no!" Reedy said. "Ajax, what did you do?" She grabbed his arm.

"Homer," said Pallas.

"I didn't mean to," Ajax whispered.

Atlas knelt at Homer's side. He was unconscious, but breathing. "Hey, Homer. You okay?" He shook his friend's shoulder.

"Don't touch him," said Nike. "His spine may have been injured."

"I'm sorry," cried Ajax. Large tears ran down his cheeks. "Please be okay, buddy!"

"Nice way to treat your *buddy*," said Pallas.

"He didn't mean to," said Reedy.

"Enough," said Nike. "Please back away so that Dr. Circe can get to him."

Oliver and his friends returned to their corner and began to drill the charge and toss again. Atlas and Pallas remained with Homer, and Reedy stood next to Ajax, holding his hand.

A moment later, Penny returned with Dr. Circe. The doctor kneeled next to Homer and poked and prodded him before scanning him with the same device she had startled Atlas with the day before.

"He's well," Dr. Circe said. "No spinal injuries. Just a concussion. I'll take him back to his room. He'll be fine tomorrow."

"I'll help you," said Ajax, wiping the tears from his cheeks. Before Dr. Circe could protest, he scooped Homer up and headed towards the dormitory.

"Is that alright?" Dr. Circe asked Nike.

"That's fine," said Nike. "I'm not sure anyone would want to spar with Ajax-Seven after this anyway."

"Ha!" laughed Dr. Circe. "Good one!" She laughed to herself as she followed Ajax and Homer.

"Let's get back to work," said Nike, shaking her head at Dr. Circe.

Most of the other students had already begun drilling again, following the example of Oliver and his friends. Atlas, Pallas, and Reedy walked back to their corner of the room.

"Sorry I snapped at you," said Reedy. "I didn't mean it to sound so harsh."

"It's fine," said Pallas.

"I told Ajax he should have practiced slowly at first. He doesn't know his own strength, especially not since he started eating the gray stuff."

"Gray stuff?" asked Atlas.

"Breakfast and lunch," said Reedy.

"We get green stuff."

"I'm red-green color blind. I get them confused with grays sometimes."

"Weird," said Atlas.

Pallas elbowed him in the ribs. "Don't be rude."

"It's okay. It is an abnormal condition. Abnormal *is* a synonym for weird. He's correct." Reedy spoke matter-of-factly, without a trace of irony. "Anyway, the *green* stuff is full of strength-building proteins and amino acids. And something else, probably, because it builds muscle and strength incredibly quickly. That's how Eugenio was able to push you and the redhead around so easily last night."

"His name is Homer," snapped Pallas.

Atlas looked at his skinny arms. He tried to flex them without making it too obvious. *Are they already bigger? Maybe.* "Cool."

"Don't be mad at Ajax," Reedy said. "He's really quite sweet."

"Did you know him before?" asked Atlas.

"We've been in the same home room for the last two years. Back home on Philadelphia, that is."

"Earth," said Pallas. "We're from Earth."

Reedy ignored her. "He was strong before, but he's gotten so much stronger in such a short period of time. He doesn't understand what he's capable of."

"No, apparently he doesn't," said Pallas.

"I understand that your friend was injured, but he's going to be fine," interrupted Nike. "Get back to drilling the defensive toss. I will change your partners if I must."

"Sorry, Sarge," said Atlas. He turned away from Nike to avoid any response. "Alright, Pallas. My turn. Come at me!"

AFTER ANOTHER HOUR of drilling defensive moves, the students were dismissed to the showers before the last class of the afternoon.

"I've taken a lot of showers today," Atlas said aloud, as the shower dried him off. "Hygiene must be very important to the Titans. No wonder their bathrooms are so fancy." Thinking about what Reedy had said about the green oatmeal, he posed and flexed in the mirror for a few minutes before retrieving his freshly folded clothing, getting dressed, and meeting up with Pallas outside Homer's room.

"Come in," said Homer. The door opened.

Atlas and Pallas entered. "He sounds fine," said Atlas.

"Hullo," said Homer. "We just started a game, but you can join us for the next one." He pointed to the cards in front of him. No one else was in the room.

"Or maybe not," Atlas said under his breath.

"Who are you playing with?" asked Pallas.

"Ajax." Homer nodded to the bathroom. "He's indisposed at the moment."

"Where did you get the cards?" asked Atlas. He was thinking about how the Thebans had made him throw away everything from home.

"I asked for them," said Homer. "They have a bunch of games and stuff on hand for us to use during free time. But you can ask for just about anything, really." He gestured to a row of books stacked on his drawer. "I asked for all of those."

"Wow," said Pallas. "Mind if I look?" She had already crossed the room and begun reading the book spines.

"Of course not."

Seconds later, the bathroom door opened and Ajax exited. He nodded and took a seat next to the bed. "That green stuff! Don't know if it's worse going in or coming out."

Pallas crinkled her nose in disgust. "You, uh, need anything?" she asked Homer.

"I'm good. They're bringing us dinner later."

"We're heading back to the Amphitheater for Astronomy," said Atlas. "Want to come with us, Ajax?"

"I won't need it," he said. He picked up his cards and scrutinized them. "I'm a combat specialist, obviously."

"That's an understatement," teased Homer.

"And anyway, I think I've learned enough about Astronomy for one day," said Ajax.

"We'll all need basic navigation—," began Pallas.

"I've been excused."

"We'll see you later, then," said Atlas. "Glad you're feeling better, Homer."

"Thanks for coming to see me," Homer called after them.

CHAPTER 10

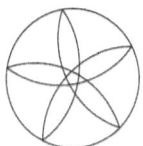

THE NEXT MORNING, Atlas's glass woke him up with a gentle buzzing on his wrist. He'd forgotten to take it off the night before. Somehow it also vibrated. He'd been under the impression it didn't have any moving parts, or any parts really, except for the single pane of glass.

How quickly it has become a part of my routine, and I have no idea how it works, thought Atlas. *How does it charge? Or does it run until the battery's dead? And where's the battery? A clear battery? How does it stick to my skin, but not to anything else? Why doesn't it leave any tacky residue? The whole thing seems impossible. Imaginary, even. Like hearing music over the radio, or making a video call on a mobile phone once were. What one generation can't imagine, the next can't imagine their life without. Here I am, many generations beyond the technology I was born to—*

The glass buzzed again, harder this time. He'd fallen back asleep. Automatic snooze detection. Practical, but also annoying. Atlas slid out of bed and pulled on his clothes. "Why am I doing this?" he muttered.

Neither Pallas nor Homer waited outside his room. Atlas assumed he was late and quickened his pace but didn't run. He was about to do plenty of that.

When he arrived at the track, no one else was there. He

checked his glass. The display said he was supposed to be at the track. Was he really that late? Surely he wasn't early?

Atlas was about to head to breakfast, believing the glass was malfunctioning, when Oliver, Penny, and Theo arrived. Close behind them were Nerissa and Eugenio. Atlas nodded to them. Oliver was the only one that nodded back.

Neither Theo nor Eugenio had paid any attention to Atlas since the incident in the dining hall, but Atlas felt a bit apprehensive about being alone with them. It was stupid, but Pallas's concern from that first night stuck in his head. She didn't seem like someone prone to exaggeration. Were they truly that dangerous?

The rest of the students began to trickle onto the track.

Atlas tapped on his glass. The time read five minutes earlier than it had the last time. So, it was malfunctioning. *No, wait...it knows I'm always late.*

"Traitor," Atlas said.

"What?" demanded Theo.

"Nothing," said Atlas. "Just talking to myself." He looked anxiously for his friends.

Finally, Pallas and Homer appeared. Reedy and Ajax were with them.

"We waited for you," said Homer. "You could have told us you weren't going to walk with us."

"Sorry." Atlas considered telling the truth about his glass. "I thought I'd get an early start this morning."

"Ajax used to have that same problem," Reedy said, as she patted Ajax on the arm. "He was always late, and so his glass set itself ten minutes ahead."

Pallas grinned but didn't say anything.

Ajax extended his hand. "Good morning."

"Good morning, Ajax." Atlas shook his hand. The handshake was firm and strong—almost painful. *Big guy truly doesn't know his own strength. Maybe we could just high-five in the future? That might also be dangerous.* "I guess you try not to be late anymore?"

"At first I just started going everywhere ten minutes later than my glass said, but then it set itself to twenty minutes ahead, and the alerts became much more annoying."

"Thanks for the tip," Atlas said.

"You're welcome."

"Here we go." Pallas nodded. Nike had begun leading them in some pre-run stretching. "Even if it kills us," Pallas reminded Atlas.

"Even if it kills us," Atlas nodded.

DESPITE ATLAS'S CONCERNS, he and Pallas were able to maintain Nike's pace for the entire run. Atlas thought he was going to die, and Pallas appeared similarly distressed, but they finished only a few paces behind the students in front of them. That appeared to be adequate for Nike and they were not required to run an additional fifteen miles.

It was such an improvement over the day before that Atlas questioned whether they'd been able to accomplish it through an act of sheer will power, or thanks to a side-effect of the green oatmeal. Maybe it improved cardio too? *Talk about a super-food.*

Homer, of course, finished near the front. Reedy and Ajax finished together near the middle of the pack. Despite having the longer stride, Ajax seemed the more exhausted of the two.

Later, at breakfast, the five of them took turns timing how fast they could slurp down the green oatmeal. They noisily cheered each other on. Somehow, it made the suffering more tolerable. *Also,* Atlas thought, *it helps knowing that this stuff's giving me super-human strength and stamina, too—maybe.*

"Have you looked at the schedule for the rest of the day?" asked Reedy between gulps of water to clear the aftertaste.

"How do you find the schedule?" asked Atlas. "Do we have Combat Training again today?"

"No, that's only on the first day of the cycle." Reedy finished her glass of water and started on Ajax's glass since he didn't seem to mind the aftertaste as much.

"The cycle?" Pallas asked.

"Yes, the Academy schedule cycles through a four-day pattern. It's like a Titan week, I guess. The schedule is the same for every corresponding day in the cycle."

"Except yesterday," said Ajax. "We don't have a boring history lecture every first day, fortunately. The whole first half of yesterday was different. It's Gymnasia, then Math, normally."

"We're taking a gymnastics class?" Atlas asked.

"No, it's a fitness class. To make us stronger."

"I'd rather sit through a lecture," Atlas said. "But again, how do you check your daily schedule?"

"Hold up your glass," said Reedy. "Think about what you want to see. Look." She lifted her arm. Reedy wore the glass on the outside of her wrist. The daily schedule appeared.

"It reads your thoughts?" Pallas pulled her glass off and set it on the table. "No thank you."

"It only reads them when you want it to." Reedy dropped her arm and the screen went blank. "See? I thought, *I want teriyaki salmon for dinner tonight.* Nothing happened. When your wrist is down, it can't read your mind. I've tested it extensively."

"So, all I do is raise my wrist and think about what I want to see?" Atlas asked.

"Exactly."

"Did you know about this?" Pallas asked Homer.

"Yes. I thought you did too. You were wearing it everywhere."

"I only used it to see the time, really." Pallas pursed her lips and wrinkled her nose. "I guess that's what I wanted to see and that's what it showed me. Creepy."

"Oh, don't worry," said Reedy. "No one else can use theirs to read *your* mind. Your glass only works for you. And no one else can access your thought data either."

"How do you know?" asked Pallas.

"I told you. I tested it thoroughly."

"So that's why you kept asking to try mine," said Ajax.

"Yes. Also, Dr. Circe confirmed my hypothesis."

"Why should you trust her?" asked Atlas. "She's loony."

"And she's a Titan," Pallas added.

"*Is* she a Titan?" Atlas asked. "She's shorter than most Titans."

"Isn't she?" asked Pallas.

"I think she's Thracian," said Reedy.

"What?" said Homer.

"From the planet Thrax. We learned about it in Astronomy last night."

"Oh," said Homer.

"She *looks* like a Thracian," said Reedy.

"How do you know what a Thracian looks like?" asked Pallas. "We also learned about Vandalus and Dorad last night. Why couldn't she be Vandalusian or Dorado?"

"She told me she was born here," said Atlas.

"I was born in America, but I'm Moroccan by heritage," said Reedy. "But even if she was Titan, why should that matter?"

"Pallas doesn't trust the Titans," said Atlas.

"Really? Why don't you trust them?"

"I just don't," said Pallas. She squirmed and elbowed Atlas in the ribs. "Why should we trust them? What's the difference between them and the Olympians? They both want the Sphere for themselves."

"I don't know," said Reedy. "Personally, I admire that they told us about their relation. They didn't have to do that."

"Let's get back to what we were talking about," said Pallas. She tapped on her glass still lying on the table. "How do you know Dr. Circe didn't tell you what you wanted to hear?"

"I told her my glass was malfunctioning, that I could hear the other students' voices in my head saying mean things about me when I walked near them," Reedy said. "She told me that was impossible because the glass only works for the student it belongs to and it must be in contact with your skin to read your mind.

Plus, it has unbreakable privacy protections incorporated throughout. No one but the owner can access it."

"So, maybe she figured out you were lying?" Atlas said.

"I was very convincing," said Reedy. "Broke down in tears and said, 'Then where are the voices coming from?' She did a full cerebral scan. Turns out I have anxiety and am prone to obsessive-compulsive fits. Already knew all of that—I like doing things well." She shrugged. "The doctor told me I was just stressed out by the new environment. It was so easy."

"I thought you didn't lie?" said Ajax. "Two years ago, you told me it was immoral."

"It is. And I don't, unless a substantially greater moral imperative compels me to lie. I needed to be sure my thoughts were private. And I wanted to make sure I get help managing my mental health. Mission accomplished."

"Sounds pathological to me," muttered Atlas.

"Morality usually isn't black and white," said Reedy. "People act like it is, but they're deluding themselves, and too often, the line where they define black versus white is subjective—it's okay when I do it, but not you."

"Isn't that what you're doing?" said Atlas.

"Not at all. I said things aren't just black and white."

"But you decided where the line for acceptable gray area stands."

"I did not." Reedy spoke firmly, but not angrily. "Lying is immoral. Violating the privacy of others is *more* immoral. When considering the one versus the other, convincing Dr. Circe that I was overly anxious and stressed was essential to gaining peace and privacy of mind."

"But you said the glass keeps your thoughts private," Atlas said.

"I didn't know that before, did I?"

"Seems like you could use hypotheticals to justify pretty much anything, right?"

"That's not what I'm doing." Reedy seemed to be losing patience with Atlas.

"Then prove it," Atlas blurted. He sighed and looked at Pallas, then back at Reedy. "Sorry. I didn't mean it like that."

"Yes, it's true some people try to use the existence of moral gray areas to justify their behavior," Reedy said. "They tell themselves their moral failings are who they are—neither good nor bad—as if the way you treat other people was an immutable characteristic like blood type or eye color. Others try to justify their actions in the name of fairness—as if calling something unfair was justification for acting unfairly. In other words, just because you can take a position within the gray area does not automatically make that position a moral one."

"That's my point," said Atlas. "How can you claim your position is a moral one when you did something you consider immoral in order to accomplish your goal?"

Reedy appeared quite pleased with where Atlas had led her. "You have to carefully and as disinterestedly as possible weigh your actions against the consequences for others. Then, you have to take the most moral position allowed."

"You're still basing everything on your own judgment." Atlas shook his head.

"That's all anyone can do," said Reedy. "I weighed the cost of Dr. Circe believing I'm an anxious obsessive against the benefits of us—all of us—being confident in our private thoughts. I did it for everyone, not just me."

"You're so weird," said Ajax, smiling.

Ajax's deflection worked. Everyone laughed, even Pallas. She seemed convinced enough by Reedy to put the glass back on her wrist. Atlas wasn't convinced by Reedy's argument. It still seemed like you could justify anything if you claimed it was for the benefit of enough people—or the *right* people. Even still, he was grateful for the peace of mind. Atlas touched the glass on his wrist.

"Show me the daily schedule," Pallas spoke to her glass.

"You don't have to say it out loud," said Homer.

"I know. But until I'm comfortable with this mind-reading thing, I'm going to." She looked at her glass. "Gymnasia is next? I thought you said it was on the first day of the cycle?"

"Gymnasia is every day," said Ajax.

"Great," said Atlas. "Because we don't run enough every day already."

"Except the fourth day," corrected Reedy. "That's Rest Day. No classes at all. Not even pre-breakfast running."

"I don't love the running, but I'm looking forward to the Gymnasia classes," said Ajax. "Especially since I learned about what this green stuff can do." He clenched his enormous fists and grinned.

"Easy, buddy," said Homer. "You gotta' give the rest of us a chance to catch up to you." He forced a smile, but his eyes looked worried. With only Eugenio and Oliver comparable in size to Ajax, it was likely that Homer would remain partnered with Ajax for all future combat training sessions.

"No worries, buddy. With my help, you'll be caught up in no time." Ajax slapped Homer on the back.

That one had to leave a bruise, thought Atlas. "What other torture are they putting us through today? Pit fighting?"

"Let's see…" Pallas said. "Science and then lunch. After lunch we have Flight Training, then—"

"Flight training?" Atlas sat forward in his seat. "That sounds fun." He sat back again and frowned. "Except there's not a lot of flying in trans-light travel."

"What? How would you know?" asked Homer.

"The Thebans explained it to me."

"Oh right," Homer sighed. "Your best friends."

"We will still need to know how to operate a trans-light craft," Reedy said. "Maybe the translator had trouble with the correct terminology."

"Maybe," said Pallas. "But remember, we have no idea what situations we'll find ourselves in while we're searching for the

Sphere. I'd bet we'll come across all kinds of vehicles we will need to drive...or fly."

Ajax nudged Homer. "She's smart. No wonder you like her."

Homer turned bright red. "That's not...why?...I meant...as a friend, that's all." He looked at Ajax, dumbfounded by the betrayal.

Ajax didn't appear to realize he'd said something he shouldn't.

"Ajax," Reedy said gently. "Maybe that wasn't something you should have shared. If Homer told you something in confidence—"

"He said as a *friend*." Pallas looked annoyed and maybe even angry, but not embarrassed. "After Flight Training, we have Xeno-Technology, and that's it for the day. I'm going to my room to read." She stood up abruptly and cleared her tray. "See you in class."

After a moment of awkward silence, Atlas quietly cleared his tray and followed after Pallas, but once he stepped into the hall, she was gone. She didn't answer the door to her room.

Almost an hour later, Atlas caught up with Pallas outside the Gymnasium. She was standing outside the door, as if unsure about going inside.

"Look, I'm sure Ajax was confused," Atlas said.

"What? No...I mean, I don't care about that."

"Okay. Worried about Gymnasia?"

Pallas looked at Atlas, then turned back to the door. "No, I'm excited about it, actually."

"Oh yeah? I'm not."

"I've always wanted to be strong." Pallas seemed lost in thought.

"Me too, but I don't like getting sweaty and gross. And it's a lot of work. I'd rather eat the green oatmeal."

"I don't think even the green oatmeal works unless you put the work in."

"Probably not. It'd be nice though." Atlas grinned, but Pallas didn't even crack a smile. *She's really serious about this.*

"Back home, I always wanted a gym membership. We could never afford anything like that. I wanted to be big and strong. I'm not tall, but I thought that being super-strong would be enough."

"You want to be a super hero?" Atlas said. "All you need is a radioactive accident."

Pallas squinted at him and crinkled her nose. "I just wanted to be strong enough to be left alone. So *they* would leave me...*let* me be a kid. But like I said, I didn't have the money." She sniffled twice and composed herself. "And now, here I am, about to begin training on an alien world with advanced, scientific training methods."

Atlas felt awkward. *How should I respond? Apologize?* He tried to lighten the mood. "Almost makes being kidnapped worth it, eh?" *That was a stupid thing to say*, he immediately thought.

Pallas looked at Atlas and studied his face for a moment. "Maybe not for you. For me, it might be the best thing that's ever happened."

CHAPTER 11

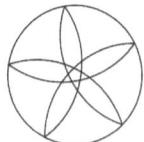

GYMNASIA WAS NOT AS terrible as Atlas had feared. Nike introduced them to a series of weightlifting, gymnastic, and calisthenic exercises that would form the basis of their training regimen. Although several of the exercises were a bit complex and demanded an athletic ability currently beyond Atlas and many of the others, Nike taught them how to modify each particular exercise. She and her assistants demonstrated the progressions the students should follow until they developed the strength and skill necessary for the more complicated exercises.

It was fun. Even though Atlas lacked the body awareness to efficiently perform even the moderately complex weightlifting and gymnastic exercises, his smaller frame helped him do better with the body-weight exercises than some of the bigger and stronger boys. His flexibility helped too. Some of the other Philadelphians could hardly squat.

Atlas had meant to keep an eye on Pallas to see if she was still excited about the class, but became so engrossed in his own workout that he completely forgot about everyone else. By the end of the class, he was lying on the floor gasping for breath, his heart racing harder than he'd ever pushed it before. His clothes were drenched with sweat and Atlas had freshly burst blisters on both hands. *This is what true death feels like,* Atlas thought.

After a few moments recovering, his body flooded and tingled with endorphins and Atlas realized he actually did like getting sweaty and dirty. He grinned. *This is a good death.*

Everyone seemed to be in a similar state of physical desperation and exhaustion as Atlas: their bodies splayed out across the floor, workout equipment littered like shrapnel. Even Oliver and his friends were sitting in their corner of the room, panting heavily.

Oliver stood first. Then he offered his hand to each of his friends and pulled them to their feet, clapping them on the shoulders and grinning before moving on. Oliver clearly cared deeply for each of them, and they relished his attention.

Atlas tried to stand up. His stomach heaved violently and he almost lost his breakfast. *The only thing worse than swallowing that green stuff is having to swallow it again*, he thought. Atlas steadied himself, then staggered across the room to get some water.

"Are you okay?" Pallas asked. She beamed with excitement.

"I will be," said Atlas.

"You look like you died."

"I think I did." He gulped down some water, then burped. "Excuse me. I almost lost my breakfast."

"Yeah, me too." Pallas jumped up and down. "Isn't it amazing? I can't believe we get to do this every day."

"Except the fourth day, and thank goodness for that."

"You didn't have fun?"

"I admit, it was a lot more fun than I expected. But I'm going to need that fourth day to be resurrected." Pallas didn't laugh. It wasn't much of a joke, Atlas admitted. "Anyway, I'm glad it lived up to your expectations."

"It was so much *better*. I feel so alive even though I was terrible. It's going to be forever before I master any of those gymnastic exercises, but I can't wait."

"Hey Homer," Atlas called to the red-fuzz-capped figure limping towards the exit.

Homer looked around. "I'll see you guys in Science." He turned back and continued limping to the exit.

"What did you do to him this time?" Reedy scolded Ajax as the two of them joined Atlas and Pallas.

"I did nothing. He must have overdone it trying to keep up with you."

"With me?" said Reedy.

"Yeah, he saw how much weight you were lifting and so he added more."

"That was not a prudent idea. I've lifted weights before. He has not, I assume."

"I don't think so."

"I am sorry I wrongly accused you."

"No worries," said Ajax.

"Looks like he's got a ways to go before he catches up to you, eh Ajax?" Atlas punched Ajax's shoulder.

Ajax looked irritated, but he didn't retaliate. He seemed more surprised by Atlas's comment than the punch. "We all have a ways to go. Homer will do well. I'll just remind him to be more prudent, like Reedy says."

"Right," Atlas said. He'd tried to banter with the guy and offended him instead. *Just like me.* He decided to change the subject and turned to Reedy. "You've lifted weights before?"

"Yes, my parents were kind of fitness buffs."

"You're so lucky," said Pallas.

"It wasn't quite like this, but it was similar," Reedy said. "Still, I don't think I've ever worked so hard in my life."

"I wouldn't have thought…" Atlas began, and stopped too late.

"Because I'm so skinny? I'm a lot stronger than I look." Reedy flexed proudly. Her biceps bulged under her Theban clothes.

"I don't doubt it. I only meant that I didn't expect it. Based on our…uh…conversation earlier, you seemed like someone more interested in philosophy."

"Why can't I be strong too? After all, Socrates said, 'It is a shame to grow old without seeing the beauty and strength of which your body is capable.'"

"Socrates said that?" Pallas asked.

"According to Xenophon," said Reedy. "Socrates was illiterate, so he never wrote anything he said down. Others like Plato and Xenophon had to do it. There's lots of evidence to support that quote, though. For example, Plato's Academy was actually a gymnasium probably a lot like this one."

"Cool," said Pallas.

Atlas felt like he'd made a fool of himself with Reedy now too. *Can't seem to keep my foot out of my mouth today.* He changed the subject again. "So, anyone got any idea what to do about these clothes?"

"What do you mean?" Reedy asked.

"They're soaked in sweat. I know they dry quickly, but after that workout, I kind of want to change my clothes. Or wash these, at least. I don't know about you guys, but the Thebans only gave me one pair of clothes, and there isn't anything but underwear in my drawer."

"Yeah. Dry or not, the idea of putting these back on after a shower is pretty disgusting," said Pallas.

"Get in the shower while you're dressed," Reedy said. "Then squeeze them out and hang them up. Otherwise, they'll fold themselves and won't dry properly. There should be a hook outside your shower. By the time you're finished showering, they'll be dry."

"That's good to know," said Pallas. "Thanks so much." She started towards the exit. "See you in Science," she called back at them.

"She's in a much better mood now than at breakfast," said Ajax.

"Ajax!" said Reedy. "It's not polite to talk about people behind their back."

Atlas agreed with Ajax. And why shouldn't Pallas be happier?

According to her, this class was a dream come true. *Good. At least being kidnapped is benefitting someone.*

"See you guys in Science." Atlas started towards the dormitory.

"Atlas?" Reedy called after him.

"Yes?" Atlas turned.

Reedy had caught up with him. Ajax, however, remained behind.

Reedy smiled nervously. "I'll be direct, since otherwise you might think I'm disingenuous." She looked him directly in the eye and became serious. "Ajax and I would like to be on your squad."

"What do you mean?"

"The prophecy says that a group of five of us will discover the Celestial Sphere. Even before we heard about the prophecy, there were rumors the Titans were going to split us into three squads. The prophecy seems to have confirmed it."

"You're probably right. But the Titans will divide us up as they see fit, don't ya' think?"

"I don't think so," said Reedy. "They want the squads to work well together. We need to be effective, and that means we need to get along well."

"We barely know each other. We don't *know* if we get along well."

"You're right. In fact, there are a number of things I find insufferable about you already. I can't imagine how badly you will annoy me once we spend some real time together."

Atlas realized she wasn't joking and he flinched. "Then why would you want to be on a squad with me?"

"I have my reasons." Reedy set her jaw and cocked her head. Then she crossed her arms and rocked back slightly. "Can we be on your squad or not?"

"Why do you keep calling it my squad?"

"Because you'll be a leader."

Atlas shook his head. "I don't know why everybody seems to think that."

"Everybody *doesn't* think that. In fact, most of the others— except Oliver's squad, of course—think they should be one of the squad leaders. But they don't understand."

"What don't they understand?"

"That people aren't drawn to them. They try so hard that they alienate people. You, on the other hand, draw people to you just by being yourself."

Atlas's mouth hung open. He didn't know how to respond, or if he should. Reedy insulted him in one breath and complimented with the next. And both seemed sincere.

"Look at Pallas," Reedy said. "She spoke to no one the two days before you arrived. But now she talks to you as if you're her oldest friend. And Homer. He talks so *much* that no one else wanted him around. Somehow, he holds his tongue—for the most part—around you."

"You said I annoy you."

"You do, and you've many annoying failings. However, I believe it is in mine and Ajax's best interest to be on your squad. In the same way, I believe it will be in *your* best interest for us to be on your squad."

"I'm not convinced that will be up to me," said Atlas. "But I like you and Ajax, even if you don't like me."

"I never said I don't *like* you," said Reedy. "I said you annoy me. There's a difference." She fiddled with the sides of her pants, as if looking for pockets. "Bottom line is people are better at being themselves around you."

"If you say so."

Atlas studied Reedy. Why did she want so badly to be on his squad? And why should it even be his squad? He arrived at the Academy last. *Since when is last picked ever team captain?*

"I have to go," Atlas said. "I don't want to be late for Science. We can talk about this when it becomes an issue, if it ever does."

Reedy nodded. "We'll see you there."

Nothing interesting happened during the Science class, although Atlas enjoyed it much more than he expected. The three

Titan teachers took turns guiding the students through a complex experiment and demonstrating the relevant principles as they went along. Learning by doing. It seemed so natural. Atlas learned more during one class than he would have in a month at his old school.

After class, Reedy and Ajax joined Atlas, Pallas, and Homer for lunch.

"Maybe it's because they know so much more, and it's easier for them to explain since they have a broader picture," said Homer as he brought his bowl of green oatmeal to his lips and prepared to gulp it down.

"Or they're better at explaining why it matters," said Pallas.

"I've never done an experiment like *that* before," said Ajax. "Seeing it work in real life just clicked for me."

"Plus, the teachers are experts and we have three of them for fifteen students," said Reedy. "Let's not be unfair. Our teachers on Earth had to handle much larger classes."

Flight Training, on the other hand, was less fun than Atlas thought it would be. Since the students couldn't leave the Academy due to the threat of Olympian assassins, all flight instruction was accomplished through simulators. The instructor made a point to emphasize that there would be no practical experience throughout their term at the Academy. She insisted, however, that the simulators were more than adequate, and capable of generating much more challenging scenarios than the Philadelphians were ever likely to face.

To Atlas, the most fascinating thing about Flight Training was that it was taught by a Theban named Bendis. Did she know the Thebans that had brought them all to Titan? Was she related to any of them? Diana, maybe? Director Themis had said that there were many Thebans now living on Titan, but Pakhet and the others didn't act like they called Titan their home. And they had all been slaves of the Olympians before coming to Titan.

Bendis appeared older than the other Thebans, even older than Diana. While Pakhet and her crew were strong and vigorous, capable of handling themselves well in combat, Bendis was smaller and almost frail, possibly due to having enjoyed most of her life in relative safety.

There were two groups, then: the refugees that managed to escape before the Olympians destroyed Thebes, and those enslaved by the conquering Olympians. *Are there any males?*

Bendis's knowledge of vehicles and transportation systems was extensive. She could recite from memory the startup sequence, range, fuel type, top speed, and mechanical idiosyncrasies of any vehicle named, including Earth vehicles. Despite the practicality of the class, and Bendis's enthusiasm and expertise, Atlas couldn't help but feel disappointed that he wouldn't get to truly test his flight skills until he was very possibly trying to escape an Olympian death squad.

Xeno-Technology scared him. As much as Atlas had grown up enjoying some of the best Earth technology available, the diversity and complexity of the equipment discussed in Xeno-Technology overwhelmed him. He hadn't been able to figure out how his glass worked without help from others, and it was far more intuitive than any of the devices the XT instructors demonstrated on the first day of class.

The instructors presented devices from thirty-five different cultures, each with their own interface system. Fortunately, of these, the class would focus primarily on only the twenty most widespread throughout the galaxy. *Only twenty.* Twenty cultures from which they would study eight classes of technology in each, including weaponry.

Twenty different systems for killing.

That's what scared Atlas the most. Of course, he knew the Olympians were trying to kill *him*—knew it better than any of them. Probably other peoples would try, as well. However, until the XT instructors demonstrated the power of a Titan ring cannon obliterating a concrete wall, Atlas had never thought that *he* might have to kill—no, he would almost inescapably have to kill.

So stupid, thought Atlas. *You should have understood that. Why else are you taking combat classes?* He'd hid from the idea, pushed it deep into the corners of his mind. Now, all of a sudden, it was unavoidable.

Kill someone who wants to kill you. Both of you believe you're in the right. But you have a family you want to get home to and you cannot let yourself be killed. Maybe your enemy also has a family at home. Can't think about that, Atlas. Think about that and you die. You want to live. You can't know which of you deserves life more, but you can decide that you will live so as to deserve life. So you choose to live. Which means you choose to kill. Two choices have become one choice. I didn't ask for this.

"Are you okay?" Pallas asked.

Atlas took a deep breath and rubbed his eyes. "Okay...yes, okay. You and Reedy and Ajax. And Homer too. I'll do whatever I have to. We're all going home alive when this is over."

CHAPTER 12

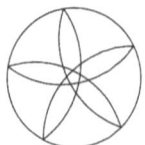

ATLAS AWOKE a few seconds before his glass began buzzing. He raised his wrist and dangled it above his face. The lights in his room began to rise and Atlas squinted at the glass. *How many days have I been here?* One hundred and eighty-four days, the display read. *Approximately six Philadelphian months,* he thought. *No, wait.* His glass calculated the correct answer. Almost seven and a half months on Philadelphia. The days on Titan were longer—approximately twenty-nine Earth hours. *One hundred eighty-four days on Titan. Just over two hundred and twenty-two on Earth.*

He'd gotten into the habit of asking this question every morning. It didn't make him feel better or worse, but he asked it every day as soon as he woke up anyway. Atlas couldn't remember why he had asked the question in the first place, but now it was a part of his routine.

What was the final score last night? Dodgers 12 - Diamondbacks 2, the display read. *They lost again. What a way to end the season.* Atlas dropped his wrist in disgust. Not the season he had hoped for, but if the Diamondbacks were going to have a bad season, at least he was 9,000 light-years away.

Several months earlier, he'd learned he could get Philadelphian sports scores on his glass. At first, Atlas had been excited, especially since the Diamondbacks started out so well. And then the season became depressing. Unfortunately (maybe fortunate-ly), he couldn't watch the games live.

Early in the season, Atlas had approached Professor Querios after Xeno-Technology and asked him how to watch a live stream of the baseball games. Apparently, it required significantly less energy for a trans-light vehicle to travel across the Galaxy than it did to transmit a live video stream. In fact, Professor Querios had explained, continuous trans-light data transmission required so much energy, the concept was completely theoretical. Streaming live sports was impossible. Atlas could, however, request an archived copy of a live event once it was over. It would arrive the next day, like his dinner order.

Atlas had accumulated dozens of game archives and only watched a few of them. *Oh well. There wasn't enough time anyway. Except on Rest Days.* He had planned on watching last night's game tomorrow, but a slaughter like that wasn't worth even fast-forwarding to the highlights. *What a season.*

Atlas rubbed his eyes and sat up in bed. He ran his hands through his hair. *I need a haircut,* he thought. There was only one type of haircut at the Academy, and he didn't want to go bald again. He sighed.

"Okay, let's get to it. Day three of the cycle." He pulled his clothes on and checked his glass again. Just enough time to brush his teeth.

The morning run went as usual. It had been months since Atlas had worked his way to the middle of the group, even as Nike continued to accelerate the pace. Atlas had begun closing in on the leaders. He had a ways to go before he caught some of them, especially Homer, but he was making progress and that made him feel good. Running was almost becoming fun.

"Great job today," huffed Pallas as Atlas knelt on his hands and knees in front of her, his chest heaving. Sweat dripped from the tight curls of Pallas's hair.

"You too," Atlas puffed. "I'm coming after you next cycle. Better watch out."

"Ha! Good luck. You'll need it." She helped Atlas to his feet and headed back to her room.

"See you in a bit," Atlas called.

"You two are so cute," Reedy whispered.

Atlas rolled his eyes. "I'm not going to have this argument with you again."

"What's there to argue about?" Reedy slapped him on the back. The pain from her slap was just below the threshold Atlas could tolerate without wincing. Apparently Reedy was taking back-slapping lessons from Ajax, because she didn't seem to know her own strength either. Reedy was still lean and thin, but if she resembled a reed, it was one made of solid steel.

"You can't deny you two have a special relationship."

"I don't deny it," Atlas said. "I'm proud of it, in fact. But it's not like what you're implying."

"If you say so."

Atlas had an idea. "Let's change the subject and talk about us?"

"What do you mean *us*?"

"Don't tell me you haven't felt it. We have a very special relationship too."

"You *annoy* me," Reedy said matter-of-factly.

"And you annoy me. It's a perfect, reciprocal relationship. Very special."

Reedy frowned. "Okay. You've made your point. I won't mention it again."

"Won't mention what?" Homer asked as he approached. Ajax was close behind him.

Atlas felt uncomfortable. Homer's infatuation with Pallas had become more and more overt the past few months. It was embarrassing, especially since Pallas refused to admit that it was even happening—or that it made her feel uncomfortable.

"I'm always teasing Atlas," Reedy said. "I agreed to stop."

"About what? His hair's long past that awkward puffy stage," Homer's red hair was almost perfectly straight and smooth. Even streaked with sweat after the run, it hardly looked out of place.

"It doesn't matter," said Atlas. "Let's hit the showers. I'm so hungry I'm even looking forward to green oatmeal."

"Me too," said Ajax. "I can't seem to eat enough lately. I had three steaks for dinner last night, and I feel like I could eat the whole rest of the cow."

Atlas thought back to when he had first met Ajax. Now, Ajax had become so big it was hard to believe Eugenio had ever been bigger than him. "Maybe not today, but someday, you *will* eat the whole cow—in one sitting," Atlas said.

Ajax slapped Homer on the back instead of Atlas, since he was closer. Homer cheerfully punched him back in the chest. The two performed their secret handshake. It mostly involved them slapping each other across the arms and legs with increasing force until one of them flinched.

Though not nearly as big as Ajax, Homer had filled out quite a bit these six months. He was still a bit lanky, but not as much. However, Reedy still lifted heavier weights than Homer.

Back in his room, Atlas hopped into the shower fully-clothed. It still seemed silly to take a shower before breakfast when he was just going to get sweaty again in Gymnasia, but that's what everyone did. The Titans were very concerned about hygiene. Otherwise, why schedule so much time to shower in between class?

After Atlas washed his clothes, he stripped them off and hung them up to dry. That was the hard part. He often kept his clothes on for the entire shower and let them air-dry. It meant sitting through part of class with slightly damp underwear, but that was better than remembering.

How are my parents?

Atlas made sure to lower his glass as he thought about his parents. It couldn't answer that question, but he didn't want it to hear the question anyway. He peeled the glass off his arm and set it on top of the soap dispenser.

So, it's one of those days.
It's been three cycles. I was due.

It only happened when Atlas was in the shower and naked. That triggered the memory. The photograph he created in his mind during that first shower on the Theban ship came back to him in exquisite, excruciating detail. Maggie. Mom. Dad. All of them smiling in the sun. Two seagulls and a palm tree in the background. And a patch of three fuzzy dandelions in the foreground growing out of a crack in the parking lot asphalt.

Atlas would never forget it and he didn't want to, but spending time thinking about it did nothing to get him home. The only thing that would get him home would be discovering the Celestial Sphere and finding a way to keep it from the Olympians forever. So, Atlas tried to keep the photograph tucked away in a drawer in his mind. For the most part, he was successful. He was only vulnerable when he showered naked.

Atlas allowed himself another thirty seconds to indulge in *saudade* underneath the shower head. *Such an interesting and appropriate word,* saudade. *Melancholic nostalgia.* Atlas had looked it up on his glass. It fit what he was feeling so perfectly. When the time was up, he dressed rapidly, wiped his glass dry on his pant leg, and went to meet Pallas, Ajax, Reedy, and Homer for the accustomed walk to the dining hall and breakfast.

On the way, they went past Director Themis's office. The office door opened suddenly and a female student stepped in front of Reedy.

"Phoebe!" Reedy said. "Dammit! Watch where you're going."

"Only an idiot walks so close to a doorway," said Phoebe.

"Says the fool walking out of a room backwards."

"Is there a problem?" said a voice from inside the office.

"No, Director Themis," said Phoebe. "Just a minor collision."

"I hope everyone is alright." Director Themis appeared in the doorway.

"We're all fine," said Reedy.

"Good. Now then, enjoy your breakfast."

"We will, thank you," said Homer.

Reedy stepped dramatically to the side and made room for Phoebe to pass. "After *you*."

After breakfast, Atlas and his friends hung out in Ajax's room for a bit, then went to Gymnasia together. In six months, they had all made remarkable progress. Reedy especially had become particularly adept at not only weightlifting, but also the gymnastic exercises.

The combination of green oatmeal twice a day, an early morning run, and the high-intensity workouts in Gymnasia had given them vastly improved strength, stamina, and endurance. When Atlas thought back on how far he had come...

"That was awful," Atlas said as he peeled himself off the floor and began to clean up his equipment. Many of the Philadelphians were still sprawled about the room. Some moaned and writhed on the floor.

"So amazing!" Pallas lay on her back wearing an enormous grin across her face, her chest heaving.

Atlas smiled. He couldn't help it. It made him happy to see how much Pallas enjoyed the workouts, no matter how painful they were. He remembered teasing Pallas about wanting super strength. Now she could lift three times her weight multiple times.

"One hundred and fifteen," Reedy declared proudly.

"Well done," said Atlas. He'd only been able to complete ninety-six repetitions. He was fine with that.

"Yes, great job," said Ajax.

Pallas didn't say anything, which usually meant she'd completed more than Reedy. Though Reedy was faster, Pallas approached the workouts more strategically, and sometimes that was enough to gain the advantage. It didn't happen often, but when it did, Pallas got quieter, even as Reedy got louder.

"How many?" Atlas whispered to Pallas as they returned to their rooms.

"One-twenty," she said.

Atlas smiled and nodded. "I guessed one-eighteen."

"You've never had any faith in me," she teased.

"None at all."

In Xenology, Professor Argo completed the unit on the Phoenician Star Empire.

Hardly an empire at all, Atlas thought. They only conquered four systems and held the third and fourth for barely half a generation. However, they were an interesting people, even if they did have a bit of a chip on their shoulder about their Empire's decline. Atlas hoped to meet one someday.

Of all the classes at the Academy, Atlas thought Xenology was the most interesting. Although the class was designed for practicality—to give the students a rudimentary familiarity with the dominant trans-light capable cultures they were most likely to interact with during the search for the Celestial Sphere—Atlas regularly found himself daydreaming about what it would be like to live among such magnificent *senti* cultures.

Senti was the only acceptable term, according to Professor Argo. Any student, even Oliver, could expect a harsh reprimand if they accidentally referred to one of the cultures or its people as *alien*.

Atlas often spent his free time or part of his Rest Day on his glass researching additional information about the various sentient cultures.

Every senti culture, Atlas had come to realize, was not that unlike the Titans—or Philadelphians, for that matter. Regardless of the level of technological sophistication, they still fell prey to the same prejudices, selfish impulses, vices, and moral lapses. Even generations after technological advances eliminated food and energy scarcity, every culture continued to suffer robberies, violence and murder, and even slavery.

Moreover, in all the cultures Atlas studied, certain people or groups, after acquiring political power, would inevitably resort to imposing their will and sensibility upon others, domestic and foreign alike. Such behavior usually resulted in polarizing the population into factions, but rarely ended in significant violence. More tragically, from time to time, each culture would fall under the control of a despotic oligarchy that had little patience for those unlike themselves. In those cases, tremendous violence and suffering followed closely behind.

Most tragically of all, even with cultures which had acquired relatively high social cohesion and cultivated a rich ideological pluralism, coming into contact with another senti culture often resulted in a race to conquest. The temptation to oppress appeared to be a galactic, or even universal, threat.

And yet, Atlas also discovered that kindness, sincerity, altruism, familial and neighborly love, and community all existed and were highly valued within every culture. Each possessed a vast and diverse library of artistic works. Each had come face to face with potential annihilation, and somehow survived.

As he studied the particularly tragic eras of each culture, Atlas easily found examples of virtue and beauty breaking through the death and despair. Even despotic tyrants loved their families and were capable of spontaneous generosity from time to time. Human nature and all its frustrating, yet beautiful, contradictions extended far beyond the confines of the Sol system, it seemed.

The more Atlas examined the differences between the cultures, the more they seemed the same. He spent many hours trying to puzzle out why there should be so many similarities between peoples separated by hundreds or thousands of light-years. The only plausible idea was that the evolutionary pressures giving rise to these virtuous human characteristics were the same or very similar throughout the Galaxy.

Strong social bonds, innovative thought, romantic and familial love, and mutually beneficial cooperation among strangers all improved evolutionary advantage on every planet. By extension, if exploiting any of these traits for selfish gain provided even a limited or temporary evolutionary advantage, the characteristics adapted to exploitation would evolve as well. As far as Atlas could tell, there were neither completely good nor completely evil cultures in the known Galaxy.

Professor Argo presented balanced discussions about most of the cultures. Atlas appreciated that the professor didn't demonize the Titan enemies. Neither did he extol the Titan allies. Notably absent from the syllabus, however, were the Thebans and Vitrians. The majority of the remaining Thebans lived on Titan, so their exclusion was somewhat understandable. Although, given how much the Titans benefitted technologically by the arrival of the Thebans, Atlas would have expected at least one class period devoted to them. The Vitrians, on the other hand, were totally uninteresting to the Titans.

Midway through the first month of classes, Atlas asked Professor Argo about the Vitrians.

"No, we will not discuss the Vitrians in this class," Professor Argo said. That was all he would say about the subject, even after Atlas pressed him later, in private. Professor Argo never answered questions asked in private conversations.

AFTER XENOLOGY, Atlas walked alongside his friends with his nose in his glass. He pounded the wall with his fist in frustration.

"It still won't let me access information on the Olympians," Atlas said. The syllabus set aside a whole month to cover the Olympians, but that was still several cycles away.

"I bet they want us to focus on our other studies," Homer said. "We've got so much else to learn before we're even ready to think about the Olympians."

"That sounds like a reasonable conclusion," Reedy said.

"Maybe," said Atlas. He looked at Pallas. She shook her head so gently he might have imagined it.

"I'm aching to train in Olympian martial arts and weapons myself," said Ajax.

"Yeah, me too," said Homer. He clapped his hand on Ajax's back and pushed him into the dining hall.

As the others went in to lunch, Pallas held Atlas back.

"Why restrict it?" she said. "They haven't blocked access to anything else, as far as I can tell. Why only the Olympians? That's what I want to know."

"Me too," Atlas said.

After lunch, the five of them walked to Survival Training. Atlas considered Survival the most practical and useful skill taught at the Academy.

The search for the Celestial Sphere might lead them to planetary systems devoid of senti life forms from which they could purchase or barter food. What if something went wrong and they were stranded on such a planet? Interplanetary food delivery wouldn't be an option.

For the first few months, Nike taught them how to identify plants and animals compatible with Philadelphian dietary requirements. Of course, they could point a glass at a plant or animal flesh and it could determine if it was edible or not, and even how much to consume in order to sustain life, but Survival assumed the worst as its first premise: no glass, transportation, communication, food, water, nor other tools. With each passing cycle, Nike prepared them for utter and total catastrophe.

Every third cycle, the students had to participate in solo or group survival simulations utilizing the skills Nike taught them. Each simulation assumed fewer tools or provisions and greater risk of death by starvation, dehydration, or exposure. Atlas and Reedy had only barely passed the last test.

Soon, an upcoming simulation would test the whole squad against the total catastrophe scenario. Above all else, Atlas wanted to pass the catastrophe. If they could survive the worst, they could survive anything. He could survive long enough—he *would* survive long enough—to go home. That was undeniably the only point to any of this. To get himself and his squad home. Saving the Galaxy by securing the Celestial Sphere would fall to Oliver and his squad. Atlas was okay with that. The Titan prophecy didn't describe the fate of the other ten Philadelphians. Atlas focused his squad's training on surviving whatever fate the ancient oracles had kept to themselves.

"Do you really think we'll ever need to know this stuff?" Homer asked.

Nike stood in front of the class, demonstrating how to prepare an eel-like amphibian that had eight stubby legs. She held the still-living creature at arms length, her hand grasping it firmly by the neck.

"I hope not," said Reedy. "I can't kill anything that hasn't tried to kill me."

"Vandalusian salamanders inject a potent toxin into their muscles when they feel threatened." Nike snapped the salamander's neck and laid it on the table. "The toxin can paralyze or kill any predator that takes a nibble." She cut into the carcass and spread it open with knives, being careful not to touch the flesh herself. "It will make your hands go numb for several hours if you touch it bare-handed. However, the internal organs of the salamander do not carry the toxin and are extremely nutritious. A Titan can live off the organs of one salamander for two days." She pulled the organs out of the body and rinsed them off in the sink. "Any of you ought to be able to survive for three to five days."

Pallas leaned over and whispered to Reedy. "After three days without food, you'll be glad to kill it just for being ugly."

"Come forward," Nike said. She lined the organs up together and sliced them into small portions.

"Finally, the good part," said Homer. He sprung out of his seat and hurried to the front of the room. He gratefully received his portion from Nike. Homer smelled it and poked at it with his finger, but didn't put it in his mouth.

"Let's get this over with," Atlas said. He grabbed Ajax by the hand and pulled him out of his seat. "At least we only have to do this once a cycle."

"That's still too often," Ajax said. He grabbed his stomach and wrinkled his nose.

Once all the students had received their portion of salamander organs, Nike nodded. They popped the morsels into their mouths simultaneously so they couldn't be discouraged by anyone else's disgust.

"Delicious," said Homer. He closed his eyes and savored his mouthful. Then he searched the table for leftover scraps.

"Really, it's not bad," said Reedy. "It sort of reminds me of tuna sashimi. Or the Cretan ground bird we ate six or seven cycles ago."

"I hate fish," said Ajax. He stuck his tongue out. "And I really hate salamander guts."

"At least Survival comes *before* Field Medicine," said Pallas.

"What do you mean?" asked Reedy.

"We're practicing amputations today."

"Wonderful," groaned Ajax.

Later, Atlas stood over his field-med dummy with a large saw in his hand. "Well Leonardo, I hoped it wouldn't come to this... but, a man's gotta eat." He dug his saw into the soft flesh of the dummy's arm. It resisted slightly, then gave way to the sharp steel. Blue fluid began to pour out of the wound. "Sorry," Atlas muttered. He adjusted the tourniquet he had set above Leonardo's elbow. The fluid stopped. Joking didn't make it easier. The dummies were so life-like. He grit his teeth and dug the saw deeper until he met the bone. The harsh grind of the saw teeth against bone made his stomach turn. Atlas grimaced, then set his weight into his cuts.

Within a few minutes he was finished. Atlas wiped the sweat from his forehead. That was much worse than sewing up a chest wound. He set Leonardo's severed hand to the side and lifted a large knife off the heating element upon which the blade had been resting. The knife glowed red. He pressed the flat of the blade against Leonardo's amputation wound. The flesh sizzled and smoked. He pressed harder, rocking and rotating the knife to make sure he cauterized the entire wound. Just to be sure, he heated the blade again and cauterized it a second time. He glanced up at the monitor where he could see Leonardo's simulated vitals were in deep distress.

"Damn," he whispered.

Atlas set the knife aside and began to bandage the wound. Once he finished, he released the tourniquet. It worked. He'd done it.

I'd have rather died, I think, than suffer through that. Maybe not months later—once it healed—but at the moment, rather than endure that pain, I might have rather died.

A pleasant, low tone chimed. Dinner. *What did I order? Ribs. Meaty bones.* He glanced at Leonardo's severed hand. *Perfect.* He sighed, then met Pallas at the door and they headed to the dining hall.

THE NEXT MORNING, Atlas woke up much earlier than he usually did on Rest Day. It was not by choice. His glass buzzed and beeped obnoxiously on his wrist.

He drew the glass to his face and squinted. Report to Nike, the display read. Urgent! Atlas rolled onto his stomach and moaned. *Not on Rest Day.* His muscles ached from the particularly challenging Gymnasia and Palaestra training of the cycle. Spreading out across the bed face-down gave them a gentle stretch which felt very pleasant. *And if I stay here for a little bit longer? Yes...just a little longer...Didn't hear...Mmm...*

A louder, piercing shriek sounded from his glass as it buzzed hard, like it was about to jump off his wrist. This time it wouldn't silence until Atlas got out of bed and stepped into the shower.

So annoying.

Ten minutes later, Atlas was walking to Nike's office. No one else seemed to be awake yet. He peeked into the dining hall. It was empty. His stomach growled. Of course. Whenever he woke up early, he always felt hungry. *Hope this doesn't take too long.*

Atlas touched the side of the door to Nike's office. No response. He touched it again. Still no response. He was about to leave when the door opened.

Nike greeted him. Her tall frame filled the doorway. Why hadn't the Titans designed this place to better match their dimensions? The doorways in the whole Academy were roughly the same size as those on Philadelphia, despite the larger stature of the Titans.

"Good morning, Atlas. You're a bit early."

"Sorry, Sarge," Atlas said.

Nike had stopped correcting him, but still couldn't hide her annoyance when Atlas called her Sarge. Atlas didn't think it was funny anymore either. It had become habit.

"It said urgent."

"And so it is," said a voice from behind Nike.

Nike stepped out of the way to reveal Director Themis sitting behind her desk. The Director waved Atlas in.

Atlas looked at Nike and chewed on his tongue as he stepped into the office. Why was Director Themis here? Atlas's stomach churned a bit as he realized the significance of a private meeting with Director Themis and Nike. *This could be good, right? Or bad.*

"Sit down," said Director Themis. He gestured to an empty chair. Nike sat near Themis in another.

Atlas hesitated for a moment, then sat down. "So, what's this about?" He slouched slightly. *Let's get this over with.*

Nike leaned forward. "As you know, we will begin full squad simulations in the near future."

Atlas nodded. It didn't sound like good news.

"In fact, the first one will be tomorrow. Your squad has done quite well in every test we've given you so far."

"I didn't know the squad selection had been formalized," Atlas said.

"It wasn't formalized," Director Themis said. "We wanted to see how you would organize yourselves."

"Oh yeah? How'd we do?"

"Well, for the most part," said Nike.

"Better than we hoped," said Director Themis. "You children organize yourselves naturally around the *best* leaders."

So that's why they had asked him to come in. Atlas swallowed the lump in his throat. *They're going to ask me to let someone else lead. That's fine. I didn't ask for this anyway. It had been Pallas's idea, really. I never wanted it.*

"However, some of the children are having a tough time organizing around a single leader," said Director Themis.

"That's where you come in," said Nike. She sat back in her chair and crossed her arms.

Is she enjoying this? Finally paying me back for the Sarge bit?

"We would like to make a transfer, in the best interest of all the squads," said Director Themis.

"I don't think that's necessary," Atlas began.

Director Themis leaned forward and pressed his fingertips together. "Let's not forget that the fundamental goal we all share is to find the Celestial Sphere and keep it out of the murderous hands of the Olympians."

"Of course," Atlas said dryly. "I don't forget that." He could never forget that. *Lanta. Dead, instead of him.*

"Good," said Director Themis. "We would like to transfer Phoebe-Ten into your squad, in exchange for Homer-Nine."

What?

"Why?" Atlas asked. He sat up in his chair and squinted at Nike, and then Themis. "No. Homer is a good friend and very loyal. I want him in my squad."

"Yes, but you don't need him," said Nike. "Gamma Squad needs him."

"More appropriately, Gamma Squad needs to be free of Phoebe-Ten," Themis said. "That will allow Daphne-Six to lead

Gamma Squad without being constantly undermined by Phoebe-Ten."

"Won't Phoebe try and undermine me too?" Atlas asked. "We don't get along well."

"She will try, but the rest of Beta Squad will not follow her. They are loyal to you." Director Themis intertwined his fingers and set them in his lap.

"We believe Phoebe-Ten will fall in line, once she sees she can't win," Nike said.

Atlas thought for a moment, then stood to leave. "So, we're Beta Squad?"

"Yes, unless the squad sims go poorly," said Nike. "But I'm sure they won't. You've assembled quite a team around you."

Atlas didn't expect anyone would ever get ahead of Oliver's squad, but he was glad to hear his squad wasn't ranked last. *No, but now Homer's squad is last. He doesn't deserve that.*

"I didn't assemble the team, and I can't make this decision," Atlas said.

"It's not your decision to make." Director Themis pursed his lips and leaned his head back.

"We need each of the teams to be as balanced and effective as possible," Nike said. "This decision is final. As Squad Leader, it's your responsibility to make this work. Please inform Homer-Nine of the transfer and help your squad to understand this."

Atlas went to the door, touched it open and exited. *No.* He turned around. "You got it all wrong. I'm not their leader. I don't get them to do anything. They do everything on their own. I just happen to be the guy in the middle."

"Exactly," said Nike.

CHAPTER 13

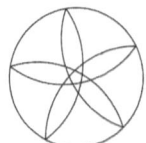

HOMER TOOK the news surprisingly well. He looked at Atlas with hurt eyes, doing his best to fight off the welling tears, but he stiffened his spine and nodded without saying a word. Atlas emphasized over and over again that he didn't have a choice—that he had refused and fought it, but Director Themis and Nike insisted on the transfer. It didn't seem to make Homer feel any better. Atlas didn't feel any better about it either.

It embarrassed Atlas that he felt compelled to apologize for someone else's decisions. It made him feel complicit and guilty. *I'll not be someone else's messenger again.*

"Congratulations on earning Beta Squad," Homer finally said. "Tell the others I'm happy for them."

Atlas watched Homer leave. Anger swelled inside. *How can I make this work when I don't believe in it? It's not fair.* In his head, he heard Pallas's voice ask, 'Since when was life fair?'

The rest of Beta Squad didn't take the news well. They yelled and cursed at Atlas. Ajax punched him in the chest, cracking three of Atlas's ribs.

"How did it happen?" Dr. Circe asked.

"I was working on muscle-ups in the Gymnasium," Atlas said. "My hand slipped off at the top and my torso slammed onto the bar. Should have chalked my hands. It was stupid really."

"That's a broad bruise for a bar," said Dr. Circe.

"I hit it more than once."

"You injured yourself and then you did it again?"

"And a couple more times too."

"What a coincidence."

"I call it consistency," Atlas said.

Dr. Circe huffed and shook her head, but didn't ask any more questions. She applied a salve to the affected area and within minutes Atlas felt better. "Your ribs will be stronger than ever in three hours. Until then, no more *consistency*."

Ajax and Reedy were waiting for Atlas outside of the medical center. Ajax hung his head and looked away. Reedy looked at Ajax disapprovingly, then pushed him forward.

Atlas shook his head. "Don't worry about it. I understand how you feel."

"Ajax is very sorry," Reedy said. "He took his anger out on you and he knows it's not your fault."

"I can speak for myself," Ajax said.

"I know you can. Like I said, I know how you feel," Atlas said. "You don't need to apologize."

"But he must," said Reedy.

"No he must *not*," snapped Atlas. "Homer is his friend. He's all of our friend. They took him from us. It's not fair, but there's nothing we can do about it. Ajax knows that and the only way he could deal with it is cracking my ribs. I'm Squad Leader, I bear the responsibility. I understand."

"It won't happen again," said Ajax.

"No, it won't, because we're never losing a member of our squad again," said Atlas. "Where are the others? We need to prepare. The first full-squad sim is tomorrow. Has anyone seen Phoebe? I would like to speak with her."

"No," said Reedy. "If I were her, I wouldn't want to be seen."

Ajax sighed. "I saw her in the courtyard, sitting by herself."

"How long ago?"

"Just a few minutes. I go out into the courtyard to cool off and clear my head sometimes. Guess I'm not the only one."

"Can you find Pallas? Let's meet in your room, Ajax. Ten minutes."

Atlas left without waiting for their response. He assumed it would take every second of those ten minutes to convince Phoebe to join them in the meeting. Her ego must undoubtably be bruised and it would take more than Dr. Circe's healing salve to fix it.

He found Phoebe in the courtyard, facing the gate, her hands fiddling with something in her lap. She didn't notice his approach.

"Hullo, Phoebe," he called.

Phoebe turned to look at him and frowned. "What do you want?" She stood up and dropped her hands to her side, fingers curled into a fist. Whatever she had been fiddling with was gone. "Here to gloat? You know that I'm smarter than you. I'm smarter than everyone here, especially Nike and Dr. Circe."

"I didn't choose this and I certainly don't like it," Atlas said. "It's just the way it is. You can focus your anger on me if you like, but that's not going to be productive. You won't provoke me, and I will not gloat. As far as you being smarter than everyone here, that may be true."

"Don't patronize me."

"I'd have to pity you to patronize you. I'd have to *like* you to pity you, and I don't like you, so do the math."

"Then why are you here?" Phoebe picked at her cuticles. Several were already raw and bleeding.

She picks her cuticles, like Maggie, Atlas thought. *She's nervous and probably feeling sorry for herself.* A wave of compassion flooded over him.

"Because you are a member of my squad," Atlas said. "The first squad sim will be tomorrow. We're having a meeting to discuss and prepare for it. We'd like you to join."

"You said you wouldn't patronize me, yet you claim that the

squad wants to meet with me. We both know they want less to do with me than I want with them."

"You're right," said Atlas. "Maybe I do pity you, after all. Either way, I need you to be there."

"If I refuse?"

"You're free to refuse, of course. I can't make you do anything. But you'll come." Atlas turned and left.

Seconds later, Phoebe grabbed Atlas by the arm and spun him around. "How do you know that I'll come?"

"Because you're smart enough to understand that finding the Sphere before the Olympians is more important than pouting." Atlas shook his arm loose and headed to the dormitory.

Back in Ajax's room, Pallas took Atlas aside. "You okay?"

"Of course," Atlas said. "Doc Circe says my ribs will be even stronger now."

"That's not what I meant, and you know it." Pallas touched him on the shoulder.

"We lost a member of our squad. There's nothing I can do about it. I have to adapt. We *all* have to adapt."

"He is our friend," said Pallas. "I know you're frustrated. We can talk—"

"Homer would be giddy to see how much you miss him already," said Atlas.

"Don't be an ass." Pallas punched him in his sore ribs.

Atlas gasped. It hurt. A lot. "I'm sorry. I shouldn't have said that." He gently rubbed the injury. "Or thought it. I was lashing out."

"Don't lash out at *me*," Pallas bristled. "I'm your friend and I had nothing to do with why you're angry. I love you and you love me. So treat me like it." She returned to sit with Reedy and Ajax on the bed.

What did she say? What did she mean? Like brother and sister love, right? Yes. Like siblings. I do love her. Like I love my sister. And my parents. She's family. So are Ajax and Reedy. Even though Reedy annoys me almost all the time. And I may never see my family again. Not if the

Olympians have their way. For now, at least, this is my family. And I love them.

The door buzzed and Atlas answered. No one was there. He looked down the hallway to see Phoebe walking away. *Let her go.*

He turned back towards the others. *Family. Phoebe doesn't have one. Not here. Pity.*

"Phoebe?"

She didn't stop.

"Phoebe!" Atlas called louder.

"I don't need to plan with you," Phoebe called back without turning around. "I can prepare on my own. I'm better that way. You go ahead and plan all you want. I'll make sure we do well tomorrow." She turned the corner and was gone.

Atlas closed the door. *So be it. Four is all we need. Especially four like us. Four like family.* He returned to the other three with a broad smile on his face.

"Where's Phoebe?" Reedy asked.

"She's not coming. She doesn't need us, she says. And that's fine with me. We definitely don't need her."

Pallas frowned at Atlas and shook her head.

"Who will navigate for me in the flight sim?" asked Reedy.

"I'll do it," Atlas said.

"You can't navigate and captain at the same time."

"I won't. Pallas will captain during the flight sim."

"Good," Reedy said. "That will work."

"What do you think, Ajax?" Atlas asked.

"That's fine with me."

"Pallas?"

"I can do it," Pallas said. "But it's not ideal."

"No, ideal would be we keep Homer." Atlas shrugged. "But this will work."

"We need Phoebe," Pallas whispered. She pulled Atlas to the side again. "We need *her*."

"What?" Atlas shook his head incredulously.

"I love Homer. He is a good friend and a capable navigator, but Phoebe is better than him at everything."

"Not at getting along with others," Atlas said.

"She can learn that. You and Reedy found a way to get along."

"It's a moot point," said Atlas. "Phoebe doesn't want to work with us. I can't force her."

"Yes she does," said Pallas. "She just needs a chance."

"Sure has a funny way of showing it."

"You'll see."

"We'll see. Tomorrow." He stepped back into Ajax and Reedy's conversation.

"It'll be real tough, I bet," said Ajax.

"But not unbeatable," said Reedy.

"No, not unbeatable," said Atlas. "We can handle it, whatever it is."

———

ATLAS'S GLASS SOUNDED A PIERCING, shrill alarm ten times louder than any he'd ever heard before. He tried to turn it off, but it wouldn't let him. *What time is it?* He looked at his glass. Alert! Beta Squad report immediately to Survival Sim, it read. Atlas rolled out of bed. *What time is it?* This time his glass responded. 3:24 AM. *Aw, hell.* He pulled on his clothes and walked out the door. Pallas was waiting for him in the hall, her hair a mess. Atlas felt his own hair. Even worse.

"Nice hair," said Pallas.

"You too." He grinned and rubbed his eyes. It was unfair, he thought, that even disheveled by sleep, Pallas's tight curls maintained a unique and complex beauty while his hair was a disaster.

Atlas and Pallas met up with Ajax and Reedy outside Survival Sim. Their hair was as messy as his. Ajax slept on his left side, apparently.

No Phoebe. *Oh well. Despite what Pallas thinks, I believe this will be better.* He touched the entrance. Pallas, Ajax, and Reedy joined their hands with his on the door. It didn't open.

"It won't open unless we're all here," said Reedy.

Dammit, Phoebe. Atlas frowned.

"Our time has already started," said Reedy.

"What if she doesn't come?" asked Ajax.

Atlas didn't answer. He looked down the hallway. Nothing.

"We fail," said Pallas.

"That is unacceptable," said Reedy. She lifted her glass. "Where is Phoebe?" She dropped her arm in disgust. "It won't tell me."

"I didn't know you could do that," said Pallas.

"That could only happen if she's in the bathroom or medical."

"Or if she's not wearing her glass," said Ajax.

"Then she'll be here soon," said Atlas. "No way she sleeps through that alarm."

Ten minutes later, Phoebe finally arrived. Unlike the others, her hair was neatly arranged and still damp.

"Where have you been?" demanded Atlas.

"Our time started almost fifteen minutes ago," said Reedy.

"Did you take a shower?" Pallas asked kindly.

"The shower wouldn't work because of the alarm," said Phoebe. "You know that. I had to wash my hair in the sink. Took twice as long. So annoying. I wish they would let you override the tardiness contingency."

"We've been waiting for you," said Atlas through clenched teeth.

"You could have gotten started without me. I would have caught up easily."

"We *can't* enter unless everyone is here," snapped Reedy. She stepped towards Phoebe angrily, her fists clenched.

Ajax grabbed Reedy by the arm and pulled her back. She tried to shake him off, then gave in.

"I'm sorry," Ajax whispered. "You asked me to protect you from immoral violence."

Pallas touched Phoebe on the shoulder. "Look Phoebe, we're just a bit anxious to get started. And…well, you can see that none of us took the time to do our hair."

Phoebe brushed off Pallas's hand. "Some of us take pride in our appearance. And by us, I mean not you, clearly. It's sad. You could be very pretty."

Pallas didn't respond.

"Just touch the damn door," Ajax said.

Phoebe tapped the door. The rest of the squad took their places and it opened.

"Thirty minutes left," Reedy said.

"Let's get to work," said Atlas.

CHAPTER 14

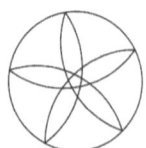

"Three acts. Thirty minutes," Pallas said. "Ten an act."

"Look at you math," said Phoebe.

Pallas took a deep breath. "No room for mistakes."

As soon as Atlas and his squad entered the room, the door shut and the lights turned on. They were on the control deck of a spacecraft.

"Reedy, what type of vessel is this?" Atlas asked.

"It's Vesuvian, an old volcano-mining vessel modified for trans-light travel."

"Get it running, please. Then, retract the heat shield. We need to figure out where we are."

Reedy sat down at the pilot station. "Atlas, this thing is not designed to withstand sustained pressure differentials."

"Why is that relevant?" Atlas asked.

"We're drifting."

"In water?"

"Negative. We're in space."

The heat shield retracted, revealing infinite stars in every direction. As the vessel drifted, rotated, and spun freely in space, the stars flew past the main viewport as if they were rising above, then setting behind the horizon.

"Phoebe, can you figure out where we are?" Atlas asked.

"Of course I can figure out where we are." Phoebe sat at the navigation console. "But I'd be much more accurate if you could get this thing to stop spinning. I can't precisely calculate our position when my *ref* points are constantly moving."

"Working on it," said Reedy. "This hunk of junk was designed to mine inside volcanos, not fly through space. The stability thrusters are more powerful than they need to be out here."

"I'll help you," said Pallas. She took a seat next to Reedy and took the thruster controls.

"No," snapped Reedy. "We're rotating on all three axes. It requires steady and precise hands to correct."

"I'm a good pilot," said Pallas.

"Not as good as me. Trust me, I got this." Reedy made small flicking motions as she operated the thruster controls. "There we go," she muttered. "Wait. No. Okay…back it off. Ugh!" She turned to Atlas. "It'll be a minute, but I'll get her under control."

Atlas turned to Ajax. "Ajax, check the rest of the ship."

"It's not a ship," said Reedy.

Atlas ignored her. "Make an inventory. Food, weapons, survival gear—we need to know what we're starting with."

"On it."

"Phoebe, we're not spinning that fast anymore. See what you can figure out by eyeballing."

"You want me to *eyeball* a billion stars?"

"Worth a shot," Atlas said. He clenched his teeth. "Maybe we'll get lucky."

Phoebe went to the viewport. "The spinning is distracting. How am I supposed to calculate anything?"

"You're the best astronomer," said Atlas "Just look for anything you recognize. Any rough idea of our location helps us understand the stakes. We can do the calculations later, when we're more stable."

"If Reedy was half as good a pilot as she claims, we'd already be stable and I'd have already calculated our exact position," Phoebe said.

"Atlas, tell her to shut up, please," Reedy snarled.

"You should concentrate on your task," Phoebe retorted.

Atlas stepped closer to the viewport and leaned against the glass. *Was that? Maybe. Yes. But not quite right.* "Pallas, take command. I'll navigate."

"Taking command," said Pallas.

Atlas sat at the navigator station and began calculating their position.

"What are you doing?" Phoebe asked. She hurried back to the navigation console and clearly expected Atlas to cede navigation back to her, but he didn't move.

"Pleiades," Atlas said, his fingers tapping across the console.

"The Pleiades?"

"Exactly. Check for yourself. You better hurry though. They're almost out of the viewport."

Phoebe went back to the viewport. "That's *not* the Pleiades. It can't be Pleiades. It wouldn't look like that from anywhere else in the Galaxy. Not unless we—"

"Not unless we're close to Earth," Atlas said.

"How close?" asked Pallas.

"Approximately a light-year or two away."

"Dangerously close," said Pallas.

"What do you mean?" asked Phoebe.

"The stakes are greater than we expected," said Pallas.

"Much greater, probably," said Atlas.

"Reedy, how close are we to stability?" asked Pallas.

"Almost got it."

"Ajax, what's the inventory?"

"Not good," said Ajax. "Only a few days of water. No food. No weapons."

Pallas sighed. "Atlas, once Reedy gets us stable enough to engage the trans-light reactor, get us to a friendly system. Far away from here."

"Xenia is our best bet," Atlas said.

A loud siren suddenly blasted in their ears and purple lights flashed a dizzying pattern.

"Reedy?" Pallas said.

"We're losing pressure!" said Reedy. "I told you this wreck wasn't designed for space."

"Can someone turn that off?" Phoebe asked. "It's hard to think."

"We need to go. Now." said Pallas. "Atlas, get us out of here."

"We're not stable enough. I can't calculate a safe place to land. We could end up inside a mountain."

"Then take us close enough to orbit the planet," Pallas said. "The Xenians can help us land."

"Affirmative," said Atlas. "This is as good as I can do."

"Do it," said Pallas.

Reedy reached forward to engage the trans-light reactor.

"No, wait!" yelled Phoebe. She lunged and touched Atlas's console as Reedy flipped the reactor switch.

A single, powerful flash of light illuminated the whole room. Atlas blinked. A large, dark afterimage hung in the center of his vision. When it cleared, he looked out the main viewport at the planet in front of them.

"This isn't right. That's not Xenia," he said. Atlas turned to Phoebe. "What did you do?"

"I took us to a better place," said Phoebe. "Xenians are arrogant."

"You've never met one," said Ajax.

"I don't need to. I've studied them."

Pallas spun Phoebe around to face her. "Where did you send us?"

Phoebe shoved Pallas away. Pallas stumbled backwards and fell.

"Don't touch me," Phoebe said. "We're safe. That's what matters."

Ajax helped Pallas to her feet. He looked at Phoebe and then at

Pallas, an unspoken question written in his grim expression. Pallas shook her head. Ajax nodded and returned to his seat.

"Phoebe, sit down!" Pallas said. "Do *not* touch anything or say anything until we are safely landed."

"I don't know about safely, but we're about to be landed," said Reedy. "We appeared too close to the planet to maneuver into an orbital vector. We're in the outer atmosphere and descending. Rapidly."

"Dammit," Pallas said. "Atlas, can we trans-light?"

"Not at this velocity. It'd be suicide."

"Options?"

"I can burn the thrusters to slow our descent. But it'll use all our reserve power. We'll be stuck on the planet."

"Is it populated?" Pallas turned to Phoebe. "Is the planet you brought us to populated?"

"You told me not to say anything," Phoebe said.

Pallas took a deep breath. "We don't have time for this...I'm going to assume it is. We'll have to find help once we land. Reedy, deploy the heat shields."

"I won't be able to see," Reedy said.

"We'll burn up if we don't."

"Maybe not," said Reedy. "This vessel was designed to mine inside volcanos, remember?"

Pallas stared out the viewport for a moment. "What do you think?" she asked Atlas.

"Worth a shot," he nodded.

You can do this, he thought. *You can do it, Pallas.*

She nodded, and then again more confidently. "Keep the shield open. Burn thrusters."

Reedy turned back to the console. "Thrusters engaged...it's not enough. We're still accelerating."

"Full thruster burn," Pallas said.

"We're too high. They'll be spent before we're low enough for a safe landing."

"Do it."

"Full thruster burn...It's—it's working. We're slowing our descent. Still too fast for a landing. Thrusters will be out of fuel before we reach a thousand feet above the ground."

"Aim for a water landing," Pallas said.

Atlas scanned the mapping data on his console. "Sixteen kilometers to the north. It's a large, fresh water lake."

"Will the ship withstand the impact?" Pallas asked.

"When it was first built, yes. Unquestionably," said Reedy. "Now? I can't know."

"That's our only option. Do it."

"Correcting flight path."

Before long, the blue of the lake came into view. The hills surrounding the lake were densely populated with hundreds of residences.

"Watch out for the houses," Atlas said. "They weren't on the map. But you should be fine." As the lake got closer, Atlas began to relax. He exhaled loudly. "We're going to make it."

Reedy stared intensely out the viewport. She chewed on her lip, as fingers and wrists made dozens of precise, twitching motions to keep the old mining vessel stable.

Suddenly, the view from the viewport began spinning erratically, a spiraling whirl of blue water, green hills, desert, and sky.

"What happened?" Pallas demanded.

"I don't know," said Reedy. She sounded defeated. "Um... thruster failure, aft starboard. There's nothing I can do."

"There's always something," said Pallas.

"What's the point?" said Reedy. "It's over." She pushed back from the pilot console.

Beta Squad watched as the Vesuvian mining vessel spun further and further out of control and hurtled towards the ground. Pallas gasped. The ship crashed into a populated hillside and exploded.

Mission failed: All dead. 253 civilian casualties, blinked across the viewport.

After a few seconds, the scene on the viewport changed. Philadelphia—no, Earth. And its moon.

Our moon, thought Atlas. *So beautiful and familiar. Serene. And peaceful. From here it looks as if all is perfect down there. Everything looks perfect from a distance. If only they knew what's going on out here. Maybe they wouldn't waste so much time and resources—and so very many lives—fighting over such petty differences. And what am I doing? What are we doing? We've fallen into the same trap—*

A dozen Olympian trans-light warships appeared in positions around Earth. There was another, unfamiliar ship with them—large and hexagonal with a circle cut out of the center. In the middle of the circle a small white sphere slowly rotated, suspended by beams of energy. The ship positioned itself above the North Pole. The sphere began to rotate faster and the beams of energy became brighter and more erratic, like lightning. Arcs of energy shot out of the corners of the ship and connected to the Olympian ships. The warships absorbed the energy for a few seconds and then sent powerful blasts at Earth.

Earth was gone.

No explosion. Just gone. Nothing but the Olympian ships and the hexagonal craft remained. Then, the Olympian crafts trans-lighted away.

"This is still part of the sim, right?" asked Phoebe.

No one answered. Pallas dropped her gaze. Atlas stood up and went to her side.

A loud explosion rumbled and shook the sim room. Fire and debris hurtled towards the viewport, originating from where the Earth had been.

"There's no sound in space," Ajax said.

"Is that the Eiffel Tower?" asked Reedy.

Sure enough, a twisted and distorted Eiffel Tower hurtled past the viewport. Then George Washington's face from Mount Rushmore. And then a section of the Great Wall of China. Finally, the torch from the Statue of Liberty came tumbling towards them, crashing into the viewport. The lights in the sim room came up and the door opened.

"Everything they do is so damn melodramatic," Atlas said. "It's almost comical."

"I don't think it's funny," said Phoebe. "You all failed. If this were real, everyone we have ever known and might know would be dead. Such a shame. I expected more from you."

"Shut up, Phoebe!" Reedy vaulted out of her seat and started towards Phoebe. Ajax grabbed her by the shoulders. Reedy shook him off and he fell backwards.

Reedy seemed surprised that she'd knocked Ajax down. "I'm not going to hurt her. I'm just going to teach her to shut her mouth."

"Why should I shut up?" said Phoebe. "You failed. Spectacularly. I could have saved you. I could have saved everyone. But Pallas put me on the bench. Brilliant. Really brilliant." Phoebe turned to Atlas. "Why did you put her in charge? She's a loser."

"Shut up," said Atlas.

"She was born a loser," said Phoebe. "You don't know. Her mom's in jail. Her dad's a drug addict. With genetics like that, it's a miracle she made it this long without getting knocked up. I mean, really…what were the—"

Reedy's fist connected with Phoebe's jaw. Phoebe crumpled to the ground, unconscious. Reedy didn't stop. She viciously kicked Phoebe in the ribs. And again. And again before Ajax was able to tackle her.

"Let me go! She *deserved* it," screamed Reedy. "I'm not finished! I'm not finished! I can do better! I can do better! I'm not finished."

Ajax lifted Reedy up and carried her out of the room. Reedy sobbed uncontrollably. As Ajax carried her down the hall, she howled in anguish.

Dazed from what had happened, Atlas checked Phoebe's pulse. Still strong. But her breathing was irregular. Broken ribs, probably. He looked up at Pallas. Streams of tears gushed down her cheeks.

"Pallas?"

It was like she couldn't see him.

He stood up and stepped in front of her. "Pallas?" He touched her arm. She reacted violently, punching him hard in the shoulder. Then she fell to the ground and scooted herself into a corner where she whimpered quietly.

"I'll get Dr. Circe," Atlas said gently. "I'll be right back."

When he got back to the sim room, Pallas was gone and Phoebe was beginning to regain consciousness. She grunted painfully. Dr. Circe and an orderly stabilized Phoebe, then took her to Medical.

Atlas was alone in the sim room. He looked around the meticulously detailed interior of a simulated trans-light craft. *What happened? How did we fail so spectacularly? Phoebe. No. Not just Phoebe. Reedy lost control. Pallas doubted herself. And I had been too proud to befriend Phoebe. Ajax was the only one who had done well. Good ole Ajax. You can always count on him.*

Atlas sighed and shook his head sadly, then left the sim room.

NONE of his squad joined Atlas for breakfast. Ajax came in briefly to retrieve his and Reedy's food. He nodded at Atlas as he left. Homer ate with his new squad. Atlas caught his gaze briefly, but Homer dropped his eyes back to his meal. No one in Gamma Squad talked to Homer. He was as alone as Atlas. But different. Worse. Atlas finished his meal in silence, cleared his table and walked to the serving area to get Pallas's meal.

Pallas wouldn't let him in. He shrugged and left the food outside her door. None of the squad came to class. Atlas went through the Gymnasia workout mechanically, without emotion. He finished well after the others. After lunch, he took Pallas food again. Her breakfast sat untouched. He buzzed once, then set the food next to the identical breakfast bowl.

"HEY ATLAS! GREAT JOB THIS MORNING," said Theo, taunting Atlas as they sparred. Nike had partnered the two of them together for Combat Training since none of Atlas's squad came to class.

"Did you see, *At-last-picked*?" Theo threw a punch and Atlas dodged. "Preliminary rankings came out." Theo swung at Atlas's head, but Atlas deflected it harmlessly to the side. "Your squad's been dropped to Gamma. Last. Where you belong." Two punches. Two blocks. "Some have started calling you Omega Squad." Theo kicked Atlas in the side. "Okay, so it's just me calling you that, but I'm sure it will catch on."

Atlas didn't counter, even though Theo's attacks left him wide open. It was only a warm-up spar, after all. Atlas began to give up ground. Before long, Theo had backed him against a wall.

"Right where I need you," said Theo. "Up against a wall, where everybody knows you fall apart." He punched Atlas in the stomach and Atlas doubled over. Theo brought his knee up quickly into Atlas's face, snapping his head back sharply against the padded wall. Atlas crumpled to the floor.

Theo pulled Atlas to his feet by the shirt collar. "Such a disgrace! Quitter!" He spit in Atlas's face. "Now maybe you've finally learned your place. Don't worry, though. Yeah, don't you worry. We got this. We'll save Earth. Alpha Squad will save all your asses. We'll save the Galaxy." He pulled his arm back to strike.

Atlas closed his eyes. But the blow never fell. He heard a thud.

When he opened his eyes, he saw Theo on the floor, sniveling. "I'm sorry, O. I didn't mean anything by it."

Oliver held Atlas by the shoulders to steady him. He looked sincerely concerned. "You okay, Sterling?"

Atlas nodded.

"Sorry about that," Oliver said. "He forgets we're all here for the same reason, sometimes." He reached down and picked Theo up, then dusted him off. He pressed his forehead against Theo's. "Do you understand, now?"

"Yes, Oliver," Theo said. He turned to Atlas. "I'm sorry for what I said. And what I did."

"And I am sorry things went so poorly today," Oliver said to Atlas. "Don't worry about it. It was only the first full-squad sim. There will be lots more, and you'll do better next time. We're counting on you to have our backs when the time comes."

Atlas looked at Oliver. "Sure," he whispered.

"It's a big job, you know—saving the Galaxy." Oliver's eyes became distant. "We're up to the task, but it will be easier if we know we can trust our back-up."

"I understand," Atlas said.

Oliver grinned. "Good." He put his arm around Theo and the two of them walked off while he explained to Theo what his punishment would entail.

"Congratulations," Atlas called after them.

Oliver turned back.

"I heard your squad completed the whole sim, and with time to spare," Atlas said. "Congratulations."

"Thank you. We've a long way to go yet, but thank you."

After dinner, Atlas once more took Pallas her meal. Grilled chicken with broccoli and carrots again. She ordered it at least twice a cycle. He buzzed and set the dinner down next to the untouched breakfast and lunch bowls.

The door opened as he stood up. Pallas stood silently in the doorway.

"I brought you dinner," Atlas said.

"Thank you," said Pallas. She stooped and picked up her dinner. Stepping backwards into the room, she smiled awkwardly, as if ashamed, and closed the door.

Atlas went to his room, stripped off his clothes, and took a long, warm shower, most of it sitting in the corner of the stall with his head buried in his arms, the streams of water beating down relentlessly. He closed his eyes tightly. *Warm. Comfortable. Familiar. The only thing that feels exactly like it did back home. If I could just sleep like this.*

As he crawled into bed, Atlas couldn't get the image of the exploding Earth out of his head. Stupid and theatrical as the simulation was, Atlas kept playing it back over and over. The Eiffel Tower. George Washington. Statue of Liberty. It was all meant so seriously it was hilarious. Like a soap opera. Atlas began to laugh uncontrollably, but the laugh rapidly descended into a desperate cry. *Mom. Dad. Maggie. All dead.* He failed. And they were dead. Not yet. Not quite. But what about when he failed for real? They'd be dead, like Phoebe said.

Please, please, please, he thought. *Let Oliver and his squad save us all. Don't let the rest of us screw it up for them.*

CHAPTER 15

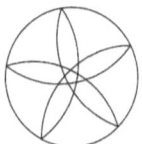

DESPITE THE FIASCO of the day, Atlas slept well and easy. He woke up in the middle of the night to use the bathroom and was surprised at how relaxed and calm he felt. For the first time in a long time, the burden of carrying the fate of the Galaxy on his back didn't lurk in the back of his mind. Oliver and his squad were so capable, and they worked together like a precision-crafted machine. He could trust them to get the job done, even if Theo and Eugenio didn't like him.

That didn't mean Atlas was going to quit. No, Atlas and his squad would recover from their stumble yesterday and work their way back up to Beta Squad status. It wouldn't be easy, but it was practically certain. Daphne was capable, but she couldn't get Phoebe to work with a team. And despite Homer replacing Phoebe, Daphne's squad had only gotten halfway through the second act of the sim before time ran out.

Atlas already had a plan to make Phoebe a functioning member of his squad. *I can do it. It will work.*

Like everyone, Phoebe needed to feel valued. Perhaps she needed it more than most, but that was a lot different than needing to feel the *most* valued. *We should have welcomed her to the squad. I should have welcomed her. And I shouldn't have taken navigation from her, or challenged her abilities.*

Undoubtedly, Atlas would prefer to have Homer back, but that wasn't going to happen. As squad leader, it fell to him to make sure each squad member felt valued. That meant trusting them all to do their jobs. He'd failed. *I'll try again tomorrow.*

Atlas fell back asleep planning his new approach as squad leader. It would begin with the morning run, and then breakfast. *Yes.* He smiled. *Yes. Good plan. Good...plan...*

FOR THE SECOND day in a row, Atlas was awakened early by the blaring of an unfamiliar alarm from his glass. Bleary-eyed and disoriented, he stumbled to his drawer and fumbled through his clean underwear, searching for his glass. *When I get home, I'm throwing away all the alarms in the house.* He realized the alarm wasn't only blaring from his glass. The bathroom mirror also screeched at him, and the lights in the room were flashing. *What's going on?*

He held his glass up to eye level. *Intruder Alert! All students report for immediate evacuation*, it read. A schematic of the Academy appeared on the glass. Several areas on the schematic flashed red with a black 'Intruder!' warning in the middle. A room adjoining the dining hall flashed yellow with 'Evacuation' spelled out in green.

Pallas!

Atlas quickly pulled on his clothes. His door buzzed. Without thinking, he opened it.

Pallas crashed into him, knocking him to the floor.

"Why did you open it?" she said.

"You buzzed," Atlas said, picking himself up.

"There's an intruder! I could have killed you."

Atlas shook his head and pointed to the schematic on his glass. "Let's get to the evacuation point."

"It could be a trap."

"Or another test," said Atlas. "They love surprise tests."

"I don't think it's a test." Pallas grabbed his hand. "This is real."

"How do you know?"

"I don't know. But I do."

Atlas studied Pallas's face for a few seconds. *Trust your squad,* he thought. "Okay. What do we do then?"

"First, we get our friends. We'll be safer together."

"Agreed."

Atlas touched his door open. Reedy, Ajax, and Homer stood there, about to buzz the door. The hall was quiet, the alarm only sounding inside the room.

"What are you doing in here?" Homer asked Pallas, looking surprised and disappointed. "I was halfway to the evacuation. Came back to get you, but you didn't answer."

"I'm glad you're here, Homer," Atlas said. "You've probably heard how much we missed you yesterday."

"Yes," Homer said. He kept his eyes on Pallas, but she looked away uncomfortably.

"Is this another sim?" Reedy asked.

"No," Pallas said. "This is real, I think."

"Has anyone seen Phoebe?" Atlas asked.

Homer sighed and shook his head.

"Why?" said Reedy.

"Because she's a part of our squad," Atlas said. "That makes her our responsibility. We need to find her. We need to be together."

"Right," said Homer. "I'd better get to my squad."

"No, you're staying with us," said Pallas. "Friendship trumps squads."

Homer looked to Atlas for confirmation.

Atlas nodded. "You're better off with us and we're better off with you." He clapped Homer on the shoulder and addressed the group. "Ideas?"

"We need weapons," said Ajax.

"Agreed," said Atlas. "From the XT lab?"

Pallas shook her head. "There's no guarantee there will be anything useful left unsecured in there."

"And it's on the far side of the evacuation," said Reedy.

"Most the weapons in Xenotech are nonfunctional anyway," said Ajax. "They're just for show. We need to get to Combat Training."

"The Combat weapons are nerfed," said Homer.

"Not the melee weapons," Ajax grinned slyly.

Homer and Ajax performed their secret handshake. While most of the Philadelphians preferred to train with ballistic and energy weapons during Combat Training, Homer and Ajax had worked diligently to master an impressive array of melee weapons.

After a loud slap across his thigh from Ajax, Homer flinched first. "Right, sounds fun."

"This isn't a game," said Reedy.

"Of course not," said Ajax. "But we're still going to win. Let's go, Homer." He broke into a run.

"We need to stay together," said Pallas.

"And we need to find Phoebe," Atlas said.

"You get her," Ajax called back. "We'll bring weapons."

"There's no time to argue," said Homer. He chased after Ajax.

"Meet us outside the dining hall," Atlas called after them.

They didn't acknowledge.

"Buzz the doors as we walk by," said Reedy. "We need to make sure everyone is awake." She touched Terry's and Polly's doors as they passed. There was no response. Reedy wrung her hands as the three kept walking. "I hope they got out."

"Did you see anyone else when you were on your way to my room?" Atlas asked.

Reedy shook her head. "No, but I went straight to Ajax's room as soon as the alarm sounded. I was already awake."

"Me too," said Pallas.

"Phoebe?" Atlas yelled through her door. He buzzed twice, then pounded on the door. "It's Atlas. Open up."

"Where is Phoebe?" Pallas asked her glass. "It says she's in the dining hall already."

"Nice of her to make sure we're okay," said Reedy.

"We need to get to her," said Atlas. "If it's a trap…"

He ran towards the dining hall. The others followed.

"It's probably too late," said Pallas. "I mean, if it's a trap…"

"Yes, but we have to try," said Reedy.

Atlas slowed to a walk just before they arrived at the dining hall. He turned to Pallas.

"You're right, the evacuation is a trap," he said.

"How do you know?" asked Reedy.

"We should have seen the others," Atlas said. "Or at least a few of them. Homer said he was halfway to the evacuation point when he decided to come *back* for Pallas. How could he have time for that?"

"He's a fast runner," said Reedy.

"Pallas is right. The evacuation is a trap. The intruders must have spoofed the alarm one squad at a time."

"Why would they alert one squad at a time?" Reedy asked.

"To make it seem like another sim," said Pallas.

"If it's a trap, the prudent thing to do would be to meet back up with Homer and Ajax and find another way out of the Academy."

Atlas shook his head. "Alpha and Beta squads need our help. Together, we might be able to overwhelm the intruders."

"We need the weapons," said Reedy.

"You wait for them, if you want," said Atlas. "I'm going."

"No," Pallas said. "We go together."

"We should wait for Homer and Ajax," said Reedy. She picked at her fingernails and chewed on her bottom lip. "That's the right way to do things. We should do it the right way. We need it *right*. Correct. Proper." Her breathing became shallow and short.

"We can't wait," said Atlas. "Take a deep breath, Reedy. I need you at one hundred percent." He stood to the side of the dining hall doors, pressed against the wall.

Pallas and Reedy did the same on the opposite side of the doors.

"Ready?" asked Atlas.

Reedy took a deep breath, swallowed, and nodded.

Atlas opened the dining hall doors. The lights were off. It was quiet inside. Atlas peeked around the doorframe. Nothing. Dark. He stepped into the dining hall. The light didn't turn on. *Wish I had a flashlight*, he thought. A light from behind him illuminated the floor. He turned to see Reedy following him, an arm held so that her glass acted as a flashlight.

"Ask for a flashlight," whispered Reedy.

Pallas switched her glass to flashlight mode and stepped even with Reedy. Atlas followed the girls' example.

"Thanks," Atlas whispered. He swept the beam of light from his glass across the dining hall. It was remarkably focused and powerful. *Thought there was nothing this thing could do that would surprise me. The little things. Always the simple, little things.*

Everything in the dining hall appeared just as it should. Nothing but empty tables and chairs arranged in their proper place. It didn't look like anybody had been here since dinner the evening before. Even the chair Atlas had sat in was slightly askew and pushed back from the table, just as he remembered leaving it.

"Everything looks normal," said Reedy.

"Except for no lights," said Pallas.

The three made their way towards the door that, according to their glasses, led to the evacuation. It was the same door Nike always used.

Where are Homer and Ajax? They should be here by now, Atlas thought. Maybe they hadn't heard him say they would meet at the dining hall. He didn't like going into an unknown situation like this without weapons, and without two of the better fighters in the Academy. But if there was any chance they could help the other students, this was how it had to be.

Atlas pressed his ear against the wall next to the evacuation door. Nothing. "Okay, last chance. If you want to go, go now. Find a way out of the Academy. We can meet up in the forest."

"Not a chance," said Pallas.

"Reedy?"

"We're not leaving," Ajax's voice called out of the darkness.

Relief washed over Atlas. His fingers tingled with adrenaline.

"You said meet outside the dining hall," said Homer.

"We couldn't wait," said Atlas. "What did you get?"

"Mostly just blunt objects," said Homer. He thrust a heavy, leather-bound, metal handle into Atlas's hand.

Baseball bat? No, a Theban battle club. The barrel was star-shaped rather than cylindrical like a bat, but otherwise weighted similarly. The wielder could easily switch between one and two-handed use.

"Since you love the Thebans so much," said Homer.

Ajax handed a Vandalusian monk staff to Pallas, and a set of Phoenician combat rods to Reedy. Ajax kept a Titan short sword for himself, and Homer carried a set of wooden short clubs.

This whole thing is absurd, Atlas thought. *Against someone capable of infiltrating the Academy, these weapons will be practically useless. Our only hope is greater numbers. Where are Nike and Themis? Not here. No more questions. No more delays.*

"On three," Atlas said. "One...Two..."

"For Philadelphia—er...Earth!" Reedy said. She touched the door open and ran into the evacuation chamber.

Atlas and the others followed close behind.

The room was so brightly lit, Atlas couldn't stop blinking. His eyes ached and watered. He heard several loud crashes, and screaming.

"Atlas! Pallas! Get out of here. *Run*," said a familiar voice. Oliver.

Atlas rubbed his eyes and squinted. Oliver stood near the far corner, brandishing a crude club of some sort. Behind him lay the rest of his squad, leaning against the walls at unnatural angles. A hooded figure stood between Oliver and Atlas.

The hooded intruder turned towards Atlas and his friends. It stepped towards them. Oliver swung his club wildly, but missed. He stumbled and grabbed his side. Blood pooled on the floor underneath his feet. The intruder ignored him and continued towards Atlas and his squad.

Atlas fixed his grip on his Theban battle club and set his feet like he was up to bat. Pallas, Ajax, and Homer readied themselves near him. Reedy ran full speed past Atlas and let out a blood-curdling howl as she leapt at the intruder, transferring her momentum into a fierce swing of the combat rods. The intruder ducked under the swing and swept Reedy aside mid-leap with one strike of its bare hand. Reedy limply hit the floor and slid hard against the wall. Another body lay near her. Phoebe. There were others too, strewn around the room. Daphne's squad.

"Arete-Twelve," said the intruder. "Designation: Slavery." It continued towards Atlas. "Atlas-Fifteen. Designation: Slavery."

"I'm nobody's slave," said Atlas.

"Atlas-Fifteen. Designation: Slavery," the intruder repeated.

Oliver's club crashed down on the intruder's shoulder, causing it to stumble forward slightly. It turned back to Oliver, who knelt on one knee, defiantly waving a wooden chair leg. His strength was failing.

"Oliver-One," the intruder said. "Designation: Death."

"You said...that already, but I ain't...dead yet," said Oliver.

The intruder reached for Oliver's club. Oliver swung it desperately, but the intruder caught it and yanked it from his grasp. "Oliver-One. Designation: Death." The intruder pressed its finger against Oliver's throat and drew a line from one side of his neck to the other. Then it turned back to Atlas.

Oliver remained still for a few seconds, staring wide-eyed at Atlas. He began to choke. A large slit opened up across his throat and a torrent of blood gushed out. Oliver fell forward onto his face, and lay still in the growing puddle of his blood.

"Oliver!" Atlas screamed. He charged forward with his club held high with rage and fear.

Pallas, Homer, and Ajax charged with him, their weapons raised. Atlas reached the intruder first. He swung at its head, but with a swift flick of its wrist, the intruder deflected Atlas's blow and upset his balance. In the same motion, the intruder kicked Atlas's legs out from under him. Atlas crashed to the floor, smashing his shoulder on the star-barrel of his club. Pallas swung at the intruder's legs. It deftly sprung into the air above her swing and spun a kick that caught Pallas across the chest.

"Pallas-Fourteen. Designation: Slavery." It ducked underneath an attack from Homer and then another from Ajax. "Ajax-Seven. Slavery."

Homer swung his other short club at the intruder's head, but he was too close. The intruder caught Homer by the wrist and pulled him off his feet while simultaneously kicking Ajax square in the stomach.

"Homer-Nine," the intruder said as it disarmed Homer.

"Designation: Slavery," Homer spat.

The intruder pulled Homer's face closer. "Designation: Blindness." Homer ceased struggling. The intruder smeared the back of its finger across Homer's eyes then tossed him aside.

Ajax stabbed his sword through the intruder's torso. It fell forward, carrying Ajax's sword with it. Homer screamed in agony, clutching at his eyes. Then he was silent.

Ajax stood above the fallen intruder. He reached down to retrieve his sword and yanked it out of the intruder's body. The intruder rolled onto its back and groaned. Ajax raised his sword and prepared the killing blow.

"Ajax-Seven," Ajax sneered. "Designation: Death-dealer." He let out a fierce yell and swung his sword down with all his might.

The intruder rolled out of the way at the last instant. It was back on its feet before Ajax could react. It ripped the sword out of Ajax's hands and lifted him off the ground by his throat.

"Ajax-Seven. Designation: Slavery."

Ajax went limp and the intruder tossed him aside. It turned its attention to Pallas, who coughed and sputtered for air.

Atlas forced himself to stand. His right shoulder felt broken. He lifted his Theban club with his left hand and set himself between the intruder and Pallas. He swung at it and connected. The intruder shrugged it off. Atlas swung again. Same. He swung at its head. The intruder stepped nimbly out of reach. *How? Ajax stabbed it through the chest. How is it still walking?* Atlas gripped his club with both hands and swung through the pain.

The intruder caught Atlas by the wrist.

"Atlas-Fifteen. Designation: Slavery."

Atlas went limp. The intruder let him crumple to the floor.

Atlas couldn't move. He was conscious, but completely paralyzed. His muscles felt like they were on fire, but he couldn't scream. He could breathe, but he couldn't scream.

"Pallas-Fourteen. Designation: Slavery," the intruder said.

Atlas heard the thud of Pallas's body hitting the floor near him, then the steps of the intruder walking away.

"Arete-Twelve. Designation: Slavery." More steps. "Eugenio-Five. Designation: Death."

Atlas tried to close his eyes. He wanted to hold his breath—make himself pass out—but he couldn't. Anything to not have to listen to this. Helpless.

"Theodore-Three. Designation: Death."

"Please, please, *please*. No." Penny's voice. "No, no, please."

"Penelope-Two. Designation: Death."

"No—no." Choking. Then the slump of another body falling to the floor. Silence.

"Nerissa-Four."

Stop! Stop! Stop! Atlas begged. *Make it stop! I can't listen...I can't! Stop!*

"I won't beg," Nerissa said. It sounded like she spat.

"Designation: Death." Another body hitting the ground. And more steps. "Edward-Eight. Designation: Blindness."

Eddie screamed as Homer had, then fell silent. The intruder continued working its way around the room. The same painful screams from Daphne, Polly, and Terry. All blinded. Agonizing screaming, then sudden silence.

The intruder lifted Atlas up and dragged him onto a pile of his squad mates, including Phoebe. *Stupid Phoebe. Her fault. We could have escaped.*

Someone else entered the room. *Help? Nike? Finally! Too late for Alpha Squad. But finally.* Atlas tried desperately to speak.

"Well done, Styx," a voice said. "You never disappoint, that's for sure. The best in the business. Truly the best. If you ever decide to leave government work, make sure you come to me. I pay obscenely well." The voice approached Atlas and his squad. "Let's see...so, these are mine, correct? Thought so. Don't look like much. Not for what I paid, at least. But they're young. Hmm...maybe a bit too young. No matter. I'm patient. They'll learn faster and recover more quickly from the work."

The voice was even closer. Bare legs. Then a face bent down, cocked sideways, and scrutinized Atlas. "Hello, there. You don't look very well. Don't worry. I have excellent physicians. They'll have you all fixed up good as new in no time. No, don't say anything. You're welcome. Wait! Now where are my manners? I'll introduce myself. I'm Apollo. You belong to *me* now."

Apollo stood up and laughed. Then he kicked Atlas in the face.

CHAPTER 16

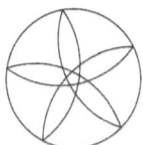

DESPAIR. Utter, desperate, all-consuming despair. The first and only sensation Atlas experienced as he floated back to consciousness. Despair like a vacuum. Despair like infinity. Despair like nothing. Despair like everything. Zero.

Atlas counted backwards from one hundred by threes. Why had all this happened to him? He was only a boy. Not even yet fifteen years old. He never asked to fulfill an ancient prophecy from a senti civilization nine thousand light-years from his home. Baseball. *I just wanted to play baseball and spend time with my friends. The only aliens I ever fought or wanted to fight existed solely in video games. My family. I want to see my family again.*

The headache hit as Atlas tried to sit up. Almost as bad as the day he'd arrived at the Academy. He felt the side of his face where Apollo had kicked him. It was swollen and tender to the touch. He winced. Wincing hurt almost as much as touching it. Atlas could only open his right eye part of the way. And his shoulder. He could barely move it, but it didn't hurt as badly as before. Maybe it wasn't broken.

He could move again. He was alive. *And not blinded. But why?*

The image of Oliver bleeding out right in front of him stuck in Atlas's mind. Though he hadn't seen it happen, he imagined the other four from Alpha Squad with their throats slit and dying as well. They stared at him with accusing eyes. Even once the life was gone, their eyes condemned him.

They were right to do so, Atlas thought.

"Pallas," someone whispered. "Pallas?"

"Who is that?" Atlas asked. It was too dark to see.

"It's me, Ajax."

Flashlight. Nothing happened. Atlas felt his arm. His glass was gone. Of course. "What's wrong with Pallas?"

"I can't find her," said Ajax.

"Where are we?"

"Some sort of detention cell," said Reedy.

Atlas turned towards Reedy's voice. She seemed close. He stretched his hand out but found nothing. "I can't reach you."

"I'm here." Reedy caught Atlas's hand.

"Are we together?" Atlas asked.

"Three of us," said Ajax. "I can't find Pallas, or Homer."

"Or Phoebe," said Reedy.

"Yes," grunted Ajax. His voice came from above Atlas. "Or Phoebe."

Atlas felt his insides turn to ice. "Was she…were they killed?"

"No," said Reedy. "The intruder…Styx…only killed Alpha Squad. Beta was blinded. But we were kept alive and whole."

Atlas touched the side of his face again. His head and shoulder throbbed. "For the most part," he muttered. *No*, he chastised himself. *Oliver. Penny. Nerissa. Theo and Eugenio. Lanta. All dead. What do I have to complain about?* He felt ashamed. "Where are Pallas and Phoebe? And Homer?"

"Pallas and Phoebe were carried out with us," said Reedy. "I know they were alive. The Olympians stacked us on top of each other. I could feel Pallas's breath on my arm. And I could see Phoebe's eyes twitching."

"Why do you think the attackers were Olympians?" Atlas asked.

"Who else would attack the Academy?"

"The murderer...Styx...didn't seem big enough to be Olympian," said Atlas.

"Apollo definitely is," said Ajax. "He kept talking about how Titan smelled funny compared to Olympus."

"I didn't hear that," said Reedy.

"I'm not making it up."

"I didn't say that you were. I said I didn't *hear* it."

"What about Homer?" Atlas asked.

"I couldn't see, but I think they piled the Betas somewhere else," Ajax said. "I heard them moving bodies. I doubt they would have bothered moving...moving Oliver."

"Unless they wanted trophies," said Reedy.

"I think *we're* the trophies," said Atlas. The three were silent for a moment.

"Ugh," said Ajax. "Why am I so sore?"

"I am too," said Reedy. "Must be from whatever Styx used to paralyze us."

"I don't feel sore," said Atlas. "But I really can't feel anything except this wicked headache."

"What's wrong with your head?" Reedy asked.

"Apollo kicked me."

"You and your head," Reedy laughed weakly. "You're like a magnet for head injuries."

Atlas wanted to laugh, despite everything, but he was afraid it would hurt too much. "Seems that way, doesn't it?" He reached up towards Ajax. "Help me up, Ajax?" He caught Ajax's hand and was immediately pulled to his feet. "Have you tried calling out for Homer, or the other Betas? Maybe they're in a nearby cell."

"I don't think they were brought aboard the same ship as us," said Ajax.

"We were the only ones designated for slavery," said Reedy. "The Olympians may have left them on Titan."

"I don't think so," said Atlas. It didn't make sense for Homer and the rest of Beta Squad to be left behind, but he couldn't decide why not. "Anyway, our priority is to find Pallas first. We need her."

"And Phoebe," said Reedy. "It's morally imperative that we find both."

"If she had—," Ajax began.

"It's not her fault," Reedy said. "None of us are at fault. We did our best. We are absolved. And anyway, we don't know her side of the story."

"I think I do," said Ajax.

"You may know less than you think."

"Stop," Atlas snapped. "Assigning or absolving blame is useless! The Titans failed. Our squad failed. Everyone failed. *I* failed. But it doesn't matter anymore. None of it matters. I don't care about *the squad* or the Titans or the Sphere or who deserves the blame for anything. Right now, the only thing I care about is finding Pallas. When we find Pallas, we'll find Phoebe. They kept us together, they'll keep the two of them together too. And then we're getting the hell out of here!"

An awkward silence lasted for almost a full minute.

"Where would we go?" Ajax finally asked.

"Anywhere," Atlas said. The sudden illumination of the hold lights silenced him. They weren't in a cell, after all. More like a cargo bay. Stacks of large crates littered the hold in irregular clusters.

"You said we were in some sort of cell," Atlas said to Ajax.

"We were," said Ajax. "I felt the walls. But now they're gone." He took a few steps forward with his arm outstretched. Nothing. He lowered his hands and took another few steps. "What the hell?"

"What?" said Atlas.

"There it is."

"There's nothing there," said Reedy.

Ajax pressed and something in mid-air resisted. "Weird. I can't feel anything. But I can't get past it."

"Pretty cool, eh?" a familiar voice said. "Just had it installed.

First time ever in a ship this small." Apollo walked out from behind a cluster of crates. "Literally turns the air into a prison." He stepped face-to-face with Ajax and put up his hand, sliding it up and down the invisible barrier, testing its strength. Without warning, he punched Ajax in the face.

Ajax retaliated, but his fist got stuck mid-punch. Apollo punched him in the stomach, and then again in the face. Ajax fell backwards onto the floor. Reedy ran to his side.

Apollo laughed uproariously. "Your face! You should have seen your *face*. Not yours, of course, Ajax. Your face was getting drilled by my fist. I mean Atlas's face. You should have seen it. Hilarious. Do it again! Please?"

Atlas glared at Apollo.

"No, that wasn't it. Try again. No? Oh well. Obviously, the barrier doesn't affect me. Had you fooled though, didn't I? That whole pantomime bit. Classic. Aw, come on, you gotta' admit it was funny." He took a step forward, beyond where the barrier had stopped Ajax. "I step inside. I step outside." He stepped backwards. "Inside. Outside. Inside. Outside. Now you try it. No? Fine. Spoil my fun."

"Where's Pallas?" said Atlas.

"She's with Phoebe," said Apollo.

"Where's Phoebe?"

"She's with Pallas." Apollo laughed again. Apparently, he was his own favorite comedian.

"If you hurt them, I'll kill you," said Atlas.

"No, you won't. But don't worry. I have no intention of hurting them. In fact, my intentions with them are quite the opposite." He grinned lecherously. "Not yet, of course. That's obscene. But later, when they're older, and when they've grown to appreciate me. I promise to tell you all about it when it happens. Maybe, if you're good, I'll even let you be there."

"You're revolting," Reedy spat at Apollo. Unexpectedly, her spittle passed through the invisible barrier and hit him in the face.

Apollo snarled and wiped it away. "Technology is never

without its flaws, obviously. But don't be jealous, Arete. You're free to join Pallas, Phoebe, and the rest of my girls any time you choose. I would have put you with them from the start, but your psychological profile indicates you're much more likely to harbor a homicidal grudge. So of course, you understand, I will have to keep you with these boys, for my own safety. Maybe once you get a taste of how difficult that life can be, you'll come to me on your own. I take very good care of my girls—that's a promise. Spare no expense."

"What other girls?" asked Atlas.

"Oh, I have lots of girls. Hundreds, from all over the Galaxy. Titans, Vitrians, Thracians, Cretans, Dorados, Phoenicians, Xenians, Thebans, Vandalusians, even a few Olympians. Your friends are my first Philadelphians, of course. How *exciting*." Apollo clapped his hands together.

"Why are we here?" asked Atlas.

"You don't remember?" Apollo shook his head. "I guess I kicked you harder than I thought. Your species seems unusually delicate." He hopped inside of the invisible barrier and outside again, then chuckled. "Isn't it obvious? You live here now. You belong to me."

"I belong to no one," said Reedy.

Apollo leaned against some crates. "You know, a lot of people think I'm crazy for bringing you here. I admit, it wasn't cheap. And you're smaller than I expected, so the work may kill you— except for you, Ajax. You'll be fine. But I'm optimistic our arrangement is going to work out, so if you'd please quickly fall in line, we'll all be better off."

"Not my style, *sorry*," said Reedy.

"Of course, if it takes too long for you to adapt, I may get bored or frustrated and kill you all instead. At least then I'd save some money on food for my animals. I have an awe-inspiring collection of intergalactic carnivores. You really ought to see it. Maybe you will." He giggled. "Most of them prefer live prey, of course. Don't worry, I would anesthetize you beforehand. I'm not a barbarian."

"I can think of a few more appropriate words," said Reedy.

Apollo smiled. "What a zinger! I take it back. You are *not* welcome to join the rest of my girls. Not after you've hurt my feelings like that."

We need more information. Keep him talking, thought Atlas. "Where are we?" he asked.

"You're on my estate," said Apollo. "It's a rather large one. So large, that if you tried to escape, you'd starve before you reached the border of my property. I see you're impressed. Well, what can I say? My workers have been good to me." He hopped in and out of the invisible barrier a few more times, amusing himself.

"Right, your *workers*," scoffed Reedy.

"No matter what you call 'em, you gotta' have good people, one way or another," Apollo smirked. "Although, if I'm being completely honest with you—and why the hell not?—the greater portion of my obscene largess comes from *strategic investments*."

Apollo pantomimed placing his hand against the invisible barrier and resting his weight against it. "Here's a bit of financial advice: the best investment you can ever make is in people—we've been over that already—but when you're ready to take it to the next level, you gotta' go big. Yep! Buy yourselves a couple of politicians. Of course, you gotta' get em while they're young and relatively inexpensive. Before you know it, you're buried in cash." Apollo sighed and grinned contentedly. "I am blessed. Truly blessed. But like I said, I'd be nothing if not for *my* people."

"Where are the other Philadelphians?" Reedy asked. "The ones that were blinded?"

"Don't know. Don't care. Some aristocrats have a quirky penchant for keeping blinded courtiers, but not me. Nothing against it. Just not my thing. I went to a dinner with Delphi, for example—now that guy is a genuine weirdo—and every servant in the dining room was blinded. Can you imagine? Not a single crumb was spilled. I was *astonished*."

Apollo's wide-eyed grin turned into a scowl. "They say Delphi sees the future, and that's the secret to his rapid ascendancy. Total reptile excrement. He can't even see the present. Lives in the past." Apollo shrugged. "Still, he's one of mine, so I love him anyway." Apollo skipped inside the barrier again, grinned, and then hopped outside. "I really need to be going. Business. You know how it is. My people will be here to collect you shortly. Don't try anything with them. They are authorized to use deadly force. Let's see...anything else I need to tell you? Seems like there is, but I just can't quite remember. Oh well, you'll figure it out." He spun around on his heel and sauntered off.

A few seconds later, four male guards arrived in the cargo hold. Two were either Olympians or Titans, perhaps one of each. Another was considerably shorter, but with orange and red hair, a Phoenician. The last had gray-blue skin like Diana. A Theban male.

They did exist.

"You will stand with your hands behind your back," said the Phoenician.

"Hi, I'm Atlas." He stuck out his hand. The Olympian-Titans snarled and drew heavy metal clubs from their belts. Atlas lowered his hand and put both behind his back, as instructed. "I apologize. I was just excited to meet some fellow slaves—I mean...um...*workers*. Anyway, I'm glad you're here. Apollo's alright and all, but sometimes you just want to be with your own oppressed caste, ya' know what I'm saying?"

"Silence, Philadelphian," said the Theban.

"You will learn to hold your tongue," said the Phoenician. He passed through the invisible barrier and stepped up to Atlas's face. "Or you will end up without one." He nodded to the Olympian-Titans, who smiled grotesquely before opening their mouths to display ragged stumps of a tongue.

"So, you guys were pirates?" Atlas asked.

"Atlas, *enough*," said Reedy.

"Listen to the girl," said the Theban. He turned to Reedy. "You may yet earn your place in the Governor's harem."

"No thanks," said Reedy.

"Many women have killed to achieve such an honor."

"And many more have died trying to attain it," said the Phoenician.

"I will kill someone, but not for that honor," said Reedy.

The Theban laughed. "It will be such a pleasure to break you. I do hope that delicious privilege falls to me."

Ajax lunged at the Theban. The Olympian-Titans hit him in the torso with their clubs which delivered a strong electric shock. With a rumbling groan, Ajax fell to the ground.

"Cowards," muttered Reedy, but she didn't move.

"Get up!" said the Phoenician to Ajax. "The game is over. Come with us peacefully and silently or we will use deadly force."

Ajax stood up and took his place behind Reedy. The Phoenician tapped something on his wrist and the invisible air barrier no longer restrained the Philadelphians. They followed the Theban out of the small, trans-light vessel and passed through a gate into an expansive garden surrounding an enormous black building.

The garden was filled with hundreds—maybe thousands—of exotic plants. No trees. The largest were barely more than bushes. A large hexagonal fountain drained its water along six narrow channels that irrigated the different sections of the garden. It really was quite lovely, Atlas admitted.

The Theban led them through the garden and past the black building.

"This, you may have guessed, is the Governor's residence," said the Phoenician. "Under no circumstances will you enter the house unless required by your duties."

Atlas estimated the house was nearly a football field long, though less than twenty meters wide. The structure rose at least forty feet before dozens of swooping peaks erupted across the length of the roof. The tallest towered almost sixty feet beyond the center of the house. Despite its height, the house revealed only two rows of windows. *Only two floors?*

The exterior surface was covered in a highly polished black stone that reflected the surrounding gardens. Ribbons of platinum highlighted each juncture and corner of the structure. Everything about Apollo's house betrayed a preference for the ostentatious.

Atlas, Reedy, and Ajax were led around the back of Apollo's house and beyond, towards a low concrete building. They passed hundreds of laborers engaged in agriculture and construction, digging and dunging, herding and chopping, fabricating and transporting.

Many of the laborers stopped to gawk at the new arrivals. *They've never seen Philadelphians before,* Atlas thought.

"I would advise you not to fixate on a particular labor," said the Phoenician. "Our system will match you to the task to which you are most apt. If you are lucky, you will remain on the compound, though it is more likely you will end up hundreds of kilometers away, working in one of the Governor's factories."

Unacceptable, thought Atlas. *We can not be separated.*

They arrived at the low concrete building.

"This is the barracks where you will sleep tonight," said the Theban. "Tomorrow you will be assigned to your division and transported to your post."

"Barracks curfew is two hours after sundown until one hour before sunrise," said the Phoenician. "A tracking device has been injected into your blood stream. If you try to remove it, or stray too far out of your designated sector, it will kill you."

The Theban led them into the barracks. Rows and rows of bunkbeds were the only furniture. All were empty.

"May I ask a question now?" said Atlas.

"Ask, Philadelphian," said the Phoenician.

"Well, um, my shoulder was injured. I'm afraid it's fractured. What can I do about that?" Atlas rubbed his shoulder.

"It is not broken, Philadelphian," said the Phoenician. "You have a large contusion, but that is all. You will be fine."

"Are you sure?"

"Yes, all laborers are examined prior to transport. There has been no permanent damage."

"Well good, I'd hate for my injury to get in the way of my slaving…I mean unpaid labor."

"If you fall behind in your duties, you will be terminated," said the Theban.

"Good to know," said Atlas. He was silent for a moment. "What if I have an itch and scratch myself where the tracker is? It's not going to interpret that as an attempt to remove it, is it?"

"The tracker moves freely through your bloodstream," said the Phoenician. "It does not remain in a part of your body long enough for you to scratch it."

"Also good to know," said Atlas. "This is officially the most informative orientation tour I've ever had. Anything else I need to know? Like, is it safe to operate a microwave?"

"Tier I laborers do not have access to microwave emitters."

The Theban laughed. "Philadelphians still cook their food in microwave ovens. I believe that's what he means."

"Yes, exactly," said Atlas.

"There are no microwave cooking devices on Olympus," said the Phoenician.

"What? No microwave popcorn? What do you do for movie night?"

"*Atlas*," Reedy hissed.

"I'm sorry," said Atlas. "I only want to make sure I don't accidentally do something that will cause my death. I've seen how inconsequentially Olympians view life, but I happen to value it an awful lot."

"Not enough to think before you speak perhaps," said the Theban. "Stay away from high-powered magnets. They may cause the tracker to overload and burn a hole right through your torso."

"That sounds improbable," said Reedy.

"I've seen it happen," the Theban grinned. "The screams were *horrifying*."

He stopped in front of a set of bunkbeds in the furthest corner of the building. "You will sleep here. The shift supervisor will distribute ration credits once you have completed your daily tasks. As you have not completed any tasks today, you will not receive ration credits."

"I recommend you seek out someone to assist with his or her duties for the remainder of the day," said the Phoenician. "There's always a slight chance they may be willing to share a crumb or two in exchange."

The four guards left, leaving Atlas, Reedy, and Ajax alone among the hundreds of bunkbeds.

Ajax climbed up to the top bunk. He sat for a minute, then jumped down. "Reedy, take the top bunk. I'll sleep below you."

"You guys see if you can find someone willing to share their work and food with you," said Atlas. "I'll meet you back here an hour and a half after sundown." Atlas walked towards the door.

"Where are you going?" Reedy asked.

"To find Pallas and Phoebe."

CHAPTER 17

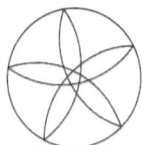

ATLAS WANDERED around Apollo's compound and the nearby fields, pausing to chat occasionally with a heavily-laden slave—that was the right term, no matter what Apollo preferred to call them—hoping to give the impression he was begging to work for rations. The burdened slaves had little interest in Atlas's smalltalk. Atlas didn't say much to the other, less-burdened slaves other than a perfunctory greeting. Sometimes he just watched them work and tried to guess which planet they were from.

Apollo owned slaves from almost every senti culture Atlas recognized, as well as dozens he had never studied. It reminded Atlas of what he had once longed for—an intergalactic spaceport filled with dozens of different senti species—when the Thebans had instead parked their trans-light vessel on an old slaughterhouse foundation in the middle of a farm. Apollo's compound was even further from a spaceport than that farm, but here, finally, was the intergalactic melting pot Atlas had wanted so badly. He wept.

As the sun began to lower, Atlas slowly circled back towards the main house. He glanced up at the many windows from time to time, looking for clues as to which section housed the harem. He shuddered. *What a disgusting word, but I don't know what else to call it.*

When the sun dropped below the horizon, Atlas decided that the harem occupied the western wing of the house. Every few moments a slender silhouette would pass by one of the windows. Not much to go on, but from Atlas's perspective, that section of the house seemed the most active. If Apollo told the truth about the number of females he kept, it seemed the most likely place to search for Pallas and Phoebe.

By itself, the western wing was enormous. And it was impossible to know which part housed the mature women apart from the girls. Atlas realized he was making a lot of assumptions about Apollo. What if he didn't care to separate the women from the girls?

Wish Pallas was here, Atlas thought. *She would know what I should do. She's so much better at reading people. Maybe I should wait a day? There's a chance Ajax, Reedy, and I will all be posted on the compound. Won't Apollo want to keep us close, for novelty's sake? I should be patient and gather more information. Make friends with others who can tell me what I need to know about the house. No. Can't risk separation. And what about the Celestial Sphere? Who cares? But look what the Olympians have done without it. What will they do if they find it? We have to stop them. The time to find Pallas and escape is now.*

There was a low wall projecting out from one side of the house, giving shade to a bed of flowers. Atlas believed he could use it to climb up to a second-level window. Perhaps a sympathetic woman would open the window for him, if he said Pallas was his sister. *No, too risky. What about the back door? Likely leads to the house slave barracks.* He'd seen quite a few slaves coming and going through the back door. The front door? He hadn't seen anyone use it. It was a terrible idea, but also the best option.

Atlas walked around to the front. It was worth a try. *I'm new here. I can claim ignorance or confusion.* No one was around. All the garden slaves had finished for the day.

He walked up the steps to the front door. It was at least twenty feet high and ten feet wide, seemingly cut from a single slab of the same ebony stone that covered the rest of the house. A complex and intricate geometric pattern, carved in relief and accented with platinum, decorated the entire door. Atlas looked closely at a minor imperfection. So insignificant he had only noticed it by chance. Any other moment of the day, and the light would have made the flaw invisible. Carved by hand.

Atlas reached for the door knob. At the slightest touch of his finger on the knob, the door swung open, nearly knocking him down. Atlas cautiously looked inside.

The crystals from the three chandeliers cast a soft, golden glow about the expansive entrance hall. The same pattern from the door —here painted in gold and other metals—covered the walls as they arched up to the central peak of the roof. Gold-banistered stairs swept up each side of the room to the second floor. A composite stone that included large flecks of gold covered the floor. Thin lines of gold held the stone tiles in place. The whole room reminded Atlas of a sunset. He felt profoundly awestruck by the beauty and grandeur.

Pallas. Atlas shook his head. He heard voices coming from one of the adjoining hallways. Atlas ran as quietly as he could up the stairs, ducking into the western upstairs corridor as the voices entered the lower hall.

"No one's here," one of the voices said.

"Why is the door open?" said another. "Security!"

"Never mind that," said the first voice. "I've been saying for months that door knob is too sensitive. A light breeze picks up and the knob activates."

"You don't know that's what happened."

"I'm sure it's what happened."

"And if there's an intruder?"

"Terapon, you worry too much. The Governor recently upgraded the spectrum scrambler. Not even Oracle Delphi can trans-light onto his estate. The borders haven't reported any visitors by land or air, and no laborer would dare to pass through the Honorific Portal. The likeliest explanation is the wind."

"If I worry, Doero, it is because it is my duty to worry. Nevertheless, I suppose you are correct. You must see about calibrating that knob, immediately."

"Of course," said Doero.

Atlas walked quietly down the corridor, Terapon and Doero's voices fading behind him. Dozens of doors lined each side of the long hallway. Where to begin? Atlas hadn't thought this far ahead. *Can't just randomly open doors. So many doors. I didn't think this through. Maybe I should go back. I'm sorry, Pallas.*

A door near the end of the hallway opened and two young women stepped into the hallway. Atlas looked frantically for a place to hide. Nothing. Not even a potted plant. The two young women stood outside the door, facing each other and chatting. They hadn't noticed Atlas. He considered running for it, but he'd come too far down the hall. He'd never make it.

Atlas tried the door closest to him on the left. It didn't open. Neither did the door on the right. Nor the next door further down. The young women hugged and gave each other a light kiss. *Out of time.* Atlas flung himself against another door to the left. It opened. Atlas slipped inside.

The door shut behind him. The room remained dark. *What if someone's in here?* He crouched down and crawled forward. *Beds. Three beds. Oh no. Good. All empty. This is hopeless. Need to get out of here before I'm caught. Such a bad idea. What a stupid move. Pallas would never have acted so rashly.*

The lights turned on. Atlas instinctively flattened himself to the floor and rolled underneath the nearest bed. His heart raced so loudly he was sure it would give him away. A pair of legs approached the bed. *One of the girls from the hall. They saw me.* The legs stopped only inches away from his face. The skin was tinted ever so slightly orange. Phoenician, probably.

A light, silky tunic dropped to the floor. Atlas blushed with embarrassment. The young woman sat on the bed, her bare feet, ankles, and calves dangling in front of him. She swung her legs ever so slightly. *So extraordinarily lovely!* Atlas was sure he had never seen lovelier lower legs in all his life. He felt himself falling in love. He wanted to reach out and bury those ankles in thousands of kisses. *What a creeper*, he thought. *Hiding under a bed, fantasizing about a woman's ankles. Focus! I need to find Pallas. Have to get out of here and find Pallas.*

"Who's Pallas?" the young woman asked. "Should I be jealous?" Her voice was sweet and sincere.

Atlas realized he'd been discovered, but his more pressing thought was that the young woman's voice was the most beautiful sound he had ever heard. *Such flawless and bewitching vocal chords!*

The young woman laughed. "No one's ever complimented my vocal chords before." She stood up and spun delicately around on perfect toes attached to perfect feet and perfect ankles. "Why don't you come on out so you can complement me to my face?"

"I'd rather not," said Atlas.

"Don't worry. If I was going to turn you in, I would have already. I know you're not here to hurt me." Her voice had a reassuring, confident lilt.

"Of course not," Atlas said. "I would never hurt you...or try to hurt you."

"I know, sweetie." She reached her hand below the bed. "Now, come on out here so I can get a proper look at my admirer."

"It wouldn't be proper," said Atlas.

"But sneaking into my room and hiding under my bed is?"

"I mean...your clothes," said Atlas.

"That was a trick, so I could hear what type of man you are. Come on out. I'm fully clothed." She fluttered her fingers.

Atlas took her hand. A charge of electricity shot up his spine. His heart pounded in his ears as he allowed himself to be guided out from under the bed.

"You can hear my thoughts?" Atlas kept his eyes down, ashamed of the hot flush in his cheeks.

"Only some of them." The young woman was dressed in an identical garment to the one she had dropped at her feet. "When you think about me, and a few seconds after, that's all." She lifted Atlas's chin to meet her eyes. "I'm Zhehera. What's your name?"

"Atlas." Her eyes were silver and grey. They were his favorite. He never wanted to look anywhere else.

Zhehera smiled. "I like that name. What happened to your darling face?"

Atlas touched where Apollo had kicked him. "I'm new here. It's been a difficult...um...adjustment."

"I see." said Zhehera. "Where are you from, Atlas?"

"I'm from Earth...er...Philadelphia."

"And Pallas? Is she also a Philadelphian?"

"Yes, she's my sister."

"You don't have to lie to me," Zhehera frowned. "She's obviously not your sister."

"You've met her? Then why ask who she was?"

Zhehera smiled. "I haven't met her. I heard you worry about finding her."

"I thought you could only hear my thoughts if I was thinking about you?"

"And a few seconds after, remember?"

"I didn't remember. This is new to me," said Atlas. "But how did you know I lied about her?"

"When I hear thoughts, I also hear the feelings that go with them. That's how I knew you didn't come here with ill intentions, and how I know that the feelings you have for Pallas are not those of a brother."

"She's my friend, and I have to find her. Apollo said she was to become one of his...women. I thought maybe someone in the harem might have seen her."

"Are you calling me a whore?"

"No." Atlas's cheeks flushed redder than they ever had before. "I mean...I just thought..."

"But you do think I am one of Apollo's *women*." Zhehera stuck her chin out indignantly. "Apollo does *not* own me."

"I'm sorry, I thought you were a slave."

"Are *you* a slave, Atlas?" Zhehera pursed her lips and crossed her arms.

Atlas thought for a moment. "I am a prisoner, not a slave."

"As am I," said Zhehera. She spread her arms wide. "This is my prison."

"I am deeply sorry." Atlas looked at his feet and sighed.

"I don't need your pity."

"I mean for what I said—for what I insinuated."

Zhehera stared at Atlas for a moment, then tousled his hair. "I forgive you. Pallas is lucky to have someone who cares for her as you do."

Atlas shook his head in embarrassment. "She's a friend."

"Yes, I know. An extremely good friend, but don't worry. I know you don't feel the same way about her as you do about me." Zhehera grinned playfully. "I'm not jealous."

"Please don't tease me," said Atlas. "I'm just young, that's all. And it's not fair that you can read my thoughts."

"I'm not teasing—okay, maybe a little. But not maliciously. I find your innocence appealing."

Atlas's chest tightened and the blood rushed back to his cheeks. "I'm not even fifteen," he said.

Zhehera brushed a shock of orange-yellow hair from her face. "Neither am I."

"You seem—I mean, I'm not saying you look *old*."

"I know I don't look it. I've lived so much more than fourteen years."

Atlas stared at his feet, unsure how to respond. "I can't imagine."

Zhehera lifted his chin again. "All who fall into such circumstances as ours bear a heavy burden. That mine is unique from yours does not diminish the weight of either."

"Yes," said Atlas. He suddenly became aware of the time he'd spent with Zhehera. "I don't mean to be rude. You already know, I guess, that I could listen to you talk and stare into your eyes forever, but I need—"

"To find Pallas. I know. You are so exceedingly loyal. I admire that. Even while I cloud your mind, you keep coming back to her."

"Do you know where she might be?" Atlas asked. "She would be with another Philadelphian girl."

"And does the other girl have a name?"

"Her name is Phoebe. We're not particularly friends."

"But you want to help her too?"

Atlas nodded.

"And they're both about our age?"

"Exactly my age," Atlas said. "We have the same birthday."

"Truly? Exactly the same birthday? Now, that is interesting." Zhehera was quiet for a moment. "They will be safe for the time being. Apollo doesn't call for girls younger than fifteen."

Then you haven't been called for? Atlas shook his head. *She can hear when you think of her, remember?*

"They will remain in Consort Training until they are judged ready. For most, it is less than a month, though for some it is much longer. Then they will be brought to live here."

"What do they...do in Consort Training?" The question made Atlas nauseous with anger and disgust.

"Almost nothing," Zhehera said. "Apollo likes his women soft, helpless, and with a taste for luxury. Everything is done for them. They mostly lie around and gossip about each other while old women prisoners bring them food, dress them, bathe them, and perform any other task the consorts-in-training would normally do for themselves. Before long, no matter what they were before being taken by Apollo, they have become completely dependent on remaining in his good graces." Zhehera's gaze became distant.

"Pallas is strong," said Atlas. "Both physically and mentally, she is strong. She will never allow herself to be made helpless."

"I hope you are right," Zhehera sighed. "I have seen many I believed strong become utterly and completely helpless."

"But you didn't," Atlas said.

"You don't know me—don't know what I once was, or how that compares to who I now am."

"Someone weak and helpless would have feared me," said Atlas. "You would have called for security if you weren't strong and confident."

"Perhaps. But I have pretended to be weak for so long that I fear I am becoming the pretense."

"Then you must help me reach Pallas and Phoebe as soon as possible," Atlas said.

"You want to escape? And you want to take me with you." Zhehera shook her head. "My dear Atlas, if I were to escape with you, then I truly would have lost all my strength."

"I don't understand," Atlas said. "It won't be easy to escape."

"No, it will not," said Zhehera. "And if you are to do it, you must do it soon, before you become complacent—before you become contented. Apollo does not treat his prisoners poorly, so long as they obey. You will have food, shelter, protection, and even recreation. All you have to do is obey. That is the danger. For many, that is enough."

"Not for me," said Atlas.

"Nor for me."

"Then why won't you come with us?"

"It is not my destiny. I have a task I must complete." Zhehera turned away from Atlas and towards the door. "I will be fifteen in two months. Then I will be called for."

Atlas watched her silently for a moment. "You mean to kill Apollo."

"Now you read *my* thoughts? Well then, now we both know each other's secrets and so we can both trust each other."

"Of course," said Atlas. "I would never betray you."

"I know," said Zhehera. "Now go. It is late. You will have to hurry to get into the barracks before curfew." She took Atlas's head in her hands and kissed him on the forehead.

Atlas melted and wrapped his arms around Zhehera. It felt as if he was hugging Pallas and Reedy, his mother and Maggie, his grandmothers, and all other women he loved at the same time. So many strong women in his life. He felt incomprehensibly lucky.

Zhehera gently pressed Atlas away. She went to the door, opened it, and checked both directions of the hallway. "The only ways in or out are through the main entrances, front and rear. Go now. And be careful."

Atlas slipped out of Zhehera's room and hurried quietly down the hall. He felt embarrassed and ashamed, both because he realized he had put Zhehera at risk, and because he had clutched her like a small, fearful child clings to his mother. He had to put space between them. *If I am caught, she must not be suspected. How precise is the tracking device? Can't give them a reason to pull the data. You've really screwed this up, Atlas.*

Before long, Atlas arrived at the stairway. He peeked around the corner and down to the entrance hall below. No one. He crept down the stairs and approached the front door. It wouldn't open. He firmly grasped the knob but nothing happened. Atlas yanked on it. Still nothing. He pressed his weight against the door, but it didn't budge.

Atlas began to panic. *Wait. The rear entrance.* But it was down another level, in the basement where he'd seen so many house slaves enter as the sun went down. Still, there was no other option. He peeked down the hallway from where Doero and Terrapon had emerged. Another hallway branched off towards the rear of the house. *Maybe that way.* Atlas took a deep breath and clapped his thighs. He hurried down the hall and found stairs to the basement. "Yes," he exclaimed in spite of himself. He clamped his hand over his mouth, checked up and down the hallway, and hurried silently down the stairs.

Atlas cautiously entered the house slave quarters. The corridors were dark except for two rows of tiny lights running along both sides. Raucous voices erupted in laughter from behind one of the doors he passed. A few drops of urine ran down his leg as he darted around a corner. He hadn't used the bathroom since the Academy, he realized. His stomach grumbled. *Haven't eaten either.*

Atlas followed the lights away from the rear exit. *Thirty seconds. I'll give myself thirty seconds.* He began to count backwards in his head. At twelve he found it. The kitchen.

There was no doorway, only a wide opening. A few dim lights illuminated a large, industrial kitchen. A basket of leftover rations from that evening sat on a counter. Atlas grabbed three ration cakes and hurriedly left.

The laughter had died down, but he could still hear an occasional hoot as he rushed to the rear door. *What a dismal place to hear laughter*, he thought. Soon, he was outside.

Atlas silently closed the rear door and looked out across the lawn. No one else could be seen. *Later than I thought. Past curfew. How long was I with Zhehera?* He walked across the field to the barracks. *Will I be able to get in? And what if I can't? How cold does it get at night?*

"What are you doing out here?" It was the male Theban. He stood outside the barracks entrance, drinking something from a small bottle that he tried to casually conceal.

Atlas didn't answer. He calmly continued walking towards the door.

"It is past curfew on your first day," the Theban called. He set his bottle in a bush as he walked towards Atlas. "You will be severely punished for this. Where have you been? You will tell me immediately. If you make me requisition your tracking data, your punishment will be even more severe."

Atlas approached the Theban calmly. "Can we talk about this tomorrow? I'm tired. It's been a long day, and I have to pee. First day as a slave really takes it out of you, ya' know?"

"You will answer me, Philadelphian. If you do not, your friends will partake in your punishment as well."

Atlas turned to the side and walked to a cluster of bushes. "Could you maybe look away for a sec—give me some privacy?"

"What are you doing?"

"I got hungry," said Atlas, as he relieved himself in the bushes.

"That is disgusting! Filthy Philadelphian."

"No one wanted to let me help them in exchange for a portion of their rations, so I snuck into the house...uh—what does Apollo call them? Servants?—into the servants' quarters, waited until they'd all gone to bed, and took some food." Atlas turned around and wiped his hands on his pants.

"I don't believe you. When I pull your tracking data and discover—"

Atlas retrieved two of the ration cakes out of a fold in his shirt and showed them to the Theban.

"You will serve a month in the mines as punishment."

Atlas took a bite out of one of the cakes. "If I'm going to the mines, better get my strength up."

The Theban smacked Atlas across the face. Atlas righted himself and took another bite of the cake. He pulled the third cake out of the fold in his shirt. "Want one? I brought plenty." The Theban swiped the cake out of Atlas's hand, then hit him again. His mouth bleeding, Atlas grinned and took another bite. The Theban knocked him down. Atlas stood up, dusted the cake off, and finished it.

"You will regret your insolence, Philadelphian. Surviving a month in the mines would have been unlikely. You will certainly not survive two."

"Care to bet on it?" Atlas asked as he stuffed the second cake in his mouth.

CHAPTER 18

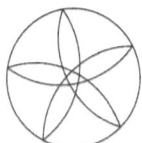

ATLAS AWOKE EARLY. His joints ached with a burning fire and his muscles throbbed as if they were about to burst. His throat and nasal passages were raw and inflamed such that every breath felt like he was inhaling hot sand and exhaling obsidian dust. He didn't even want to think about what was going on in his lungs.

Trace gases released during mining processes caused his discomfort. At first, it was a tickle in the back of his throat, similar to when he had first arrived on Titan. Unlike on Titan, however, Atlas's symptoms became worse with every day he spent down in the mine. Some species didn't react to the gases at all; for others it was fatal after a few weeks. As the first Philadelphian to work in the mine, every day was an experiment. And every day, the prognosis became less optimistic.

It was always hot in the mine. That was the most unexpected detail. Atlas had believed that the temperature underground was supposed to be cool. Not this far down. Even his Theban clothing couldn't keep him cool.

Atlas pulled off the stiff canvas that served as his blanket and rolled onto his stomach. He lifted his legs above the edge of his sleeping trough and carefully lowered them out of the narrow hollow he had carved out of the hard, volcanic stone. The bunk was barely long enough to fit him, but deep enough to prevent him from rolling out, and only wide enough for his shoulders. He'd cut it like that particularly, so no one else would want it. Too small for almost anyone else.

His toes found the footholds he had carved to precisely fit his feet and Atlas slowly lowered himself the thirty feet to the ground. He had spent a week of his few off-hours carving the footholds into the wall of the main shaft. It took another week for the bunk.

The dangerous trace gases were relatively dense and the highest concentrations settled near the mine floor. By carving his bunk so high up, Atlas avoided exposure to the gases while he slept. If not for his Theban shoes' capacity to adjust their soles to different surfaces, Atlas would never have been able to climb the wall. If he couldn't climb, he never would have been able to carve out the footholds or his bunk. The Theban shoes had probably saved his life. *Little things keep you alive.*

Apart from his clothing, that dirty piece of canvas was his only possession. Every night, Atlas soaked the canvas in water and slept underneath it. By morning, it was completely dry, but Atlas hadn't sweat himself to dehydration.

He had taken the canvas from another miner who died in a cave-in shortly after Atlas had arrived in the mine. Two Vandalusians and a Cretan tried to take it from him, and Atlas had to fight them off. They were also dead now, but it wasn't his fault.

On the ground, Atlas made his way along the narrow mine passageways to the supply depot. He stepped carefully over the nearly nude bodies of other miners sprawled out wherever exhaustion had overcome them. These were new to the mines— less than two weeks—and hadn't yet had a chance to finish carving their own bunks, or take one from the dead. Some were drenched in sweat. Others dry as a bone. A few of them probably wouldn't wake up.

One of the bodies began to bark the harsh, squealing cough that identified his species and also signed his death warrant. Thracian. Hearty and strong as they were, the mining gases turned their lungs to bloody mush. Atlas estimated this particular Thracian had six, maybe seven days left. That is, if the heat didn't get him first.

The supply depot was closed. Pickle hadn't opened for the day yet. *Guess I woke up earlier than I thought. Oh well. At least I'll be first in line.* Atlas leaned up against the steel doors and closed his eyes. He let himself slide down until he was sitting with his back against the door. Seconds later, he was fast asleep.

Atlas awoke to a sharp kick in the ribs. He sprung to his feet and prepared to fight. A short line had formed.

"Get up, Philadelphian!" said the nearest Vandalusian—who Atlas assumed had kicked him. "You're keeping us from our rations. Go in, or get out of the way."

Atlas nodded and went inside the supply depot. The Vandalusian and other miners pushed past him to get to the rations dispenser. Atlas waited patiently behind them. When it was his turn, he retrieved his rations and went to collect his tools for the day. The other miners sat in the middle of the floor and greedily devoured their meal.

"Morning, Pickle," Atlas said.

The Vitrian stepped out from behind the racks of picks, shovels, and sledge hammers. "Good morning, Atlas. I wish you would not call me that."

"Well, Piquamamanturuftix Elpurtistazug is a bit too many syllables for the morning. Pickle's easier."

"My species does not appreciate nicknames," said Pickle.

"Liar, you forget I've met other Vitrians before."

"General Orsetulidex. I did not forget," Pickle huffed.

"That's right. And he introduced himself to me as Taco, which he said is a popular nickname for Vitrians, and on Earth it's a popular, and delicious food. That's why I call you Pickle."

"It is dishonorable to refer to Vitrians with food terms," said Pickle. Compared to Taco, Pickle had much shorter tusks that were also a deeper shade of red, and Pickle's head horns were almost non-existent. He was obviously much younger than Taco.

Still, his long limbs were enormous, like an elephant. Atlas didn't know how they compared to Taco's.

"Taco didn't mind."

"General Orsetulidex has no honor," said Pickle.

"So you've said," Atlas said, his mouth stuffed with rations.

"Had he died along with those he led to their unnecessary demise, he might have preserved some. But fleeing as he did, while those under his command died by the thousands...I doubt any Vitrian children will receive the name Tachonamewharuts for many generations."

"And yet, you still call him General," said Atlas.

"That is how I knew him," said Pickle. "He was once a great man, and an acquaintance of my father. Since I will not see my home again, it does not matter if I choose to remember him for the great man he once was instead of the coward he became."

Atlas changed the subject. "Any news from the topside?"

"Not much new." Pickle prepared his daily inventory register as he spoke. "The last legal challenge against Potentate Delphi has been dismissed."

Atlas nibbled on his ration biscuit. "So, he's in there for good, eh?"

"It appears so. There was never much doubt he would beat the challenge. After all, he is the Great Deliverer. The Savior of the Olympians." Pickle spoke without a trace of irony.

"Yeah, and all he had to do was kill a bunch of kids," Atlas said bitterly. "The Olympians are sure impressed easily."

"The Potentate prophesied that he would defeat the Philadelphians spoken of in the ancient prophecies," said one of the miners sitting in the middle of the room, eating. "That makes him the most powerful Oracle to have ever lived."

"Saying you're going to do something and then doing it is *not* a prophecy," snapped Atlas. "And I don't remember seeing him at the Academy that night. He sure didn't fight me." Atlas narrowed his eyes and took a few menacing steps towards the Vandalusian who'd spoken.

The miner stood up and sneered at Atlas, but shoved the remains of his rations into his mouth and left the supply depot. The other miners returned their attention to their food.

Atlas returned to his conversation with Pickle. "Saying you're going to do something and then sending someone else to do it isn't a prophecy."

"I am a laborer," said Pickle. "It does not matter what I think. But the Olympians believe in Potentate Delphi because...well, because you are *here*."

Atlas grumbled, "So, what now?"

"Well, now that he is free of political barriers, I imagine the Potentate will continue with his plans."

"Invade Titan," said Atlas.

"Yes, I expect the invasion will begin soon."

"Even without the Celestial Sphere?"

"By defeating you, Potentate Delphi proved the Sphere is irrelevant."

"So *he* says," said Atlas. "What do you think?"

"I have told you it does not matter what I think."

"It matters to me. Do you think the Sphere is irrelevant?"

Pickle set down his inventory register and looked at Atlas. His skin shimmered, but he remained visible. "I think the Celestial Sphere is a myth used as an excuse to destroy and enslave other species."

"And yet, it makes you nervous," said Atlas. "I saw you shimmer. You wanted to become invisible, but the implant stopped you."

The other major difference between Taco and Pickle was the latter's habit of wearing clothing. Taco hadn't needed it since he spent most of his time invisible. Pickle, being unable to become invisible, wore loose, flowing clothing in an effort to retain his modesty.

Pickle shimmered again. "The power of myth is often more dangerous than the power of reality. Look at the damage the myth of the Sphere has done to the Galaxy already. I shudder to think of the destruction that could arise should such a powerful device actually exist."

Atlas chewed his rations and thought for a moment. "How do you explain the myth's emergence among hundreds of distinct planets?"

"Very few of which continue to adhere to the myth," said Pickle.

"Whether they believe in the Sphere or not, the emergence of such similar prophecies on so many planets, thousands of light-years apart, can't be mere coincidence."

"No," said Pickle. "Because if it was coincidence, that would mean the death of your friends, and your capture, only served the purpose of bringing Potentate Delphi to power. Or, more broadly, that your abduction from Philadelphia was nothing more than a ruse to stoke tensions between the Titans and Olympians."

Atlas thought about when he had worried Taco might be a conspiracy theorist. Pickle could be the real deal. *Perhaps it's characteristic of all Vitrians? Taco did say they were prone to nervousness.* And yet, Pickle's words stuck in his head. Even if the Sphere was real, what if there was some truth in Pickle's conjecture? Were the Philadelphians just pawns being sacrificed as a means to interstellar war? Pallas would appreciate Pickle's skepticism. *Pallas.* Atlas hadn't thought about her for a few days. He quietly finished the rest of his rations.

Pickle handed Atlas his tools for the day. "Try not to get hurt. It would be a terrible shame to die today."

"Why should today be any different?"

"Because it is your last day, of course," said Pickle.

"Really?" Atlas was stunned. He'd stopped counting several weeks ago. Could it really be the end of his sentence?

"You did not remember?" Pickle said. "By the sound of you, it is just in time. Another few weeks and your lungs would never recover."

"Yes." The mention of his lungs made Atlas cough. "Just in time." He took his tools and headed out to work his last day in the mines. *Last day in the mines.* He thought of Pallas. And Ajax and Reedy. And Zhehera. And even Phoebe. What had become of them during these two months? How would he establish contact with Pallas and Phoebe? His last attempt landed him here. He would need to be more careful, more cautious. But it needed to be soon. They all needed to escape. Whether the Celestial Sphere was myth or fact, Atlas was done playing the pawn in the game between Titan and Olympus.

Zhehera was right. Even in the hellhole of the mine, Atlas had become complacent, droning through each day without a thought for the future, intent on survival. *Survival only.* Survival was day-to-day, moment-to-moment. Every moment. Survival kept him alive, but it wasn't a life. The only hope for life was away from here. *Find the Celestial Sphere. Stop the Olympians. Save Philadelphia. If the Sphere even exists. It has to exist. I need it to be real.*

With his thoughts occupied by his friends, the Sphere, and dozens of impossible escape plans, the daily work passed rapidly. Atlas got into a minor fight with a Dorado over water rations, but other than that, the day was uneventful. Was it really the last day of his sentence?

At the end of the workday, Atlas turned in his tools to Pickle. It was a strange feeling, taking his headlamp off for the last time. Despite its simplicity, the headlamp seemed more essential than his glass ever had. Atlas held the small puck-shaped light in his hand and turned it over. So simple, yet without it, he would have died. It had saved his life twice: once, when a cave-in had trapped him in a narrow passageway, waist-deep in water, and the only way out was to swim under the cave-in; and again when a falling stone had hit him square in the headlamp. The lamp barely had a scratch, but the rock would have killed him. Apollo didn't believe in helmets. At least not for mine workers. Atlas chuckled to himself. *Reedy was right, I am a magnet for head injuries.*

"If it means that much to you, go ahead and keep it," Pickle said. "We got hundreds of them."

"What?" Atlas asked.

"Keep it. The headlamp. You know, as a memento of your time here."

"No thank you." Atlas handed the headlamp back to Pickle. "No offense, but this has been an experience I would like to forget, but never will."

"No offense taken. I understand." Pickle returned Atlas's pick to its place on the tool rack, but he set the headlamp on a separate, mostly empty, shelf. "You know, you should be proud. No one has ever survived this long down here."

Atlas shrugged. "That's only because no one's ever been sent down here for this long."

"I have been here for three years, but I understand your point. I do not live here. I have a comfortable bed on the surface."

"Since it's my last day, you want to finally tell me what you did to get sent down here in the first place?"

"Not unless you want to be down here another two months," Pickle said wryly. "It is a long story."

"Another time, then," said Atlas. He stuck his hand out to Pickle.

"So, you want to keep your headlamp after all, then?"

"No, I want to shake your hand. It's a Philadelphian custom. A sign of respect."

Pickle eyed Atlas suspiciously, but stuck his hand out to meet Atlas's. Atlas grabbed his hand and shook it firmly.

"Thank you," said Atlas. He released Pickle's hand and turned to go. As he was about to exit the supply depot, he turned around. "See you later."

Pickle nodded, then returned to organizing the mining tools.

Atlas began the slow ascent to the guard station. There was only one entrance to the mine, but a million ways to die once you got inside. That made it difficult to make friends with other miners, or care about them one way or another. First and foremost, you had to make sure you survived. Caring what happened to others was a distraction. Distractions got you dead. A tear rolled down his cheek. What had he become? Would he even be able to care about others anymore? Or had the mine killed him from the inside?

"Philadelphian!" someone yelled.

Atlas ignored the voice. He wasn't about to get into a fight on his way out the door.

"Philadelphian," the voice repeated. "I'm talking to you, Atlas."

No one called him by his name down here except Pickle. The voice sounded familiar, but Atlas continued walking to the guard station. If he got there after curfew, they wouldn't let him out. He'd be stuck in the mines another night. And if he didn't report to the barracks by morning…

"Please," the voice pleaded. "I'll die in here."

Atlas turned around. It was automatic, involuntary. A Phoenician miner climbed towards him. As he got closer, Atlas realized he must be new to the mines. His face and clothes were still relatively clean and he wasn't wheezing as he climbed. Then Atlas recognized him. It was the Phoenician that had escorted them to the barracks. One of Apollo's most trusted workers. *Well, perhaps not so trusted anymore.*

"I am in a hurry," Atlas said and turned back to his climb.

"Please help me," the Phoenician said. "You have survived longer than anyone down here. Please, tell me what to do. I'll die."

"Don't die," Atlas called back as he continued to climb.

"Zhehera," the Phoenician sputtered.

Atlas spun around and took a few angry steps towards the Phoenician. "What does that mean? Is it a curse? Because I have been cursed a dozen times by Phoenicians down here and I have outlived every single pathetic one of them."

"It is the name of my cousin," said the Phoenician. "She told me to find you. Zhehera said you would help me. That you were a good person."

"I have never heard that name before," said Atlas. This was

obviously a trick. Had they discovered where he had been that night? Zhehera could be in trouble.

"Her birthday was yesterday," said the Phoenician. "She turned fifteen. Apollo will call for her any day now. I tried to change her records. But I was caught and now I am here."

"Sounds like an appropriate punishment," said Atlas. No way he could trust this Phoenician. "I am sorry for your misfortune, but you made a choice and now you must suffer the consequences. I'm going to be late."

"She told me to tell you goodbye," the Phoenician said desperately. "Zhehera said she goes to fulfill her destiny and that you must go to fulfill yours as well."

"My destiny is to leave the mine," said Atlas. "And I will do exactly that. I suggest you get back to the sleeping area and stake out a spot to sleep before all the good ones are taken." He walked about ten meters, then stopped. What if the Phoenician was telling the truth? *Wasn't I just wondering if I was still capable of caring about others?* Atlas dragged his fingers through his hair. *When did my hair get so sticky? This mine! I nearly lost myself here.*

He turned back to the Phoenician. "Sometimes the best places to sleep are away from the others—up high, out of the way, and they require a bit of work to reach. It's possible one such space may have recently opened up. Also, try and find a way to stay cool at night."

"Thank you," sniffled the Phoenician. "Thank you, so much."

Atlas started to climb again, then turned around one last time. "If you want to know how to survive down here, it's simple. You gotta' have a reason to keep living and it's gotta' be a good one—so good that even when you forget it, it's still there, deep down, compelling you to move forward, one day at a time, until the last day comes and you finally leave the same way you came in." Atlas climbed the rest of the ascent to the guard station with a smile on his face.

The guards checked his identity and frisked him for stolen ore or other contraband. They gave him an injection to help neutralize the effects of the dangerous gases. Then they opened the gates and let him out.

An hour later, Atlas finally exited the mine. It was dark, and he was miles away from Apollo's compound and the barracks. He had no other choice, so he stepped onto the road that led back to the compound and his friends. He breathed in the refreshing smell of the woods. His lungs felt much better already. *One step at a time. I should be there by dawn. Tomorrow's a big day. The biggest day yet.*

CHAPTER 19

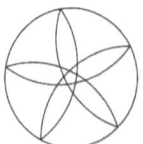

SHORTLY AFTER THE first break of dawn, the roof of the laborer barracks came into view. Atlas was exhausted. He sat down against a tree to rest for a minute and watch the sunrise, but almost immediately began nodding off, so he stood back up and began the final descent. *Can't risk missing check-in. Rest later.* His throat burned differently than it had down in the mines. *Thirsty.*

He tried to swallow, but couldn't muster the saliva. Hours earlier, a stream had passed under the road. Atlas had drunk his fill, but there hadn't been any water since then, and he didn't have time to search for a spring or creek. *So close. Drink later.*

During his time in the mines, Atlas had seen only a few dozen survive long enough to be released and sent back to Apollo's compound. Of those, six had been sent immediately back to the mines because they hadn't reported to the barracks before the next work day began. It was a rule no one told you about. You had to see someone break it, or break it yourself, to know it existed. None of those six survived their return to the mines.

Atlas looked at the barracks roof. He looked at his feet. *One foot in front of the other. Then I can take a shower. Drink water. Eat rations. Take a nap. And escape.* He yawned. *Find Pallas and Phoebe. Escape. Get Ajax and Reedy. Find Pallas. Escape.* He quickened his pace.

Today. It has to be today. Atlas began to run.

He had spent the night-time journey imagining various escape plans, their risks, and chances of success. None of them seemed feasible. Apollo's estate was too big, and Atlas knew next to nothing about it. But they had to escape soon. Today. He'd already delayed it enough. Hopefully the others had been successful learning about the estate. *They will be angry at me, probably,... because I got myself into trouble,...but, I had to protect Zhehera... Zhehera who will be called for soon...*

Escape. Today. Or die trying. Atlas sprinted the last four-hundred meters. He felt free already.

Atlas checked-in with the head laborer-on-duty who made no effort to hide his disgust at Atlas's appearance and smell. He didn't say a word, just grimaced and motioned for Atlas to enter the barracks. The morning wake-up bell hadn't yet sounded, and the rest of the laborers were asleep.

Atlas made his way to the showers. He was thankful there weren't mirrors in the barracks so he wouldn't have to look at himself after two months without bathing. What did he look like? He couldn't remember, but he also didn't want to know. Not until he was clean, at least.

He entered the shower fully dressed. Warm water. He lifted his face, opened his mouth, and drank freely from the shower head. He didn't care that it was warm. It was cleaner than the water in the mine, and it didn't have that sulphur aftertaste. And he was so thirsty.

With only a light scrub, all the dirt and grime washed right out of his clothing. Remarkable. Even after the abuse of the mine, the Theban clothes looked brand new. *Little things.* He peeled the wet clothes off, hung them up to dry, and began the more difficult task of cleaning himself. The dirt of the mine stuck to his skin and required scrubbing to remove. He had to wash his hair five times before the tacky residue rinsed away.

Clean and refreshed, Atlas dressed quickly. He felt so much better now that he was clean. Even his joints and muscles felt better. The steam from the shower had felt so good in his lungs. *That injection was effective.* The burning in his throat and nasal passages had diminished to an unpleasant irritation.

If they had the cure all along, why not administer it to the workers in the mine? The answer was obvious, Atlas realized. Working in the mines wasn't the punishment. The looming threat of impending death was the punishment. Certainly, there were extremely few repeat offenders. Surviving the mines meant guaranteed compliance in the future. And the stories told by the few who returned would all but guarantee the compliance of others.

Atlas had survived. *But I haven't learned my lesson,* he smirked. The excitement of reuniting with his friends and escaping together energized him. He wasn't even tired anymore. He yawned. *Maybe I have time to lay down. Just a few minutes. Before the wake-up bell sounds.*

He made his way to the back of the barracks where Ajax, Reedy, and he had been shown their beds two months earlier. The bunks were empty. No Ajax. No Reedy. Maybe they'd moved beds. He could find them later.

Atlas lay down on the nearest bed, but he couldn't get comfortable. It was too soft. Compared to the mine, the barracks were paradise. This was going to take some time to get used to— *No! I can't get used to it. I'm leaving. Escape. I'm so tired. And uncomfortable.* He turned from side to side and then onto his back. Atlas tried lying on his stomach, which was worse. He considered climbing out of bed and lying on the floor. Instead, he decided to force himself to remain still, no matter the discomfort. It worked. His eyes soon closed and he fell asleep.

Almost immediately, the wake-up bell sounded. Atlas rolled onto his side and ignored it. He'd already showered, after all. *I have time. Just a few minutes, please.*

Soon, the incessant shuffling and early-morning laughter of the other laborers made him self-conscious. It was unfamiliar and unsettling. He couldn't remember the last time he'd heard laughter like that. Were people normally this friendly and cheerful? He climbed out of bed and made his way to the front of the barracks.

The head laborers were in the middle of a shift change. The one that had admitted Atlas walked into the sleeping quarters as Atlas was about to exit. The head laborer yawned. So did Atlas. He peeked through the open door at the new head laborer-on-duty. The Theban male. *The one who sent me to the mine. Just my luck.*

"Reporting for assignment," Atlas said.

The Theban looked surprised. "So, you survived. And you hardly look the worse for wear. How unfortunate."

"I clean up real nice," said Atlas. "My lungs, joints, and muscles still ache, even after the injection they gave me, if that makes you feel better."

The Theban narrowed his eyes. "Yes, I believe it does. Perhaps you have learned your lesson, then."

"I learned a lot of things that I didn't know before," Atlas said. "But I don't expect most of them to be of any use out here."

"Perhaps we should send you back?. We wouldn't want to waste your expertise."

"Ah, but I have already passed the torch, you might say."

"What do you mean?"

"Your colleague, the Phoenician," Atlas said. "He was gracious enough to take my place."

The Theban scowled. "He did not deserve such punishment. The fool! Throwing away his position for a family member."

So, the Theban *did* care about somebody. And what's more, perhaps the Phoenician had told the truth and truly was Zhehera's cousin.

"I gave him my bed, and a piece of canvas I used to soak in water to keep me cool at night. It's no guarantee of survival, but it's better than nothing."

The Theban's face softened. "Your bed?"

"Yes, I carved it into the wall, high above the densest gas concentration. Took me weeks. Now it's his."

"Why would you do that?" the Theban demanded.

Atlas shrugged. "Well, I'm not using it anymore. And it'd be too small for anyone else to sleep in. Your friend is a bit on the small side, even for a Phoenician. Plus, he didn't seem like the hard-labor type. He'll need every advantage he can get if he's going to survive."

The Theban was silent for a moment. "I expect you will demand special treatment now?"

"I honestly hadn't thought about it. But, if you're offering, it would be nice to be assigned to the same division as my friends."

The Theban laughed. "You're not Apollo's type."

"What do you mean?"

"The girl. She has been sent to Consort Training. And well, the other two were already there." The Theban laughed again. "I guess she decided the amenities were better in the house—the food certainly is. But I suppose I can assign you a position alongside the brute." The Theban consulted the screen on his desk. "Philadelphian Ajax, report to the head laborer-on-duty, immediately."

A moment later Ajax appeared, shirtless and wet. He was enormous. How could he have grown that much in only two months?

"Ajax reporting, sir." He pulled on his shirt

"Ajax, you are assigned a new apprentice." The Theban pointed towards Atlas. "I believe you know each other."

"Hey Ajax," Atlas said. "Good to see you. They're feeding you well, looks like."

Ajax turned away from Atlas. "I do not need an apprentice."

"No, you do not," said the Theban.

"Has my work been unsatisfactory?" Ajax asked.

"Not at all. In fact, your work has been exemplary. And now, it is my decision that you should take on an apprentice."

Ajax frowned. "Respectfully, sir, if that is your wish, I request a different Tier I be assigned as my apprentice."

"What?" said Atlas. "Why? Ajax?" He looked bewilderedly at

his friend, but received no response.

"Not what you expected?" the Theban asked Atlas. "A lot has changed during your absence. Ajax here is a Tier IV now. He has responsibility over all of Metallurgy. An impressive rise in such a short time, I admit."

"Which I have earned through my blood, sweat, and loyalty," Ajax said. He looked disapprovingly at Atlas. "This one is only loyal to himself. He cannot be trusted."

"And that is exactly why I am assigning him to you," said the Theban. "I know you'll keep an eye on him."

Ajax sighed. "Very well. If that is your will."

"It is," said the Theban. "Take him to rationing. I have authorized today's rations for him. Then take him with you to Metallurgy before the daily delivery."

Ajax nodded. He turned and left the room. Atlas followed.

When they were out of earshot of the Theban, Atlas let out a whistle. "That was pretty good. Very convincing."

Ajax stopped and turned to Atlas. "You should understand something. I do not want an apprentice. And I especially do not want *you* as my apprentice. I do not trust you. You are weak, and ill-suited to my work. I can only hope that you will injure yourself or die in an accident. Barring that, should you give me a reason to report you, I will not hesitate to do so. Either way, I shall be rid of you.

"If I am wrong, then you will have to prove it to me. This work is back-breaking and dangerous. I demand a lot of my workers and I do not tolerate ineptitude or laziness. And in case I am not being clear enough, I do not play favorites."

"But, we're—" began Atlas.

"That we once were friends is not significant. Things are different now. You are my apprentice and I am the head of Metallurgy. Much is demanded of me and I will demand much of you. I suggest you request a transfer as soon as the initial ten-day term is complete."

Atlas watched his friend walking away. What had happened

to Ajax? Had he broken so easily? How had he become head of Metallurgy so rapidly? And why had Reedy been sent to Consort Training? Apollo was afraid Reedy would carry a grudge despite the brain-washing. Had she been broken so tragically that Apollo no longer considered her a threat? Impossible. But how else to explain it? What might have happened to Pallas and Phoebe? Would any of them even wish to escape anymore?

A tear fell from his eye. *I need to know. Today. Tonight. With or without the others, I'm leaving tonight.*

Atlas jogged a few steps and caught up with Ajax.

After devouring his daily rations, Atlas followed Ajax to a small transportation depot. They drove to Metallurgy aboard self-driving, self-balancing motor-bikes. Neither spoke to the other during the trip.

The more Atlas thought about it, the angrier he became. How could Ajax give up on everything? Had he forgotten what the Olympians did at the Academy? Atlas wanted to punch Ajax in the face, but escape was the priority, and that was more easily accomplished from the compound than in the mines. He'd learned that lesson, at least.

Metallurgy was housed in a large building about fifty kilometers northwest of the main house. The trip took about fifteen minutes. The facility was much cleaner and less industrial than Atlas expected. There were no smoke stacks belching noxious fumes nor heavy machinery rumbling loudly. The building was attractive and clean with pleasing architectural details and lots of windows. It reminded Atlas of a library.

A rail system running behind the Metallurgy building delivered the daily load of unprocessed stone and ore from the mines. Ajax supervised the daily delivery from a catwalk along the backside of the building. Atlas stood with him and watched as the stone and ore he had helped mine the day before were dumped into giant, underground hoppers. He was surprised at how much material the railcars carried.

"And that's just one day's worth?" Atlas asked.

"Yes," said Ajax. "Most of the mining is done by machine." He pointed to a much smaller railcar. "That's your contribution. Next to nothing."

Ajax nodded and the two continued the inspection tour. Specialized machinery analyzed the raw material for valuable metals and sorted them for extraction. Another series of machines pulverized the stone and sent it through a final series of equipment where the individual atoms of the desired metals were separated from the slag and then condensed into solid blocks of purified metal.

That's where the work began. Each block had to be individually catalogued, tested for purity and density, weighed, and stored by laborers. This involved carrying the blocks of metal by hand from one station to another, recording the relevant data, and storing them in the appropriate container for later shipping. Depending on the metal, some of the blocks had a mass upwards of fifty kilograms and each Tier I laborer was responsible for handling one hundred and fifty blocks daily, including Atlas—apprenticeship duties notwithstanding. Ajax left to continue his duties, leaving Atlas in the supervision of the Cataloguing foreman.

It was exhausting work, but not as difficult as mining. The biggest difficultly Atlas had was staying awake while he waited for the testing equipment to deliver the results. He tried to keep his mind active by planning how to contact Pallas without putting himself at too great a risk. *If she's been turned like Ajax…No, not her. But just in case…Zhehera. I can trust her. I know where to find her.* She may be able to help contact Pallas. She may even be able to speak to Pallas's state of mind.

"Philadelphian," someone shouted.

Atlas shook off the sleep that had been creeping upon him. He picked up the block of metal he was testing and turned around. A Cretan female approached him—the first female he'd seen of her species. She was short but sported enormous, bulging muscles. But no horns. As she got closer, Atlas could see that she *did* have horns, but they had both been cut short, nearly even with her skull. Why? The males he had known in the mine still had their horns.

"It's not polite to stare," the Cretan snapped.

"I'm sorry," said Atlas.

"Never seen a Cretan before?"

"I have," Atlas said. "I knew a few in the mines. They didn't make it."

"Not surprising," said the Cretan. "Our males are embarrassingly delicate." She spat on the ground. "They're suited for little else other than breeding."

Atlas felt disgusted by her comment, but rather than challenge it and force the Cretan to double down, Atlas chose to ask a disarming personal question, like his dad would have. "Will they grow back?"

"What?"

"Your horns. Will they grow back?"

"None of your business," said the Cretan.

"I apologize," said Atlas. "Did you need something from me?"

"You will finish your shift in Alloys. Report immediately, by order of Ajax."

"I haven't met my quota yet."

"It will be added to your quota for tomorrow," said the Cretan.

"Point me in the right direction," sighed Atlas. He set down the silver block he was carrying. *I won't be here tomorrow*, he thought.

The Cretan grunted and walked away. Atlas assumed she meant for him to follow her. The Cretan's movements were powerful, yet graceful. This was a woman who'd achieved a command of her body most people didn't realize they lacked. *Who was it Reedy quoted? Plato? No, Socrates. '...beauty and strength of which the body is capable...'* Beautiful, but not like what Earth media had taught him. *A better beautiful.*

"What's your name?" Atlas asked.

The Cretan didn't answer.

"It's just, I know someone who would love to meet you," Atlas said. "If I knew your name, I'd feel more comfortable telling her about you."

"Why would she want to meet me?"

"She admires strong women." Atlas stepped up alongside her. "I'm telling you, she would love to meet you."

"My name is Tora," the Cretan said. "You can introduce us this evening. Bring her to the Metallurgy section of the barracks. What division is she in?"

"That's the problem. I haven't seen her for two months. I just got out of the mines."

"You were in the mines for two months?" Tora raised her eyebrows. "Perhaps you aren't as delicate as you look."

"Thanks, I think."

"And you met this girl in the mines?"

"No, she and I arrived together. But I was sent to the mines shortly after. Last I heard, she was in Consort Training."

Tora was silent for a moment. "If she remained in Consort Training, she no longer admires strong women. Apollo does not allow such thinking."

"You don't know Pallas," Atlas said.

"And you do not know what they do to girls in Consort Training."

"And you do?"

Tora furrowed her brow and walked in silence.

Atlas realized Tora knew about Consort Training first hand. He felt ashamed and tried to think of something to say to pull his foot out of his mouth. Nothing. At least, nothing that wouldn't make it worse.

"They don't grow back," Tora said.

"What?"

"My horns. They will not grow back. Apollo didn't like them, so the consort attendants cut them off. And then, when my muscles came in, he disliked them even more than my horns. He sent me here."

"I'm sorry," said Atlas.

"Don't be sorry. Apollo is a weak and delicate man. I scared him. And when he couldn't make me conform to his ideals, I scared him even more."

Atlas wanted to ask Tora more questions, but they had arrived at Alloys. Tora pointed to the entrance, grunted, and left.

"Nice to meet you," Atlas called after her.

The Alloys foreman greeted Atlas inside. Two of his laborers had been sent to serve a week in the mines after getting into a fight, and now he was short on workers. For the remainder of the workday, Atlas hauled blocks of metals to and from alloy machinery. He would have liked to know how they worked, but the only accessible sections of the machines were the input and output chutes, and no one answered his questions. All Atlas knew was that he would load the purified metal blocks into the machines and later he would haul the resulting alloyed blocks to their new storage containers.

Finally, the workday ended. Atlas completed his last assigned alloy. He wiped the sweat from his forehead and looked around the facility. All the other workers had left. *Rations.* Atlas realized he was starving. Strangely, he didn't feel tired. *Second wind.* Or fourth, maybe. He'd lost count.

The only other transport bike still parked outside Metallurgy belonged to Ajax. Atlas waited a few moments for his friend, just in case, then mounted his bike. It automatically strapped him in, and left.

As the bike drove him back to Apollo's compound, Atlas thought again about how to best contact Pallas. Zhehera was clearly the best option. But how to get to her?

I could try the front door again. It worked once. I only need it to work once more. Yes, that's the only real option. I'll need to be more careful, but I can do it. Get to Zhehera. Now, while everyone is preoccupied with their rations. Not quite dark yet...maybe by the time I get back to the house...doesn't matter. There's no time to waste.

CHAPTER 20

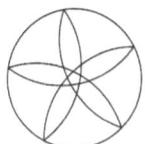

ATLAS AGAIN STOOD at the front door of Apollo's house—the Honorific Portal, Doero called it—as the sun began to set. All the garden laborers had gone to rations. Atlas touched the door. It required greater force than before to trigger the automatic open. Doero must have had the sensitivity recalibrated, like he said he would. Atlas cautiously peeked inside.

No one in the entrance hall. *Easy. Just like before.* The hall's exquisite craftsmanship dazzled him as it had the first time. Such a resplendent entrance, and yet it seemed hardly used at all. Perhaps only when Apollo received dignitaries.

Atlas crept up the stairs and down the western corridor to Zhehera's room. All was quiet. He tried the door. Locked. He looked up and down the hallway, counting the doors to make sure he was at the right room. *Yes, this is it. She must not be in. Or maybe this isn't her room anymore. Has she been called for?* Would Zhehera have moved to another part of the consort wing after her birthday?

Then Atlas had an idea. *Zhehera,* he thought. *It's me, Atlas. I'm here to find Pallas. Can you help me?*

He tried the door again. Still locked.

"Zhehera, it's Atlas," he whispered. "I need to speak with you. Please unlock your door."

Still locked. Atlas sighed in disappointment. It was a long shot anyway. He had no idea what the range of her ability to hear his thoughts might be.

Atlas headed back towards the stairs. Better not push his luck any more. He felt utterly defeated and exhausted. He needed rest. Yes. He'd been too hasty. A good night sleep, in a real bed, and he'd be able to think more clearly in the morning, make a better plan. The idea of escaping today was too rash. A decision made from exhaustion. Escapes took time and planning. How would he deal with his tracker, for example? He hadn't even thought about it. *How stupid.*

As he approached the top of the stairs, Atlas realized he was most disappointed about not seeing Zhehera. So many nights in the mine he had thought about her. Her silver and grey eyes. Orange-tinted skin. Orange-yellow hair like fire. The sweet and subtle tones of her voice. And...her ankles. Atlas felt his cheeks flush and his spine tingle.

"Atlas?" a voice whispered.

Atlas turned around. Zhehera stuck her head into the hall. She smiled at him. Atlas's insides turned to goo.

"Get in here, quickly," she said.

Atlas practically skipped back down the hall and into Zhehera's room. He was giddy and light-headed. His joy in seeing Zhehera overwhelmed all other concerns.

"What the afterworld are you doing here?" Zhehera asked.

"I just got back from the mines. I need to speak with Pallas."

Zhehera cast her eyes down. "Always Pallas. She's nice, but I hoped you'd be happy to see *me*."

"You've met her, then?"

"Yes, we've met," said another, happily familiar voice.

"Pallas!" Atlas turned to see his friend sitting on one of the beds. He started towards her, but remembered Zhehera and stopped.

"What are you doing here?" he asked Pallas.

"Don't worry," Zhehera smirked. "I was teasing. I'm not jealous."

Pallas stood and walked to Atlas. She was dressed in fine, silky clothing, similar to what Zhehera wore, and her hair was different. It was long. Much longer than it should have been after only two months. Her long, tight curls stuck out in every direction, tamed only slightly by gravity.

"This is my room," Pallas said. "I'm the one that should be asking what *you* are doing here." She gave Atlas a hug. Her embrace was strong.

"What? How?" Atlas turned to Zhehera.

"I knew how important she was to you," said Zhehera. She smiled and put her arms around Atlas and Pallas. "As soon as she was released from Consort Training, I made her my roommate."

Atlas released himself from the embrace. "Then, you... um...*graduated* from Consort—?"

"Yes," said Pallas. "It was easy."

"Oh," said Atlas. His heart sank. So, they'd changed her, like Tora had warned him.

"Now don't do that. I'm still the same." Pallas shook her head. "Look, to graduate from Consort Training, all you have to do is convince them that you're docile and compliant. That happens one of two ways: you resist and they do whatever is necessary to break you, or you accept it and resign yourself to your new life."

"You see, Pallas and I have much in common," said Zhehera.

"But..." stammered Atlas.

"He doesn't get it," Pallas said to Zhehera. She turned back to Atlas. "It's not hard to accept the consort lifestyle. It's posh and easy. There are very few things we can't have. If you accept the luxury and allow yourself to enjoy it, just like that, you've completed Consort Training."

"That doesn't seem like you," said Atlas.

"You've never had to pretend to be something you're not," said Pallas. "The trick is you gotta' keep your disgust for the whole thing buried deep. You have to let a part of you enjoy the pampering. But that other part of who you are, the part that takes pride in hard work and hard-fought accomplishment, you have to hide, but not too deeply. You don't want to lose it."

"How do you not lose it?" Atlas asked.

Pallas flexed her arms and grinned. "Train while everyone else sleeps." She looked at Zhehera. "Find a supportive partner."

Atlas smiled at Pallas's well-earned pride. He felt grateful to know her.

"It was Phoebe's idea."

"Where is Phoebe?"

"In another room several doors down the hallway, with Reedy."

"That's something else I don't understand," said Atlas. "How did Reedy get into Consort Training? Apollo believed she would carry a grudge forever."

"She does, but after you disappeared, Reedy thought it would be better if the three of us were close together."

"Of course, but how did Apollo allow it?"

"She didn't ask Apollo. She walked right up to one of the head eunuchs, smiled politely, and asked to enter Consort Training." Pallas grinned. "I still don't think Apollo even knows Reedy's here."

"And that's his fatal flaw." Atlas's mind raced. "No one dares step out of line because doing so means likely death in the mine, or being fed to his carnivores. Anyone with a bit of daring could waltz right into this house and kill him."

"It's not that easy," said Zhehera. "His wing of the house is extremely secure. No one gets in unless he calls for you." Her voice fell slightly as she said this. "You have to wait until he calls for you, if you want to get close to him."

"There's got to be some other way? Bribe a guard or something like that."

"Though they are prisoners like the rest of us, the guards will not be bought, and they are empowered to immediately execute anyone who attempts bribery," said Zhehera.

"Why are they so loyal to Apollo?" Atlas shook his head in disgust.

"Because he lifted them above us."

"Give a little power to the powerless and they forget they were once like you," said Pallas.

"Apollo is an arrogant fool," said Atlas. "Who does he think he is, a god?"

"He is mortal," said Zhehera. "That makes us equals." She stuck out her jaw and pursed her lips.

Atlas turned to Pallas. "You explained how she got in, but how did someone with Reedy's...um, personality make it through Consort Training?"

"She lied, of course," Pallas laughed. "She lied so convincingly even I thought she was serious."

Atlas laughed with Pallas.

"Why is this so funny?" asked Zhehera. "It wasn't funny when you heard of the lies Pallas told."

"Reedy doesn't lie—according to her," said Atlas. "Except, I've never met anyone better at it."

"Which reminds me..." Pallas punched Atlas in the chest. "Why did you get yourself sent to the mines? I had a plan. Phoebe and I were all ready to implement it as soon as we got out of Consort. Then, you go and delay it. It was an excellent plan. A perfect plan."

"It still *is* a perfect plan. Except for one thing."

Atlas froze. Ajax stood in the open doorway.

"You just don't learn, do you, Atlas?" Ajax stepped menacingly towards Atlas. The door closed behind him. "Barely a day out of the mines, and you've already violated at least a dozen rules. Apollo will not be pleased. You'll be executed. *All* of—"

"Ajax, listen to me, please," Atlas pleaded. "It was me. All me. I snuck—"

"Do not interrupt me. All of you *will* be executed. All..." Ajax paused.

Atlas held his breath and watched Ajax, wondering if he and Pallas could overpower him. *Maybe with Zhehera's help.*

"...of *us* will be executed if we're caught." Ajax grinned slyly.

Atlas eyed Ajax suspiciously. Pallas gave Ajax a hug and he enthusiastically hugged her back. Only when Ajax extended his hand did Atlas take a tentative step towards his friend. Ajax lunged forward and shook Atlas's hand with his typical brutish strength. Atlas rubbed it afterwards.

"What about earlier today? What you said to me?" Atlas said.

"I didn't know if I could trust you."

"Well, you made me believe I couldn't trust *you*."

"Really? Ain't that something?" He turned to Pallas. "So, are we doing this?"

"Yes," said Pallas.

Ajax turned to Atlas. "We need to go. Now, before the others in the barracks notice we're not at rations."

Atlas turned to Pallas. "What's going on?"

"You're escaping," said Zhehera. "Tonight."

"But we need a plan," said Atlas.

"We *have* a plan," said Ajax.

"We were just talking about this," sighed Pallas.

"Sorry," said Atlas. "I'm really tired."

"The four of us figured it all out while you were away. We had plenty of time to consider every detail," Pallas teased. "Zhehera helped, of course." She winked at Atlas. "I really like her," she whispered.

Atlas was overwhelmed with sleepy confusion. Then he grinned. Oh, how he loved these people! Pallas doubted herself. Ajax was overzealous and brusque. Reedy was a scold. And Phoebe was an insufferable know-it-all. For all their flaws, Gamma Squad had risen to the occasion and made up for his mistakes.

He turned to Zhehera. "You'll come with us?"

"No dear," Zhehera smiled sadly. "I haven't yet completed my mission."

"Don't," said Atlas. "It's too dangerous."

"No more dangerous than yours."

A tear rolled down Atlas's cheek. "Be careful," he whispered. "I'll see you again."

"I *can't* promise," Zhehera said. "Both are impossible promises."

"Atlas. We need to go," said Ajax.

"Okay," said Atlas. He wanted to kiss Zhehera on the forehead, but didn't.

"Don't forget me," she said. She lifted one foot and twisted it delicately so that he could see each side of her ankle. She giggled softly.

"What was that?" Pallas asked.

"Never mind," said Zhehera.

Atlas followed Ajax out of the room. He should have been embarrassed, but he was too happy. And also miserable. He must see Zhehera again, or he would never be free of the nagging void opening up in his heart. *I will complete my mission. And Zhehera will complete hers.*

CHAPTER 21

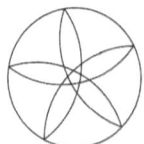

ATLAS AND AJAX made it out of Apollo's house unseen and walked in the early moonlight towards the barracks. "What about Phoebe and Reedy?"

"They know the plan," Ajax said. "We have a system. I was in the garden, signaling them, when I saw you walk up to the front door. Gutsy move. No wonder you got caught last time."

"I missed curfew last time. That's the only reason I got caught."

"Well, anyway, I had to make sure you didn't ruin our plans," said Ajax. "When I saw you make it to Pallas and Zhehera, I thought I'd have a little fun with you. Scare you a bit."

"Yeah, thanks for that."

"You deserved it for the hell you put us through these last two months. We thought you were dead, for sure."

Atlas shrugged. "There were times when I thought I *would* die in there. I don't know why I didn't, really. So many others did."

"I know why you didn't die," Ajax said.

"Oh yeah? Why?"

"Because we need you to lead us to the Celestial Sphere."

Atlas thought for a moment. "You don't need to lead. You've done fine without me. In fact, if it wasn't for me, you'd be long gone." He shook his head. "You probably should have left without me."

"Pallas would never leave without you. Believe me, I tried to convince her."

Atlas felt a pit in his stomach. "Good," he managed to say.

"Just teasing," said Ajax. "You were sent to the mines because you tried to contact Pallas. We understand. You were looking out for your team, and protected your friends by bearing the consequences yourself. That's what a good leader would do. That's why we need you." He hesitated. "Besides, you're the one who brought us together, the one who taught us to work together."

"Did you forget about the simulation fiasco?"

"Phoebe was new to the team. She felt betrayed and vulnerable. So did the rest of us. She understands now. We all do. And if it wasn't for that *fiasco*, we'd have kept Beta squad. We'd be blind."

"Yeah, I thought about that too," said Atlas. "You think our ranking determined what they did to us?"

"Otherwise, Homer'd be with us, and Phoebe'd be blind."

"That was my thinking," Atlas said. "Thank God for Phoebe's fiasco."

"It was all of our fiasco," Ajax said.

"You performed exemplarily," said Atlas.

"No, I only did what I was asked. No more. I didn't volunteer even when I thought I could help. And before that, I didn't apply myself in areas that weren't my strengths. I pigeon-holed myself as a combat specialist and convinced the rest of you—and myself —that was all I was good for."

"Well, that *is* all you're good for," Atlas deadpanned.

Ajax faced Atlas and scowled.

"I'm joking," said Atlas. "You deserve it."

Ajax hit him in the shoulder, but not too hard.

Atlas sighed. "What were you going to do with me? You know, if you decided you couldn't trust me to go with you?"

"Knock you out and carry you," said Ajax.

Atlas laughed nervously. "Alright, what's next?"

"We eat," Ajax said.

"Didn't we miss rations?"

"It's common for some of the slaves to work late. They serve rations until an hour before curfew."

"I wish you wouldn't call them slaves."

"They *are* slaves, often in more ways than one."

"They don't know any better. Many have never known anything but this."

"What should I call them?" Ajax asked.

"They're prisoners, like us," Atlas said.

"Maybe. Prisoners retain the hope of escape…or release. These don't. They don't even think about it." He looked crestfallen. "If they keep their head down, they are safe and well fed. They don't know there's any different."

"But if we escape, we can show them hope," said Atlas. "That there's more than this."

"*When* we escape, I will be happy to call them prisoners," said Ajax.

"Of course, sorry. I'm so tired. I know we'll escape."

"You don't even know the plan."

"But I know the people who made it."

Ajax nodded. They had almost arrived at the barracks. "We'll go in separately, and eat separately. After rations and before curfew, we make our separate ways to Metallurgy. Do you remember how to get there?"

"Yes, I mean the bike does all the work, right?"

"Make sure you pick the same bike you rode earlier. The others won't work this time of day."

"Okay."

"The others will meet us there."

"What's in Metallurgy?" Atlas asked. "How will the others get there?"

Ajax stopped a few dozen yards away from the barracks. "It's taken care of," he said. "I'll go in first. Wait a minute, then you come in." He didn't wait to be acknowledged.

Atlas stood outside the barracks door for a few minutes, then entered and made his way to rations. The ration crew were about to close down for the evening. Atlas took his food to an empty table and ate quietly by himself. Ajax had already gone.

When he finished his meal, Atlas made his way to the front of the barracks. The other prisoners were chatting and laughing, telling each other stories from the day. As he passed the various groups, Atlas realized that none of them were children. The youngest besides him and Ajax looked like older teenagers, practically adults. He hadn't paid attention to that before. In the mines, it didn't matter how old you were. If you woke up in the morning, you were a day older than the day before. That was all that mattered. It had been a long time since Atlas had thought of himself as young.

He certainly didn't feel like a child. At least, not most of the time. There was still a lot he hadn't experienced, large gaps in his maturity, and Atlas knew it. And yet, as he watched the teenage prisoners horsing around and flirting with each other, he couldn't help but feel melancholy. He hadn't asked for this responsibility. It had been forced upon him. He didn't want it. Even as prisoners—or slaves, if they preferred—these teens found ways to be young, to indulge themselves, to experience life. Not him.

Some old dude on a faraway planet scribbled some gibberish hundreds of years ago, and now Atlas and his friends were here, on Olympus, as prisoners. Oliver was dead. And Penny. And Theo. And Nerissa. And Eugenio. Also probably Nike, Themis, and Dr. Circe. And Lanta. Brave Lanta, who died for him. Homer and the Betas were blinded. *All to prevent the Titans from using us to find a mythical Sphere that may not even exist. So stupid. And senseless.*

Atlas shuddered. *Believe. Believe in the Sphere. If it's true, there's hope. If it's true, there's a way home. Find the Celestial Sphere and keep it from the Olympians for good. It has to be true.*

There was no more room for mistakes. Atlas's last mistake had cost them two months. Not again. *Never again.*

Atlas nodded to the head laborer-on-duty as he passed through the barracks check-in. "I'm going for a short walk." The supervisor barely looked up from the book he was reading. Atlas slipped out into the cool evening air and walked to the transportation depot.

No one was there. Just the bikes. *Which one was mine?* He yawned and closed his eyes, trying to recall where he'd left his bike earlier. Atlas climbed aboard the nearest bike. Nothing happened. *No, that's where it was this morning. This evening I parked over there.* He swung his leg over the correct bike. It strapped him in and took off.

Ajax stood outside the Metallurgy entrance, waiting for him.

"I was about to go look for you. The others are waiting for us."

Atlas looked around, but didn't see any other bikes. Was this a setup? *No, you're just tired. Tired and paranoid, like in the mines. Trust Ajax. He's your friend.*

Ajax led Atlas to a room near the back of the building. Atlas felt his heartrate quicken and his armpits begin to sweat. Ajax opened the door.

Phoebe, Pallas, and Reedy were inside.

Atlas sighed in relief. *See! Friends. You have friends.* This was really happening. Pallas—and also Reedy and Phoebe, he assumed—had changed from consort garb into Theban clothing.

"About time you got here," Phoebe said. "We've been waiting for *months.*"

Reedy gave Atlas a hug. "How were the mines?"

"Wonderful this time of year. You should really go." Atlas coughed at the memory of the mines.

"We will, if we don't get going," said Phoebe.

"First things first," said Pallas. She held up a small white box. "We need to remove our tracker chips."

"How?" asked Atlas. "They circulate freely through the bloodstream."

"True," said Pallas. "But they're also extremely sensitive to magnets."

"That's why we're here," said Ajax. He walked to a large, white machine with a cylindrical opening that sat in the corner of the room. "This is a magna-forge. It uses oscillating magnetic fields to heat steel for shaping. You know, like a blacksmith."

"When exposed to a magnetic field, the tracking unit heats up," Phoebe said. "You can actually feel it getting hot inside your body." She held out a magnet and put it in the palm of her hand. "It should only take a minute. Oh! There it is." She winced slightly. "A magnet like this won't do much but hold the tracker in place. But you can feel it get uncomfortably warm. That's why we need that thing."

Pallas handed out magnets to the others. "Apollo will be notified when the trackers go offline. We have to do it all together. Otherwise, he could activate the air prison."

"Or terminate us," said Reedy.

"Or terminate us," sighed Pallas. She wrinkled her nose.

"The magnetic field from the magna-forge should jam the termination mechanism," said Phoebe. "We'll be fine. I suggest you place the magnet in your non-dominant hand." She adjusted the magnet in Atlas's hand. "Keep it in your palm. It's the safest place."

Atlas looked at the small, circular magnet. *Little things.* He followed his friends to the magna-forge. "So, when the tracker gets really hot, then what?"

"It burns through your hand," said Reedy. "Right?"

"Exactly," said Phoebe. "The magna-forge heats it up and pulls it out. It's the only way. I've thought about this for weeks. There's no other way to do this."

"And once it's gone, the air prison can't work?" asked Atlas.

"The tracker *is* the air prison," said Phoebe.

Atlas looked at Phoebe. Her eyes begged him to trust her. "Okay, let's do it."

Phoebe smiled. "Does everyone feel the heat in their hand?"

"Yes," Pallas said. She stuck her hand into the cylindrical opening.

"Yes," said Ajax. He did the same.

"Yes," said Reedy.

"Yes," said Atlas.

Phoebe stuck her hand into the cylinder. "We should start at the lowest setting. Hopefully, it will be enough. Too high and the magnetic field could be deadly." She bit her lip hard in anticipation. "Remember to keep your palm open, no matter how much it hurts."

"Here it goes," said Ajax. With his free hand, he turned on the magna-forge.

Almost immediately, the heat within Atlas's hand intensified. He looked at the faces of his friends. Pallas squeezed her eyes tightly and clenched her teeth. Reedy bit one of her other fingers. Ajax stared at the forge's power indicator.

"Higher," said Phoebe. "Put it higher, before it cooks our hands."

Ajax turned the setting up two notches. The magnets flew off their hands and clanged against the walls of the forge.

"*More*," said Phoebe. "Get it over with!"

Ajax raised the power six more notches. Atlas's hand was in excruciating pain. He focused on his breathing. Phoebe bit her lip until it bled. Reedy began to shake. Pallas whimpered.

"Still more," sobbed Phoebe. "It needs to pull it all the way through."

Ajax turned the magna-forge up to fifty percent. Instantly, their hands were pulled forcefully against the inside walls of the magna-forge. Atlas could feel the tracker begin to move through his hand. Then, it was out.

With a shriek, Atlas pulled his arm out of the magna-forge. He clutched his injured hand. There was less blood than he expected. The super-heated tracker had cauterized the wound as it passed through his flesh.

Pallas howled and fell to the ground, sobbing. Then Reedy. Ajax was next. Shaking his freed hand, he wiped tears from his cheeks, but made no sound.

Phoebe's hand remained stuck inside the magna-forge. "Turn it off!" she wailed. "It *burns.* I can't do this anymore. Turn it off!"

"Just a little more," said Pallas.

"Turn it off. Leave me behind. Go! Before they find you."

"No," said Reedy. "We won't leave you." She wrapped her arms around Phoebe and held her close. "Higher, Ajax. Make it quick."

Ajax turned the magna-forge to seventy-five percent. Phoebe screamed shrilly then collapsed backwards, knocking Reedy to the floor with her. She clutched her wrist desperately. Blood spurted through her fingers.

"It must have nicked an artery," Pallas said. She retrieved her small box and opened it. "Keep pressure on it." Inside were a roll of bandages and a metal canister. Pallas quickly wrapped Phoebe's wrist in the bandages. Blood soaked through the bandages.

"What happened?" asked Ajax.

"My magnet slipped," sniveled Phoebe. "I tried to adjust it with my fingers, but when I did, I guess the tracker moved down to my wrist." Tears streamed down her face. "I'm going to die, aren't I?"

"Don't be stupid," said Reedy. "You're going to be fine."

"I can't stop the bleeding with this, only slow it," said Pallas "We'll need to get her medical help."

"You need to *go*," cried Phoebe. "Before Apollo's goons get here."

"Hold on," said Pallas.

"No!" Phoebe pushed Pallas aside and stood up. "You need to go, now." She grabbed Atlas and pushed him towards the door. "Leave me here."

"Not a chance," said Atlas. He put his arm around Phoebe.

"We escape together. Or we get caught together. Whichever outcome, we do it as a team."

"This way," said Ajax. He led them to the rear of Metallurgy. "There's a railcar we keep on site for when we process more dross than usual. It's self-powered."

"Where do the rails lead?" sniffled Phoebe.

"To a construction materials plant," said Ajax. One of the biggest on Olympus. It's responsible for almost thirty percent of Apollo's income."

"How fast is the railcar?" asked Atlas.

"Fast enough." Ajax flung open the doors to a large railway hangar. Several large cargo cars sat empty on one side of the room. On the other side was a large rail vehicle. The back two-thirds of the vehicle was a bed for hauling dross. At the front was a control cabin large enough to fit all five of them. "I separated the engine from the extra cars earlier today." Ajax climbed up into the cabin and began the ignition sequence.

Atlas climbed into the cabin last. He looked at his injured hand. It throbbed with every heart beat, but any bleeding had stopped. He tried to make a fist, but couldn't move his fingers more than a few millimeters.

"This should help," said Pallas. She held up the canister from her first aid kit. "Hold your hand out for me.

Atlas gave her his hand. Pallas pressed the canister against the wound. There was a short hiss and what felt to Atlas like a mild electric shock. Pallas removed the canister. The pain in his hand was nearly gone. Atlas tried to make a fist again. He couldn't close his hand all the way, but at least he could use it to grab and hold onto the railcar guardrail.

Reedy and Ajax fared slightly worse than Atlas and couldn't quite close their hands around anything, even after the injection. They had to work together to operate the controls that started the vehicle and opened the hanger doors. Phoebe couldn't even wiggle her fingers. She sat down on the floor of the cab, against the wall, her bandage dripping with blood.

The railcar lurched forward as Reedy and Ajax guided it out of the hangar. Seconds later, they were traveling along the rails towards the materials plant. The headlights of the railcar were the only illumination along the railway, but they cast a long and wide beam that provided ample light. Atlas watched as the trees along the railway suddenly appeared bathed in light, rushed by, then faded into the shadows. Gradually, the forest became more dense.

Pallas stooped near Phoebe, re-dressing her wound. Phoebe was breathing shallowly and crying.

"I don't want to die," she moaned.

"Hush," said Pallas. "You're not going to die. You've just lost some blood, that's all." She wiped her forehead with the back of her bloodied hands. "Wish I had a tissue-bonder."

"It should have worked," wailed Phoebe. "It should have worked. It *should* have worked."

"It did work," said Pallas. "Now, just stay calm. We'll get you some help soon." She wrapped her arms around Phoebe. "Breathe deeply and slowly. We don't want you to go into shock."

Atlas approached Ajax. "We need to get off the rails. They'll follow the railcar as soon as they see it's gone, and we're not moving fast enough."

"Trust the plan," said Ajax. "Another few kilometers and we jump. There's a lake. With any luck, they'll try to intercept us at the materials plant and find the railcar empty."

"Good," said Atlas. He turned back to Pallas. "I'll take Phoebe."

Pallas nodded. "I'll go before you, so I can help bring her to shore."

The trees disappeared as the railcar burst out of the forest and onto an open bridge. On both sides of the rails, a lake appeared below, illuminated by the stars and moonlight.

"Here we are," said Ajax. He opened the door of the cabin. A gust of air roared into the cabin as the railcar continued to gain speed. "We have approximately twenty seconds," he yelled and pointed across the lake. "Swim that way."

"Hold my hand," shouted Reedy. She grabbed Ajax's hand and the two jumped together.

Pallas helped Atlas lift Phoebe and walk to the open door. She kissed him on the cheek, then jumped.

Atlas carefully stepped to the opening. He looked down. The lake was at least fifteen meters below them, and the railcar was rapidly approaching the end of the bridge. "Hang on, Phoebe," he whispered, then stepped out into the empty air. *Hope it's deep enough*, he thought.

The fall seemed like an eternity. He didn't dare look. Atlas tightened his grip around Phoebe and tried to keep his feet pointing straight down.

The impact jarred him fiercely and the water tore Phoebe from his arms. It was too dark to see anything. Atlas flailed his arms wildly through the water, hoping to catch a foot or wrist. Nothing. His lungs began to burn. The fall had knocked much of the air out of them.

As Atlas swam towards the surface, Phoebe suddenly wrapped her arms desperately around his neck. She squeezed tightly and wrapped her legs around his, making it impossible to kick. Atlas managed to get his head above the surface for an instant, but Phoebe dragged him back down before he could get a breath. They began to sink.

———

THE NEXT THING ATLAS KNEW, Reedy was kissing him. He spat water into her mouth and sat up with a start, knocking her backwards into the mud. He coughed repeatedly, then fell back into the sludge again.

Atlas lay on the bank of the lake. Ajax stood over him, smiling. Beyond Ajax, Atlas could see the rail bridge in the distance, backlit by the moon.

"Thanks for sharing your drink with me, but I wasn't thirsty," sputtered Reedy. "Help me out of the mud, Ajax."

Ajax offered one hand to Reedy and the other to Atlas. With a single heave, he lifted both to their feet. "We need to get into the woods."

"You swam with me all that way?" Atlas asked. "Thank you."

"No big deal," said Ajax.

"Phoebe? Pallas?"

"I'm here," said Pallas. She stood ten meters up the embankment, on the edge of the woods. "I have Phoebe. She's okay, but not for long if we don't get moving."

"What's next?" Atlas asked.

"Apollo has a hunting cabin near here," said Reedy. "He likes to bring his favorite consorts there for long holidays."

"If there's any place we can get the supplies we need to make it out of Apollo's estate, it'll be there," said Ajax.

"There should also be medical supplies," said Pallas.

"Is it well-guarded?" asked Atlas.

"No need for guards, we think," said Ajax. "We're still deep within his estate." He climbed the embankment and joined Pallas.

"Apollo wanted this place to be private," added Pallas. "Just him and the consorts. No one should be there."

"How can you be sure he's not there tonight?" said Atlas.

"Because he called someone to his residence tonight." Reedy held her stomach. The thought clearly disgusted her, and Atlas decided not to pry any further.

"We can talk on the way," said Ajax. He stooped and picked up Phoebe, cradling her in his arms. Then he disappeared into the woods.

"Thank you for saving me," Atlas said to Reedy.

"It was Ajax."

"He pulled me to shore. But, you...um...gave me CPR."

"Only you could make me regret something like that," Reedy teased. She tripped and fell on her face, slipping down the muddy embankment until she was waist deep in the water.

Atlas slid down and pulled Reedy back to her feet. "Nice

moon, eh? I suppose this is as good a place as any to fall for each other, doncha' think?" He smirked.

Reedy smiled back. The two of them helped each other up the embankment. At the top, Reedy began to laugh. Atlas joined in and the two continued laughing until they caught up with the others.

CHAPTER 22

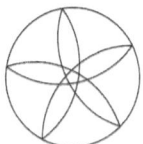

THE LOW DRONING of insects and the sound of the Philadelphians' feet crunching in the undergrowth and fallen leaves were the only disturbances of the otherwise still night. No search vehicles skimming above the forest canopy. No land vehicles approaching on nearby roads. Atlas sighed with relief. No indication Apollo's goons had discerned their destination.

Atlas and his friends walked quickly and quietly through the woods of Apollo's hunting reserve. Occasionally, a wild animal cried out in the distance, as if warning other animals to stay away from that part of the forest.

All became eerily quiet as Atlas and his friends approached Apollo's hunting cabin. Even the drone of the insects disappeared from the background.

"We need weapons," Atlas finally said.

"There should be some in the cabin," said Ajax.

"Ballistic or energy, most likely," Atlas said. "Hunting weapons. We'll need melee also, if we're going to make it across the estate without becoming a predator's lunch."

"Any weapons are better than none," Pallas said.

"Apollo's hunting cabin is only our first pitstop," said Ajax. From there, it's at least ten days to the next one. The *estate* is about as large as a mid-size country, and we have to zig-zag our way through it in order to avoid all the factory towns. We'll need hunting weapons as well, if we're going to make it."

"Let's hope Apollo is a collector of senti weapons and not just senti slaves," said Reedy. "Most modern Olympian weapons can only be used by Olympians."

"Shhh," whispered Ajax. "There it is." He crouched and motioned the others to get low.

The cabin was dark except for a few landscape lights along a pathway leading up to a door. It was smaller than Atlas had imagined, barely larger than his house back on Earth. Designed for privacy. Just Apollo and a consort or two.

"Looks empty, but let's not be overconfident," Atlas said. "That's Apollo's trademark."

Pallas crept up alongside Ajax to check on Phoebe. Blood continued to drip from Phoebe's saturated bandages. "She's in shock and has lost a lot of blood. And who knows what alien microbes might have been in that lake. We're past caution. We need those medical supplies. Now." She stood up and strode towards the cabin.

"*Pallas*," Ajax whispered. "Get back here!"

Pallas didn't turn around.

"She's right," Reedy said. "We have to risk it. Phoebe will die if we don't."

"No," said Ajax. "If we're caught, you think Apollo will save her? He'll let her die to punish us."

"If we're caught, he'll kill us all," Atlas said. "Saving Phoebe is worth the risk. We would have left her in Metallurgy if we didn't believe that." He stood and offered his hand to Ajax. "Let's go."

Ajax shook his head and frowned, but let Atlas pull him to his feet. Phoebe moaned and gave a loud, hissing sigh. Her head fell limply backwards and her injured arm slipped off her chest and dangled freely.

"Phoebe?" Ajax said desperately. "She's barely breathing." He ran after Pallas.

Atlas and Reedy followed close behind. Pallas stood at the

door to Apollo's cabin, her hand hesitating above the door knob. She looked back nervously at Atlas. He nodded and Pallas opened the door. Atlas held his breath. Silence. They exhaled as one.

Atlas stopped Pallas from walking into the cabin. "Reedy and I will go first, make sure the cabin is empty. You and Ajax find a place to attend to Phoebe. "

Reedy nodded. "Any idea where we might find medical supplies?"

"Medicine cabinet, maybe? I don't know. Check everywhere," said Pallas.

Atlas and Reedy spread out in different directions. Atlas moved slowly through the darkness to avoid crashing into furniture. *This is impossible. Phoebe is dying.* At this rate, they'd never clear the whole cabin in time.

The lights came on. Atlas wheeled around. Kitchen. White and clean. Elegant, even.

Reedy stood near a control interface on the far side of the adjoining dining room. She shrugged and mouthed, *"No time."*

Atlas motioned for Pallas and Ajax to enter. He pointed to the dining table near Reedy. Pallas hurriedly cleared the candles and place settings and Ajax carefully lay Phoebe down. Pallas checked Phoebe's pulse, frowned, and began chest compressions.

"Put pressure on her wound," she told Ajax.

Atlas found a rack of knives. He grabbed the two largest and brought one to Reedy. He motioned for her to continue through the doorway near the control panel. Atlas took the stairs.

At the top of the stairs, Atlas felt along the wall until he found the control panel. It illuminated at his touch. He scrutinized the interface. The text was Olympian. He grunted in spite of himself. He'd never learned how to read Olympian in the mines. That was a problem Reedy didn't have, apparently. She had no trouble turning the lights on downstairs, but Atlas had no idea which controls would turn them on here.

Atlas gritted his teeth and touched a part of the screen that kind of looked like a power button. The lights upstairs turned on much brighter than necessary. Atlas had to squint to see anything.

He was in a hallway. There were three doors.

Atlas cautiously opened the first door, clutching his knife and preparing to attack. The lights were just as bright inside. The room was elaborately decorated with fine fabrics, soft pillows, and hardwood inlaid with platinum. Astonishingly beautiful. No one was inside. *Guest room. Or...consort quarters*, he decided.

The second room was the same as the first, only a little bigger and with even finer furnishings. No one.

The third room was the biggest, but rather than soft fabrics and hardwood, it was decorated with exotic animal hides and elaborate stonework. Four large mirrors positioned in the center of each wall made the room seem even larger as they reflected each other into infinity. A square and comparatively simple bed sat in the exact center of the room. Apollo's quarters, obviously. This whole level was nothing but sleeping quarters. No weapons or medical supplies. Wasting time.

"Well, there you are, buddy!" Apollo appeared in the mirrors. "I've been looking all over for you."

"Die in the Underworld," said Atlas. He moved to leave the room.

"Hold on! I need to ask you a few questions, if you don't mind."

"I'm a little busy at the moment, sorry," said Atlas.

"Aw, come on. It will only take a second. It's been so long since we've talked."

"It's just not the right time," said Atlas.

Apollo narrowed his eyes. "Don't you understand? There will be no *other* time. Styx is on her way. She'll be there soon. Personally, I'd have rather handled this little internal matter on my own, but the Olympian Central Council—meddlesome pests that they are—they don't want to risk you getting away. Apparently, it would be embarrassing for...*Potentate* Delphi." Apollo smirked. "Can you believe that guy? Insists everyone call him Potentate, no matter what...no matter how long you've known him. It's a capital crime if you don't, even when he's not around. After everything I've done for him! Do you think that applies to his mom too? Wonder what she calls him? I know for a fact he wasn't the favorite."

"What do you want?" scowled Atlas.

"Simple," said Apollo. "I want you to surrender."

"Not going to happen."

"It is your best option. I have people that can get there before Styx. If you surrender to them, I think I can convince the good *Po-ten-tate* to let me keep most of you alive. The girls, at least. To be perfectly honest, I'm most interested in saving them. But hey, I can promise you a swift, painless death. That's better than you'll get from Styx."

"No thank you," said Atlas.

"You have less than twenty minutes to think it over. I under-stand. It's a big decision, but not a hard one. My men will be there soon. If you surrender to them, some of you live. If not, you'll all die."

Atlas walked out of the room.

"Think about it!" Apollo called after him. "I'll be busy until tomorrow morning—celebrating with a new girl—but I hope we get another chance to talk once I wake up. *Think* about it."

The doors to the room finally snapped shut.

Atlas hurried back to the stairs, stopping only to grab a blanket from the first room. As he reached the top of the stair-well he noticed a red triangle flashing in the middle of the control console. *What? That wasn't there before.* He hurried downstairs.

"What did you do?" said Reedy. She met him at the bottom of the stairwell.

"Nothing. I just turned the lights on."

"You turned *all* the lights on, inside and outside," said Ajax.

"You triggered the emergency alarm," said Reedy. "They know we're here!"

"I can't read Olympian. I'm so sorry." Atlas thought about telling them what Apollo had said. *No time for that now.*

"Well, it's done," said Reedy. "At least we know they're coming now. It's been driving me crazy not knowing—wondering if a whole squad of Apollo's goons were about to jump out of the woods."

Atlas pushed past Reedy to the table where Pallas and Ajax were treating Phoebe. Atlas covered Phoebe's body with the blanket. Reedy had found medical supplies. Phoebe breathed easily through the help of a breathing machine.

"I messed up," Atlas said. Ajax looked up at him, but didn't respond. He was holding Phoebe securely so Pallas could work.

"We needed the light," Pallas said dryly. She continued working on Phoebe's wound.

"The light is useful," Ajax said. "Unfortunately, the weapons vault is locked down now. Only Apollo can open it."

Atlas felt defeated. He'd ruined everything. The team had planned and executed a nearly flawless escape, but he'd ruined the whole thing at the touch of a button.

"What do we do now?"

"Phoebe needs blood," said Pallas. She pointed to a metal object on the corner of the table. "Reedy found a body-fluid replicator. I already put a sample of Phoebe's blood into it, but she'll die before it replicates enough. She needs a transfusion now, but I don't know what type she is."

"I'm O negative," Atlas said. "Universal donor."

"We don't have time," said Reedy. "We need to leave."

"Phoebe will die," said Ajax.

"The math is simple. We leave and she dies, or we stay and we all die."

That's not the only equation at play, Atlas thought.

"I'm not leaving," said Ajax. He looked angrily at Reedy and shook his head in disappointment.

Reedy shrunk in shame for a fraction of a second, but then set her feet and stood tall, asserting confidence in her assessment.

Atlas watched Pallas work on Phoebe. The bleeding had stopped. She was closing the wound with a tissue bonder. Phoebe's face and skin were pale, her breathing shallow. She would likely die no matter what. It was too late. They would all die when Styx got here. It made sense to leave. *Leave Phoebe. The rest of us have a chance—a small chance, but a chance—if we leave her. Let her die. Not our fault. This is on Apollo and the Olympians. We can avenge Phoebe's death. We* will *avenge her. So many have already died. So many. No. No more. Not Phoebe. Not any of us.*

"We're not leaving Phoebe," Atlas said. "We got this far as a team, and whatever happens from here on, we'll do as a team."

Reedy opened her mouth, but Atlas shut her down with a glance. Ajax smiled in gratitude.

"You and Reedy secure the cabin," Atlas told Ajax. "Barricade all points of entry. Improvise whatever weapons you can." He handed the knife to Ajax. "I'll secure Phoebe while Pallas performs the transfusion." Atlas thought about what else they should do. "That's it. Lock us down as tightly as you can. Pull together whatever defenses you can find. We'll take care of Phoebe."

Ajax nodded and began pulling the curtains over all the windows. Reedy stared at Atlas for a second, but nodded approvingly and joined Ajax.

Atlas gently held Phoebe's head between his hands. "How much will she need?"

"One unit ought to buy us enough time to start transfusing directly from the BFR," Pallas said. She searched the medical kit and pulled out two needles and some sterile tubing. Pallas connected the needles with the tubing. "Here we go." She poured a small amount of disinfectant over Atlas's left forearm and did the same for Phoebe's uninjured arm. "Make sure you keep your arm raised. Gravity has to do all the work. Pull that stool up. You can lean against it, if you get dizzy."

Atlas did as Pallas told him. "Okay, I'm ready."

With his free arm, he secured Phoebe. It was an awkward position, but Atlas thought he could hold it long enough to complete the transfusion.

Pallas tied off Atlas's arm with another bit of tubing. "You're going to feel a prick. There...dammit. Missed. Sorry. That's going to be a nasty bruise. I'll have to try a different vein."

Atlas winced and bit his lip, but remained still.

"Trying again. Okay. Keep still. Good. Got it." Pallas smiled and released the tubing around Atlas's arm. Blood flowed down the tubing until Pallas arrested it with a small kink near the end. "Okay, now for Phoebe. The vein's barely visible. Okay. You can do this, Pallas. Careful. Almost. Almost. There. Good. Done. Ha!" She inserted a syringe into the tubing and evacuated the trapped air. Then she released the kink in the tubing. Blood flowed from Atlas and into Phoebe.

"Now what?" Atlas asked.

"We wait," Pallas said. Perspiration poured down her forehead and temples, mingling freely with tears. "We've done our best."

Moments later, Pallas disconnected the tubing from Atlas and connected Phoebe to the BFR. Phoebe's synthesized blood began to flow into her veins. Pallas sat down heavily and wept for a moment. Atlas rested briefly, then went to help Ajax and Reedy stack the furniture in front of the downstairs windows and doors.

"I don't suppose you can turn some of these lights off?" Atlas asked.

"No," said Reedy. "We already tried that."

"Well, that's everything except the table," said Ajax. "We don't have weapons, but at least it won't be easy for them to get to us."

"Of course, they could blow up the cabin," said Atlas. "If they want us dead, I doubt they'll care much how it's accomplished. Apollo can always build a new hunting cabin."

Reedy and Ajax looked dumbfounded at Atlas. Reedy dropped her hands in resignation. Her chin quivered as her nostrils flared. Pallas stood and swatted Atlas on the back of his head.

"I'm sorry," said Atlas. "I don't know why I said that. I'm a bit lightheaded, I guess. We'll figure something out. We'll get out of here."

Reedy and Ajax continued to stare at Atlas with blank expressions.

Atlas felt profoundly uncomfortable. How had he let those thoughts slip out? What stupid things to say. *Another failure. You can't un-say something like that.*

"We *are* going to get out of here," Atlas said.

"No," said Reedy. "You were right. The minute you triggered the alarm, you signed our death warrant." Her words were drenched in bitterness.

"Reedy," Pallas said. "It wasn't—"

"No! Do not defend him. It is his fault. If not for Atlas, we would have escaped months ago. He triggered the alarm because he never learned to read *rudimentary* Olympian. He never learned to read because he was sent to the mines. He got sent to the *mines* because he flirted with a pretty alien girl when he should have been looking for you and Phoebe."

"Don't call her that," said Pallas.

"It's his fault we had to come up with an escape plan and then sit and wait for his sentence to end, meanwhile a dozen windows of opportunity opened and shut," Reedy continued. "It may not be his fault Phoebe's injured, but he made us stay instead of leaving her. Now we're all going to die and it's his fault! All your fault, Atlas! And now? Now it's your fault I'm giving up. It's hopeless. Totally hopeless, and that's all your fault."

"Reedy, that's not fair," said Ajax quietly.

"It isn't fair, but it's understandable," said Atlas. "More importantly, it's irrelevant. This is the situation we're in. There's no point getting upset over how or what might have been different." He placed his hand on Reedy's back. "We will survive this. *And* we will succeed in finding and securing the Celestial Sphere."

"You can't know that," sniffled Reedy.

"But we all know that. The prophecy said five will rise above the other ten. Here we are now, five Philadelphian youth. The other ten are dead or blind. At least that much seems to have come true. Whether you believe the prophecy now, or never have believed in it, here we are. We're the five that will find the Sphere. We don't have to believe in the prophecy to make it come true. We have to keep going, and believing in ourselves, despite our failures."

"But Atlas, you've forgotten something," said Reedy. "We've all forgotten something very important. *We are kids.* Just kids. Not even fifteen years old yet. We're not allowed to think about that, because every moment threatens to destroy us, but it's still true. The fate of the Galaxy shouldn't be up to us. We're just kids. It's not fair. They can't push something like that onto us because *they* don't want to deal with it. It's not fair."

"No, it's not fair. But if we do nothing, we're no better than those who laid the burden on us." Atlas put his arms around Reedy.

"A hug won't make me feel better," Reedy said.

"This is a thank you," said Atlas. "Because what you said makes *me* feel better."

Reedy wiped her eyes and looked up at Atlas. "What?"

Atlas smiled. "I'm glad I'm not the only one who thinks this whole thing is absurd and unfair. You don't know how reassuring it is to know I'm not the only one with doubts."

"Of course we have doubts," said Pallas. "That's what's kept us alive. We doubt the Titans. We doubt the Olympians. We doubt the prophecy. But we don't doubt each other." She put her arms around Reedy and Atlas. "I don't know if we can succeed. But I know we're not going to give up."

"It will take more than our best to get us out of this mess," said Ajax.

"Come join us, Ajax," Reedy said.

"I'm not much of a hugger." Ajax fidgeted and looked away.

"Me neither," whispered Phoebe.

"Phoebe!" Pallas ran to Phoebe's side and grabbed her hand.

"I was so worried—we were so worried. I thought the transfusion was too late."

Phoebe smiled weakly and closed her eyes. "Did we jump out of a train?"

"Just rest," Atlas said. "We'll talk about it later." He stepped away from Phoebe and motioned for the others to follow him.

"I'm sorry," said Reedy.

"No need to apologize. I understand your frustration. And I do bear some blame for how things have turned out so far. I only hope I also bear some of the blame for everything that's gone right."

"Of course. I sometimes forget—"

Four loud, heavy knocks sounded from behind the barricade Reedy and Ajax had placed in front of the door. The Philadelphians instinctively crouched down.

"Ajax, help me with Phoebe," Pallas whispered. She crawled back to the table. "We need to get her down."

Without a word, Ajax crept after Pallas. Together, they gently lowered Phoebe to the floor.

"Careful with the BFR tubing," Pallas said.

Four more loud knocks.

Here's Apollo's men, Atlas thought. *Should I tell everyone else? Save the girls' lives?*

"Why are they knocking?" Reedy asked.

"Maybe they want to give us a chance to surrender," Ajax said.

"We should take it," said Reedy.

"Are you crazy?" asked Pallas. "We'll never get another chance to escape."

Six knocks, louder and faster than before.

Why keep knocking? It didn't make any sense. Atlas looked at Reedy, then back at the door. He looked at Phoebe, comfortably sleeping. She'd survived, but was helpless. If they tried to fight their way out, they would have to leave her behind. If they gave themselves up…

Two more knocks. And a voice...barely audible...but familiar. Atlas stood up and walked towards the door.

"Atlas? What are you doing?" Pallas raised her voice a bit. "We need to fight. That's our only option."

"We don't know that," said Reedy.

"I'm with Pallas," said Ajax. He stood and picked up a chair, preparing to smash it.

Another two knocks. The voice again. *I know that voice.*

"Hold on." Atlas raised his hand to halt Ajax. "Help me with this." He took hold of the largest piece of furniture blockading the door and violently heaved it out of the way.

Reedy jumped up to help. Atlas tossed the pieces aside with abandon while Reedy tried not to unnecessarily damage anything. Ajax smashed his chair several times until he had recovered two large clubs from the debris. He handed one to Pallas. The two crouched in front of Phoebe and prepared to fight.

The entrance was clear. Atlas flung open the door.

A black-clad individual quickly stepped inside.

"Atlas, Apollo's men are very near. We must go now," she said.

Atlas threw his arms around the woman. "Ata! So good to see you again."

Another woman entered.

"And we are glad to see *you* again, Philadelphian," said Pakhet.

CHAPTER 23

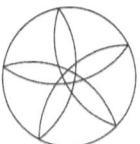

THE AIR WAS thick and heavy. Dense clouds extinguished the moon. Distant thunder rumbled through the forest. A storm approached.

Atlas could only barely discern the silhouettes of those running in front of him. Their dark clothing made them nearly indistinguishable from the forest. Shadows running through shadows.

An explosion roared through the trees. The shockwave raced past Atlas and the others, carrying with it the souls of Apollo's men. Pakhet's surprise. Atlas looked back towards the cabin. He couldn't help it. Instinct. Even knowing it was going to happen, he wasn't prepared. The woods behind them glowed in the light of the burning cabin. It was beautiful, and also macabre.

Atlas wished Apollo had been in the cabin. The poor men who triggered the explosion would be nobodies—Tier II's and III's—whose only crime was conditioned obedience to a tyrant with absolute power over their lives. Never again would they return home to their families. Atlas rubbed his eye. Those men died so that he and his friends might live. *Live to be worthy of life.*

He was surprised how much thinking about the victims of the explosion upset him. They wouldn't have hesitated to kill him and his friends, given the order. It was their job to kill. Sudden death—meted out or received—was part of the job description. And yet, they wouldn't have died except for Apollo. Their deaths were on his head. Apollo remained safe and alive and powerful because he sent others to do the hard work of death.

Up ahead, Reedy stumbled and fell. Atlas almost tripped over her. Instead, he crashed into Ajax, who had turned to help Reedy. Struggling to keep his feet, Atlas slammed his shin against a tree stump.

"Get up, Philadelphians," Pakhet snapped as she ran past, carrying Phoebe on her back. "The survivors will be upon us in minutes."

Atlas helped Ajax to his feet. Reedy was already up and running again. Atlas bent to examine his shin. There was a large tear through his clothing and the cloth was wet and slightly sticky. Blood.

He probed the wound with his finger. The gash was deeper than he expected. He put some weight on his injured leg. *Not bad. I can do this.* He ran after Ajax. *Ouch—okay. It's okay. I can do this.*

Pakhet and Pallas had disappeared. Atlas could only barely make out Reedy's silhouette and Ajax was catching up to her rapidly. Atlas was hobbling—almost skipping—as the pain in his leg grew. *Keep moving. Just keep moving.*

As Atlas began to lose sight of Ajax, the pain started to fade. Atlas quickened his pace. Soon, the pain was gone. Atlas realized he couldn't feel the injury at all. His lower leg was almost totally numb, but it wasn't like any numbness he'd experienced before. It didn't make him clumsy or awkward, just blocked the feeling from the wound. How? Atlas could only assume the Theban clothing was responsible, because he was soon running again at almost full speed. *Little things keep you alive.*

A loud buzz zipped overhead. Someone behind him cried out sharply and crashed into the underbrush, then was silent.

"Atlas! Get down. *Now.*" Aura dropped out of a tree and ran towards the cry, holding a large spear to her face like a rifle.

Atlas dropped flat into a tall patch of underbrush. He could hear Aura's footfalls running across the fallen leaves, but then everything was silent. His heartbeat pounded in his ears.

"Atlas?" Pallas whispered. "Where are you?"

"I'm here," Atlas whispered back. "Where are the others?"

"Up ahead, with Pakhet and Ata. I turned back when I realized you'd fallen behind. Are you okay?"

"I hurt my leg, but I'm fine. I can hardly feel the pain anymore."

Someone yelled angrily in the woods behind them, the cry cut short. Loud buzz. Another yell. Metal against metal. A loud thud. Someone cried in pain, possibly Aura. Another buzz and a pop. Then silence again.

"Should we go?" Pallas asked. "Or wait for her?"

"Just a minute longer," Atlas whispered. He listened carefully for any other sounds. Nothing. Not even insects.

Atlas crept onto his knees and looked above the undergrowth. He could barely see more than shadows, but none of them seemed to be moving. "Let's go," he said, standing up.

A shadow stood near him. "I'm here," said Pallas.

"Which way did everyone go?"

Pallas pointed to the left of the tree where Aura had appeared. "That way, I think."

"After you," Atlas whispered. He took a few steps towards Pallas.

Pallas turned to meet him. "Look out!" She lunged at him, knocking Atlas to the ground.

Another shadow fell next to them, thrown off balance by the swing of its heavy weapon.

Atlas scrambled towards the shadow, grasping for the weapon. Pallas also darted at the shadow, but the assailant kicked her sharply in the side. She fell to the ground, gasping. Atlas tried to wrestle the weapon away, but couldn't jerk it free.

He bit the attacker's arm until it bled. The blood burned Atlas's mouth like acid. A fist pummeled the back of Atlas's head, but Atlas didn't relax his bite until he felt the attacker's grip on the weapon slip.

Atlas wrenched the weapon free but lost control and accidentally flung it into the forest shadows. He reflexively reached for the weapon. The assailant's boot connected with Atlas's stomach and he fell next to Pallas, winded and vulnerable.

The shadow retrieved its weapon and stood over Pallas and Atlas. It raised the large, broad weapon high above its head. A glint of moonlight broke through the clouds and struck the weapon's tip. *This is it*, Atlas thought. He rolled over and shielded Pallas with his body.

The air buzzed twice and the attacker's arms exploded, splattering Atlas and Pallas with blood. The weapon stuck harmlessly in the ground. The shadow howled in pain. There was a high-pitched hum and a bright green spike burst through its torso.

The shadowy assailant slumped to the ground, revealing another dark figure holding a spear with a bright green head. The spearhead faded to black as their rescuer stooped to help Pallas and Atlas.

"The blood is a potent acid," said Diana. "Quickly, use your clothing to neutralize any that touched your skin."

Atlas wanted to greet the Theban, but his mouth burned from the attacker's blood. He pulled up a corner of his sleeve and stuck it in his mouth. The Theban clothing neutralized the acid and numbed the pain of the burns.

Fortunately, most of the assailant's blood spatter had landed on Atlas's clothing. A few drops had landed on his neck. Atlas neutralized the acid and held his sleeve to the wound until the pain was gone.

"We need to move," Diana said. "There will be many more on their way." She pulled Atlas and Pallas to their feet.

Atlas tried to ask Pallas if she was okay, but the chemical burns on his lips and tongue prevented him. Instead, he patted Pallas on the shoulder and guided her to follow Diana.

Diana led them swiftly through the forest. She scanned both

sides of the dark woods constantly and fell back to check behind them every thirty seconds. Finally, they reached a meadow at the edge of the woods.

In the middle of the meadow, its contours accented by red lights, stood the Thebans' ship. In the darkness, it appeared as if floating through space, like a proper interstellar spacecraft. How foolish Atlas had been to be disappointed that interstellar travel failed to meet his expectations. And what he wouldn't give to be home right now. *In my bed. Safe and sound. My parents and sister in their rooms down the hall.*

Heavy rain began to fall. Diana turned to watch for anyone else daring to venture out of the woods. She waved Atlas and Pallas onto the ship. As Atlas passed, he looked at Diana's weapon. It was the same spear she'd carried when escorting him to the Academy. The same one she had prodded him with when he back-talked the Thebans.

She could have blown a hole clean through my chest, he thought.

Banka greeted them at the ship's entry port. "Hurry Atlas! Pallas! We must go now."

Atlas and Pallas slipped inside the ship. Diana followed close behind. She slammed the hatch shut. There was a high-pitched whine, a flash of light, a loud clap like thunder, and then silence.

"What happened to your face?" Banka asked. She touched Atlas's mouth delicately.

"Thracian blood," Diana said. "A Thracian male attacked them before I could reach them. I ended him, but they were too close to the target." She stepped closer to examine Atlas. "Although it appears Atlas learned about the properties of Thracian blood on his own. Did you bite him?"

Atlas nodded.

"Well done," Diana said.

"We need to get you to Dr. Circe immediately," said Banka. She turned to Pallas. "You too, my dear. Judging from your gait, you probably have a few broken ribs."

"What about the other one?" Pallas wheezed.

"The other Philadelphians came aboard before you," said Banka. "Phoebe is—"

"No, the other Theban. She jumped out of the tree. We heard fighting."

"Aura knows how to take care of herself," said Diana.

"We can't leave her behind." Pallas went to the hatch and tried to push it open.

"We have already left Olympus," said Banka. "And arrived on Titan."

"Then let's go *back*. We can trans-light right back and get her."

"I'm afraid it's not that simple," said Banka.

"Aura knows how to take care of herself," Diana repeated. "We'll go back for her, I promise."

"But first, we need to take care of you," Banka said. "Please come with me to the medical bay."

AT LEAST NINE HOURS LATER, Atlas woke to find himself recovering in the medical bay of the Theban ship. He touched his lips and gums. The acid burns were healed. He opened and closed his mouth several times and inspected his mouth with his tongue. Everything seemed back to normal. The gash on his shin was also healed. No scars.

Atlas's clothes had been removed and disposed. After everything he'd been through with them, they were gone. It was silly to get sentimental over a set of clothing, especially after everything else he had lost, but that one set of clothing had been with him through it all, literally saving his life on multiple occasions, especially in the mine. Now it was gone. Someone had even changed his underwear. *Hopefully not Dr. Circe.* She was such a weirdo.

"Good. You're awake," said Reedy.

"Finally," said Phoebe. "You slept forever. I was starting to think you were trying to convince us to go after the Sphere without you." She and Reedy sat near Atlas's hospital bed. Phoebe held a paperback book.

Atlas was so glad to see Phoebe alive and well that he jumped out of bed and gave her a hug. "I'm so glad you're okay."

"This is uncomfortable," Phoebe mumbled against his bare chest. "And inappropriate."

"We thought we lost you," Atlas said.

"You're not *that* lucky."

"No, I guess I'm not." Atlas smiled stupidly.

"Can you put some clothes on now?"

"Here." Reedy handed Atlas a bundle of new Theban clothing.

"I'd like to take a shower, if I could," Atlas said. He didn't feel dirty. In fact, he felt antiseptically clean. *After everything,* he thought, *it would just be so great to take a nice, long shower.*

"There's a bathroom over there," said Reedy.

Atlas took the bundle of clothing and trotted off to the shower. His leg felt great. No pain. He stopped.

"Where's Dr. Circe? Does she need to discharge me, or something?"

"She's sleeping," said Phoebe. "Between me, you, and Pallas, she's had a busy day. She said you're free to go as soon as you wake up."

"Pallas is alright?"

"Of course," said Reedy. "Dr. Circe is very good."

"She's fixed me up quite a few times. Pallas's broken ribs should be a piece of cake."

"Yes," said Reedy. She shifted her weight nervously. "Like I said, Dr. Circe is very good."

Atlas went to the shower. Something about the way Reedy had responded seemed odd. *Oh well. As long as Pallas is fine. We're all back on Titan. And alive. These past two months seemed like an eternity. But we're back on Titan.*

Atlas climbed into the shower and let the water wash over him for several minutes without moving, or thinking.

Eventually, one question forced its way into his consciousness.

How did the Thebans find us?

He'd been so happy to see them. The situation had been so desperate, Atlas hadn't even thought about how the Thebans had been able to locate them. That was an answer he was going to get at the first opportunity.

Pakhet. I need to speak with her.

Several more thought-free, motionless minutes passed.

It feels so good to be back on Titan, Atlas thought. *Freedom. Safety. Food. Well, not food yet, but maybe Banka could get me a pizza from Aldrighetti's like she did before. I'm really hungry. How amazing is it to feel hungry and be able to do something about it whenever you want? For the last two months, that wasn't an option. That's what's next. Questions can wait. I'm going to eat. Eat and think about how good it is to eat as much as I want. Sleep as much as I want. Use a clean bathroom…but, it's not over yet. Not by a long shot.*

The Sphere. How are we going to find the Sphere? No one even knows if it really exists. But we can't go home—back to Earth—until we find it. No place is safe until the Olympians can't acquire the Sphere. So many have died because of that damn Celestial Sphere.

And Homer. Poor Homer. I haven't thought about him for such a long time. Was he still alive? We're not going home until we find him, or at least know his fate. If we can find the Sphere, we can find Homer.

A knock on the bathroom door interrupted Atlas's thoughts. "Hello?"

The door opened a crack. "Are you almost done?" Reedy asked. "Pallas is asking for you. And we're hungry, so we're going to go eat."

"I'll be right out. Um…Where can I find Pallas?"

"Out the doors and to the left. Third—no, fourth door down."

"Thanks."

"They brought in Earth food! Can you believe it?"

"Sounds great," said Atlas. Truthfully, he wasn't sure his stomach would be able to handle Earth food after two months of mine rations. But he was anxious to prove himself wrong. "Go ahead and start without me." He heard the door shut.

A few minutes later, Atlas finished his shower and dressed in his new clothing. It was nearly identical to the old clothing, but different somehow. The texture, or maybe a slightly different shade of black. Once the clothing conformed to his body, it fit as well as his old clothes.

Theban clothing slowed bleeding, neutralized acid, and anesthetized wounds, but Atlas still thought the most remarkable thing it did was transform from quadruple extra-large to a perfect tailor-fit without any change in texture, thickness, or other properties. Oh, and it could fold itself. *Little things.*

Atlas left the medical bay and went to find Pallas. Fourth door down. As he was about to knock, the door opened. Pallas almost walked right into him.

"Atlas, I was just coming to find you. They said you were talking a shower. That was almost an hour ago."

"No, it hasn't been that long, has it?" Atlas's cheeks reddened slightly.

"At least. What took so long?"

"I was thinking."

"Me too," said Pallas. "On Olympus, I was so consumed with planning our escape and avoiding suspicion that I didn't have time to truly think these past two months. Least, not think how I used to."

"I know the feeling. And I have some serious questions that I want answered."

"Like what?"

"Let's go eat with the others. We should talk about this together. As a team."

"Agreed," said Pallas. "But first, there's something I want to talk about with you. Alone."

"What is it?"

"It's about Zhehera." Her tone was serious but tentative, almost nervous.

Was Pallas jealous of Zhehera? *How ridiculous! Why would she be?* "What about Zhehera?" Atlas asked.

"I'm worried about her," Pallas said. "I'm afraid something bad may have happened to her."

"Why do you say that?"

"She volunteered to be the distraction for our escape. In fact, she insisted."

"She was going to kill Apollo."

"That was the plan, yes."

"She'd have to get access to his private wing. How would she get in?"

"She volunteered."

"Volunteered for what?" Atlas knew the answer but didn't want to admit it.

Pallas didn't answer.

Atlas stared at the floor, his cheeks filled with rage and sadness. "Then Apollo is dead. Good riddance."

"That's the thing," said Pallas. "I'm not sure he *is* dead. No one would have come after us if he was dead."

Atlas thought about Apollo's last words to him through the mirror-com at his cabin. Zhehera was the girl he spoke of. *I'm so stupid*, Atlas thought. *Should have realized. Every clue.* He clenched his jaw and swallowed the lump in his throat.

"They might have still come after us, if he sent them before…"

"Yeah. Maybe," said Pallas. She looked at her hands, then rested one on Atlas's shoulder.

Atlas put his hand over Pallas's hand. "Apollo is dead," he insisted. *Zhehera wouldn't fail*, he thought. She couldn't fail. Apollo was dead.

"Atlas, I hope you're right, but—"

"Apollo is *dead*." He brushed off her hand.

"Saying it louder doesn't make it true. She wanted you to know—"

"No." said Atlas. "Apollo is dead. He sent his men after us before he called for Zhehera."

"You don't know that."

"Yes I do," said Atlas. Why did Pallas want to convince him Zhehera had failed? "I spoke to him."

"To whom?"

"Apollo," Atlas sighed. "At his cabin. Upstairs. He appeared on the mirror-com in his bedroom."

"You talked with him?" Pallas's jaw dropped. "Why didn't you say anything to us?"

"There wasn't time. Phoebe needed help."

Pallas crossed her arms. "What did he say?"

"He said Delphi sent Styx to kill us all. He said that his men would arrive first, and if we surrendered to them, he'd work a deal with Delphi to keep you three."

"Us three?"

"You, Reedy, and Phoebe."

"Oh." Pallas stared at the floor.

"I'm sorry, but I couldn't stand him taking you three back to the...western wing. I would rather all of us die, together. Maybe it wasn't my place to make the decision, but that's the decision I made."

Pallas was quiet for a moment. "What does this have to do with Zhehera?"

"Just something he said," Atlas replied.

"What?"

"I'd rather not think about it." Atlas clenched his fists.

"Zhehera made me promise not to tell you until we were safe. She didn't want you to try to save her"

"Zhehera doesn't need saving. Apollo is dead, and nobody will mourn him. Zhehera killed him. She fulfilled her destiny, and I'll congratulate her after we fulfill ours."

Pallas smiled sadly. "You're probably right."

CHAPTER 24

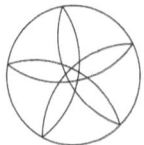

ATLAS AND PALLAS joined the other Philadelphians around a table covered with pizzas—stacked three boxes wide and four boxes tall—from Aldrighetti's Spaghetti Ghetto. The others had already begun eating, but over half the boxes were unopened.

"They got two of everything," said Reedy. "What a criminal waste of food."

"To be fair, Banka said there was a problem with the translator," Phoebe said. "They only meant to get a half pizza of everything on the menu."

"What a fortunate mistake," Atlas said. He found both pepperoni, pineapple, and jalapeño pizzas untouched and promptly pressed two slices together like a sandwich and took an enormous bite. Atlas closed his eyes and forced himself to savor that first exquisite mouthful. Then he devoured the two slices together, only barely pausing to breathe in between bites. It was a perfect moment. Sheer ecstasy.

"I wish they'd bought Pizza Boutique instead," said Phoebe. "This stuff is so greasy."

"It's wonderful," said Atlas. He made another pizza sandwich and took a bite.

"It is pretty good, but it's no Pizza Trough pie," said Ajax.

"Pizza Trough is disgusting," said Reedy. "It's basically just a large, soggy cracker soaked in grease and ketchup."

"You don't even like pizza," said Ajax.

"How do you not like pizza?" Atlas asked with his mouth full.

"I just don't," said Reedy.

"What do you think, Pallas? It's the best, isn't it?" Atlas was almost finished with his second pizza sandwich.

Pallas finished chewing before quietly answering, "It's good."

"But not your favorite? That's okay. Everyone's entitled to their opinion. What's your favorite pizza place?"

"I don't have a favorite," Pallas said. "But this is good. Very good."

"You gotta' have a favorite," Ajax said. "Everyone does."

"Maybe she doesn't," said Reedy. "Let her eat."

They ate until they couldn't eat anymore. Even Reedy ate nearly half a pizza, which Atlas thought was impressive for someone who claimed not to like pizza. There was ASG Root Beer to go along with the pizza, which everyone enjoyed, but Atlas thought was a bit flat and bitter. *Must be a bad batch.* That happened every once in a while at Aldrighetti's since they brewed their own, in-house. Overall, it was the best meal Atlas had eaten in months, and he was sure the same was true for his friends, their personal pizza preferences notwithstanding.

After a few moments silently basking in their overindulgence, the Philadelphians began to clean up. Pallas and Ajax gathered the dishes and utensils and returned them to the sanitizing cabinets. Reedy tried to consolidate the pizzas as best she could, declaring they could be stored for later and not wasted, but she couldn't find a refrigerator in the galley and was forced to leave the boxes on the table.

Atlas found himself wishing he could send the leftovers to the workers in Apollo's mine, and he didn't even like most of those guys. It did seem like an awful waste to throw that much food away. Hopefully the Thebans had some way to store it.

"Do you think anyone else survived?" Phoebe asked.

"Do I think who survived?" Atlas asked.

"Anyone else at the Academy," Phoebe said. "Director Themis, Nike, Professor Bendis—the others. Dr. Circe survived. Do you think anyone else did?"

"I'm not sure you want to know the answer to that question," said Pakhet, her distinctive, metallic voice revealing her entrance.

Four Thebans entered the mess hall behind her. Diana, Ata, Banka, and…Aura? No, the fifth Theban was much older than the others Atlas had met. She carried herself as someone used to being treated with great deference.

"Of course we want to know," said Phoebe. "That's why I asked."

"We've already lost so much," said Pallas. "No need to spare our feelings."

"Professor Bendis, at least, did not survive, I am sorry to say," said the fifth Theban. "She met her end at Styx's hand, as have so many others."

"How do you know Styx?" asked Atlas.

"She is the chief assassin of the Olympians," said Pakhet. "We have crossed paths before."

"And we have killed many of her acolytes," smirked Diana. "Your Thracian acquaintance, for example."

"Yes, but Styx has also killed many of our sisters," said Banka.

"I have not forgotten," retorted Diana.

"Of course not," said Banka.

"As for Nike and Director Themis, we don't know where they are," said Pakhet. "We assume they were taken by the Olympians."

The older Theban raised an eyebrow. "Since I am denied a proper introduction, I shall introduce *myself*." She raised her head high, pointing her chin towards Atlas. "I am Neith, Prime Matriarch of Thebes, and I have information that will lead to your discovery of the Celestial Sphere."

Ajax stood, then bowed. The other Philadelphians awkwardly followed his lead.

"Please, please, none of that," said Neith, beaming with false modesty. "I am a mortal like anyone else. And Thebes, in its current state, is little more than a wasteland." She laughed ironically. "I am the First Mother of a deserted and barren wasteland. So, do not stand nor bow to me. Once, long ago, I deserved such respect, but no longer." She sighed.

Diana shook her head. Pakhet brought Neith a seat, but dropped it in front of her rather than holding it for her to sit upon. Banka looked embarrassed.

Neith gestured towards the other Thebans. "You see? Even my subjects show me nothing but disdain."

"We are not your subjects," said Pakhet. "Nor would we recognize your authority were you still sitting atop your throne of oppression on Thebes."

"No, indeed," said Neith. "You recognize no authority but your own, do you, my dear?"

"I need no other," said Pakhet.

"*This* is awkward," Atlas whispered to Pallas.

"Anyone else getting uncomfortable?" asked Phoebe.

"Like watching one of your parents fight with their parents," said Ajax.

Neith sat down. "And yet, you have invited me here, so I am not completely useless to you."

"You are here only because you cling to your monopoly on *state secrets* more desperately than you clung to the protection of our home world and the safety of our people," said Pakhet.

"You know nothing, *child*," said Neith. "You were not even born when Thebes fell."

"But I was," said Diana. "And though only a little girl when we were taken from Thebes, I remember the words of my parents, telling me how you bargained the freedom of one third of our people and the lives of another third in exchange for your own safety."

"You know nothing!" screamed Neith. "The Olympians would

have killed us all. Though I could not save Thebes, I saved our people."

"By consigning us to slavery and slaughter," said Pakhet.

"Some of you, yes. That was non-negotiable. They made it exceedingly clear. One third of the population as slaves and another sacrificed, or extermination of all."

"But not your third of the population, of course," said Diana.

"Enough!" yelled Banka. "This is not the time to rehash such old and tired arguments." She pushed Pakhet to a seat on the other side of the room. "I have already forgiven you for your foolish bickering. Let us hope the Philadelphians can do the same."

Atlas sat down, happy to have a break from the awkward tension. Phoebe let out a low, lilting whistle as she sat. Ajax chuckled under his breath. Pallas watched Neith with pity and compassion mingling on her face. Reedy shook her head.

"You are right, Banka," said Neith. "And for my part, I apologize. You must understand, dear children, when I was taught about the Celestial Sphere as a child in the royal court, the tales were quite different than the events we have observed these last several generations." The old matriarch sat quietly for a few moments with a slight smile on her face, perhaps reminiscing. Then she became very serious. "Though Pakhet does not believe it, I care very deeply about my people. I wake every morning carrying the burden of all the suffering resulting from my treaty with the Olympians. It was a decision not made lightly, and not a morning passes that I don't weigh anew the consequences of my actions against what might have been—and every morning I am convinced that I made the only acceptable decision."

"Excuse me...um...Madame Matriarch," said Phoebe. "The five of us just escaped from an Olympian slaver. Before that, we watched as our friends were slaughtered and blinded by an Olympian assassin. We know all about Olympian savagery. Forgive us, but we're not particularly interested in the guilt burden you bear as a consequence of your deal with them."

Neith narrowed her eyes. "Is that right, young Philadelphian?" Her words dripped with understated, yet potent, venom. "Well, it seems that the stories I once learned about the events surrounding the discovery of the Celestial Sphere were not the only ones exaggerated. The geniality of your species was also highly misrepresented."

"This is a waste of our time," Phoebe addressed her friends. "She cares more about perceived slights to her dignity than about giving us any useful information. And worse, she resorts to hurling insults like a child. We have more important things to do." She stood to leave.

"Please, Philadelphian," Pakhet said. "Return to your seat. This is my fault. I provoked the Matriarch. I will remove myself. Perhaps in my absence, the Matriarch might be found in a more agreeable disposition."

"Ha!" laughed Neith. "Suddenly such formality. So you *are* capable of demonstrating respect on occasion. Very well. I accept your terms."

"No, Pakhet," said Phoebe. "You stay. Either she shares the information with all of us, or the...um...Matriarch leaves." Phoebe's voice betrayed sudden uncertainty. She looked at Atlas apologetically.

Atlas nodded for her to continue. "You don't need my permission."

Phoebe grinned, then turned back to Neith. "Either way, we need to plan our next steps. The Olympians could launch an invasion against Titan at any moment." Phoebe took a few steps towards the Matriarch, her palms facing out. "Please understand, Madame Matriarch. We mean no disrespect, but we have neither the time nor patience to fuss about your feelings. So help us, or don't. But if you don't, please understand that should we fail and the Sphere fall into Olympian hands, you will be responsible for many billions more deaths. How easy will it be to fall asleep at night, knowing *that* burden awaits you at the dawn of every morning?"

All eyes were on Phoebe, whose eyes didn't deviate from Neith's.

Atlas couldn't help but smile. Clever as he might be, Homer never would have come up with that speech, let alone have the nerve to confront the Matriarch. As much as Atlas missed Homer and regretted what happened to him, he was equally proud that Phoebe had found her place.

"Very well," Neith finally said. "You will indulge an old woman the opportunity to provide some context for the information I am about to share, I hope?"

"Go ahead." Phoebe sat back in her chair.

"The tale I am about to share has been passed exclusively from Prime Matriarch to Prime Matriarch for generations and is—or was—considered one of our most sensitive state secrets." Neith wrung her hands together. "It has never been written down and every Prime took an oath to die any unimaginably excruciating death our enemies could devise before revealing the secret to anyone other than the next delegated Prime. Perhaps now you understand the hesitation with which I share this. Although, as there is no Prime designated to take my place, and since I have already lived longer than most Matriarchs, perhaps it is better the information does not perish with me."

"We will not share your secret," said Atlas.

"Thank you," said the Matriarch. She inhaled deeply. "Many generations ago, Thebes was visited by citizens of a distant, highly-advanced civilization. They revealed themselves only to the ruling Prime Matriarch, a direct ancestor of mine. The visitors called themselves Ciencians and claimed they were peaceful explorers, interested only in studying our people and culture, as they had previously studied the citizens and cultures of hundreds of other worlds."

"It always starts with the best intentions," muttered Pallas.

"My ancestor granted the Ciencians' request. She reasoned that with such superior technology at their disposal, the Ciencians could have easily carried out their observations in secret.

Since they had instead sought her permission, the Prime believed their motives to be friendly. The only condition my ancestor stipulated was that the visitors inform her periodically of their activities."

Diana huffed indignantly.

"Of course," Neith continued, "the Prime was motivated by both personal curiosity and her sacred responsibility for the welfare of our people to learn as much as she could about the Cienciants and their technology. She asked them endless questions each time they reported on their research. However, the Cienciants refused to answer the large majority of her questions, claiming that doing so would cause irreparable harm to the development of our civilization. And yet, the Prime persisted.

"The Prime was, of course, an extremely beautiful and cunning hunter. Once she sighted her quarry, her patient persistence was destined to succeed. Over several solar cycles, she gleaned as much about the visitors as she could by carefully choosing her questions and listening intently to what they did *not* say even more than what they did say. The more the Cienciants equivocated, the more she learned."

Curiosity and cats, thought Atlas.

"The Cienciants were an unusually inquisitive species, and also deeply passionate about their research. But for all their idealistic dedication to acquiring knowledge and understanding, their seemingly single-minded zeal for studying new forms of intelligent life was nothing more than a permutation of the same fascination with novelty which often inaugurates romantic endeavors." Neith smirked lewdly. "The Prime noticed that one of the Cienciants tended to offer more detailed reports when it was his turn to present. Additionally, his gaze often lingered on her when he thought she did not notice. Her prey selected, the Prime requested that this Cienciant be her exclusive liaison."

"Ugh! I hate these stories," whispered Pallas to herself.

"In time, the Prime gained an intimate trust with the liaison. Little by little, as the relationship between the two continued to develop, he began to share details about the Cienciant civilization. Among other things, the Prime learned that at the core of Cienciant culture was an object called the Globe of Heavens."

"It's always a woman," whispered Ajax. "No secret has a chance once a woman gets involved."

Reedy elbowed him in the ribs. "Proof of our superiority."

"The Prime attempted to learn more about this Globe, but all the Cienciant liaison would say was that it was the source of all their technology and culture; that it possessed nearly infinite power; but that even with all the time, energy, and resources the Cienciants had dedicated to studying it, they had acquired only minimal understanding."

"Excuse me, Matriarch," Phoebe said. "We're already aware that nobody really knows anything about the Sphere."

"You must have patience, my dear," Neith said. "If you skip to the end of a story before you earn it, you've broken a universal law, for which the punishment is eternal ignorance."

Phoebe looked confused and irritated.

Neith laughed. "Cause and effect, my dear. It is the law by which one observes the web of history unfold."

"You are a pedantic and hypocritical fool!" said Pakhet. "Neither these Philadelphians nor the billions of Thebans you condemned to death or slavery need learn anything about cause and effect from you. We have *earned* our understanding, while the meager knowledge you have acquired came merely by *observing* our suffering."

"Pakhet," said Ata. "Let Neith finish. There is no need to censure or attack her. She's just an old woman. Let's not give the Philadelphians reason to sympathize with the Matriarch." She looked at the Philadelphians, who all squirmed uncomfortably in their seats.

"We only want to know whatever the Matriarch can share about the location of the Celestial Sphere," said Atlas.

"She doesn't know the location," said Pakhet.

"Then what are we doing here?" said Reedy. "Why waste our

time with this story? It's imperative we don't waste any more time."

"Pakhet is correct," said Neith. "I do not know the location of the Sphere. Nor do I know how to find the Ciencia system, which would be the most logical place to begin a search."

Phoebe opened her mouth to say something, but Atlas stopped her with a touch on the arm.

"However, I do have information critical to your mission," said Neith. "If you'll indulge me the rest of my story, I promise you will find it worth your while."

"Of course, Matriarch," said Phoebe.

"Thank you, my dear. Now, where was I?"

"Nobody, not even the Cienciants, know what the Sphere is," said Phoebe.

"Yes. Thank you," Neith said. "The Prime was disappointed that her Cienciant wouldn't entrust her with more information about the Globe of Heavens. However, by this time, her attempt to manipulate the Cienciant's romantic interest as a means to information had backfired. She had fallen in love.

"As time went on, the two developed a deep and passionate love for one another. Of course, had the other Cienciants learned of the affair, they would have returned to Ciencia immediately, taking the Prime's lover with them. Their love had to remain an absolute secret."

"Secrets don't keep," whispered Pallas.

"Of course, secret relationships cannot remain secret forever. Eventually, the other Cienciants learned about their colleague's indiscretions. They withdrew from Thebes immediately without allowing the Cienciant the chance to say goodbye."

"How sad," said Reedy.

"The Prime scoured every location on Thebes where the Cienciants had studied Theban culture. She found no trace of the liaison or his expedition. Soon after, a child was born. Her daughter. The next Prime. Destined to rule Thebes. And she was half Cienciant."

"That must have caused a scandal," said Reedy.

"No one knew that the baby was half alien. Deprived so unexpectedly of the great love of her life, the Prime had not even told the father of the impending birth," said Neith. "As I said, this was a closely guarded state secret, passed only from Prime to Prime."

"That's not what I meant," said Reedy under her breath.

"If the people had known the baby's parentage, it could have led to civil war," said Neith.

"If the people had known, we might have rid ourselves of the tyranny of the Matriarchs," said Pakhet. "Instead of constructing elaborate vanity projects to honor the Matriarchs and their *greatness*, the people could have engaged their time and resources in other enterprises, like interstellar defense. Thebes might not have fallen."

"As the web of history unfolds, it is easy to speculate on what might have been," Neith said mildly. "We imagine that only a few minor changes would output a much improved present. But taking a step back to look at a greater portion of the web, we understand that we cannot predict the impact any single action may have on the greater whole."

"Spare us your tired philosophizing, old woman," said Pakhet.

"Pakhet," chided Banka.

"What?"

"That was unnecessary and mean. You will apologize to the Matriarch, or I shall not forgive you."

Pakhet stared at Banka, then turned to the Matriarch. "I apologize."

"You are a descendant of the Cienciant," Atlas said to Neith.

"I am," said Neith.

"How does that help us?" asked Phoebe.

"Because of something the Cienciant said to the Prime shortly before they were separated," said Neith. "She asked him if Ciencia had ever had visitors from another planet. He replied 'No one can visit without a destination.'"

"What does that mean?" Reedy asked.

"It means Ciencia can't be found," said Pakhet. "It's a ghost system. It might as well not exist."

"Or it's a myth," muttered Phoebe.

"How can you know that?" Reedy asked Pakhet. "You *knew* about Ciencia?"

"I thought you said it was a state secret?" Ajax accused Neith.

"It was," said Neith. "I told Pakhet about Ciencia and the Globe of Heavens in order to convince her to accept the retrieval contract."

"You told me about the planet," said Pakhet. She turned to the Philadelphians. "She did not tell me she was an alien."

"Do not use that vile term in my presence," said Banka.

"Why didn't you tell the Titans?" Phoebe asked Neith.

"Because keeping the secret gave the Thebans an advantage," interjected Pallas.

"An advantage for what?" asked Ajax.

"To use us to get the Sphere," said Pallas.

The Thebans became silent. Ata squirmed in her chair.

"Is this true?" asked Phoebe.

"Of course it is," said Atlas. "It was part of the plan from the beginning, wasn't it? Once the Titans had trained us and sent us to search for the Sphere, Pakhet and friends would conveniently show up and tell us about Ciencia. That's why they miraculously showed up at Apollo's cabin."

"How did they find us?" Reedy asked.

"The translator," said Atlas. It was so obvious. Why hadn't he figured it out sooner? "When you first brought me to Titan, Banka mentioned it couldn't accurately translate everything she was telling me. I didn't think of it at the time, but since then I've assumed you must have embedded a tiny device somewhere in our heads. It must have tracking functions as well."

"Then why didn't Apollo remove it?" asked Ajax.

"Because the translators we gave you were designed to appear like standard Titan translators which neither transmit nor receive data," said Banka. "We fashioned them after a model very familiar to both Titans and Olympians."

"Fortunately for all of us, Apollo has always been exceedingly over-confident," said Ata.

"When the Olympians scanned you for tracking signals, they couldn't have found any," said Diana. "The modified translators were programmed to commence broadcasting your location once you had finished training at the Academy."

"We did not know if any of you were allowed to live," said Banka. "The Olympians have a longstanding tradition of enslaving one third of those they conquer, but they have made exceptions before. We couldn't risk a rescue without knowing where to find you." Her voice dropped. "Or knowing how many of you were alive. All we could do was wait for the tracking function to activate."

"They activated just four days ago," said Ata.

"Then you know if Homer is alive?" asked Pallas.

"Yes," said Banka. "He and four others are also alive."

"Then why did we leave them behind?" Reedy asked angrily.

"Because they're scattered," said Atlas. "We were together. They had one shot at a rescue. It had to be us, right?"

"Yes," said Banka.

"In fact, two of the others have been taken to other planets," said Diana.

"Where?" said Reedy. "We must go after them."

"Their trackers are no longer functioning," said Ata. "Shortly after we rescued you, their trackers went silent."

"Does that...does it mean they're dead?" asked Pallas.

"We don't know what it means," said Pakhet.

The room was silent for a moment. Atlas thought about Homer. *Apollo said Delphi had ordered us killed. Did that order include the Betas? Why wouldn't it? One hundred. Ninety-seven. Ninety-four. Ninety-one. Eighty-eight. Eighty-five...*

"Thank you again for rescuing us," said Phoebe. "But if we can't find Ciencia, why does any of it matter? Why rescue us?"

"If you didn't interrupt me so often, you would already know the answer," said Neith.

"I am sorry," said Phoebe.

"It's not only your fault," said Neith. She cast an irritated glance towards Pakhet. "As I was saying...when the Prime learned that Ciencia couldn't be found, she asked the Cienciant how he and his colleagues would ever get home. He told her, 'Ciencia knows her children and makes herself known to them.'"

"So we need to take you with us?" Reedy sighed, irritated. "Great."

"Oh no. Not at all. I'm far too old."

"Then what are we supposed to do?" asked Ajax. "If we need a Cienciant to find Ciencia, but you won't come with us, how will we find it?"

"And how will we even know where to look?" asked Reedy. "The Galaxy is far too big."

"I know someone who knows which region of the Galaxy to search," Pakhet said judiciously. "He just needs to be properly persuaded."

"Taco," whispered Atlas. But how would Taco know where to look? He *was* very old. And he did say he'd been to many far-flung parts of the Galaxy and had heard many of the Celestial Sphere myths. Maybe Taco discovered something about Ciencia during his travels? But would he tell the Thebans after they'd kept him captive for so long?

Atlas suddenly realized why Taco had been captured and held by the Thebans. For the same purpose that he and the rest of the Philadelphians had been abducted.

"Restore Thebes," Atlas said quietly.

"What?" asked Pallas, leaning close.

"From the very beginning." Atlas continued under his breath. "That's what they've wanted us to do."

"What? I didn't hear."

"Nothing. I'll tell you later." Atlas stood and walked towards Neith. "We have interrupted you again, Madame Matriarch. I am sorry for that. We are very anxious to get started. So, can you answer this one last question? How do we find Ciencia without you? How will the unfindable planet reveal herself to us?"

"Simple," said Neith. "Take my great-granddaughter with you."

Atlas scrunched his face and frowned, confused. He scratched his chin. "I thought the Prime Matriarch had no heir?"

"I do not. My granddaughter does not deserve the position, nor would she accept it were it offered to her. In truth, she does not know she is my great-granddaughter."

"No? Why not?" asked Phoebe.

"For her protection, of course," said Neith. "And because it was a state secret."

"Inconvenient facts always are," Reedy huffed.

"Where can we find your great-granddaughter?" asked Pallas, reproving Reedy with a sidelong glare.

"You already have found her," said Neith. "She is right here."

Neith pointed at Pakhet.

CHAPTER 25

"Better let me talk to him," Atlas said.

Banka tapped the pattern that unlocked the last door to the detention bay. "I have never been unkind to him. He has no reason to distrust me."

"You're part of the crew that's holding him prisoner. Kind or not, he will not want to speak with you."

"You may be right. I will remain outside."

"No, we should both be there, for transparency. I'll talk."

"As you wish," said Banka.

The last detention bay door slid open and Atlas stepped through. He turned to Banka. "Pakhet didn't know she was related to Neith, did she?"

"That is insignificant," Banka said.

"It *is* significant if it affects her state of mind as we search for Ciencia. I can't have her distracted, even if she is just the key that opens Ciencia for us."

"Pakhet is not just a key."

"Of course not. But as far as this mission is concerned, that's the only reason she's coming with us."

"We will all be with you, for protection," said Banka.

"For *your* protection, you, Ata, and Diana will stay here on

Titan. If you have to do something, make a plan to rescue Aura." Atlas began walking towards Taco's cell.

"Is this really the best place to talk about this?" Banka asked.

"I asked a simple question. Did Pakhet know she was related to Neith? Yes or no?"

Banka stopped Atlas with a touch of his shoulder. "If I tell you, that is the last we will discuss it?"

"For now."

"No, she did not know. None of us knew. We assumed the Olympians had killed the entire Prime lineage, save the Matriarch. Neith's revelation, if true, would explain a few things."

"Such as?"

"Pakhet's stubbornness, for example." She smiled wryly.

Atlas laughed.

"What is so funny?" a nearby voice said. "Ah! Atlas Nodzhor-doraneetheen! You have returned to see your old friend, Taco. What luck you caught me. I was just about to step out for an errand." Taco chuckled and made some rattling sounds against the cell bars. "Then we would have missed each other. Fate, it seems, had other plans. And how are you, my friend?"

Atlas smiled as he approached Taco's cell. The Vitrian was invisible. Atlas couldn't even find his smudge. "Hello, Taco. Good to *not* see you again."

"Ha! Clever as always, of course. It is good to see you, though I am troubled to see you in the company of one of those horrible women."

"Don't be rude, Taco. Banka is very kind. And she's a friend of mine."

"Your parents need to have a talk with you about picking better friends," Taco said. "Of course, that is impossible thanks to your friend here—who, I will remind you, helped kidnap you."

"We've moved past that," said Atlas.

"You forgive easily."

"It's not really your business, but the Thebans have saved my life and the lives of my Philadelphian friends several times," Atlas said. *Brave Lanta*. "One of them died while protecting me. And another may also have died or been captured by Olympian assassins while defending us."

"That is unfortunate," said Taco. "We have our disagreements, obviously, but I do not wish the Theban women dead." Taco was silent for a moment. His smudge appeared briefly, but then disappeared again. "You are right. There is no need to be rude. I apologize, Miss Banka."

"Just Banka. And I forgive you," Banka said.

"Right, you are the one that forgives everyone. Do you genuinely forgive them, or do you only say that you do?"

Banka smiled.

"Listen, Taco. We need your help—your expertise," Atlas said. "We need to get to a system called Ciencia."

"I am afraid I cannot help you," said Taco. "I have never heard of Ciencia."

"Most people haven't," Atlas said. "It's a hidden system, shielded from detection and intrusion, apparently."

"If you cannot detect it, how do you know it is there?" Taco asked.

"We've heard the tales about an ancient Vitrian spacecraft test," said Banka. "It resulted in the craft and her pilot being instantly transported over a thousand light-years off course."

Taco laughed loudly. "As I have told Pakhet many times, that is nothing more than an old folktale of my people."

"We know it is more than that."

"Oh you do, do you? Well, my dear, then you know more than I do."

"With all due respect, General Orsetulidex, you know more than you're sharing," Atlas said.

Taco took a moment to answer. "There is no respect due to General Orsetulidex." He paused. "Would you mind telling me where you heard that name?"

"It's a long story," Atlas said. "The short version is I met another Vitrian by the name of Piquamamanturuftix Elpurtistazug. I called him Pickle. He told me about General Orsetulidex."

"Then you know why the General deserves no respect."

"I know one side of the story. I don't know yours. Nor do I need to hear it, honestly. Everyone has a past."

"You are assuming I am the General. I told you before that Tachonamewaruts was a very common name on my planet."

"You did."

"Then why do you think I am the General? There are more than a few Vitrians who bear the shame of that name, though by no fault of their families other than succumbing to popular naming trends." Taco sounded slightly agitated.

"You *are* General Orsetulidex," Banka said. "That is the reason Pakhet captured you and has held you here." She took a step forward and stared as if she could see Taco.

Do Thebans have ultraviolet sensitive vision? Atlas watched for a clue that Banka could actually see Taco, and wasn't just trying to intimidate him. Atlas couldn't decide one way or another.

"She did not *capture* me. I came willingly. It seemed appropriate, considering I deserved far worse."

"Do not lie," said Banka. "I watched her capture you."

"Had I not wished to be captured, I assure you, you would still be mourning Pakhet."

Banka grimaced angrily. She closed her eyes, breathed deeply, and grabbed the bars of another cell—the one Atlas had occupied. "I forgive you, Vitrian. But I do not forget. And I will never allow you to hurt her."

After a few seconds, Banka relaxed and stepped back. Atlas wished Taco was visible. It was hard to endure the silence without being able to read Taco's emotional state.

"Elpurtistazug?" Taco asked. "He related to Colonel Elpurtistazug?"

"I believe that was his father," said Atlas.

"So, he survived. That's more than most. And where is his son now?"

"He runs the dispensary in a mine on Olympus. He and I became friends."

"Then he is a slave," said Taco. "What a shame. It would have been better for his father to die fighting the Olympians than for his generations to end up as their slave."

"So, there was a war between the Vitrians and Olympians?"

"With whom have the Olympians *not* waged war? Ever since they destroyed Thebes, they have believed themselves destined to rule the Galaxy. But they *will not* rule Vitros."

"You defeated them?"

"Hardly," said Taco. "More of a stalemate. A very, very costly stalemate." His voice trailed off.

"Here is your chance to strike a blow against the Olympians," Atlas said. "Tell us the location of the failed trans-light test."

"Now you say it was a trans-light test?" Taco said. "As I said before, you seem to know much more than I do about my people's space-faring history."

"General Orsetulidex!" Banka snapped. "We don't have time for these games. Your rank afforded you full clearance to know the complete details of the test and the follow-up investigation."

"There is no need to yell. Just because you cannot see me does not mean I cannot hear you." Taco's tone became serious. "Release me. I will tell you everything I know."

"That is not possible," Banka said. "But I am sorry for losing my temper. Please forgive me."

"If you do not release me, then I am afraid that we are done talking," said Taco. "I am tired of imprisonment and am ready to rejoin *polite* society."

"Taco, please tell us," Atlas pleaded. "We need to find the hidden system. It's the only way to stop the Olympians."

Taco didn't respond. After waiting a full five minutes in silence, Atlas turned and walked to the detention bay exit. Banka followed.

"Why can't we release him?" asked Atlas. "I trust him."

"Pakhet does not. We will figure out another way," said Banka as the last security door slid shut behind them.

"I thought he would tell me," Atlas said. "What a waste of time."

"We as yet have an advantage. The Olympians don't know they need a Cienciant to find Ciencia."

"Unless the Cienciants left descendants on other systems as well," said Atlas. "If they studied as many planets as Neith's story claims, I doubt Thebes was their only indiscretion. And not all of them may have been as good at keeping secrets as Neith and her ancestors."

"That is a possibility," said Banka.

They walked in silence. Atlas looked at Banka and then away. Then he looked at her again.

"Is there something on your mind?" asked Banka.

"I wanted to…um…thank you…for avenging Lanta's death."

"Oh," said Banka. "It was necessary in order to—"

The lights in the corridor went out. Absolute darkness enveloped Atlas and Banka.

"Atlas?" Banka said. Her voice sounded worried.

"I'm okay," said Atlas. "Doesn't this thing have emergency lights?"

"It has three emergency light redundancies, each with isolated power systems. They should have…unless the whole ship…Stay here. I'll find out what's going on."

"I'll come with you," Atlas said.

"It will be safer if you *stay here*. Just in case…" Banka's nimble footsteps echoed down the corridor.

Alone, Atlas suddenly panicked. *They've found us. They disabled the ship and now we're sitting ducks.* His heart pounded in his ears and his breathing became shallow and rapid.

One series of emergency lighting finally engaged, illuminating the corridor floor.

Have to find the others. Now! Before the Olympians find them. Where are they? They could be anywhere. So many rooms on this ship.

Atlas stopped and kicked a door. Maybe it was the one leading to the preparation room. The beginning of everything. His hands began to shake, so he pounded on the door. I'm tired! So tired of all this! Didn't ask for any of it. I just want to go home. Please, please, please let me go home.

"Pallas? Ajax? Pakhet!" He continued bashing on the door. "Reedy! Ata! Phoebe? Diana!" Atlas slammed his whole body against the door in desperation. Then again. And again. Altas let himself slide to the floor. Sweat poured down his face. By now, it was too late. All his friends were dead, and he'd be next. *Let it be quick. I hate the Olympians. Forever.*

No! No, wait…Why disable the Theban ship? Blowing it up would be more effective, if they want us dead. Disabling the ship means they're attempting to recapture us. That means there's an opportunity to escape. My friends are alive! We'll escape. As soon as I find them, we'll escape. Like we did before.

"Atlas!" Reedy yelled.

Atlas looked up to see Pallas and the rest of his friends running towards him.

"Get up! Hurry," said Pallas.

Before Atlas could respond, Ajax grabbed him by the shoulders and heaved him onto his feet.

"We need to get to the rear exit," Ajax said. "Let's go!"

Atlas and the others followed close behind.

"We're surrounded," said Phoebe. "There's at least thirty Olympians outside."

"How'd they get so many on-planet?" Atlas asked.

"How should we know?" said Reedy. "Does it really matter?"

Pallas ran up alongside Atlas. She met his gaze briefly and offered a weak smile, then accelerated past him. They passed the detention bay, and then a door with bright and colorful warning symbols on it. *Must be the fusion reactor*, Atlas thought. *No, Taco said there was a bathroom beyond the detention bay.* Seconds later, the corridor terminated in a dead-end.

"I don't understand," said Phoebe. "The purple one said there was an exit back here."

"Her name is Banka," said Atlas.

Ajax pressed his hands against the wall. "I can't find it. It's supposed to be here."

"Are you sure you heard her right?" asked Pallas.

"Of course I'm sure," defended Phoebe. "She said it was at the very back of the ship. A secret hatch."

"There's nothing here," said Ajax.

"Maybe we missed it," said Reedy. "What about that door back there?"

"No wait," said Atlas. "What's that?" He pointed at the floor underneath Reedy's feet. "Right there." A small metal ring glinted in the emergency lighting.

Reedy stooped down to examine it. She touched the ring and it swiveled up to meet her hand. She looked behind her and adjusted her feet outside the floor panel. "I can't move it. It won't budge."

"Let Ajax try," said Phoebe.

"Try turning it," said Ajax. "I bet you have to release the locking mechanism."

Reedy tried clockwise first, but it wouldn't budge. She got it to move a few millimeters when she turned it counter-clockwise, but no more.

"Try pushing down as you turn," said Pallas.

"I am," said Reedy.

"I told you to let Ajax try," said Phoebe. "He's the strongest."

"Try pulling up," said Ajax.

Reedy looked at the others and shook her head in frustration. But she didn't yield her position. Instead, Reedy stomped her right foot, then her left, clapped her hands together, and squatted. She jammed as many fingers as she could through the ring, tightened her core with a deep breath, and pressed with her legs. Her face grimaced and the tendons of her neck strained from the effort. "Aaaaggghhh!"

There was a loud series of clicks, followed by a whoosh of air as the floor panel fell out from beneath Reedy, sending her tumbling backwards. Ajax tried to catch her, but she knocked him against the corridor wall. Reedy stood up, laughed, and helped Ajax to his feet. Triumphantly, she twirled the ring around her finger.

Atlas looked down into the opening. Slivers of sunlight from beyond the rear of the ship revealed the edge of the landing pad and the tall grass of the meadow beyond. The escape hatch had landed quietly on the grass. Atlas closed his eyes and tried to remember the first time he had arrived on Titan. *Which direction were we pointing? How was the old slaughterhouse foundation situated in the field?* "We're near the woods, I think."

"The Thebans are trying to draw the Olympians to them by defending the primary hatch," Pallas said.

"They'll think we're trying to escape through the secondary hatch," added Phoebe.

"With any luck they won't suspect this exit and there will only be a few Olympians for us to worry about," said Pallas.

"With any luck, there will be *more*," said Ajax. He smashed his fist into his open hand.

"I'll go first," said Atlas.

"You should let me go," said Ajax.

"No, I'll go," Atlas insisted. "I'll wait for you before advancing. The old engine nozzles should provide enough cover for three of us. Once Pallas is down, we go. Straight into the woods. Only engage hostiles if they're directly in your path. Reedy and Phoebe, you'll have to drop down and follow us out immediately. Stay close. We can't risk getting separated."

"What about the Thebans?" asked Reedy. "We can't leave them."

"We have no weapons." Ajax frowned. "With the power out, the doors to the armory are sealed. The Thebans only have what they carried."

"Get to the woods," said Atlas. "That's first." He stepped up to the opening in the floor and looked straight down. Half of the fallen floor hatch was illuminated by sunlight. *Better be quick about getting into the shadows once I drop.* "Watch your head as you go down." He stepped forward and dropped through the hole, landing on a dark corner of the floor panel. The panel shifted and slipped in the tall grass, flinging him against one of the engine nozzles. It rang like a loud, low church bell.

"Dammit!" Atlas said under his breath.

He recovered and pulled the floor panel out from under the opening. It was heavy and almost nine inches thick, but Atlas was able to slide it under another of the nozzles.

Ajax dropped down and quickly stepped into the little remaining shadow. Atlas held his hand up to signal Pallas to hold position. He sidled to the edge of the nozzles and peered out towards the woods. It was further than he remembered, but he didn't see any Olympians. He edged out slightly into the sunlight and looked as far to the left and right as he could.

"Two on each side," he whispered to Ajax. "They're not that close. If we're fast, we'll be past them before they can cut us off."

"Ranged or melee weapons?"

"Ranged. But I think they want us alive. Otherwise they would have blown us and the ship to hell. Their weapons will be set to non-lethal."

"Slower and less precise. We have the advantage," said Ajax.

Atlas nodded. "Ready." He signaled Pallas. She dropped immediately. "Go!"

"Reedy! Phoebe! Now!" Ajax hissed.

Pallas ran on Atlas's right and Ajax on his left. Atlas looked ahead, focused on the woods. *We have to make it. We will make it.* He heard yelling from the Olympians on both sides, and then the loud, high-pitched hiss of non-lethal energy bolts zipping around them. *Strange how much louder non-lethals are than lethal bolts. Almost to the woods. Just a few more seconds.*

Ajax pulled slightly ahead of Atlas. He turned to look back at Reedy and Phoebe. "Reedy, duck!" He peeled off and ran back.

Atlas and Pallas stopped less than twenty feet from the safety of the woods. They turned and crouched to see what had happened. One of the Olympians engaged Phoebe in hand-to-hand combat. Reedy lay still in the grass. Three other Olympians were closing in on the two girls. Ajax was too far away. The Olympians would get there first.

"Let's go!" said Atlas. He and Pallas rushed to their friends' aid.

The second Olympian was almost upon the two girls. He raised his weapon to fire at Phoebe. At that range he wouldn't miss. As he put the weapon to his shoulder, the Olympian's head snapped sharply to the side and he dropped to the ground.

"Wooo! That's right!" Ajax yelled. He hurled several more rocks at the other advancing Olympians, scooping the stones from the ground as he ran and letting them fly in one fluid motion. The other two Olympians crouched and fired at Ajax.

"Help Phoebe," Atlas said, as he scooped up a rock and hurled it at the crouched Olympians.

Pallas nodded and sprinted towards Phoebe.

Atlas continued to hurl rocks as he ran. He wasn't as accurate as Ajax, but he hit close enough to the Olympians to draw some of their fire. One of his stones hit an Olympian in the shoulder, just in time to disrupt his aim as he fired a shot that narrowly missed Ajax.

Then Ajax was upon them. From close range, he hurled his last fist-sized rock at the furthest one, hitting the Olympian squarely in the chest, causing him to drop his weapon and stumble backwards. In the same motion, Ajax leapt into the air and tackled the other Olympian.

Atlas ran at the Olympian who'd caught the rock in the chest. The Olympian picked up his energy rifle and leveled it at Ajax. Atlas screamed and lunged at the Olympian, pushing the rifle into the air as it fired. Atlas fell to the ground and rolled away.

From his back, Atlas kipped back to his feet and rushed the Olympian. He swatted the Olympian's rifle to the side and punched him in the throat. The Olympian dropped the weapon and grasped at his throat with both hands.

Atlas scooped up the rifle and aimed it at the Olympian. "This is for Oliver. And Lanta." *Brave Lanta.* He switched the rifle to lethal and pressed his finger against the trigger.

"More incoming!" Ajax yelled.

Atlas removed his finger from the trigger and lowered the rifle. Several other Olympians ran towards them. They were almost in range. He looked around. Ajax carried Reedy over his shoulder and was running to the woods. Phoebe and Pallas collected weapons from the downed Olympians.

"Atlas! Let's go!" called Pallas. She carried two rifles in her arms, and had a metal staff of some sort slung across her back. "Hurry."

Atlas looked back at the Olympian, now on his knees, still clutching his throat. *For Lanta*, he thought. Atlas raised his rifle, but then lowered it again and switched it back to non-lethal. He turned and ran after Pallas and Phoebe.

Soon, Atlas and his friends were underneath the cover of the Titan woods. Ajax stooped over Reedy, trying to revive her by patting her cheeks. Atlas watched as the Olympian reinforcements approached their fallen comrades. Pallas offered one of the rifles to Ajax, but when he wouldn't take it, she laid it on the ground next to him.

"At least we know how there are so many of them," said Pallas. "These are older Olympian weapons. It's another sleeper cell. Probably several."

"Lucky for us they're older weapons," said Atlas. "Didn't Reedy say something about only Olympians being able to use their modern weaponry?"

"Yes," said Ajax, still trying to revive Reedy.

"Here, you take this one." Pallas handed the other rifle to Phoebe.

"No good for me," said Phoebe. "Arm's broken." She held up her left forearm. It was twisted and discolored. "Same damn arm," she laughed and pointed towards the metal staff Pallas had slung on her back. "That thing packs a wallop." She pulled a side-arm out from the waist band of her pants. "Anyway, I got this."

"That's it, Reedy. No, don't get up," said Ajax.

Reedy brushed Ajax's hand aside and sat up anyway. "I'm fine."

"You were hit by a non-lethal," said Ajax. "No blood."

"Then I'm not dead. Let me up."

The reinforcements had reached the Olympian that Atlas had spared. He was writhing on the ground, desperate for air. One of the reinforcements raised his weapon at his comrade and fired. The injured Olympian jolted violently and was still.

"We need to go," said Atlas.

"Alright, let's go," said Ajax. He tried to pick Reedy up.

She pushed him away. "No." She lifted herself slowly to her feet, leaning on a tree for support. "I can carry myself."

"Here." Pallas handed Reedy the other rifle. "Can you manage?"

"What about you?" Reedy asked as she took the rifle.

"I have this," Pallas said, indicating the metal staff. She pulled a side arm out of her waistband. "And this."

"I'll hang back and slow them down," said Atlas. "Stay close together, but not too close. Wait for me at the road." He turned and fired at the approaching Olympians. "Hurry! Go!"

Reedy trotted after Pallas and Phoebe, but stumbled after a few steps. Ajax rushed to her side, but she pushed him away again. She started trotting again, but slowly, and with a bit of a limp in her right leg.

The reinforcements had slowed as a result of Atlas's cover fire, but they weren't stopped. They crouched low in formation and fired back as they advanced upon him. The incessant barrage of energy bolts prevented Atlas from aiming properly when he exposed himself to fire back.

Atlas fired six shots in rapid succession and ran deeper into the woods. Energy bolts buzzed all around him. Trees exploded into splinters. Those weren't non-lethals anymore. *I need to get deeper. Stay low. Zigzag around the trees.*

After leading the Olympians deeper into the woods, Atlas swung back towards the road. Several minutes later, he was back with his friends. The sounds of the fight between the Thebans and the Olympians could be heard in the distance.

"Keep an eye out," Atlas said. "I tried to lead 'em into the woods, but I don't know if they saw me change direction."

"I got it," said Ajax. He stood up with his rifle and took a position behind a pair of trees grown closely together.

"What now?" asked Reedy.

"We help the Thebans," said Atlas.

"Of course," said Phoebe. "We can't get into Ciencia without Pakhet."

"And we can't find it without Taco," said Atlas.

"He didn't tell you where it was?" asked Pallas.

"No, he didn't." Atlas looked down the road towards the Theban landing pad. "Not yet."

"We better move, then," said Pallas.

Atlas nodded. "Ajax, we're moving out. Watch our rear for a minute, then join us."

Ajax gave a thumbs up as he scanned the woods for Olympians. "Reedy?"

"I'm fine," she huffed.

The Philadelphians ran along the road, just within the protection of the trees. Phoebe steadied Reedy as they ran. The sounds of the fighting grew louder and louder. Then everything was silent.

"Oh *no*," said Pallas.

Atlas sprinted past her and didn't slow down until he got to the edge of the woods. His heart fell as he took in the scene.

The Thebans clustered together near the ship's sealed hatch with their hands in the air and their weapons on the ground. Several defensive energy barriers were scattered in front of them, sputtering and fading.

Olympian soldiers in a semi-circle formation advanced on the Thebans. They kept their weapons trained on the Theban women, as if begging for an excuse to shoot. Multiple motionless Olympian bodies lay strewn across the field and concrete.

Another figure strode past the cautiously advancing Olympians and into the middle of the semicircle, facing the Thebans.

Dressed in black. Hooded. Styx.

CHAPTER 26

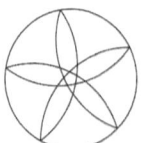

"WE'RE TOO LATE!" lamented Phoebe. "They're dead."

Ajax ran up behind the others. "Nothing behind us," he said.

"They're not dead yet," said Atlas. "Reedy, cover our six." *Brave Lanta.* "I'm not going to let them die." He picked up his rifle and left the cover of the woods.

"Now we're talking!" cried Ajax as he darted after Atlas.

Pallas and Phoebe caught up with them and Ajax signaled to fan out and surround the Olympians. Pallas and Ajax took the left. Atlas and Phoebe went right. The four ran as quietly and quickly as possible, weapons raised.

The Olympians remained unaware of the Philadelphians' advance. Atlas counted twenty. *Five for each of us.* Atlas lusted for revenge, but checked his rifle again to make sure it was set to non-lethal. Couldn't risk catching the Thebans in the cross-fire.

The Philadelphians were nearly within range for Pallas and Phoebe's side-arms. The Thebans had seen them but kept their eyes directed on Styx.

The assassin stood in front of Pakhet, obscuring her from view. Atlas could hear Styx speaking, but couldn't distinguish the words. Styx viciously back-handed Pakhet, knocking her to the ground. Pakhet quickly stood back up and faced Styx. Her helmet was gone.

Multicolored scars criss-crossed most of Pakhet's face and scalp. One eye was completely scarred over, and part of her lips were missing, revealing missing teeth. She spat at Styx, who grabbed her around the throat and lifted her high, turning her from side to side, seemingly reveling in Pakhet's disfigurement.

Banka let her eyes meet the approaching Philadelphians—only for a second, but long enough to be noticed. An Olympian turned to see Pallas barreling down on him.

The Olympian yelled, but his warning was cut short by an energy bolt from Pallas's pistol. Atlas fired three shots from his rifle and three more Olympians fell to the ground. The other Olympians returned fire and Atlas dropped and rolled to avoid their attack. He popped back to his feet and strafed as he fired.

Two other Olympians succumbed to Phoebe's pistol. She continued shooting as she ran towards the far side of the Theban ship. With her left arm broken, Phoebe had to rely on her less dominant hand. Many of her shots missed their mark. Phoebe pressed against the ship within a shallow hollow in the fuselage as three Olympians began advancing on her position.

Atlas brought down two more Olympians and engaged two others in a firefight from behind a boulder. Pallas and Ajax fought four Olympians in close combat. Two others lay near them. Pallas threw her empty pistol and hit one of the Olympians in the face. She drew her staff and connected with the gut of another. Ajax must have also run out of ammo because he was using his rifle as a club.

Where are the Thebans? Atlas fired two shots as he peeked around the 'boulder. Diana and Banka lay sprawled across the concrete, crawling below the crossfire towards their discarded weapons. Ata crouched near the open hatch of the ship, behind the only remaining energy barrier. *Pakhet?*

Styx dragged an unconscious—or immobilized—Pakhet behind her as she tried to escape in the confusion. One of the Olympians advancing on Phoebe pulled back to cover Styx's escape, pinning Atlas behind the boulder.

Where is Styx going? The woods? Atlas concentrated his fire on the Olympian covering Styx, but after a few shots his rifle started beeping. Energy depleted. *Dammit!* He was trapped behind the boulder, taking fire from two sides. The boulder trembled with every energy bolt impact. Splintered stone chips rained down on him. *How much more can it take?*

Suddenly, Atlas heard energy bolts buzzing over his head in the opposite direction. He looked up to see Reedy steadily limping towards him, firing at the Olympians. Her face was calm, almost serene, but her eyes moved from target to target with a furious intensity. She lowered her weapon as she reached Atlas and collapsed next to him behind the boulder.

Atlas took her rifle and sprung to his feet, ready to fire. The shooting had stopped. All the Olympians were down. Diana and Ata rushed to help Pallas with an injured Ajax. Atlas lowered his rifle. Banka ran towards him—no, to the left of him. *Pakhet!* Atlas wheeled around towards where Styx had been escaping. Pakhet lay sprawled on the ground. Atlas ran to her.

Further on, Styx was running away. A small trans-light craft appeared in front of her. She tripped and fell hard, but nimbly rolled onto her back and raised her arms as if to fend someone off. Then, the empty air lifted Styx by her feet and tossed her twenty feet away. She lay there still for a moment.

Ajax stood and ran towards Styx's fallen form, one arm hanging limply at his side. Well before he got to her, Styx leapt up and violently slashed the air with a long knife. The air let out a blood-curdling howl and began to bleed profusely. Styx hobbled and skipped towards her ship.

"No!" yelled Atlas.

Diana and Ata ran after Styx, but they were too far away. Atlas was closer, but he ran directly for the bleeding air which had collapsed onto the grass and was becoming less and less invisible. With a flash of light, Styx's ship was gone.

"Taco." Atlas dropped to his knees beside the Vitrian.

"Atlas, my friend," wheezed Taco. He smiled weakly, then

winced. His body fluttered between visibility and transparency. He held his stomach with both hands. Blood gushed over his naked stomach from beneath his fingers.

"Get Dr. Circe," Atlas called. "Quickly! Taco's been injured."

Ata turned and ran back to the ship. Diana knelt to examine the wound. She tore a strip of her shirt and tried to press it against Taco's stomach.

"Do not bother," Taco sputtered. "There is nothing...can...be done. It is...okay."

"Dr. Circe is the best," said Atlas. "She's saved my life twice. She will save yours."

"There is...no time. I must tell you...where to find the... hidden system."

"Don't worry about that," said Atlas. Tears rolled down his cheeks. "You'll take us there when you're better."

Pallas, Ajax, Reedy, and Phoebe arrived at Atlas's side. Reedy shook her head when she saw the wound and touched Atlas's shoulder. Pallas began to cry.

"I must keep...my promise."

"What promise?" asked Atlas.

"I...am...freed. I keep...promise."

"Don't give *up*. Stay with me. Keep your promise later."

"Black hole. Near center...of Galaxy. Not black...hole. Not... center of...Galaxy." His body had become nearly completely visible. One foot was severely maimed, a painful, ancient wound.

"Shhh!" said Atlas. "Just rest. The doctor will be here soon."

"Don't get...close. Vitrian ship...bounced."

"It bounced?" asked Phoebe.

Reedy elbowed Phoebe in the ribs.

"One hundred...light-years outside...the Galaxy," wheezed Taco. "Bounced. Many generations...ago. Barely more than...story now. But true. Best tales...always true."

"Yes, of course," said Atlas.

"Be safe...Atlas. Be good. Be...happy. Be...compas...sionate. Be...Be...Be..." Taco let out a slow sigh and was still.

Pallas stooped and closed Taco's eyes. She stood and placed her hand on the back of Atlas's head. He leaned against her leg and wept.

A few minutes later, a large Titan security force arrived and began processing the scene. Atlas remained at Taco's side until the coroner had to prepare the body for transport.

"I'm sorry about your friend," Phoebe said. She tentatively reached out with her good arm and put her hand on his shoulder, then withdrew it. "How did you know him?"

Atlas stood up and watched as the Titans loaded Taco's body onto a transport. *Finally, a flying car in real life. How odious.* "I met him when the Thebans first brought me here. On the ship. He was in the cell next to mine. We talked. Didn't you meet him?"

"No," said Phoebe. "The other cells were empty when I was brought here. Though I suppose he may have been invisible." She stifled a frown. "Guess I wasn't worth talking to."

"I'm sure that wasn't it," said Atlas.

"No, it's the truth. I *wasn't* worth talking to back then. I didn't like me. Why would anyone else?"

"Your parents?"

Phoebe shook her head. "Nah, they're the career type. Real workaholics, you know. It's cliché, but that's how they are."

"What about your friends?"

"I didn't know you back then." Phoebe shrugged and smiled, but Atlas could see the pain in her eyes. "I'm an annoying know-it-all. No one likes those."

"Well, I think you're worth talking to and I like you fine."

"I still think you're a pain in the butt," said Reedy. She walked up behind them, apparently recovered completely. She wrapped her arms around Phoebe from behind and lifted her up.

Phoebe laughed. "Careful of the arm—and thanks." She turned back to Atlas. "I feel like a selfish idiot, though. Your friend died, and I somehow made this moment about me."

"Just things we should have talked about before now, but didn't have the time," said Atlas.

"We don't have much time for it now either," said Reedy. "We're needed back at the Academy."

"By whom?" asked Atlas.

"I'm not sure," said Reedy. "One of the security officers said we needed to get there as soon as possible."

"I'm not ever going back to that graveyard," Phoebe said.

Atlas looked at Phoebe and thought of Oliver. Penny. Nerissa. Theo and Eugenio. "No. We're not going back there," said Atlas. "Our priority is to find Ciencia."

"And how will you get to Ciencia?" Banka asked as she approached the Philadelphians. "Not on our ship, unfortunately. Ata says it may never run again."

"I'm sorry to hear that," said Reedy.

"That's extremely inconvenient," said Phoebe.

"I am sorry, but we were never going to take your ship," said Atlas. "How's Pakhet?"

Banka smiled. "She is being a very difficult patient for Dr. Circe right now."

"Poor Dr. Circe," said Reedy. "At least that means Pakhet is okay."

"Don't worry about Dr. Circe," said Atlas. "I feel sorry for Pakhet."

Banka laughed softly. "I suppose Pakhet will learn the hard way."

"Yes, I suppose she will." Atlas grinned as he imagined Dr. Circe expertly prodding Pakhet's every annoyance, both physical and psychological. *Taco would have liked to see that*, he thought. "Banka, we need a ship."

"Yes, you do."

"Any ideas where we can get one?"

"Perhaps you should consider attending the meeting at the Academy."

"No," said Atlas. "Like Phoebe said, it's nothing more than a graveyard. Whoever it is wants to talk with us, they can come here. Or meet us somewhere else."

"As you wish," said Banka. She nodded and went to speak to a security officer.

Atlas watched as the officer looked over at them, then back at Banka and nodded. He stepped aside and spoke into his glass.

"You think we'll ever get our glasses back?" Atlas asked. "First week in the mine, I kept looking at my wrist out of habit."

"I'm not sure why we'd need them," said Phoebe. "Not anymore. Not for what we're doing."

"Why not?" asked Reedy. "You don't think they could be useful in finding Ciencia."

"No, I don't," said Phoebe. "It's a hidden system. Unfindable. The best clue we have is based on an old folktale."

Atlas was annoyed. "Taco said it's near the center of the Galaxy, that it looks like a black hole. He was a General. He knew what—"

"That's still thousands of cubic light-years to search," said Phoebe. "Little glass toys won't help us."

"So, you think we should give up?" Reedy asked Phoebe.

"Of course not," said Phoebe. "I just meant to point out all we've accomplished in the last two months. We did all the hard work by ourselves—nothing but our wits and intuition to help us. We don't need those silly rectangles on our wrists."

"Sorry I brought it up," Atlas said.

"Well, I'd like to have one again," said Reedy. "There were a lot of times during the last few months that my glass could have been very useful."

"Did you forget that the Olympians hijacked them and lead us directly into a trap?" Phoebe said.

"That is a good point," said Atlas.

Reedy glared at him.

"Anyway, we have more important things to worry about." Atlas nodded towards Banka, who was returning from the security officer. "Why won't they speak to us directly?" he asked Banka.

"They are intimidated. And perhaps a bit afraid. They can't

believe that you children killed and captured so many Olympians by yourselves."

"Killed?" Atlas felt his stomach turn to ice. *But we used non-lethals.* "How many did we *kill*?"

"Eighteen dead. Four by us, fourteen by you," said Banka. "The rest captured, except for that coward, Styx."

Fourteen dead. Too many for one person, or two people. Am I the only one that hasn't taken life? Atlas looked at Reedy and Phoebe. Why hadn't it messed them up? How were they able to carry on a normal conversation? Atlas couldn't process that right now.

"Why did Styx try to take Pakhet captive?" he asked.

"Styx wanted information," Banka said. "Pakhet told her we didn't have any. Styx didn't believe her."

"That's all?" Something didn't seem right about Banka's explanation. Too simple.

"That's all Pakhet would say. Although, there was something else strange."

"What?" Atlas asked.

"When that coward shamed Pakhet by removing her helmet, something…I don't know. It was as if she was surprised. I do not know why. I can't imagine a vile creature like Styx would be shocked by the marks of suffering Pakhet bears."

"No, I don't think so," said Atlas. This troubled him too.

"The security officer reports that an alternate location is acceptable," Banka said. "I apologize for allowing myself to become distracted."

"No worries, Banka," said Reedy.

"Where? What location?" asked Phoebe.

"Neith's house."

"Not *her* again," moaned Phoebe. "She drives me crazy."

"That will be fine," said Atlas.

"What?" said Phoebe.

"Thank you, Banka. Please give Pakhet our condolences," said Atlas.

"Condolences?"

"Yes, for having to put up with Dr. Circe."

Banka smiled. "I will tell her." She nodded and left.

"Why do we have to go to Neith's house?" said Phoebe. "That uppity old hag drives me crazy."

"You already said that," said Atlas.

"And don't call people old hags," said Reedy. "It's rude and disrespectful."

Phoebe frowned. "I'm sorry, but I don't like her. She's so elitist and self-important, all because of who her ancestors were. I bet she's never worked a day in her life."

"You don't have to like her," said Atlas. "I don't care for her much either. But I trust Banka. And we need a trans-light ship. I don't think there are any other options. We're meeting the Titans at Neith's house."

"How's your arm?" Reedy asked Phoebe.

"Fine," said Phoebe. She lifted it and winced. "I should probably see if it's my turn with Dr. Circe yet."

"I'll go with you," Reedy said. "I'm going to ask her to replace my translator, anyway. We all should, so we can't be tracked again."

"Good idea," said Atlas.

The two girls left Atlas staring over the field where Taco had uttered his last words.

Pallas approached Atlas from the cluster of security vehicles, her metal staff slung across her back. She favored her right leg as she walked towards him.

"Are you alright?" Atlas asked.

Pallas nodded. "Just a mild sprain. Nothing to worry about."

"Ajax?"

"He's resting. The energy bolt missed the bone and major arteries. He'll have limited range of motion for a few hours, maybe a day. But other than that, he'll be fine."

"Good." Atlas rubbed his eyes with the palms of his hands and yawned. "Reedy thinks we should have Dr. Circe replace our translators."

"That's a good idea, but it might take a while."

"That's fine," Atlas yawned again. "We're meeting some Titans at Neith's house once we're done here. Hopefully they'll give us a ship."

"They'll try to send chaperones," Pallas said. "They'll want to make sure we don't keep the Sphere to ourselves."

"I know."

"We can't let them take possession of the Sphere."

"I know."

"Good."

Atlas grinned. He reached out and grabbed Pallas's hand. "I'm glad you're here with me, Pallas. You're the best friend I've ever had."

Pallas blushed. "You *must* be tired. You're getting sappy."

"Maybe. But I'm also telling the truth. Any of us could have died today. We could have died a million times since we were first brought to Titan. But we're still here. We're still alive. And we're all together because of you. I'm grateful."

"Stop." Pallas fidgeted nervously. "Zhehera will get jealous."

Atlas dropped Pallas's hand.

"I'm so sorry, Atlas. I don't know why I said that." She grabbed his hand back. "I'm not used to sincere praise, I guess."

Atlas looked up at the first stars that were beginning to appear above the sunset. Pallas entwined her fingers into his and joined him staring into the emerging infinite.

"Do you think she's still alive?" Atlas asked.

"I hope so," Pallas answered. "Yes. Yes she is. Zhehera's the toughest person I've ever known."

Atlas nodded and smiled.

Pallas turned to Atlas. "And the prettiest, too."

Now Atlas blushed.

"Too bad she thinks you're odd and creepy."

Atlas's head sunk. "She said that?"

"I'm sorry. I shouldn't have said that. It was unkind, and a breach of trust. You won't tell her I told you, will you?"

"No," Atlas said. His heart was in his toes. *Oh well. It was impossible, anyway.*

Pallas watched Atlas wallow for a moment, then a large grin crept across her face. "Wow! You got it *bad*." She slapped him on the back. "I'm sorry, but I couldn't pass up the chance to tease you."

"What?"

"Zhehera never said you were odd and creepy. She thinks you're cute and sweet. But I'm *really* not supposed to tell you that, so please don't ever tell her."

Atlas playfully pushed Pallas away. She shoved him back. The two laughed, then embraced.

"I'm going back for her," Atlas said. "When this is over—once we've found the Sphere—I'm going back, and I'm going to free her and all the others Apollo has enslaved."

"I'll go with you," said Pallas.

"I know." Atlas kissed Pallas on the forehead. "That reminds me...I met someone during my brief stint at Metallurgy I know you'd love to meet."

"If you're trying to set me up with someone—"

"No, I just think you'd like her. She's super-strong and has enormous muscles. Her name is Tora."

"So now you don't want to be my best friend anymore either?"

"Now who's being sentimental?"

Pallas turned back to the stars. A meteor streaked across the sky. She sighed deeply. "I told him this would happen."

"Whom?"

"Oliver. The night you and I first met. When Eugenio was about to kick you out of the dining hall. I told Oliver this is how it would happen."

"What do you mean? How could you know?"

"It made sense," said Pallas. "If the Alphas were the Titans' pick to find the Sphere, they'd also be the first the Olympians would try to kill. I told him that."

"Oh," said Atlas.

"We agreed that the best strategy would be for the Alphas to be the target, giving the rest of us an opportunity to succeed. Misdirection."

"Oliver knew they were going to die?" Atlas asked, appalled.

"We all knew death was a possibility," said Pallas. "After we heard the prophecy about the Five Philadelphians, Oliver accepted it. He made sure his Alphas were the most obvious target." Pallas touched one of the tears on her face and rubbed it between her fingers.

"We will succeed," said Atlas. "Their deaths won't be in vain." It sounded hollow as he said it. It was still impossible. They were five kids against an entire civilization. *How can we possibly succeed?*

"I told Oliver you'd say that," said Pallas. She wiped her eyes and smiled into the heavens. "And I promised him I'd help you believe it."

CHAPTER 27

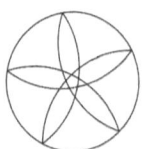

"WHAT'S WRONG?" Pallas asked Atlas as the Philadelphians walked through the halls of Neith's expansive, yet austere home. Everything was neat and clean, and the workmanship was meticulous, although nothing about the house's construction or decoration was ostentatious.

"Just thinking," Atlas said. "For a Prime Matriarch, she lives pretty simply. It's pretty sparse in here." He'd expected something much more extravagant, maybe not quite like Apollo's homes, but more than this. For someone who claimed such a remarkable history, there was no trace of that past adorning the walls. The Olympians had done their best to erase the Thebans' future and their past, Atlas realized. Neith probably had nothing to display.

"Did you already forget the enormous gate and the dozens of guards?" Phoebe said. "She may not decorate extravagantly, but Neith still believes her own life is more valuable than her guards' lives. Typical, pompous aristocrat."

"Hush," said Reedy. "We are guests here. Be polite."

Ajax laughed. "I'm glad you're around, Phoebe. Reedy spends a lot less time correcting me now that she has you."

"Or maybe I just gave up on a hopeless case," Reedy said.

"That's enough," said Atlas. "I'm going to bite the next person that says something mean, joking or not."

Pallas raised her eyebrows. "You're going to *bite* us?"

"That's what my mom and dad would say to get my sister and I to get along. They would bite hard too." Atlas grinned as he looked at his forearm.

"I've never heard of that one before," said Ajax. "My brothers and I were sent to our rooms without dinner when we fought."

"You must have gotten along pretty well, because you sure didn't miss many meals," Atlas said.

"That wasn't nice," said Pallas.

"You're right," said Atlas. He bit his own forearm, leaving deep toothmarks in his skin. "Ow!"

The others laughed. Phoebe grabbed his arm to examine the bite.

"I hope you've had your rabies shot," said Reedy, offering her arm to Atlas at the same time.

"What are you doing?" asked Ajax.

Atlas smirked and bit Reedy's arm.

"Yeah, Ow!" howled Reedy.

"If you had any meat on your bones, it wouldn't hurt so much," said Phoebe.

"Better skinny with a low pain tolerance, than injury-prone with a high pain tolerance," Pallas said.

Both girls offered their arms to Atlas. He bit them. Phoebe winced, but didn't yelp or whine.

Pallas cursed several times and punched Atlas in the shoulder. "Sorry. I didn't expect it to hurt so bad. Dammit!" She shook her arm vigorously.

"Okay, Ajax. Your turn," said Phoebe.

"Why the hell would I want to do something so stupid?" said Ajax.

"Does that count?" asked Phoebe.

"I don't think so," said Reedy. "That was more truthful than mean."

"Thank you," said Ajax.

"But I still think you should be bitten for what you said about me constantly correcting you and Phoebe," said Reedy.

"Again, less mean, and more truthful," said Ajax.

"Now that definitely counts as mean," said Pallas.

"You're all a bunch of children," complained Ajax. However, he rolled his sleeve back and offered his arm to Atlas.

"Dammit!" yelled Ajax. "You bit me harder than the others!"

"No, I didn't," said Atlas. "I bit everyone the same. You're the one that rolled your sleeve up. You didn't have to do that."

Ajax massaged his arm gingerly and scowled. "What a stupid game."

"Sorry to interrupt your...game, but we have limited time," spoke a familiar voice.

The Philadelphians followed the voice to a nearby room. Inside, Themis sat in a plush and ornate hover chair. Six armed Titan bodyguards stood along the walls. There were five chairs arranged in front of Themis.

"Director Themis!" said Phoebe. She pushed past the others into the room.

The bodyguards moved to stop her, but Themis halted them with a raised finger. They grudgingly obeyed. Two of them stepped a few paces closer to Themis, just in case.

Phoebe bounced up to Themis and took his hand. "I am so glad to see you. We thought you were dead."

"As am I glad to see you, my dear," said Themis.

"May I ask how you survived?" interrogated Pallas. She crossed her arms.

"That matters little," said Themis. "And as I said, we have precious little time."

"It matters to us," said Atlas. "We watched friends be killed and blinded. No one tried to help us. *No one.* We were enslaved, and still no one came to rescue us. We assumed no one came because everyone was dead, yet here you are."

"Young man, I do not have to answer you and I will not," said

Themis. "You will sit down. All of you, sit! We have little time for talk."

The others remained awkwardly quiet as they moved to take their seats in front of Themis. Phoebe squeezed Themis's hand again and sat. Atlas remained standing.

"Atlas-Fifteen, you will take your seat."

"No," said Atlas.

"Atlas?" Phoebe nervously whispered. "What's going on?"

"I'm not going to sit because this won't take that long."

"Suit yourself," said Themis. "First, let me—"

"You misunderstood," said Atlas.

"Excuse me?"

"We did not come here to listen to you," Atlas said. "You are here to listen to us."

"Am I?" Themis glowered.

"Yes."

The bodyguards moved towards Atlas, but Themis waved them off. He leaned back in his hover chair and pressed his palms together. "Please go ahead."

"We need a ship," Atlas said.

"Yes, I know," said Themis. "I can provide one for you, along with additional support throughout the duration of your mission."

"What kind of support?" Pallas asked.

"A pilot, of course," said Themis. "And a security detachment for your protection."

"That will not be necessary. Your Academy taught us to be self-sufficient," said Atlas. "We need nothing from you but a trans-light capable vehicle. Something small that won't attract a lot of attention."

"And you expect me to loan you such a ship?"

"No, I expect you will *give* us a ship."

"Will I? Without compromise? Without oversight?" Themis leaned forward and squinted at Atlas. "I am more than happy to procure you a ship which will be more than adequate. But if you think I am willing to trust custody of the Celestial Sphere to a group of children, you are mistaken. You will be accompanied by an elite squadron of specially trained Titan soldiers."

"Unfortunately, you don't get to dictate those terms," said Atlas.

"And why not?"

"Atlas, what are you doing?" asked Phoebe. "He's not the enemy."

Atlas tried to reassure Phoebe with a quick glance. He turned back to answer Themis. "Why not?" Atlas smirked. "Because you do not get to make decisions for us anymore, Themis. Our lives don't belong to you. Our actions don't belong to you. And the Celestial Sphere, especially, does not belong to you!"

Themis studied Atlas for a moment, then pressed his hands against the armrests of his hover chair and lifted himself to his feet. "Tell me, young Philadelphian, to whom does the Celestial Sphere belong? To the Thebans? The Philadelphians, maybe? Perhaps the Olympians deserve control of the Sphere. Or *maybe* you want the Sphere's power all for yourself?"

Atlas stepped forward and locked his eyes on Themis. *Your height doesn't intimidate me, old man.*

Themis turned to his bodyguards. "Detain him. He has been corrupted by the Olympians and is a traitor."

Ajax, Pallas, and Reedy immediately leapt to their feet. The bodyguards hesitated.

"Why are you being like this?" Phoebe stood slowly, obviously conflicted. "Both of you?"

"Seize him!" Themis commanded. "Why do you hesitate?"

"They are afraid," said Atlas. "And with good reason. They heard about what we did today—about how many Olympians we overwhelmed."

"And *killed*," interjected Ajax. "With their own weapons."

The guards took defensive positions, but didn't advance on Atlas. Ajax raised his fists to mock them and taunted the closest bodyguard with a quick lunge and a threatening jab at the air. The bodyguard flinched and steppped backwards.

"We are leaving now," said Atlas. "If anyone tries to stop us or follow us, they will regret it." He turned and walked towards the exit. Pausing, he turned to face Themis again. "You call me a traitor because I will not deliver the Sphere to you. So be it. But let me be clear. Neither will I deliver it to the Thebans, nor the Olympians, nor *any* other civilization. I wouldn't even hand it over to the President of the United States. The Sphere, if it really is as powerful as everyone fears, is too dangerous for any one person or culture to possess."

He walked out of the room.

Reedy and Pallas followed close behind. Ajax continued to taunt the bodyguards as he made his way out. Phoebe hesitantly followed.

"Phoebe, you would follow him?" asked Themis. "Can't you see he wants the Sphere for himself? He'll destroy us all."

"No, he won't. You are wrong." Phoebe hurried and caught up with the others.

"What was that?" Reedy asked Phoebe.

"What was what?"

"Your whole best friends routine back there," said Pallas.

"I like Director Themis," Phoebe said. "He's a friend."

"He's old," said Ajax. "That's creepy."

Phoebe turned red. She spoke softly, almost inaudibly. "I didn't have any friends in the Academy. Director Themis was kind to me."

"You didn't want friends," said Reedy.

"Everyone needs friends," said Phoebe. "I used to go to Director Themis twice a day and beg him to send me home. He wouldn't, of course. Said I wouldn't be safe. Over time, we became friends. He helped me, when he could."

Reedy stopped. She clasped her mouth with one hand and clutched Ajax's arm with the other. Pallas grabbed Phoebe by the shirt and threw her against the wall.

"He *helped* you?" Pallas snapped.

"What does that mean?" asked Reedy.

"He helped me study, talked with me about my problems. Stuff like that," said Phoebe. "What did you think I meant?"

"Don't be dense," said Reedy.

"Did he help you take Homer's place?" asked Pallas.

"No—no, of course not," stammered Phoebe. "At least, I don't think so. I never asked him to. Please believe me—I never asked to take anyone's place."

"Why should we believe you?" asked Pallas. She slammed Phoebe against the wall again and again. "We lost Homer because of *you*."

Phoebe shook her head rapidly, her face contorted in fear and pain—although Pallas wasn't slamming her very hard. Phoebe let Pallas continue to bash her against the wall.

"Pallas!" Atlas grabbed her wrists. "Stop this."

"She lied to us," Pallas said. "She's *still* lying." Enormous tears rolled down her cheeks.

Atlas gently pulled Pallas away from Phoebe. "I don't think Phoebe lied to us. And even if she did, it doesn't matter. She's not that person anymore."

"How can you say that? How can we trust her?"

"Because she chose you over me," Themis said from down the hall.

Ajax and Reedy whirled around, ready to fight, but Themis was alone, driving his hover chair towards them.

"What's going on out here?" Neith emerged from a side room. In her casual, sleeping clothing, she appeared older and more frail than she had earlier in the day, aboard the Theban ship. However, her movements were spry and confident. "That's the wall to my bedroom you're banging against."

"I'm afraid this is my fault," said Themis. "I allowed myself to become suspicious and distrustful; the children were antagonized as a result."

"So your meeting is over then? I hope you've come to an agreement."

"Indeed we have." Themis made sure he had Atlas's attention before continuing. "I will provide the Philadelphians with a personal ship appropriate to their mission. The rest of the mission will be up to them. The Titan High Government needn't know. The Philadelphians have my complete trust."

"Good." Neith smiled. "Will you come to bed now? It's been a long day and I am exhausted. You don't want me to fall asleep before you come to bed." She winked.

"Yes, dear. I'll be there shortly."

"Gross," whispered Ajax.

"Good night, children," said Neith. "Please take care of my great-granddaughter." She closed the door before they could respond.

"You changed your mind?" Phoebe asked Themis.

"Someone showed me the error in my thinking. And after all, shouldn't I, of all people, exercise some faith in the prophecy of my ancestor?" Themis stared at Phoebe. "I am proud of you, Phoebe-Ten. You have finally found your place."

"You know I hate being called that," said Phoebe.

"I do." Themis took her hands. "You'll indulge an old man his terms of endearment, won't you?"

"No, *that's* gross," mouthed Reedy to Ajax.

"Of course," said Phoebe. She suddenly gave Themis a big hug. He was caught off guard, but gradually softened as Phoebe clung to him. "Thank you for listening to me all those times in the Academy," she said. Phoebe turned to the others. "I told you he wasn't a bad guy."

Themis straightened his robe. "Yes, well...you had better get going. There is no time to waste."

"Yes," said Atlas grabbing Phoebe by the arm. "Director Themis has another engagement to attend to."

Ajax grimaced and shook his head violently.

"Outside the far edge of town, almost directly east of the

Theban landing pad, there is a ship ready and waiting for you," said Themis. "It's a small ship with only minimal defenses and its space-flight capabilities are quite limited, but it is trans-light capable. And it cannot be tracked by the Titan High Government. I will grant you sole and total access. The ship is yours."

"Thank you," said Atlas.

"Please treat her well," said Themis. His eyes sparkled. "She is a good ship. A very fine ship, indeed."

"We will," said Reedy. "I promise."

Themis nodded and showed them to the door.

Pallas grabbed Phoebe's hand. "I am so sorry, Phoebe."

"I never asked to be transferred to another squad."

"I believe you," said Pallas. "Please forgive me."

Phoebe kissed Pallas on the forehead and hugged her shoulders. "Only if you forgive me—for being so terrible for so long."

"A long time ago."

Themis arranged for secure transportation to take them to the ship. This made Atlas nervous. He didn't like the idea of anyone, even trusted bodyguards, knowing where they were headed, or when.

Styx had survived and Atlas knew the Olympians wouldn't stop coming for them. Delphi had built his entire political career on the capture and murder of the Philadelphians from their ancient myths. Atlas and his friends could never go home as long as Styx and Delphi were after them. Then there was Apollo. *How many Olympians want us dead? Possibly all of them.*

If we find the Sphere, that would change everything. Delphi would be exposed. I could save Zhehera. With that power, I could free all Apollo's slaves—no, we—we could free all the slaves on Olympus. We would avenge all the horror the Olympians have wreaked upon the Galaxy. And that's only the beginning. With possession of the Celestial Sphere, we could rid the entire Galaxy—

Atlas shook his head. *No, we can't be trusted. I can't be trusted with that much power. Given the chance—the opportunity—we will* destroy it. *That is, if Ciencia exists. If the Cienciants exist. If the Celestial Sphere exists.*

The information Taco had given them only narrowed the search to a few hundred thousand cubic light-years. Atlas couldn't help but feel a bit hopeless, even after everything. Had they survived this long, just to spend the rest of their lives on an endless, wild goose chase across the Galaxy?

The security detail dropped the Philadelphians off near Themis's ship. Pakhet and Banka were waiting for them. Pakhet had wrapped some dark cloth—a scarf maybe—around her face and head. Only her good eye was visible.

"Did Themis arrange your transport, too?" Reedy asked.

Banka looked shamefaced. "No, we already knew about this ship. We—"

"We were about to steal it," Pakhet said. Without her helmet distorting it, her natural voice was pleasant, almost melodic. "But it looks as if that old fool has changed the access."

"You weren't going to leave without us?" asked Pallas.

"Of course not," said Banka. "In fact, we were hoping Director Themis would offer it to you. Stealing was a last resort."

"Well, he *did* give it to us," said Phoebe. "And he's not an old fool."

Atlas stepped between Pakhet and Phoebe. He touched the ship and a previously invisible hatch opened near the center of the hull. From under the port, a long ramp extended to the ground.

"Why didn't you tell us about the ship, if you already knew about it?" Atlas asked Pakhet.

"Would you believe we wanted you to have plausible deniability?" Pakhet said.

Atlas stared intensely at Pakhet. "No. And if you're going to come with us, there are two rules I'll expect you to follow."

"You can't find Ciencia without me."

"No matter. You agree, or you don't come on board."

"Fine. What are they?"

"First, you tell the truth and you don't hide any information from us."

"Okay," Pakhet said. "What else?"

"You respect my orders and the orders of my crew. This is our mission, and we will retain operational control."

"Of course. Um…Yes, *Captain*." Pakhet said.

"This is not a joke!" said Ajax.

Pakhet waved him off. She touched Atlas on the shoulder. "Do you remember when we first met?"

"You smacked me so hard I fell to the ground," said Atlas.

"I never heard that story," said Pallas.

"You tried to strike back with a swift kick—at Banka no less—and missed." Pakhet sounded amused, almost nostalgic. "You looked like a Thracian sea scorpion flopping about on land."

"What's your point?" Atlas's neck was starting to get hot.

"My point is that I knew…even then…I knew it would be you leading this mission."

"You didn't treat me like it."

"I didn't coddle you," said Pakhet. "If I had, you might have felt entitled to special treatment. You wouldn't have fought so hard. You would have become weak."

"You don't know that."

"Maybe not," said Pakhet. "But I know you're who you need to be—who *we* need you to be. The whole Galaxy. We all need you five to be exactly the people you are right now."

CHAPTER 28

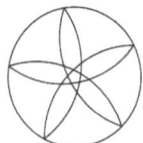

REEDY STOOD behind the controls of the small spacecraft that Themis had given them. She surveyed the control board and settled into the pilot's chair.

"Wow! This thing is a classic! It still has all the original controls."

Having been designed for Titan pilots, the chair looked almost comically oversized with Reedy's slender frame nestled in it. After a bit of fiddling with the seat controls—itself a bit of slapstick comedy—she was able to adjust the seat to a more appropriate position. After it all, however, she still looked like a small child sitting in an adult's chair. "Most repurposed ships like this have had total gut-jobs to make room for the trans-light system. They kept this one vintage."

"But Themis said it was trans-light capable," said Pallas.

"It is, but the old controls have been reworked to correspond to the trans-light system. I'm guessing that's why Themis said it had limited space-flight capability. Even the analog controls have been repurposed." Reedy was practically bouncing in her chair with excitement. "She's so beautiful."

"That's not what you were saying outside," said Phoebe.

"You called it a piece of old junk," said Ajax.

"Well, I've never been happier to be wrong," said Reedy,

bringing the console and monitors to life with the flick of a switch. "And she's all mine...er...ours."

"When you're at the helm, she's yours," Atlas said.

"Perfect." Reedy spun around two full circles in her chair. "She needs a name."

"What about *The Philadelphian*?" Ajax suggested. "Since that's what they call us anyways."

"It ought to reflect her heritage," Reedy said. "It can't just be about us."

"The *Titanic* is probably not a good name," quipped Atlas.

The others laughed, except for Reedy.

"But it should also honor her current mission," Reedy mused.

"*Esfera* means sphere in Spanish," said Phoebe. "I've always thought it's a pretty word."

"I got it," said Reedy. "*Gaia*. Her name is Gaia."

"Goddess of the Earth." Pallas nodded. "Mother of the Titans *and* Olympians in Greek mythology."

"I like it," said Atlas.

"It's very pretty," said Phoebe.

"Yes," said Reedy. "And it's also kind of a joke. Biting our thumb at the Olympians and Titans."

"I hope the translators can properly convey the nuances of the joke," said Atlas.

"Probably not, but it can still be funny to us," said Ajax.

"Then we agree?" asked Atlas. "Good." He turned to Pakhet, who had remained quiet during the conversation. "Welcome aboard *The Gaia*, Pakhet."

"Just *Gaia*," said Reedy. "We don't call you *the* Atlas."

"Welcome aboard *Gaia*," said Atlas.

"Thank you, Captain," said Pakhet. She held one arm gingerly. Apparently, Dr. Circe hadn't been able to fully heal all Pakhet's injuries—or Pakhet hadn't had the patience to be completely healed. "Now that you have named it, where will it take us?"

"Working on it," said Phoebe. She was seated at the navigation console, reviewing holographic star maps of the Galactic Center. "Give me a minute."

"No problem," Atlas said. "Let me know when you have something." He gestured for Pakhet to take a seat against the bulkhead. "Pallas, take co-pilot."

"Got it." Pallas giggled when she sat in the enormous co-pilot chair.

"Ajax, watch the monitors. I don't want to be surprised by uninvited guests again."

"Okay, but Themis wasn't being modest when he said this thing has few defense capabilities," Ajax said. "It's hardly more than a bee-bee gun."

"What is a bee-bee gun?" asked Pakhet.

"It's a toy," said Reedy.

"Please don't exaggerate, Ajax," said Atlas. "I need to know exactly what capabilities we have."

"Sorry, Atlas. Only a pair of energy rifles. Relatively low yield. Might not even penetrate modern infantry armor. Useless for anything other than a brief distraction."

Atlas frowned. "Phoebe, prepare an emergency jump, at least three hundred light-years away. In case we need to make a quick exit."

"Got it." Phoebe's fingers flew around her console. "Done. Emergency trans-light jump to Xenian orbit standing by."

"That's only 284 light-years, but it'll do," teased Atlas. He joined Phoebe at the navigation table. His eyes met Pakhet's. She nodded. Atlas wondered if he had done the right thing by refusing Banka's offer to assist with the mission. At the very least, she could have kept Pakhet in line. *No. It's better that Banka stay on Titan.* Plus, there weren't enough bunks.

"Need any help, Phoebe?"

"Another pair of eyes could be helpful, thanks."

"Where are you so far?"

Phoebe dug her fingers into the holographic stars and rotated the map so that both of them could see it better. "Taco said it looked like a black hole near the Galactic Center, right?"

"Yes, but that it wasn't the Center and that it wasn't a real black hole. But it was an old story, likely distorted over time."

"Exactly," said Phoebe. "Which got me thinking. The Vitrians were experimenting with trans-light, right?"

"That's what the Thebans believe. Right, Pakhet?"

"According to several sources, yes," Pakhet said. "The Vitrians have possessed trans-light technology for at least a dozen generations longer than most other civilizations."

"Well, if you were experimenting with trans-light, why would you look for a black hole? Trans-light only lets you travel to points where EM breaches of the Space-Time fabric carry enough bandwidth for emergence."

"I understand how trans-light works," Atlas said. "I took the same classes you did."

"I know. My point is, why would they search for black holes, which are basically light vacuums within the fabric of Space-Time?" Phoebe rubbed her eyes and squinted at the map. "Except for the region immediately leading up to the event horizon, the EM bandwidth near the black hole wouldn't be any better than anywhere else, but it would be much more dangerous."

"What are you thinking?"

"They must have been looking at the gamma bursts. Since black holes create conditions where gamma bursts may be emitted FTL, some have speculated that such high energy bursts could enable trans-light beyond the Galaxy."

"I don't remember reading that," said Atlas.

"I read ahead."

"Gamma bursts go right through normal shielding like it was tin foil," said Reedy. "And coming from a black hole, they'd be too irregular to be viable for trans-light. How would you modulate fast enough? It would be suicide."

"Maybe that's the key," said Pallas.

"Exactly," said Phoebe.

"What do you mean?" asked Ajax. "I'm not looking to kill myself."

"I mean that the gamma bursts from a real black hole would be far too dangerous to approach," said Pallas.

"That's what I said," said Reedy.

"But what if the Vitrians discovered a less dense gamma burst source?" Pallas said. "Maybe just below the threshold of their shielding capacity?"

"That would be tempting," said Reedy.

"That's what I'm searching for," said Phoebe. She switched the galactic map to radiation mode. "That's what the *not black hole* from the story means. It means a source of gamma radiation bursts too weak and too stable to be from a black hole."

"Brilliant," said Pakhet.

"Let's hope the cartographers picked it up when they charted the Center,'" said Reedy.

"Yes. Yes," Phoebe answered distractedly. Her hands and nose were buried in her maps. "Hopefully, your girlfriend's people didn't write it off as galactic noise and omit it, Atlas."

"What?" said Atlas.

"The Phoenicians. They charted the galactic maps the Titans, Thebans, and most other sentis use."

"I know that," said Atlas. He glared at Pallas.

Pallas swatted Reedy on the shoulder. "You told her?"

"Was that a secret?" Reedy said. She looked at Atlas. "Oops."

Phoebe enlarged a particular area of the map and leaned close to it. "Hmm...nothing. But there should be something," she muttered, then sat up in her seat.

"You got something?" Atlas asked.

"Yeah, I think I do." Phoebe pointed to a section of the map. "What do you think?"

"It's a bit further from the Center than I expected, but yeah, I think you may have found it."

Phoebe beamed. "Setting a course. Reedy, what's our space-flight range? I don't want to get too close and end up bouncing us out of the Galaxy like the Vitrians."

"We have ion thrusters that can provide some propulsion, but are hardly useful for anything other than setting and maintaining orbit," said Reedy. "The big impulse engines were removed to make room for the trans-light modulator. In other words, the closer the better."

"I have to guess?" lamented Phoebe.

"Not guess," said Ajax. "Deduce. You can do it."

"Yes, Phoebe," added Atlas. "You can do it."

"You heard what Reedy said, didn't you?" said Phoebe. "We have no real space-flight engines. If I get too close and we're bounced out of the Galaxy, there may not be enough EM band-width out there to trans-light back. It could take hundreds of years to make it back to the Galaxy. We'll be stuck out there in the black, eating the bodies of whichever of us succumb to hunger first."

"And you heard what I said," said Ajax. "I'm not looking to kill myself. I trust you. We'll be fine."

"You can't know that," said Phoebe.

"I don't, but I believe it. I didn't *know* we'd escape Apollo. I didn't know you'd survive your wound. I didn't know we'd defeat the Olympian kill squad. But I *believed* in all of those things. And they happened. This will be the same." Atlas shrugged. "If I'm wrong, I'll volunteer to be eaten first."

"Gross," said Reedy, looking as if she might throw up.

Phoebe took a deep breath and dove back into the map. She expertly manipulated the different force and spectrum views of the area surrounding the newly-discovered Ciencia Abyss. Phoebe's fingers danced among the stars as she dug into the forces swirling about that region of space. The inside of the ship came alive with the light show from Phoebe's map.

"Anyone else have an urge to dance?" asked Ajax. "No? Fine."

"Okay," said Phoebe. "This could work, I think. We may have to travel around space for a few days, but I think we'll be fine."

"Good," said Atlas.

"We'll arrive on a plane perpendicular to the gamma bursts," said Phoebe. "Just in case that's what triggers—"

"Someone breached our sensor perimeter," yelled Ajax. "Multiple breaches. Whole helluva lotta' breaches!"

"Phoebe, set the course," said Reedy.

"Hold on," said Phoebe.

"We're taking hits," said Ajax.

"Do it, Phoebe," said Atlas. "Hurry!"

"One sec. Got it. Go!"

Reedy punched the trans-light lever. Every surface in the ship, including the Philadelphians, flashed intensely. Then, everything was quiet.

"Did we get away okay, Ajax?" Atlas asked.

Ajax checked his monitors. "Looks like it, yes."

"Well done," said Pakhet. She stood behind Phoebe, looking over her shoulder at their position on the galactic map. "We're probably only a couple hours away from contact."

"We still might get bounced away," said Phoebe. "Although probably not outside of the Galaxy at this speed."

"I don't think so," said Pakhet. She spoke slowly and quietly, as if deep in thought. "Ciencia makes herself known to her children."

No one said anything for a moment. Pakhet went to a porthole and stared out into space. Atlas joined Pallas and Reedy looking out from the helm into the Ciencia Abyss.

"I was right," said Phoebe. "No event horizon. It's not like a black hole except for the FTL gamma burst and the apparent lack of other EM."

"What?" asked Ajax.

"There's no sun," said Atlas.

"There's no *visible* sun," said Phoebe. "At least, not visible to us. No EM or gravity waves escape that entire region."

"That shouldn't be possible," said Reedy.

"Don't ask me how they did it," said Phoebe. "But it's what

they did. According to all sensors, that whole region of space is an energy-matter vacuum. A black hole that's not a black hole. Except for the gamma bursts, that is."

"They gotta' come from somewhere," said Ajax.

"But if they appear FTL, it could be impossible to pinpoint their exact origin," said Reedy.

Phoebe buried her face in her hands. "I thought there would be something here—anything. Once we got here, I was *sure* there would be something to guide us."

"There is," said Pakhet.

"What?" asked Phoebe.

"I see it," said Pakhet. She stepped alongside Reedy and bent to access the controls. "Do you mind?"

Reedy looked at Atlas for confirmation. "Be my guest." She stood up and made room for Pakhet to slide into the pilot seat.

"What do you see, Pakhet?" asked Atlas.

"The sun." She corrected the yaw and pitch of *Gaia* and primed the ion thrusters. "Straight ahead."

"There's nothing ahead for at least a few light-years," said Phoebe, peeking through her fingers.

"No, it's much closer than that. Trust me."

"You see the Ciencia sun?" asked Pallas.

"I do. Just barely. That is, I don't see it like I see the stars or you children, but I know it's there. When I look towards it, I see it, even if you step in front of me." Pakhet paused and put her hands in front of her eyes. "Like this. I still see it, in *both* eyes. It's been so long since I've seen anything…but I turn away from the sun, and it's gone." Pakhet turned to face the wall.

"Ciencia makes itself known to its children," said Atlas. "Pakhet must possess a gene cluster that allows her to see through the shielding."

"Seems like it helps her see through more than that," said Pallas. "She says she can see it through organic tissue."

"I can," said Pakhet. "I can't explain how. But I know it's there. I don't know how else to explain it."

"Okay," said Atlas. "You have the helm. Take us in."

Reedy looked surprised, and even hurt. She scowled. "I should take co-pilot."

"Yes," said Atlas. "Pallas, you're relieved."

Pallas made room for Reedy and sat next to Ajax. Pakhet signaled and Reedy ignited the ion thrusters. *Gaia* jolted forward, throwing Atlas off balance. He landed in Ajax's lap.

"It's alright, Atlas," teased Ajax. "Don't be afraid."

"Sorry about that," said Reedy. "The bulk of the inertial damp-ening system was removed along with the impulse thrusters. Makes sense. Not needed for trans-light."

Atlas picked himself off Ajax and made his way to an empty chair. "You might have mentioned that before."

"Yeah, sorry."

"I thought the ion thrusters were barely more than stabiliz-ers?" said Ajax.

Reedy nodded. "Well yeah, compared to impulse engines, they're nothing. Still, we just went zero to two hundred kph in less than two seconds. Guess they have more juice in them than I thought. Looks like we'll top out at approximately three thousand kph."

"How are we doing, Pakhet?" Atlas asked.

"Very well, Captain," said Pakhet. "Based on the size of the sun, I estimate we should arrive at its habitable zone in ten days, more or less."

"Sorry about that," Phoebe frowned. "That's as close as I dared."

"There's nothing to apologize for," said Ajax. "You didn't bounce us out of the Galaxy, so now I don't have to be your dinner."

"Let's hope the planet's not on the far side of the sun this time of year," said Phoebe.

"That would be unfortunate," said Pakhet.

"I'll say," said Reedy. "It could take months to travel safely to the other side of the sun. Longer if we end up chasing the planet in orbit."

"Okay then," said Ajax. "I'm going to see about something to eat. Anyone else want anything?"

Gaia lurched forward again, this time more forcefully than the last, but quickly stabilized.

"What did you do?" Reedy asked Pakhet. "Hey, I don't have control! You locked me out."

"I don't have control," Pakhet said calmly. "You well know *Gaia* is not capable of accelerating this rapidly."

"Then what's happening?" asked Ajax.

"They're bringing us in," said Phoebe.

"That is how it appears," said Pakhet.

"Good," said Atlas. "I was hoping for something like this."

"You might have mentioned that before," Reedy mimicked him.

Atlas grinned. It was a pretty decent imitation. "I didn't want to get your hopes up based on pure speculation."

"Guys? Look!" Pallas said.

The inside of the ship became brightly illuminated. Directly in front of them was an enormous sun. They had passed through the barrier. Here it was—the hidden system. Ciencia, home of the Celestial Sphere.

"What do we got, Phoebe?" Atlas asked.

"Um…Give me a sec…wait, that's not right."

"What's up?" Atlas joined Phoebe at the navigation console.

"Nothing," said Phoebe. "I've got nothing. No sensor data of any kind."

"How can there be nothing?" said Reedy.

"There just isn't. No planets. No asteroids. Not even space dust."

"That can't be right," said Pallas.

"There has to be something," said Reedy.

"What's pulling us in, if there's nothing?" asked Ajax.

"Pakhet, can you see anything? Is this another trick?" Atlas asked.

"Only the sun," said Pakhet. "But the real sun. Not like before."

"This doesn't make any sense," muttered Atlas. They'd found the hidden system. How could there not be any planets? He stood up and walked to the helm to get a better look through the viewport. Nothing visible. They appeared to be heading directly towards the sun in a straight line. No, it was a gradual arc. *Maybe Ciencia is on the far side of the sun? That explains the arc. But why doesn't it appear on the sensors? Wait, is that? Yes. A planet.*

"There it is!" said Atlas. "Look."

"I see it," said Reedy.

"The sensors still don't show anything," said Phoebe.

"How interesting," said Pakhet.

"But there it is," said Pallas. "*Gaia*, magnify starboard segment. You can see a crescent of light."

"We're passing it?" said Ajax.

"It's a bit small," said Pakhet. "And probably outside the star's habitable zone."

And then it was gone. *Gaia* sped past the planet and continued towards the Ciencia sun.

"Lights!" said Ajax. "I saw lights on the dark side of the planet. Right near the border of night and day."

"I didn't see anything," said Reedy. She got up and stood near Pakhet, asking for her seat back.

"Well I did."

"Lights?" said Pallas. "As in artificial lights?"

"That's what it looked like," said Ajax. "Like cities or towns, maybe."

"If it was a city, why weren't we taken to it?" asked Phoebe.

Pakhet stood up from the pilot seat and returned to the seat near the bulkhead. "There are many systems with multiple inhabited planets. Though I am surprised a colony could survive this far out from the star's habitable zone. That's assuming those were indeed lights from a colony."

"I know what I saw," said Ajax.

"I believe you," said Atlas. "And it looks like we'll have a chance to verify colonization." He pointed out the viewport. Another planet appeared on the port side.

"Looks like we're going to get a closer look at this one," said Ajax.

"No," said Reedy. "We're further away. It's bigger. Magnifying port segment."

"Look for lights," said Pallas. She returned to the co-pilot seat.

They approached the second planet at a shallower vector than the first, and approximately a third of the planet was in daytime. Even though it was a bigger planet, the greater distance and the reduced visible area experiencing night would make it difficult, if not impossible, to spot the lights of a minor colony like those Ajax claimed to have seen on the first planet. Yet, as they approached, it became obvious that there were several large colonies spread out across the dark side of the planet.

"I see them," said Phoebe.

"Yes, me too," said Reedy. "Must be quite a few people down there. Especially if the light side has a similar number of colonies as the dark side."

Gaia continued past the second planet without any indication of deceleration.

"Um...I've done some calculations," said Phoebe, puzzled. "We're traveling at nearly half light-speed."

"How is that possible?" asked Reedy. "We should have been smeared all over *Gaia's* rear hull after accelerating to that speed without inertial dampening."

"You think I have any idea how any of this is possible? But apparently it is."

"Hey guys," said Ajax. "Starboard porthole." He pointed out into the blackness. "Is there a way we can magnify from back here?"

"I'll put it on the main viewport," said Pallas. The view from the starboard porthole appeared on the screen. "Here's the magnification."

"Yep, I knew it," said Ajax. "It's another one."

They were nearly directly in line with the third planet. Approximately half the observable planet was dark. Hundreds of colonies were clearly visible at this magnification. Each colony was connected to the others by faint lines, forming a web of light. But Gaia continued past with no sign of slowing down.

Shortly, they passed a fourth planet on the port side. They passed much nearer to it than any of the previous planets. It was roughly the same size as the third planet and had approximately the same number of colonies clearly visible on it. With the port-side magnification, they were able to discern colonies in the daytime regions as well.

"Okay, this is really weird," said Phoebe. "The last two planets appear to have exactly the same orbital path?"

"How is that possible?" asked Atlas.

"Again, how am I supposed to know how it's possible?" Phoebe shrugged. "My calculations put them one quarter revolution apart, and their orbital speeds are identical."

"Amazing," said Pakhet. She stood at the viewport. "It's designed."

"You're saying someone *designed* it this way?" asked Reedy. "How?"

"I don't know," said Pakhet. "Perhaps they moved another planet from their system into alignment with their primary world."

"They moved a planet?" said Ajax. "Unbelievable."

"Astounding," said Atlas.

"Looks like they moved at least two planets," said Reedy. "Here's a fifth. It appears to have the same orbit as the last two."

"Yep," said Phoebe. "And so do we, now. Also, we've decelerated to a tenth of light-speed."

"When did that happen?" said Reedy.

Phoebe shrugged and sighed.

"This must be it," said Atlas. "We're coming in for a landing."

A sudden thought came to him. "Reedy! Will this thing survive reentry?"

Reedy laughed. "Of course she will, as long as we decelerate to re-entry speed. Hopefully, whoever's guiding us has an accurate reading of *Gaia's* limitations." She turned in her seat to face Atlas. "And don't call her 'this thing!'"

As they approached the fifth planet, *Gaia* began to obviously decelerate. They still couldn't feel it, but the size of the fifth planet in the viewport wasn't increasing as rapidly as it had been. They seemed to be aiming for a landing near the border of night and day.

Eventually, several details of the planet came into focus. There were large oceans, and at least three bright green continents on the light side of the planet. However, there was little light pollution along the night side of the planet. It seemed to be considerably less populated than its two orbital sisters.

Gaia entered the planet's atmosphere. Flames covered the portholes of the ship. Atlas scrambled for his seat and searched the chair for any means of restraint. *Seriously? No seat belts? Not needed for trans-light.* He gripped the arm rests as tight as he could. After a few moments, the flames cleared. They were descending through the stratosphere.

"It's so pretty," said Phoebe. "Even at evening, it's so pretty."

Gaia lurched again as she suddenly slowed in preparation for landing. Atlas, Pakhet, and Ajax were nearly thrown from their seats. The last thirty seconds were an even slower, almost perpendicular, descent. Finally, *Gaia* touched down.

"Let's go," said Atlas, but he didn't move. Neither did anyone else. *We made it*, he thought. After a few seconds, he stood and left the bridge. The others followed him.

Atlas rushed to the exit. He unlocked the hatch and prepared to open it, then paused. This was a team effort. They had found Ciencia together. They would take their first steps on Cienciant soil together. Atlas smiled. Soon enough, it would all be over. The

Sphere would be safe from the Olympians. Atlas and his friends would be able to go home.

He opened the hatch.

To his surprise, there were four people in brightly colored robes waiting for them beyond *Gaia's* ramp. Atlas looked around the area for others. None. No buildings either. *Gaia* had landed in the middle of a stony plateau.

"Hello," said Atlas. He stepped out onto the ramp. "Um...I wonder if you could help us find something?"

One of the robed persons stepped forward. She reached a hand out, palm facing up, fingers cupped.

"We know why you have come, Philadelphians. I entreat you, allow me the pleasure of being the first to welcome you to Ciencia."

CHAPTER 29

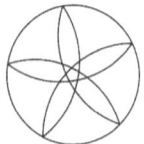

ATLAS OFFERED A HANDSHAKE. The first Cienciant looked at him awkwardly at first, then mirrored Atlas's posture—arm outstretched, palm open—but didn't touch his hand.

Maybe they don't like physical contact, Atlas thought. *Or they think we have germs. Makes sense. As advanced as their civilization may be, our pathogens could very possibly decimate their civilization. How terrible that would be.*

Atlas decided to continue standing awkwardly with his hand outstretched for a few more seconds rather than risk xenocide. He forced a smile and when he could no longer tolerate the awkwardness, he nodded and dropped his hand.

The Cienciant turned to face Pallas and imitated what she had seen Atlas do. Pallas looked sideways at Atlas. He shrugged. She played along, mimicking Atlas, but adding extra mechanical stiffness to the ritual.

"What was that?" Atlas whispered when the Cienciant moved on to Reedy, who also played along.

"You started it," snickered Pallas.

The Cienciant began the ritual with Ajax. When she stretched out her hand, Ajax grabbed it and gave it a hearty shake.

"Ajax, no!" said Atlas.

The Cienciant snatched her hand back and touched it gingerly. The other Cienciants hurried to her side.

"I'm sorry," said Ajax. "Sometimes I don't know my own strength."

"That's not the problem," said Atlas. "You may have infected them with Earth, Titan, *and* Olympian germs. We may have just destroyed their entire civilization!" He spun to the Cienciants. "I'm so sorry. *We're* so sorry. We didn't mean to infect you. Antibodies… right—you can get antibodies from our blood and use them to synthesize a vaccine. We've never made first contact before. We had no idea what to expect, or how to act, or what the right protocols are. To be honest, I didn't even think about the possibility that we shouldn't touch you, or that you might not want to be touched, until after I had already offered you my hand. Again, I'm so sorry. How can we help? Take our blood. It'll be okay. Just take our blood."

"Atlas," said Phoebe. "Calm down."

"But our germs could kill millions," Atlas panicked. "Like when Europeans first arrived in the Americas."

"I think they'll be fine," said Reedy. She pointed to the Cienciants, who smiled broadly.

"Do not worry, young Philadelphian," said the first Cienciant. "You carry no pathogens that are a danger to us. However, we appreciate your…*zealous* concern for our well-being."

The other Cienciants laughed much harder than Atlas thought the joke deserved.

"Next time you promise our blood to a new senti species, get our permission first," Reedy scoffed.

"I'm sorry," said Atlas. "We've come so far and gone through so much to finally get here. I guess I'm overwhelmed."

"That is understandable," said the Cienciant. "But let me assure you that all is well now that you have arrived."

"You've been expecting us?"

"Eventually. We did not know when you would come, but we knew that you would."

"How?" asked Pallas.

"That is a question for another time," said the Cienciant. "First, please allow me to greet you according to our custom."

"Of course," said Atlas.

The Cienciant placed her arms on Atlas's shoulders and leaned her head close to Atlas's face. "I am Citlali. I am your equal." She gently squeezed his shoulders, inhaled deeply, then blew her full breath directly onto Atlas's nose.

"Yuck," whispered Reedy.

"Now it is your turn," said Citlali. "Take my shoulders."

Atlas placed his hands on Citlali's shoulders. He was surprised by how strong, powerful, and full of life she felt.

"Now lean close so that your mouth is near mine."

Atlas leaned in close to her lips. *When in Rome...* He closed his eyes. Somehow, it felt less awkward when he couldn't see Citlali.

"Good," said Citlali. "Now, tell me your name."

"I am Atlas...um...I am your equal."

"Excellent!" said Citlali. "Now allow me to sense your exhalation, so I will know that you bear me no ill will."

Atlas inhaled as deeply as he could and then slowly exhaled as much air as he could force out of his lungs. He held his breath for as long as he could, then tried not to gasp as he opened his eyes and stepped back.

Citlali smiled warmly at him. Her smile felt so friendly and familiar, it almost seemed like a hug. She stepped back and nodded, then moved on to Pallas.

As soon as Citlali began to greet Pallas, the next Cienciant approached Atlas. His robe was mostly pink, ornamented with a fine geometric design in black. He put his arms on Atlas's shoulders and leaned close to Atlas.

"I am Astrophel. I am your equal," he said. He exhaled on Atlas as Citlali had.

Atlas put his arms on Astrophel's shoulders and introduced himself. The other two Cienciants presented themselves to Atlas and the other Philadelphians in turn.

"But where are the others?" asked Dara. Her green robe was the darkest of the four, while her skin tone was the brightest.

"What others?" asked Pallas.

"Where is Pakhet?" said Atlas.

"She didn't come out," said Reedy.

"Pakhet is Theban?" asked Itri, the other male Cienciant.

"She is," said Atlas. "And also a distant descendant of one of your people. That's how we were able to find this place." He paused. "She could...uh...see your sun through the barrier."

Citlali nodded. "Ciencia makes herself known to her children."

"I don't know why she didn't come out with us," said Atlas. "Maybe she thinks her role is completed now that she got us here."

"No one who arrives in Ciencia has fulfilled their role," said Itri.

"And what about the *other*?" asked Dara, clearly agitated.

"There wasn't anyone else," said Atlas. "Just the five of us, and Pakhet."

Dara looked at Astrophel and shook her head.

"That is concerning," said Citlali. "We observed a seventh person in the ship—possibly also Theban."

"Pakhet was the only other person with us," insisted Phoebe. "I'll go get her. You'll see." Phoebe ran back into the ship.

"You scanned us?" asked Atlas.

"Yes," said Citlali. "I apologize for compromising your privacy, but visitors to our world are extremely rare. We prefer to...*understand* who has discovered the route through the barrier. Please rest assured, now that you are here, your privacy will be absolutely respected."

"I understand, and I wasn't objecting. But there were only six of us on that ship. Your scanner must be malfunctioning."

"Our scanners do not malfunction," snorted Itri.

"Nor are they scanners, technically," said Astrophel. "Scanners are active and invasive. Our technology works passively. The sensor arrays do not act. They are acted *upon*. When you passed near them, you distorted their quantum reality."

"It's neither necessary nor important for you to correct our visitors' understanding of our sensor array, Astrophel," said Citlali.

"You made it sound as if we had invaded their privacy. Our sensors detected them, that is all."

"And then we observed the data," said Citlali. "One could argue therein lies our invasion."

"Are we really having this argument here?" asked Astrophel.

"I am sorry that I misspoke when I called them scanners," said Itri.

"That was very imprecise of you," Dara jibed.

"And I said I was sorry. Can we stop talking about it now?"

Atlas had to bite his tongue to keep from laughing out loud. Advanced civilization they might be, but they bickered as if they were siblings.

"But what about the *seventh* person?" Dara said.

"Yes, call them what you may, our *sensors* do not malfunction," said Itri.

"Atlas says there were only six persons aboard," said Citlali. "We all sensed his exhalation. He is not prone to deception."

"Unless he knows how to deceive his exhalation," said Dara. She crossed her arms. "I'm just saying…it's been done before."

"By highly trained Cienciant monks," said Citlali. "He is a child. They are children."

"We *are* highly trained children," interjected Reedy. "Not in… uh…exhalation deception, but in the interest of full disclosure, we have been trained on Titan for this specific mission. Also, we're almost fifteen. In some cultures that practically makes us adults."

"Of course you have been *trained*," said Astrophel. "How else would *children* like you have made it this far?"

"I only meant to be forthright," stammered Reedy.

"Astrophel!" said Citlali. "You have embarrassed our guest with your rudeness."

"Hey guys," Phoebe called. She ran down *Gaia's* ramp and pointed back to the ship. "Here comes Pakhet."

"Thank you, Phoebe," said Atlas.

"Well, where is she?" asked Dara.

Phoebe turned back to the ship's port. "I don't understand. She was right behind me."

Phoebe took a few steps back up the ramp. Inexplicably, she lost her balance and tumbled off the side. She fell hard, only barely managing to protect her head.

Reedy was the first to her side. "Phoebe! Are you alright?" She rolled Phoebe onto her back. "You're bleeding!" A large splash of blood streaked across her chest.

"That's not my blood," said Phoebe. "It's gray. I'm fine, really."

"Are you sure, dear?" asked Citlali. "That was quite the tumble."

"Then whose blood is it?" asked Ajax.

"Kinda' clumsy for being so highly trained," Astrophel said.

Reedy glared at him furiously. Pallas put her hand on Reedy's shoulder.

"I didn't stumble," Phoebe retorted. "I was pushed."

Astrophel rolled his eyes. "By whom? There was no one on the ramp but you."

"Whose blood is it?" repeated Ajax.

Atlas examined the ramp. A trail of gray blood led from the exit hatch to about the spot where Phoebe claimed she'd been pushed.

Pakhet stumbled out of the ship. She clutched her side with one hand. With the other, she held up something wrapped in dark fabric. A hand! But not her own. There was something familiar about the long, slender fingers.

"Styx," said Pakhet, her voice pained. "She attacked me. Where...? I don't...know how...She stabbed..." Pakhet lifted her hand from her side. It was covered in gray blood. A river flowed down her side. She stumbled a few steps down the ramp, then collapsed.

Atlas leaped onto the ramp and crouched at Pakhet's side. Citlali followed close behind. Pallas drew her staff and she and Ajax ran into the ship.

"I *knew* there was someone else on the ship," said Dara.

"This is not the time," snapped Citlali. She examined Pakhet's wound and frowned. "Call for a healer. Quickly."

"But there is an unfriendly intruder—," said Dara.

"Our sister has been severely wounded!" said Citlali. She tore a strip off her robe and applied pressure to the wound. "We will deal with the intruder later." She looked around the perimeter, worry contorting her face. "We need to get to a secure location. Contact Sitara."

"You want to take them to the Temple now?" Astrophel asked incredulously. "No. We haven't confirmed their intentions. I won't allow it!"

"This is not an argument, Phel," said Citlali. "I'm taking them to the Temple."

"We can't trust them," said Astrophel. "They lied to us about how many people were with them, and now—"

Citlali stood abruptly and faced Astrophel. "This is not an argument. Now, go away and leave us alone, or help us save the life of our sister." She stooped to tend to Pakhet, but Astrophel tapped Citlali on the shoulder and offered to take her place. Citlali moved aside.

Ajax and Pallas returned from inside the ship. Pallas carried a small cylinder.

"Gaia's clear," said Ajax. "But Styx destroyed the only weapons we had."

"And most of our medical supplies," said Pallas. "This is all that's left." She stooped next to Pakhet and pressed the cylinder against her arm. "This will put her under. And hopefully slow the bleeding some." Pakhet's breathing slowed.

Itri ran up to Citlali. "She...it—whatever it was—is no longer in the area. But I can't be sure without knowing what type of cloaking technology it may be using."

Citlali turned to Atlas. "Is there anything you can tell us that may be of help?"

Atlas shook his head. "I don't know—*we* didn't know. How could she have gotten aboard? We would never...please. Please, save Pakhet."

Citlali nodded.

"A local volunteer security force will be here momentarily," said Dara.

"No," said Citlali. "Contact them again and tell them it was a false alarm."

"Why? The people deserve to know there is a dangerous outsider in the area."

"Yes, but first we must get the Philadelphians to Sitara in the Temple. Then we will have time to speak with the security officers. Did you contact a healer?"

"As you wished."

"He or she must meet us at the Temple. There is no time to waste." Citlali stooped to help Astrophel with Pakhet.

Dara and Itri left hurriedly.

Astrophel had fashioned a bandage from the hems of his and Citlali's robes and tied it around Pakhet's wound. He muttered something Atlas couldn't hear.

"Atlas?" Pallas pulled Atlas aside. "If that was Styx..."

"I know," said Atlas. He turned to Citlali. "You need to lock the system down. No travel in or out for any purpose."

"That is not possible." Citlali forced a smile.

"You need to *make* it possible. I don't think you understand how dangerous Styx is."

Citlali pulled Atlas close. "Atlas, my dear...I understand. I do. But what you ask is impossible. There's no time for further discussion right now. We need to get to the Temple."

"But Styx has killed so many," Atlas pleaded. "Your people are in grave danger—not just from Styx, but also from her employers."

Citlali sighed. "Atlas, you have sensed my exhalation, as I have sensed yours. I believe you to be honest and sincere and I am grateful for your concern for my people. But you must trust me." She touched him on the cheek with her index finger. "Do you trust me?"

For some reason, as she asked the question, Atlas relaxed. He felt a wave of peace sweep over him. "Yes," he said.

"Then come with us to the Temple. Speak with Sitara. She will help you to understand."

"Okay," said Atlas.

Astrophel finished whatever he had been muttering and easily lifted Pakhet into his arms. He carried her down the ramp.

Atlas rejoined his friends. Phoebe had her arm around Ajax's shoulder. "How are you, Phoebe?"

"I'm fine," she said. "Really, I can walk on my own, but Ajax won't let me. It's only a mild sprain. Barely anything at all."

"Reedy, secure the ship," Atlas said. "We may not be coming back here for a while."

"You want me to secure *Gaia*?"

"That's what I said."

"No, it's not."

Atlas shook his head in frustration. "Please secure *Gaia*, dammit."

Reedy programmed a security protocol into *Gaia*, then returned to the others. "Where are we going?"

"With Citlali to the Temple."

"Wonderful," sighed Reedy sardonically. "After all we've been through so far, I genuinely don't have any more patience for strange, senti religion."

The group walked towards a waiting vehicle, Atlas alongside Citlali.

"The Temple is not a religious site," said Citlali. "Although, it is considered by many to be the most sacred of all places within the Ciencia system."

"Sounds like a religious site to me," said Reedy under her breath.

"To some, maybe. I prefer to think of it as a place of truth, rather than superstition."

"As would any true believer," said Reedy.

"Perhaps."

"What, exactly, is it the temple of?" asked Ajax.

"Of?" asked Astrophel.

"To what is the Temple dedicated?" asked Pallas. "Some deity? Or to an abstract idea, like wisdom?"

"Or to some heavenly object?" Phoebe added snidely.

"It has many names in many legends and languages," said Astrophel, as he carefully set Pakhet on the Cienciant vehicle.

The vehicle appeared to be little more than a levitating metal slab about ten meters long. No seats. It reminded Atlas of a giant surfboard. It made absolutely no sound. Not even a hum.

"Some call it—" Astrophel said.

"Just tell us what *you* call it," interrupted Reedy. "I don't need to know what others call it."

"Reedy, don't be rude," said Pallas.

"We call it the Temple," Citlali said gently. "But in most other languages and legends, the name translates to roughly the same thing, The Temple of the Celestial Sphere."

CHAPTER 30

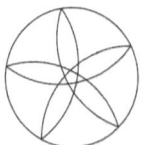

THE CIENCIANT VEHICLE raced across the Ciencia landscape. Even at such a high speed, the vehicle made no sound.

Atlas realized he couldn't feel the wind on his face. Nor did he feel the inertial force as they traveled around sharp curves and down steep grades. It was as if there was an invisible bubble around the vehicle which kept everything within it perfectly stable. It was disorienting, not being able to feel the movement, even when he walked to the rear of the vehicle to check on Pakhet.

"Hang in there, Pakhet," he said, kneeling beside her. He put a hand on hers, but recoiled when he realized Pakhet still clutched Styx's severed hand. The hand that had killed Oliver and blinded Homer. Atlas's stomach heaved in disgust and hatred.

Atlas returned to his place next to Pallas. She carried the metal staff slung across her back. Their only weapon. It was probably best they hadn't made first contact with the Cienciants while heavily armed. But with Styx out there...

His thoughts on Styx, Atlas reached out and squeezed Pallas's hand. No matter what, he wasn't going to let his friends die. That was first. Whatever was necessary.

After a short journey, they arrived at the base of a solitary mountain. As he exited the vehicle, Atlas looked up at the enormous thrust of natural stone rising beyond the clouds. Midway up, snow covered the various crags and cliffs even though the temperature at the base was comfortable, almost warm. The surrounding terrain was eerily flat. Not even eroded foothills had met them as they approached the mountain. The only explanation could be volcanic, Atlas thought. It didn't look like any volcanic mountain he'd ever seen. More like a pyramid.

"How's she doing?" Phoebe asked Astrophel.

"She's lost much blood," Astrophel said. "Her clothing has slowed the bleeding, but such a wound..." He shook his head. "I will carry her to the healer." He adjusted Pakhet's weight in his arms, then ran up the narrow path towards the mountain.

"I'm going with you," said Phoebe. She hurried after Astrophel remarkably fast considering her injury.

The remaining group began the walk up the path. Atlas was anxious to hurry along. He didn't like being separated from Pakhet and Phoebe, but Citlali walked calmly and without haste. She seemed almost relaxed.

"I thought we were going to a temple," said Ajax.

"We are here," said Citlali.

"A mountain?" said Reedy.

"It certainly is pretty," said Pallas.

Atlas looked at Pallas. "Yes. It is very beautiful. And perfect."

"So, you built the temple in a mountain?" Reedy asked Citlali.

"We built the mountain," called Dara as she and Itri came down the path to meet them.

"The healer is ready to receive the Theban inside the Temple," Itri said.

"You built the mountain?" said Ajax. He whistled. "Now that is impressive."

"Yes," said Reedy. "Even from here, it looks like it's natural."

"From any distance it looks natural, even microscopic," said Itri. He stuck his chest out proudly.

"That's not entirely true," said Citlali. "The Temple is so old the transmogrific filaments are easily visible at moderate magnification."

"But not with the naked eye," insisted Itri. "Microscopic is a broad term, and unless you know what you're looking at, you won't recognize the filaments. I assert the accuracy of my statement."

"It may be accurate, but it's also misleading," huffed Citlali. She tried to mask her annoyance, but couldn't keep the glint of frustration out of her eyes.

They had almost reached the end of the path and arrived at the wall of the Temple. Astrophel and Phoebe must have already gone inside, because they were nowhere to be seen. *But where did they go?* The path terminated at a sheer rock face. Atlas pressed his hand against the wall, but it didn't give way. *Solid as…well, solid as a rock.* He blushed and shook his head, embarrassed.

"Is something wrong?" asked Citlali.

"I guess I expected it to let me walk right through it," said Atlas.

"That would be silly," said Dara. "It's not magic."

"I didn't think it was magic. I'm just unfamiliar with the limits of your technology."

"Our technology has no limits," said Itri.

"And yet, you couldn't find Styx," said Pallas.

"That's different," said Dara. "And we can. We just need to know what to look for."

"All technology has limits, even ours," said Citlali.

"Then we haven't reached them yet," said Itri.

"That's not true," said Reedy. "You pulled your research team off Thebes after one of your researchers fathered a child with their Prime Matriarch."

"That was a matter of ethics," said Itri.

"Ethics *are* limits," said Reedy.

"Yes," said Citlali. "The most important kind." She placed her hand on Reedy's shoulder. "I have very much enjoyed our short time together, young Philadelphians." She leaned in closer to

Reedy. "And I have especially enjoyed the way you challenge Itri and Dara."

"I'm not trying to be contentious," Reedy said.

"Of course not."

"Are you leaving us?" asked Pallas.

"We have much to do," said Citlali. "If we are to find Styx before she presents a serious threat to Ciencia, my children and I must go now."

"Styx already presents a serious threat," said Pallas. "Do not underestimate her. That was the Titans' mistake."

"Your children?" said Ajax.

"Itri and Dara are your children?" asked Reedy.

"And Astrophel, who is my oldest."

No wonder they bickered like siblings, thought Atlas. "You must forgive us," he said. "But where we're from, you wouldn't look old enough to have children as old as them."

Citlali laughed. "What would you say if I told you I was already a great-grandmother?"

"Soon to be great-great-grandmother," said Dara.

"No way!" said Ajax.

"Yes," said Citlali.

"Um…Congratulations," said Reedy.

"Thank you, but I had nothing to do with it," said Citlali. "Apart from serving as a witness, I was not involved. It was my great-grandson—Dara's grandson—and his mate that performed the ritual."

"Oh…no…" Reedy blushed. "That's not what I meant."

"*Witness*?" Pallas mouthed to Atlas, frowning.

"Citlali," said Itri. He looked up at the waning sunlight. "We must go."

"Ah yes. You got me talking about my family and I became distracted. I apologize." She faced the mountain wall and closed her eyes. Stretching her arms out towards the wall, Citlali brought her hands together until her thumbs and forefingers touched, forming a triangle. Then she spread her hands apart, and as she did, a passageway opened up in the wall. There was no movement of any kind, no door sliding or swinging open, no fading transition from solid rock to nothing. Where once there had been solid rock was now a long and well-lit passageway. "Go now. Phoebe is waiting for you outside Sitara's chambers. You must all enter her chambers together."

"And Pakhet?" asked Ajax.

"I told you, she is with the healer," said Itri.

"No you didn't," said Dara. "You said the healer was waiting for her."

"That's the same thing," snapped Itri. "Phel took her ahead. The healer was waiting. Obviously, she's with the healer now."

"But that's not what you *said*," said Dara.

"Children!" Citlali said. "Enough."

"Sorry, Mother," said Itri.

"I apologize, Citlali," said Dara.

Citlali sighed. "Pakhet is with our healer. She will live and *we* will apprehend Styx. Go now, Philadelphians. Unburden your minds. This moment is for you. You are my equals."

Atlas and his friends stepped through the entrance to the Temple and into the mountain passageway. A band of light ran the length of the passageway along the top of each wall. Atlas turned to wave to the Cienciants.

"You need to go a bit deeper, so we can close the portal," said Dara.

Atlas stepped further inside. Citlali brought her thumbs and fingers back together. There was a slight delay, and then there was a wall where there had been no wall.

Ajax slapped his open palm against the surface. "Solid. Cool."

"Let's go," said Pallas. She started down the passageway.

"This is amazing," said Reedy. She reached up to touch the part of the wall that illuminated the passageway. "It's so bright. What would you say? Fifty-six…fifty-seven hundred Kelvin?"

"Almost sunlight," said Atlas.

"And yet, it's cool—almost cold—to the touch," said Reedy.

Ajax reached his hand up to test for himself. "And it has the same texture as the wall. Like it's stone."

"Look," Pallas called back. "We don't have time to be awed by every little wonder right now. It's an *ultra*-advanced civilization. Of course the technology is cool and interesting and almost magical, but we don't have the luxury to marvel at the moment, no matter what Citlali said. We are here for one reason. It's time to make the Prophecy come true."

"You're right," said Atlas. He jogged to catch up with Pallas.

Reedy and Ajax joined them as they exited the passageway and entered an enormously vast chamber extending nearly the full length and width of the mountain and rising up nearly to its peak. The floor was polished and translucent white stone, lit from below. Looking down, Atlas estimated the floor was at least several feet thick of solid stone. On the interior walls of the Temple, alternating ribbons of platinum and the illuminating substance from the passageway spiraled upwards. At the peak, the ribbons were so tightly woven together that the confluence of light and reflection made it impossible to look at directly.

A focused beam of light from the peak illuminated the center of the chamber more brightly than the rest. Other than the center, the chamber was completely uniform. Empty.

"Atlaaassss!" Phoebe called. They could only barely hear her. A shadow partially obscured the light in the center of the chamber. "Over here!"

"How did she get all the way over there so quickly?" asked Ajax. "She didn't get that much of a head start."

"She's fast," said Pallas.

"I'm faster," Reedy muttered.

"It doesn't matter. Let's go." Atlas sprinted towards Phoebe.

Ajax and Reedy zoomed past him almost immediately. They howled as they passed. Then Pallas passed him. She laughed. *That was quicker than I expected,* Atlas thought. Had the two months in the mine left him that out of shape? *No. What?* Pallas looked like she was walking.

Atlas stopped.

Ajax and Reedy also appeared to be walking leisurely, yet they moved away from him at an astonishing pace. The ground underneath the three shone brighter than the rest of the floor with little tails of light trailing behind them like a comet.

Atlas stepped casually towards the circle and was instantly rushed fifteen feet across the Temple floor. Despite the rapid velocity changes, he didn't lose his balance. He took another step, this one slower and more tentative. He was whisked nearly thirty feet. *Whoa!* He took two rapid steps, but only advanced ten feet.

He grinned broadly and took three slow, relaxed steps. He moved almost a hundred feet. Altas continued that pace and darted across the Temple floor. *How absurd*, he thought. *But so incredibly cool! The slower I walk, the faster I go.* He slowed his walking pace even more, yet his speed across the floor increased again. The distance between him and Pallas began to diminish.

Atlas slowed his pace once more, this time to a comical, pantomime-like speed. He zoomed past Pallas almost without realizing it. And then he passed Reedy and Ajax. He turned to look at them. *Tortoise and the hare*, he thought. Atlas laughed to himself and turned back around. He couldn't see the light in the center of the room any more. He stopped and turned around. *Damn. I passed it.* He started back towards Phoebe and the center light. Four steps later he arrived.

"That was so cool," said Ajax.

"How did you go so fast?" asked Reedy.

"Easy," said Atlas. "I walked slower than you."

Pallas grinned and turned to Phoebe. "So what now?"

"It's like an elevator," Phoebe whispered and pointed to the brightly lit floor. "The circle."

"Why are you whispering?" Reedy asked.

"I'm trying to be respectful."

"You were yelling earlier," said Ajax.

"That was only to get your attention. I felt really bad as soon as I did it."

"Don't be silly," said Reedy. "It's just a large, empty room."

"An *extremely* large, empty room," said Ajax.

"But not to the Ciencians," said Atlas.

"Exactly," said Phoebe.

Ajax squinted up at the light confluence. "You said it was an elevator?"

"That's what Astrophel said. He told me to wait here for the rest of you and then he carried Pakhet onto it and went down."

"Why would he go down?" asked Ajax.

"Everything must be down," said Reedy. "There's nothing up there but light. Down is the only option."

"But there's so much space up here. Why not use it?"

"Who says they don't?" asked Phoebe. "They might use it differently than we would."

"We could discuss it forever, or we could learn for ourselves," said Pallas. She stepped into the center of the circle.

"Hurry, before she goes down without us!" said Phoebe. She jumped into the circle, but nothing happened. "Hmm...it went down immediately with Astrophel and Pakhet. So fast."

Atlas, Reedy, and Ajax joined the other two. As soon as Ajax stepped into the light, the floor began to descend. It dropped rapidly, sending Atlas's stomach into his throat. He sat down and hoped he wouldn't throw up. His friends seemed unaffected.

"Are you okay?" asked Reedy.

"A bit motion sick, that's all."

The circle came to a stop. The Philadelphians found themselves nearly surrounded by the same translucent white stone that comprised the floor of the Temple. Atlas looked up. They were hundreds of feet below the Temple's primary chamber.

A narrow hallway led them out of the elevator and into a wide room full of ancient books, scrolls, maps, globes, star charts, and other anachronisms. The room smelled of mildew, dust, and aged leather. The smell made Atlas happy. *Like an old book shop*, he thought.

There was no direct path through the shelves and tables that filled the room, so they had to take a careful, meandering route through the ancient texts and charts.

"These are from all over," said Pallas. "I've seen dozens of senti languages already. Some I recognize, but most are completely foreign to me."

"Look at those stars," said Phoebe, pointing to a nearby star chart inscribed on a clay tablet. It was clearly very old, but still in excellent condition. "That is from Earth."

"How can you know from a single glance?" asked Ajax. "You're a good astronomer, but you're not that good."

"Because the writing is cuneiform. Probably from the Old Babylonian Empire."

"Yes, that star chart was drawn on Philadelphia," said a voice from behind a nearby stack of moldering books. "I'm impressed that you recognized it so quickly, especially with so many other, more interesting, maps and books competing for your attention."

"Thank you," said Phoebe.

"We are looking for Sitara," said Atlas. "Are you her?"

A short woman with long gray hair stepped out from behind the stack of books. Like the other Cienciants, she wore a brightly colored robe, but while the others wore robes of primarily one color, Sitara's bore every shade of the rainbow in narrow stripes interspersed with broad white lines. "I am indeed Sitara, young Atlas. And I am exceedingly happy to have finally made your acquaintance."

Sitara was undoubtedly very old, but her visage and composure belied her age. She reminded Atlas of his kindergarten teacher, Ms. Tucker, whose kindness and wisdom had made him think that her grandchildren must be among the luckiest in the world. It wasn't until a few years later that he learned Ms. Tucker had neither grandchildren, nor children. *What a weird thought to have right now...*

"Have you been expecting us?" asked Ajax.

"For most of my life." Sitara stepped close to Ajax and touched his cheeks and chin with her palms. Then she wrapped her long, thin fingers around his wrist and lifted it to eye level. She scrutinized it for several moments, then frowned and dropped his hand.

"Is something wrong?" asked Ajax.

"No, no, no. Not at all," said Sitara. "However, just because something is not wrong does not mean that all is right. And even if it is right, that doesn't make it good, or ideal."

"I don't understand," said Ajax.

"No, but you will. In time."

Atlas stepped forward and prepared to greet Sitara in the manner they had learned from Citlali. Sitara didn't seem to notice and she performed the same examination on Phoebe. She scrutinized Phoebe's wrist, then frowned and dropped it. Next, she examined Reedy and Pallas with the same result. When she reached Atlas, he offered to greet her again.

Sitara shook her head kindly. "No, not with me, my dear." She snickered to herself. "I don't indulge in that hollow ritual. It's a bit platitudinous, don't you think?"

"I think it's a beautiful ritual and sentiment," said Reedy.

"Of course you do, my dear." She examined Atlas's wrist, then released it, seemingly pleased.

"I don't understand," said Atlas.

"It's quite simple and obvious," said Sitara. She placed her hands on Atlas's shoulders and leaned in close. "We are *not* equals," she mocked. "And making a grand pronouncement to the contrary doesn't automatically make it so. The whole idea is absurd. Just look at us. Look at all the differences between us. I am short. Ajax is tall. You are young and inexperienced. I am older than you imagine and I have seen more than I could relate to you during your lifetime. You are Philadelphian. I am Cienciant. You and Ajax are male. Phoebe, Reedy, Pallas and I are female."

"Equality does not mean sameness," insisted Reedy.

"It doesn't?" Sitara feigned disbelief. "And yet mathematically, it does."

"Mathematically, there are an infinite number of ways to arrive at the same sum," Reedy said.

"You're assuming every being adds up to the same sum, my dear. It's simply not true."

Reedy stood silent, her mouth agape. She shifted her weight from side to side, uncomfortably admitting she had no response.

"What's wrong with being different?" Phoebe interjected. "Just because some of us may not add up to much right now, doesn't mean we're worthless. And we can always change. We can make ourselves better."

"Exactly," said Reedy. "Speaking *mathematically*, a being whose value at any given point is low, or even insignificant when compared to another being, the first being—as a sentient entity—possesses the capacity to improve. Given sufficient time, such improvement could potentially be infinite. Therefore, as you approach infinity, every being is equal."

"But we are not infinite beings," said Pallas. "Even Sitara, healthy as she appears, will die someday."

"Of course she will," retorted Reedy. "That's not what I'm saying."

"How do you know she's going to die?" asked Ajax. "What if the Cienciants are immortal?"

"Because death is a universal constant," said Pallas. "Everything dies. It's basic entropy."

Sitara seemed amused by their debate. "Yes. Yes, I will die. Someday." She looked deeply into Pallas's eyes for a moment, then laughed. "But entropy—the tendency towards disorder—is not alone in influencing the Universe."

"Of course not," said Pallas. "Gravity, EM, and the two nuclear forces hold it all together."

"An oversimplification, as you are aware, but more or less accurate," said Sitara. "However, I am speaking of something more basic and fundamental."

"What can be more fundamental than the fundamental forces?" asked Ajax.

"Strings," said Phoebe. "The vibrations of open or closed *strings* generate the observed mass and force particles that build the universe. According to String Theory, at least."

Sitara held Phoebe's hand delicately. "String Theory, as it has developed on your world and others, is an elegant and beautiful approximation of the Universe. However, I speak of a force even String Theory does not predict. A force of creation, of purpose, of action. It permeates the entire fabric of the Universe. To the study and veneration of this force was this grand edifice—The Temple of the Celestial Sphere—built and dedicated."

Reedy shook her head and frowned in disgust. "I knew this was going to turn out to be some silly, senti religion."

"Reedy, don't be rude," said Atlas

"I'm not being rude," said Reedy. "I'm just saying it's the same thing as always: a belief system emerges claiming to explain a particular phenomenon—and to be fair, it may be more accurate than what preceded it—but all too promptly, it attempts to assert itself above all other belief systems.

"It doesn't have to be explicitly spiritual or religious," Reedy ranted. "It could be a political or economic system, for example, but it's the same thing that's been happening on Earth since forever. It's the root cause of our wars and other conflicts. It's the excuse we give for so many of the horrible things that we do to one another. It's why we were kidnapped, and it's why the Alphas are dead. It's the same reason why Sitara believes herself better than us." Reedy sighed. "We all think we know better than everybody else."

Sitara smiled serenely and compassionately at Reedy. "I never said I was better than you. I said we were not equal." She embraced Reedy, who resisted at first, but when Sitara did not yield, Reedy relaxed and accepted the embrace. Sitara released Reedy and looked her in the eyes. "I love you, Reedy. Is not that better?"

Reedy stood agape for the second time. Atlas felt the urge to gloat at the humbling Reedy had endured. After all her heavy-handed moralizing, she deserved a bit of a comeuppance. However, the smug sense of justice was promptly routed by an overwhelming feeling of compassion, empathy, and appreciation. Reedy wasn't perfect. But she didn't need to be.

"I love you too, Reedy," said Atlas.

"And I love you," said Pallas. She embraced Reedy.

"Me too," said Ajax.

"And me," said Phoebe.

Sitara wiped a tear from her eye and joined the Philadelphians in their embrace. "Come now, children. It is time for you to learn the truth about the Celestial Sphere."

CHAPTER 31

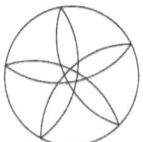

THE PHILADELPHIANS FOLLOWED Sitara back through the clutter of ancient maps and books to the elevator. Pallas touched Atlas's wrist. He slowed his pace until the others were several meters ahead. No one seemed to notice.

"So, what now?" whispered Pallas.

"I have to destroy it," said Atlas. "It's too dangerous for any one person or civilization to control."

"You don't even know what it is. I mean, obviously we can't let the Olympians or Titans have the Sphere. The propaganda alone would lead to war. But what if none of the rumors about it are true? It could be utterly powerless."

"Then why build a temple around it?"

"Because they believe it has supernatural powers, maybe," said Pallas. "Reedy could be right about this. This whole thing might just be a myth. And we are its children crusaders."

"I don't believe that," said Atlas. "I can't. I have to believe that all those deaths—our friends *and* all the Olympians we killed—I have to believe their deaths have greater meaning. They died. And we killed. It can't be for a myth."

Pallas squeezed his hand. "I understand. But it might also just be the same story as always—two opposing powers sending proxies to die so that they can become more powerful."

"That's exactly what this is," said Atlas. "But we have the chance to change things. If the Sphere is real, it must be destroyed. It won't stop them from fighting, but at least neither side will wield unlimited power. That's something. We have to do *something*. We have to destroy it."

"How do you plan on doing that? What if it can't be destroyed?" Pallas stopped him and feigned examining a nearby globe. "What if Sitara tries to stop us? Or...what will the Cienciants do to us if we're successful? I mean, they built a temple around it."

"Then you'll help me?"

"I didn't say that."

"You said *us*."

Pallas nodded that they should catch up to the others. "I think we need to know what we're dealing with first. If it turns out to truly be as powerful as everyone says, I'll help you destroy it. Somehow."

"Thanks," Atlas said.

"Of course."

The two friends caught up to the others as they reached the elevator. Sitara took her place in the center. Recalling his first trip in the elevator, Atlas sat down.

The elevator began to rise. It went up more slowly than it had gone down, but it was still unpleasant for Atlas. He tried not to think about the dizzying heights they were ascending to, or the fact that the elevator seemed to be freely levitating without obvious support. *After everything—the mine, flying through space, all that training—and it's just like I'm having a bad day at the fair.* Atlas put his head between his knees and counted backwards from one hundred by threes. Pallas stood near him and rested a hand on the back of his bowed head. The light from the narrowing temple walls became more and more brilliant, until squinting wasn't enough to block the light and Atlas had to cover his eyes with his hands.

Eventually, almost halfway through his second cycle down

from one hundred, they came to a stop. The elevator glowed from below, having lifted them above the Temple light source. Atlas looked up. Only then did he realize the elevator had carried them outside the mountain. They were now on a wide, flat outcropping a hundred feet below the highest peak of the mountain.

The platform reminded Atlas of a large helicopter landing pad. Had it not appeared of identical composition as the mountain, Atlas would have expected the outcropping was artificial, jutting out so far from the rest of the mountain as it did. *Of course it is artificial*, he thought. *This whole mountain is artificial. That's what Dara said. But it looks so real.*

Beyond the mountain peak, broad, bright stripes of millions of stars painted the sky. It was much broader, denser, and brighter than the Milky Way appeared on Earth. *We're much closer to the center of the Galaxy.* It reminded Atlas of the spiraling, luminescent stripes along the Temple's interior walls.

Pallas lifted Atlas to his feet. "Wow."

"Yeah, wow," said Atlas. Despite their high altitude, the temperature on the platform was warm and comfortable.

"I know of no sight more beautiful," said Sitara. She walked to the center of the platform and beckoned them to join her.

"No," said Phoebe. "Nothing more beautiful."

"Do you come up here often?" asked Reedy.

"Only once before. A long time ago," said Sitara.

"Just once in your entire life?" said Phoebe. "I would come up here every night. I'd probably sleep out here. That is, assuming I could sleep. I think I'd probably stay up all night counting the stars."

"That would be pleasant, but it is forbidden."

"Forbidden?" asked Atlas.

"One visit is all that is needed. Any more could be...dangerous."

"Why?" asked Reedy.

"Because of the sphere." Sitara pointed over her head.

The Philadelphians looked up. Atlas didn't see anything.

"It's in space?" asked Phoebe.

"No, it is small," said Sitara. "But it is there. I can feel its presence, even after all these years."

"I thought it would be bigger," said Ajax. "Like, a lot bigger."

"At least big enough to see," said Phoebe.

"And so, it just...kind of...*floats* up there invisibly?" said Reedy.

"You will see it, when it is time," assured Sitara.

"Time for what?" asked Atlas. He stopped looking for the sphere and studied Sitara's face. "When it's time for what?"

Sitara smiled warmly. "Before I can answer that, I must explain to you the nature of the Celestial Sphere."

"Please do," said Pallas.

"If you would please sit," said Sitara.

"I prefer to stand," said Reedy, rolling her eyes.

"I must insist." Sitara pointed up towards where she said the sphere was.

Reedy looked to Atlas. He nodded and sat down. Reedy scowled and flopped to the ground near him. "Was it going to smite me for not sitting?" she said under her breath.

"You'll recall I spoke of a grand creative force that works upon and throughout the entire Galaxy," Sitara began. "We call this force the *Epignosis*." She paused, as if she regretted something she had said. "I am unsure of how your translators will communicate that term. Quite likely, the languages of your planet lack an adequate expression. Our term conveys both the impulse to create and a sense of self-awareness. It is important that you understand that. Young Arete accused me of evangelizing for Cienciant religion..."

"How does she know my real name?" whispered Reedy.

"I do not blame her for this, of course," said Sitara. "It is difficult to believe in something with which you have little or no experience. Hers is a prudent response and I do not trivialize her reluctance to accept my word alone on the matter. Had we sufficient time, I would expound the tomes and tomes of research we have accumulated, and the details and results of over a million experiments conducted in our attempts to better understand the nature and functions of the Epignosis. The Temple Archives contain the full breadth of our understanding of this very natural force."

"Then why hasn't any other civilization discovered any of this *evidence*?" challenged Reedy.

"Because they have not known where or how to look. Or rather, the Epignosis permeates all things and everything so completely that it is difficult *not* to overlook. Its ubiquity conceals it." Sitara grinned. "And yet, we have discovered that the Epignosis is the greatest and most powerful of all the forces we have been able to measure. Its strength, we believe, is also a function of its ubiquity."

"So, what does it do?" asked Ajax. "Or, I should say, how does it act? That's the scientific term, right?"

Reedy nodded.

"My dear Ajax, the Epignosis does not *do*," Sitara said. "Nor does it act. It *is*. The entire purpose and function of the Universe is derived from it."

"I don't understand," said Ajax.

"Me neither," said Reedy. "If it's a force, it must do something. That is the definition of a force. It influences matter."

"Your last statement is correct," said Sitara. "Matter does according to the influences exerted upon it, not the other way around. The Epignosis is the prime force. It is the prime influencer, and matter obeys its influence."

"Then what does the Epig...nosis influence matter to do?" huffed Reedy.

"The *Epignosis* influences the development of sentience."

"Wait...what?" said Pallas.

"It influences the emergence of sentient beings and sentient thought."

Pallas scooted closer to Sitara and scrutinized her face. "If I understand you correctly, you're saying that the Epignosis compelled the Universe to create intelligent life?"

"Sentient life is not always particularly intelligent," Sitara said. "But when comparing sentient beings to animals driven solely by instinct, I suppose your understanding is accurate. The Epignosis compelled the emergence of sentient beings."

"I *knew* it," said Reedy. "It's an absurd religion. After everything that's happened to us, the Celestial Sphere is a myth. A lie!"

Sitara smiled, but it seemed a bit forced. "You shall quite soon understand for yourself that the Epignosis is not superstition, and the Celestial Sphere is certainly not a lie." She pointed up again, and then down, indicating the Temple. "This great edifice is called the Temple of the Celestial Sphere. It is dedicated to the study and veneration of the Epignosis and its influence upon the Galaxy. Above us *is* a sphere of immense power, but it is *not* the Celestial Sphere."

Dammit, thought Atlas. *So, it's not here after all.* His heart sank. He had begun to believe their mission was almost over. That he would be able to return home soon. That he would be able to see his parents. Watch a baseball game. Be a kid again.

"Then where is it?" demanded Phoebe.

"And why are you wasting our time trying to convert us to your religion?" said Reedy.

"The true Celestial Sphere to which the Temple was dedicated and from which emanates the greatest power in the Universe resides within…the *mind* of every sentient being." Sitara looked as if she had successfully played a prank on them.

"Our brains?" said Ajax.

"Precisely," said Sitara. "Or rather, somewhat imprecisely. The physical matter of the brain is but the focal point around which consciousness is organized. It is simple matter. However, it obeys the influence of the forces it is subject to, and the sentient brain is uniquely susceptible to the Epignosis."

"What a bunch of feel-good, pseudoscientific, metaphysical, horse—"

"Reedy!" said Atlas. "We know how you feel about this. Please let us come to our own conclusions."

"But Sitara's trying to convert you to see things her way."

"So are you. Trust us enough to make up our own minds."

"And be willing to change yours gracefully, Reedy," said Ajax.

"Each Celestial Sphere is unique and individual to the person in which it resides," Sitara continued. "It has the power to look beyond itself and its quotidian needs, and gaze into the heavens with wonder, awe, and an unquenchable thirst for greater under-standing. It is creative and curious. It possesses the capacity to learn and adapt, to correct and restore. Conversely, it also possesses the ability to denigrate and destroy. Each Sphere may govern itself with grace and humility, but it may also oppress other beings by seeking power over them, thereby disparaging and demeaning their sentience. And each Sphere, being unique, is by definition *not* equivalent to any other Sphere." Sitara pointedly looked at Reedy. "Yet, by virtue of that same uniqueness, each also possesses intrinsic value above and beyond any imaginable treasure."

"In other words, the Celestial Sphere is everything that the legends say about it," said Atlas. "But nothing like what people believe."

Phoebe leapt to her feet. "So we were kidnapped and murdered and blinded and enslaved and forced to...forced to *defend* ourselves against people trying to possess the Celestial Sphere." Her voice broke. "And all this time, everyone who did all those terrible things had their very own Celestial Sphere?" Her voice trembled and cracked with frustration and rage, and her hands shook uncontrollably. "So now what? What are we supposed to do now? Who's gunna' believe us?" She turned and waved to imaginary people. "Oh hello, Olympian death squad. I know you're here to kill us because you think we found the most powerful weapon in the Universe and you want it for yourselves. Well, guess what? You're not going to believe this, but this whole time—this whole damn time—the power was *inside* you! Oh, and it's also not an all-powerful weapon—sorry about that. It's the *power of your mind*." She began laughing hysterically. "Isn't that great? We don't have to kill each other anymore. I know it's difficult to believe, but trust me, it's true. Some old lady on a mountain told us all about it."

Pallas stood and approached Phoebe cautiously. She put an arm around Phoebe's shoulders and urged her to sit back down.

"It's not fair," Phoebe sobbed. "We're going to die. We're going to *die.* They're going to find us. They have an entire planet. They have an *empire.* And we're just five kids. We'll kill some of them. Then they'll kill us. And then they'll kill anyone and everyone else who keeps them from controlling the Celestial Sphere, which will be everyone because everyone is their own Sphere." She glared at Sitara. "You brought us up here to tell us that we're going to die for nothing. Nothing!" She collapsed into Pallas, weeping uncontrollably.

"No," said Sitara. "That is not the reason you are here. And you will not die for nothing. I haven't finished telling the story, so you don't have all the information."

"Please continue then," said Atlas. "But spare us the religious overtones."

The tension was beginning to get to him. And there was the doubt. Before, even when he doubted the Sphere's existence, it had been easy to keep going. It was something to focus on—an end goal—no matter how improbable. Even in the mine, Atlas had kept the glimmer of hope that somehow they would find the Sphere and stop the Olympians, rescue Homer and the Betas, and bring peace to the Galaxy, at least until everybody found something else to fight about. That was the only way any of it had meaning. All those deaths.

If he was successful—if *they* were successful—then there was meaning to Lanta's last breath, to Oliver's execution, to Taco's sacrifice. Success meant going home, even if he would never be the same. Atlas would bury himself in Diamondbacks games, and

ASG Pizza, and high school, and family, and he would pretend he was normal and happy until it came true.

But now, all of that seemed impossible. It seemed like a bad joke.

"…in high concentrations, bonded to high-density elements in a structure called an Epignoscent," Sitara was saying. "For many years, we believed this was nothing more than a theory, barely more than idle speculation and a complex equation. In order to be detectable in such a form, the concentration would have to be higher than we believed possible. We calculated that only an expired and critically collapsed galaxy could generate the energy needed to produce more than a few grams of Epignoscent. Discovering only a few grams of the substance within the endless expanse of space should be impossible."

"As likely as discovering a unicorn," snarked Reedy.

"And then, we *did* discover one," said Sitara. "Almost a full kilogram of Epignoscent in the form of a perfect sphere."

"The sphere," whispered Atlas. *It's real.*

He looked up, and there it was, floating freely, less than twenty feet above their heads. It had a shiny, metallic appearance, like a ball bearing, but it also seemed transparent. He could see through it to the stars beyond.

"Where did…?" said Phoebe.

"What does it do?" asked Ajax.

"It doesn't *do*, dearest Ajax—it *is*," said Reedy. "Remember?" She rolled her eyes again at Sitara. "Smoke and mirrors."

Sitara laughed. "The Epignosis *is*, but the Epignoscent *does*."

"But you said—"

"It is an aberration," said Sitara. "Force and matter eternally merged, and thus it is capable of action."

"Are you saying it is sentient? That it has consciousness?" asked Atlas.

"No, it is sentience, though it does not possess it for itself."

"Now *I* don't understand," said Phoebe.

"Who does?" muttered Ajax.

"The Epignosis force only influences matter to bring forth sentient lifeforms. It is not sentient, nor is it sentience. However, the Epignoscent incorporates Epignosis into matter in a wholly unexpected and seemingly unnatural manner. Force and matter are so tightly interwoven that the boundaries between them have dissolved. For this reason, we could not see it earlier. Unlike normal forces and matter which simply influence and react, the Epignoscent can act for itself. However, it is more like an emotional thunderstorm than a rational, self-aware being."

Sitara wrung her hands and pursed her lips. "That's not quite right. I'm doing a terrible job describing it. As I said, the Temple archives are full of literature explaining everything we currently know about the Epignoscent. If we had more time—"

"So, what does it do?" asked Reedy.

Sitara looked at Reedy, expressionless. "It will help you all fulfill your destiny."

"Argh!" Reedy cried. "Just be straight with us. Tell us what you mean."

"That is exactly what I mean. It helps people to fulfill their destiny."

"Everything I do helps me *fulfill* my destiny," said Reedy.

"Of course," said Sitara. "And the Epignoscent will take you further and faster than you ever could have imagined." She crossed to the side of the mountain and pressed both her palms against it. "We cannot control the Epignoscent, but we have learned how to coax it to respond somewhat predictably."

The sphere began to glow and hum, and it appeared to grow as it descended. When it stopped a meter above their heads, Atlas could see that it hadn't grown at all. The original sphere remained the same size as it had always been, but another sphere—seemingly comprised of some type of energy—encased the original.

"If you could live a thousand years without physical impediment or deterioration, you would not have accomplished what the Epignoscent will help you accomplish in less than a tenth of that time." Sitara returned to the Philadelphians, who had seated themselves around the Epignoscent. "Everything of which you are each capable—to the extreme limits of your mind, personality, and all other genetic traits—you will achieve through the amplifying influence of the Epignoscent...which is why I must warn you of the risks."

Sitara sighed heavily. "You have shed blood and taken the lives of sentient beings. All but Atlas have death on their hands." She preempted Reedy's protests with three raised fingers. "I do not judge you. However, taking a life has changed you. Even if you do not yet admit the change to yourselves, the Epignoscent will not let you forget the lives you have extinguished or how you felt when you terminated them."

"Do you mean that we'll be haunted by those we've killed?" Phoebe's voice betrayed how close she was to bursting into tears again.

"In a way, yes. You will never forget those who lost their lives by your hands. In time, you will learn to live with it, but each death will be with you always."

"You're assuming we're going to let you perform this proce-dure...rite—whatever—on us," said Reedy.

"But you must."

"No, I mustn't," said Reedy.

"If you don't, the Olympians will hunt you down until they have killed every last one of you, and anyone else they believe gets in their way," said Sitara. "Your deaths will be for nothing. And many more will die also."

"Smoke and mirrors," Reedy sighed as she looked at Pallas, then Atlas. Doubt, fear, and pain flickered in her face. Her eyes lingered on Ajax. He nodded reassuringly and reached for Reedy's hand.

"Okay, how does this work?" Reedy asked Sitara.

"One at a time, you will stand directly below the Epignoscent with your hands raised high in the air," Sitara said. She walked back to the mountain wall. "I will slowly lower the sphere into your hands. Keep your hands still. If they move too quickly, they'll go right through the exosphere and make contact with the Epignoscent, which you must not allow to happen. I have set the exosphere field to the maximum safe diameter. When the exosphere touches your hands, the Epignoscent will lose its ability to suspend itself. You must support its weight by yourself. You will feel as if a mild electric current is passing through your hands. It will become uncomfortable, but you must suspend the Epignoscent above you for at least ten seconds at this diameter."

Sitara touched the mountain wall with both hands. "There may be minor fluctuations in the diameter of the exosphere, and if they occur, the apparent mass of the Epignoscent may increase. For your own safety, it is crucial that you maintain the Epignoscent suspended above your head. And for all of our safety, you must not *drop* the Epignoscent."

"Why?" asked Ajax. "I mean, I won't drop it, but what would happen?"

"The energy exosphere destabilizes inorganic molecular bonds on contact. Should you drop it, the mountain could disintegrate, causing us to fall thousands of feet into a pile of radioactive sand," said Sitara. "Apropos, I would roll up your sleeves above the elbow if you do not want your clothing to be ruined."

Atlas looked for a smile, but Sitara gave no indication she was joking.

"When the requisite time has passed, the exosphere will retract and the Epignoscent will return to a suspended state. I will then prepare the Epignoscent for the next child."

"Why does the diameter matter?" asked Phoebe. Her gaze remained fixed on the Epignoscent.

"I'm sorry?" replied Sitara.

"You said you'll set the exosphere to its maximum safe diameter."

"The greater the diameter, the greater the intensity. Any larger than this, and—" Sitara gasped.

Atlas jerked around towards Sitara. Her head was turned back towards them while her body faced the mountain, arms still outstretched, hands pressed against the wall. Her mouth was fixed open in surprise, unmoving. Blood soaked through the back of her robes and began to pool on the platform.

From behind Sitara, a hooded figure appeared, holding a long, bloody knife. The other arm was shorter—the hand missing.

Styx.

CHAPTER 32

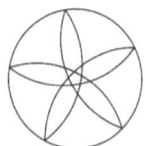

AJAX SPRUNG to his feet and rushed full-speed at Styx with his arms outstretched, ready to tackle her. Styx set her feet and adjusted the knife. Just as Ajax was almost upon her, she shuffled to the side and swung the knife with tremendous force. Ajax dropped backwards to the ground and slid underneath the swing.

Styx was thrown off-balance by the miss. Before she could recover, Pallas smashed her staff across Styx's back, knocking her down. Reedy was instantly upon Styx, pinning her weaponed hand to the ground. Ajax and Pallas quickly piled on top of the assassin and held her face-down.

Reedy slammed Styx's hand against the ground several times, but Styx refused to release her knife. She snarled and snapped, flailed and fought like a vicious animal, but the Philadelphians were able to keep her pinned. The hood slipped from her head, revealing Styx's bald, heavily marked scalp.

Atlas rushed to Sitara. Except for her eyes, she couldn't move. *Just like that night at the Academy,* Atlas thought. Sitara looked at Atlas and then beyond him—towards the Epignoscent—over and over again, frantic and desperate. *She's afraid to die,* Atlas thought. *She's lived so long. But she still isn't ready to die.*

He examined her wound. Styx's knife had gone all the way

through. The wound bled even more profusely from the front. The platform was slick with Sitara's blood.

Atlas pulled his sleeves up over his wrists and pressed the Theban cloth against both sides of Sitara's wound. Her blood quickly saturated his sleeves. He tore two clean strips of cloth from Sitara's robe, folded them quickly, and pressed them into the wound. "Phoebe! Help me, please."

"Atlas, something's wrong," Phoebe said.

"Phoebe! She's dying."

"The Epignoscent, Atlas. Something's *wrong*."

Atlas turned to Phoebe. She stood between him and the Epignoscent, staring up at it.

The Epignoscent pulsed erratically and the exosphere fluctuated wildly from color to color. The edges of the exosphere flickered irregularly. Atlas looked back at Sitara. She was in shock.

Atlas had a thought that didn't feel like his own. The Epignoscent recognized Sitara's desperation.

"How do I relieve the paralysis?" Atlas snapped at Styx.

Styx struggled to free her knife hand from Reedy's grip. Reedy slammed it violently into the ground.

The makeshift bandages Atlas had fashioned were already completely saturated with blood. He pressed his fingers deeper into Sitara's wounds, hoping to somehow find the right pressure to make the bleeding stop.

"If she dies, *you* die," Atlas told Styx.

Styx snarled at him. The snarl morphed into a hideous and mocking laugh that raised the hairs on the back of Atlas's neck.

Shaking his head in desperation, Atlas looked up at Sitara. She met his gaze and held it for several seconds. The fear and distress in her eyes disappeared. They almost looked peaceful. Sitara looked at the Epignoscent one final time, then collapsed.

Atlas tried to catch Sitara as she fell, but slipped in the blood and fell backwards against the mountain wall. He saw Sitara's head strike the stone ground. There was no reaction in her eyes or face. Dead.

Atlas stood up, leaned over, and closed Sitara's eyes, which had remained fixed on the Epignoscent. He clenched his teeth and fists and took a step towards Styx. *For Lanta,* he thought. *And the Alphas. For Taco.*

"Atlas, now it's getting bigger," Phoebe said. She circled anxiously around the Epignoscent. The exosphere field had nearly tripled its radius, though the Epignoscent remained the same size.

"I see it." Atlas looked at Styx, shook his head and took a deep breath to clear his anger, and moved towards the Epignoscent for a closer look. The exosphere continued growing, though the erratic pulsing had ceased.

A sudden shockwave ripped across the platform, hurling Atlas against the mountainside. He collapsed near Sitara's body, his ears ringing and stars flashing in his eyes. *What was...?* He saw Styx, now standing—alone. *Where are...?* Styx pulled aside her cloak and discharged a smoking cartridge from a device strapped to her side.

The dark overtook Atlas.

A few seconds later, he startled back to consciousness. *Pallas.* She lay sprawled on the far side of the platform, unconscious, or worse. Reedy lay near her, in a similar state. Closest to Atlas lay Phoebe. Her head bled profusely, and the left shoulder and back of her shirt was missing. *Ajax?* Atlas turned to see a disoriented and stunned Ajax strike clumsily at Styx with Pallas's staff.

Styx dodged the awkward attack and smashed the hilt of her knife on the back of Ajax's head. His face crashed into the ground, the staff clattering out of reach. Styx cackled, but didn't attempt to finish Ajax off. Instead, she waited until he had pulled himself back up on all fours, then kicked his arms out from under him.

Atlas tried to stand, but couldn't summon his strength. *I have to help him.* He rolled onto his stomach and tried to pull himself towards Ajax and Styx.

Shaking his head, Ajax slowly lifted himself to his feet. He swung a wild punch at Styx, who easily ducked and slashed his side with her knife. Ajax collapsed again, but didn't clutch at the wound. Styx raised her knife to deal the killing blow.

The exosphere of the Epignoscent flashed many shades of green and doubled in size again. The energy field now extended nearly a third of the way to the platform. *If it reaches the platform, we're all dead,* Atlas thought.

Styx withheld her final blow. She seemed transfixed by the Epignoscent's frantic flashing. Lowering her knife, she kicked Ajax in the head. He fell with a thud. Styx cocked her head sideways as she approached the Epignoscent. She crouched low until she was nearly squatting underneath it. The exosphere field flashed above her head. Styx dropped her knife and tentatively lifted a finger to the exosphere field.

"Don't touch it!" Atlas yelled as he pulled himself to all fours. "You can't support it with one hand. If you drop it, we all die." He crawled towards Styx and the Epignoscent.

Styx hissed at Atlas and turned back to the Epignoscent. She reached up to touch the exosphere field with both arms. As she did, her maimed arm began to glow. Two bones burst out of the bandages. Muscles and nerves snaked their way up the bones until they reached the wrist. The bones of her hand and fingers sprouted, and skin grew over the sinewy new hand.

Atlas stood. He eyed Pallas's staff and slowly inched towards it.

Styx held the new hand in front of her face and tested its mobility. She grinned and reached up with both hands to touch the exosphere. Styx shuddered as the weight of the Epignoscent settled upon her.

She remained crouched underneath the sphere. The radius of the exosphere expanded again. Styx's arms wobbled under the immense weight, but gradually steadied. With a fierce howl, Styx stood up underneath the Epignoscent. She grinned in malignant ecstasy, the sphere pressed high above her head. The exosphere field turned a deep red and began to pulse in rhythm with Styx's breathing.

Suddenly, Styx collapsed, dropping the Epignoscent. Atlas dove forward and caught the Epignoscent with his outstretched hands. As Atlas fell forward onto his knees, the Epignoscent slid onto his shoulders and neck, almost slipping out of his hands. But Atlas refused to let it fall.

The immense weight on his neck felt like a painful jolt of electricity running up and down his spine, crushing him. Atlas resisted with all his strength. He felt tendons and muscles in his back, shoulders, and legs straining under the mass of the exosphere field. He grit his teeth. *No matter what, I'm not going to let it drive me into the ground.*

Atlas slowly raised himself into a lunge. The pain in his muscles began to subside and the exosphere began to feel lighter. In front of him lay Styx, her own knife stuck into her back. Above her stood Pakhet, her face and head exposed.

Styx stirred slightly. Pakhet retrieved the knife with a twist, causing Styx to writhe in agony and flop onto her back. She looked up at Pakhet and laughed.

Pakhet readied herself to strike again.

"Sister," Styx hissed. "Make it quick."

"You are not my *sister*."

"Blood is blood." Styx sputtered gray ichor from her mouth.

Pakhet lowered the knife. She stared at Styx, then raised the knife again. When Styx didn't attempt to defend herself, Pakhet lowered the knife once more.

"Do it, sister!" yelled Styx. "Finish me, coward!"

Pakhet stood motionless and indecisive. Ajax stumbled over to her, blood streaming down his side. He took the knife and knelt over Styx. Pakhet turned away.

Ajax spat. "I got you once before and you still managed to kill our friends. I'm not letting that happen again." He gripped the knife above his head with both hands.

Styx grinned and closed her eyes.

Reedy stopped Ajax with a touch of her hand. Ajax burst into tears. He tossed the knife away and moved to stand.

Styx grabbed Ajax's shirt and head-butted him. In a flash she was on her feet, knocking Reedy to the side and leaping upon Ajax. "Fool!" Styx hissed. "Now you die with me!" She drew a line across his throat with her finger.

Pakhet yanked Styx's head backward and gave it a violent twist, snapping her neck. She let Styx fall heavily to the platform. Styx twitched twice and lay still.

"Hurry, Ajax," yelled Reedy. "It healed Styx. It will heal you." She helped Ajax stand and dragged him towards Atlas and the Epignoscent.

"Quickly," said Atlas. "I don't know how much longer I can hold it."

Ajax clutched at his throat as the tissue separated and blood began to spurt from the wound. He slumped to his knees, then fell on his face.

"*No*," cried Pallas. She grabbed Ajax's legs and helped Reedy drag him under the Epignoscent. The two girls lifted Ajax to a sitting position and raised his arms towards the exosphere. Ajax went limp and fell backwards, his eyes open, but vacant.

Atlas roared at the Universe and pressed himself up to both feet, but the mass of the exosphere drove him back to one knee.

"Ajax!" Reedy beat on his chest. "No! No! No! Don't leave me. No!" She continued pounding on his chest until Pallas pinned her arms in an embrace.

"He's gone," Pallas said. "He's gone."

The exosphere expanded again. Atlas felt his muscles rip and tear and several bones fracture, but he didn't drop the Epignoscent. The exosphere field pressed the back of his head down, driving his chin into his chest.

"Help!" said Atlas. "It's too heavy." He winced as he felt a ligament in his knee snap. Immediately, he felt the same ligament grow back and re-attach itself inside his knee. Then it snapped again, forcing him to both knees. "Hurry! *Please*."

A thought, clear and plain—but not his—popped into Atlas's head.

"Pakhet! Not you. Don't touch it! It has to be us! It can only be us."

Pallas wiped the tears from her face. She helped Reedy to her feet and the two girls positioned themselves on either side of Atlas. Reedy crouched low, also pressing her back against the exosphere, and lifting with her legs. Pallas faced the sphere and squatted lower, lifting with her hands above her head.

The exosphere immediately increased its size and mass again, forcing the girls to their knees. Pallas pressed the crown of her head against the exosphere. The mass continued to steadily increase, slowly crushing them closer and closer to the ground. The Epignoscent now rested on Atlas and Reedy's bare backs, their clothing disintegrated by the exosphere field. Pallas fell backwards into a seated position, yet continued to press the Epignoscent with her arms and head.

"I said *no*, Pakhet!" Atlas said.

Pakhet backed away.

Atlas screamed in pain as he felt his vertebrae shatter, then restore, then shatter again and again under the simultaneously destructive and restorative influence of the exosphere field. Pallas and Reedy also shrieked in agony. Atlas's heart broke as he listened to his friends' suffering. He squeezed his eyes shut and counted backwards from one hundred by threes.

Suddenly, the Epignoscent felt much lighter. Atlas was able to lift himself back into a lunge. He opened his eyes. Ajax stood next to him with his face and chest pressed hard against the exosphere and his arms reaching deep underneath it.

"Lift!" said Ajax. "Now!"

Atlas positioned his legs squarely underneath him. All four Philadelphians heaved upwards with all their might. Slowly, the Epignoscent began to rise. As it rose, the exosphere's size and mass began to shrink. Before long, the Philadelphians stood upright with the Epignoscent pressed above their heads.

Phoebe lifted herself off the ground near them. She stumbled across the platform until she stood under the Epignoscent, in between Atlas and Reedy. She touched the exosphere with her finger, then stepped back from it. Her head was completely healed. She looked up at the Epignoscent and smiled. Then, she spread her arms wide, palms open. She brought her hands together with a thunderous clap. The Epignoscent trembled and disappeared.

All five Philadelphians fell as one, unconscious.

ATLAS AWOKE IN A BED. Too soft to be his own. His head hurt terribly, so he closed his eyes again. He rolled onto his side and moaned. Every muscle in his body was more sore than he had ever known was possible.

"Good morning," said Citlali.

Atlas opened his eyes to see the Cienciant seated next to the bed. "How long have I been asleep?"

"For four days," said Citlali.

Four days? I could use another week, Atlas thought. "Where are my friends?"

"They are recovering, just as you, though they have been awake for nearly a day." Citlali closed the book she had been reading.

"And the sphere—I mean…the Epignoscent?"

"It is gone," Citlali said sadly.

"Where did it go?"

"I was hoping you could tell us."

"I don't know." Atlas closed his eyes again and thought back to the last thing he remembered. "One second it was there, and the next it was gone."

"That is disappointing," said Citlali. "Although perhaps it is for the best."

Though it was extremely difficult and painful, Atlas rolled back onto his back. "Why us?"

"I don't understand."

"Why did it have to be us? Why a bunch of Philadelphian kids?"

"I still don't understand what you refer to."

"Yes, you do," said Atlas. "You could have picked any planet, but you chose Philadelphia."

"I didn't choose anyone," Citlali said.

"Your people did." Atlas grimaced as a sudden throb of pain passed through his head. "And you know why, so please tell me."

Citlali sighed. "It's a long story."

"Tell me the short version."

"Very well." Citlali stood and set her book on her chair. "Of all the species we studied during our brief period of intergalactic exploration, Philadelphians were among the least technologically advanced. And yet, in many ways, you were substantially more advanced than any other civilization of comparable sophistication."

"Such as?"

"Well, art for one," said Citlali. "But closely tied to that was what truly drew our attention—your empathy." She sat on the edge of the bed. "Compared to the other sentient races we have studied, including our own, the Philadelphian capacity for empathy is uniquely broad. In most species, empathy is relatively consistent from one specimen to another and it remains fairly static throughout the specimen's life. For Philadelphians, empathy is like a muscle. If you exercise it, it becomes stronger. If you neglect it, it atrophies. As a consequence, there is a much broader empathetic spectrum on Philadelphia than on most worlds."

Atlas sat up slowly. He pressed his fingertips to his temples and rubbed them for a few seconds. He was wearing a lime green Cienciant robe. He remembered his Theban clothing had been partially destroyed by the Epignoscent exosphere.

"While some Philadelphians allow their empathy to atrophy and nearly disappear, others grow it to extraordinary degrees far beyond that observed on other worlds," Citlali continued.

"This is the short version, right?" Atlas pressed his hands over his eyes, inhaled deeply, and exhaled slowly.

"I am almost done," said Citlali. "As we explored the Galaxy, we discovered the tragic reality that while many sentient species attained sufficient empathy to cooperate within their own species in order to develop intergalactic space travel, such an accomplishment typically exposed the limits of their empathic capacity. As soon as they made contact with other worlds, they sought to exploit and oppress the unfamiliar sentient species, often going to war over trivial matters."

Atlas winced. "You're using too-big words for my headache right now."

"Perhaps your translator is malfunctioning," said Citlali.

"Yeah, maybe."

"We knew that if the Galaxy were to ever achieve meaningful peace, it would have to be led by a species capable of greater empathy than ours," said Citlali. "Serendipitously, soon after we identified your species as the likely future heralds of galactic peace, we discovered the Epignoscent."

Atlas yawned. "I'm sorry. I'm so very tired."

"I'll be finished soon," huffed Citlali. "We seeded various rumors and clues around the Galaxy, all pointing to Philadelphia. And then, we waited. Many of the clues died out quickly. Others attained religious significance, such as that Titan prophecy, though it was later lost for many generations."

"How long did you wait?"

"Thousands of years. And even still, according to our projections, you arrived several centuries too early."

"How rude of us," said Atlas. "And now you expect us to bring peace to the Galaxy. I've heard that before." He grunted as he rolled onto his other side, facing away from Citlali. "Do you mind if I go back to sleep for a while?"

He was asleep before he heard her answer.

HOURS LATER, when Atlas awoke again, his headache was gone and his body felt as well as it ever had. His stomach, however, rumbled desperately. He climbed out of bed and went searching for food.

"Atlas!" Phoebe ran up behind him and wrapped her arms around his neck. "About time you finally woke up."

"Yeah, well...it's been a rough couple of months," Atlas said. "You know where I can get some food?"

"Of course," said Phoebe. She wore a pale yellow robe. "Follow me." She clapped her hands excitedly.

Atlas remembered what had happened before the Epignoscent disappeared. "Phoebe, can I ask you a question?"

"Sure."

Atlas stopped her. "What did you do to the Epignoscent?"

Phoebe fidgeted nervously. "Nothing. I just...um...gave it permission."

"Permission to do what?"

"To diffuse into the Universe, I guess."

"It asked you to let it do that?"

"Yes...well, kind of. I guess it didn't ask, but I knew that's what it wanted, so I gave it permission."

"But how did you know, and how did you do it?" Atlas touched her arm. "What happened to you when Styx detonated the repulsor?"

"I hit my head."

"I saw you bleeding. You hit your head on the ground?"

She shook her head. "On the Epignoscent." She grimaced. "Not the energy field. The metal part. Or whatever it is."

"And it knocked you out?"

"It didn't knock me out," said Phoebe. "I was... uh...elsewhere."

"Where do you think you were?"

"I don't want to talk about it."

"Why not?"

"Because I *don't*." She wiped her eyes.

"Okay, I'm sorry."

Phoebe wiped her nose with a sleeve. "It's alright. Here. Dining room is just down the hall. Last door on the left." She left.

Atlas watched Phoebe walk away and decided she wanted to be left alone.

The dining room was empty except for a woman with long, dark-red hair. She wore a light-purple, Cienciant robe and was seated facing away from the entrance. An assortment of food was laid out on several tables at the back of the room. Atlas made his way to the food and began stuffing his face.

"Philadelphian. You're finally awake," Pakhet said.

Atlas turned around, but couldn't see Pakhet. The red-haired woman smiled broadly at him. She was young, but her eyes were wise. Her skin was gray-red. Theban.

"Pakhet?" He realized the woman's hair wasn't dark red, after all. Rather, it was red with narrow, black stripes. Or black with narrow, red stripes. It was hard to tell.

"You didn't recognize me? You must have hit your head harder than I thought."

"No, sorry," Atlas said. "It's just, I've never seen you like..." He sat across from Pakhet.

"Like I used to be," said Pakhet. "Well, here I am. As I once was. Before Apollo."

"You were a prisoner of Apollo?"

Pakhet smiled weakly. "Let's not speak of those things now. I did not ask to be restored, for my oath of vengeance is not fulfilled. Yet I am grateful." She sighed. "It's been so long since I saw the Galaxy without that cursed helmet—with both my natural eyes. The Cienciants have given me a gift." She pulled some of her hair back from over her ears, revealing a long, jagged scar that ran nearly the length of her head. "However, I am glad to be left a few scars. Some things I can't allow myself to forget."

"I assume someone explained to you the Celestial Sphere isn't what the legends claimed?" asked Atlas. "We can't use it to restore Thebes."

"Itri explained the nature of the Celestial Sphere to me, yes," said Pakhet. "But that doesn't mean we can't use it to restore Thebes." She spread her arms wide. "I've seen a civilization that possesses the technology to move planets into the same orbital path...and to shield their entire system from detection. Restoring Thebes should be trivial in comparison." She tapped her temple three times. "It will just take some time."

Atlas ate quietly for a few moments. "So, what's next for you, then?"

"I'm allowed to stay, if I want, on account of my special, Cienciant DNA," she said.

"Will you?"

"No. Although I am surprised to admit that part of me wishes to stay. Maybe someday I'll yield to the temptation and return to stay, but for now I have wrongs to right and questions to answer."

"Yeah. Listen...about what Styx said—"

"The Cienciants confirmed it," Pakhet sighed. "I never knew her, or knew that she existed, but yes, she was my half-sister." She looked down at the table and rubbed the inside of her left eye with one finger.

"How did she do what she did? I mean, can you—?"

"She had been genetically augmented," said Pakhet. "Her cloaking. Her method of assassination. Those are not Theban abilities, or technologies."

"I'm sorry you had to..." Atlas choked on his words. Brave Lanta. Oliver. Taco. Penny. Eugenio. Nerissa. Theo. Sitara. "*Thank you* for what you did. For what you *had* to do." He returned to his food, but wasn't hungry anymore. After playing with his meal for a minute, he stood up. "I'm going to get some sleep. We're leaving tomorrow, first thing."

ONLY CITLALI CAME to see them off.

"The others remain in mourning for Sitara," Citlali explained.

"I understand," said Atlas. They stood at the foot of *Gaia's* ramp. His friends were already aboard.

"I must ask you again to stay. We have many questions, and there are some who say the price we've paid is too high. If you would willingly submit to their interrogations, I am sure they can be convinced of your integrity."

"I'm sorry," said Atlas. "We've already been here too long." He forced a smile. "Thank you for your...um...*hospitality*." He offered Citlali a handshake.

Understanding the gesture, Citlali took his hand and smiled back. "Be patient."

"For what?"

"For the Manifestation."

"The what?"

"Sitara didn't tell you?"

"She didn't have the chance."

"Of course." Citlali steeled herself. "Then, I must explain." She was silent a moment. "The *Manifestation* is the moment the power of the Epignoscent reveals itself in you."

"It *reveals* itself? Does it give us special powers or something?" He laughed uneasily.

"We call them Amplitudes," said Citlali. "It takes what is in you and amplifies it."

Atlas nervously shifted his weight onto the ramp. "Well, I think the Epignoscent has already revealed enough. It healed us all—as it was breaking us, of course—but, we're good as new now, so no hard feelings. It brought Ajax back to life. I have no idea what it did to Phoebe, but she's alive and seems fine. That's all the manifestation I need in my life."

"It will come," Citlali said. "No one has ever survived even a tenth as much exposure to the Epignoscent as you children. It would be impossible to predict how the Manifestation might appear in you. The only thing we can be sure of is that it will be unique to each of you."

Atlas watched Citlali for a moment. *Why would you put us in this position? It's too much,* he thought. "You expect us to bring peace to the Galaxy—to *save* it," Atlas said, shaking his head. "We're just kids."

"Yes," said Citlali. She smiled.

"Perfect." Atlas walked up the ramp.

"Do not fear, Atlas," Citlali called. "It may be difficult, but do not fear the change that will come upon you."

Atlas tried to mask his irritation as he waved goodbye and sealed *Gaia's* hatch. He let out a long, deep sigh.

"Captain on the bridge," said Pallas.

The other Philadelphians snapped to attention as Atlas arrived. Everything looked different. The control stations, seating, and finish were all new. Cienciant upgrades, apparently.

"C'mon guys," Atlas said. "I told you not to do that. It's not funny."

Phoebe tittered. "I think it's funny."

Pakhet laughed from her seat in the corner.

"Sit down, everyone," Atlas said.

"Sir, yessir!" said Phoebe. She giggled again.

Atlas winced. "Tell me about these upgrades, Reedy."

"They're *incredible,*" Reedy beamed. She wore a plain white Cienciant robe. "I mean, at first I was a bit upset that all the vintage controls were gone, but come on! She's so much more capable now. We have full space and atmospheric flight capabilities as well as a far more efficient trans-light modulator."

"They upgraded our weapon systems as well," said Ajax. He wore a sky-blue robe. "Nothing destructive, of course. That's against their beliefs. But we can disable just about any ship I know about without causing loss of life. And the hull has been reinforced, so we should be able to withstand significantly greater firepower."

"Wow," said Atlas. "All that in less than a week?"

"They did it all *yesterday,*" said Reedy. "They couldn't get past my security protocol, so they had to wait for me to wake up." She grinned smugly. "Guess there are limits to their technology, after all."

"I hope you thanked Citlali for all of this."

"Of course I did," said Reedy. "When she explained *Gaia's* upgrades to me, I cried." She sniffled. "I couldn't help it. I was ecstatic."

"Don't forget about the navigation system," said Phoebe. "The new database has fifty times the stellar detail of our old one. That's better than anyone."

"Except the Cienciants," said Atlas.

"Well, yeah. Of course."

Atlas looked around the bridge at his team. *Gammas. Last place. Nothing but a bunch of failures. Five failures. Five like family.*

"Thank you all," he said. "Thank you for believing in me. But more importantly, thank you for believing in yourselves. Even after everything."

"Don't get sappy on us," said Pallas. She took her place at his side. Her red robe was the darkest of them all. "It will make it difficult for us to respect you, Captain."

"Too late for that, I'm afraid." Atlas sat in his chair. "As your captain, I order you to call me Atlas instead of Captain. That includes you, Pakhet."

"So, what do we do next, Atlas-Instead-of-Captain?" said Phoebe.

Atlas shook his head and sighed. "We decide what's next together."

"Then what are your suggestions?" Reedy asked.

"I'd like to hear your thoughts first."

"Homer," said Pallas. "We need to find and rescue Homer."

"And the other Betas," said Reedy.

"Agreed," said Atlas. "Ajax? Phoebe?"

"Absolutely," said Ajax.

"Of course," said Phoebe. "But I'd also like to pick up some new clothes. These Cienciant robes are not nearly as flattering as Theban clothing."

"Nor are they as practical," Pakhet added. "May I make a suggestion?"

"Of course," said Atlas.

"You will need weapons and additional warriors if you are to free your friends. My crew and I can provide you with both. We can also supply you with multiple sets of clothing, if you wish."

"Yes," said Phoebe. She held up a fold of her yellow robe between her pinched fingers and scowled. "Yes, please."

"Theban clothing is designed to last a lifetime, but you Philadelphians treat them very harshly," Pakhet teased.

"Then it's settled," Atlas said. He thought for a moment. "But first, before we regroup and go after Homer and the Betas, there's a quick stop I'd like to make, if you all don't mind."

"Anything," said Pallas.

"Sure," said Reedy.

"Fine with me," said Phoebe.

"Yep," said Ajax.

CHAPTER 33

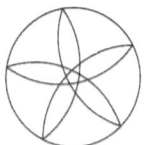

PETE STERLING WALKED from room to room, checking all the window and door locks before bed. It had been ten months since his son, Atlas, had been kidnapped and since that day, Pete couldn't feel comfortable lying in bed unless he had checked every lock in the house at least three times. It didn't help him fall asleep any faster, but at least it kept him from tossing and turning.

Mena Morandi-Sterling stood in the living room, watching out the front window and counting backwards from one hundred by threes, as she did every night while Pete performed his evening ritual. She stared out onto the front lawn and thought about years ago, when Atlas and Maggie would play outside for hours at a time, unsupervised. Nothing ever happened. She was a terrible mother. Nothing ever happened, but she had allowed that to lull her into feeling secure. *You are a terrible mother.* And now, Atlas was gone.

"Mena?" Pete said. "I'm done."

"I'm coming," Mena said. "I'll be right there." She waited until she heard Pete leave, then she wiped the tears from her eyes. *Ten months. Might as well be ten thousand years.*

The detective had said aliens kidnapped Atlas, but when he'd brought them to the station to look at the surveillance video from the Luna family home—their daughter had also disappeared—he couldn't find the footage showing the spaceship. When they asked the Luna family if they could review the original footage, there was no evidence at all of a spacecraft or aliens.

Something strange was unquestionably going on, but Mena had a hard time believing Atlas had been kidnapped by aliens. *How absurd!* Mena clenched her teeth when she thought about that imbecile detective and his obnoxious theories.

She and Pete had filed a very strongly worded complaint. When they delivered it to the station, they were told that the detective no longer worked with the department. *Why did they say 'with' and not 'for?' Shouldn't they have said he no longer worked for the department?* They had likely misspoken. Or she had misheard. Did it matter?

Atlas was still gone. What had happened to him? And to the other fourteen kids with the same birthday? They couldn't have all run away. Atlas would never do that. He was happy. *We were happy. Not perfect. But we loved one another. We love one another.*

"Hi, Mom!"

Mena shook her head. Now she was hearing his voice. *One hundred…ninety-seven…ninety-four…*

"Mom!"

Mena whirled around to face the archway that led to the kitchen. Only seconds before, her husband had been there. But now, it sounded like…and looked like…

"Atlas?"

Atlas ran to his mother and gave her a hug. Mena collapsed into him, sobbing uncontrollably.

"Did you say something, hun?" asked Pete, peeking into the room. "Atlas?"

In less than a second he had joined in the embrace.

"Where have you been?" asked Mena. She wiped her eyes and held Atlas's face. *He's real! But bigger! A lot bigger. Why is he wearing a strange bathrobe?*

"You won't believe me," said Atlas.

"Please don't tell us you were in outer space," said Pete. His insides were bursting with joy and relief. He couldn't remember feeling that joyous since the first time he had held Atlas as a baby. Despite the moment, Pete felt a tinge of shame. Atlas's birth was a miracle, and now his return to them was a miracle. *Why didn't I treat all the days in between as miracles as well?*

"I wasn't in outer space," said Atlas. "Well, at least not for most of the time I was gone. Interstellar travel doesn't work like that anymore."

"What?" said Pete.

"I don't understand. Where were you?" asked Mena.

"On several different planets," said Atlas. "I was in a special school on the planet Titan for most of the time, but I also spent two months on Olympus working in a mine. And I spent a little less than a week in a hidden planetary system called Ciencia, though I was uncons—ah…I was *sleeping* for most of that."

"This is not the time for jokes," said Mena.

"I'm not joking, Mom. And I'm not lying." He wriggled out of his parents' embrace. "I'll show you."

Atlas led his parents to the back of the house. It looked exactly the same as he remembered it. Had it really only been ten months? It seemed so much longer. To him, of course, it had been just more than eight months, but since the days on Titan and Olympus lasted between twenty-eight and twenty-nine Earth hours, that worked out to approximately ten Earth months.

"Where are you taking us?" asked Mena.

"To the back window. There's something I want to show you."

"I was looking at the backyard not five minutes ago," Pete said. "There's nothing there."

"There is now." Atlas pulled back the curtain and revealed a small spaceship that only barely fit within the backyard fence.

Mena shrieked.

"There's a spaceship in my backyard," said Pete. Just beyond the spaceship stood the treehouse where Atlas used to spend summer evenings studying the stars through his telescope.

"It was a spaceship, years ago. Now, it's primarily a trans-light craft," said Atlas. "Like I said, interstellar travel doesn't work like that anymore. Mom and Dad, meet *Gaia*."

"*Gaia*?" Pete asked.

"Reedy named her. I wasn't sold on it at first, but it's grown on me."

"Who's Reedy?" asked Mena.

"Arete Nejem," said Atlas. "She goes by Reedy. Her mom's law office is downtown."

"The Nejem girl was with you?" said Pete. "What about the rest? Were all the missing kids with you?"

Atlas was quiet for a moment. He spoke slowly and grimly. "No. Well, for a while we were all together. At the Titan Academy. Now there's just five of us together. Reedy, Phoebe Luna, Ajax Samson, Pallas Zenith, and me. Actually, that's what I came here to talk to you about."

"You came here to talk?" asked Pete. He didn't like Atlas's choice of words. "Why not come here because it's your home?"

"It *is* my home," said Atlas. "And I can't wait until I get to finally sleep in my own bed again. But right now, it's not possible."

"Why not?" asked Mena.

"There are people that need me. I can't abandon them."

"Your *family* needs you," said Pete. "I will bite you, if I have to."

"I know," said Atlas. It broke his heart to see his parents so happy one moment, and then so desperately sad the next. "But right now, there are people who need me more. They need the five of us."

"You're just children," said Mena.

"So are they," said Atlas. "And my friends and I are the only ones that can do this."

"What, exactly, can *you* do that others couldn't just as easily?" asked Pete.

"Well, I'm not sure yet," said Atlas. "I was told it might be some time before I manifest."

"What does that mean?"

"It would take too long to explain right now," said Atlas. He fidgeted uncomfortably.

"The ones that need you...they're the other kidnapped children?" asked Mena.

"Some of them. And a few others we met along the way," said Atlas. "They helped us, and now it's time for us to help them."

"They're in trouble?"

"Yes."

"And you're going to bring them home to their families?" Mena asked.

"If we can, yes," said Atlas.

"Will it be dangerous?" asked Mena. "Never mind, I don't want to know."

"We'll be as careful as we can," said Atlas.

"And the Nejem girl? You can count on her? And the other three?" asked Pete.

"I trust them with my life," smiled Atlas. "And they trust me with theirs."

"Then go," said Mena. "Go bring those children back to their mothers."

Atlas nodded. He stared at his mother for a moment, then dropped his eyes and sighed. "Thank you, for understanding." He slapped the sides of his thighs. "Well, I better get going. I have to go pick up the rest of my crew."

"Wait..." said Pete. "You know how to fly that?"

"I do alright. Reedy's the best pilot, actually. But I'm kind of in charge."

"Cool," said Pete. He smiled through his tears and gave Atlas a hug, then kissed the top of his head. "I love you, son. And I don't want you to leave. But I trust you. If people need your help, go help them." He grimaced, then composed himself and placed his hands on Atlas's shoulders. "I'm proud of you."

Mena couldn't get any words out, so she nodded and stifled the hole being ripped in her soul.

"And I love you two." Atlas wrapped his arms around his mother and closed his eyes to help him remember the moment. He kissed her on the cheek and stepped back. "Tell Maggie I love her too."

"Of course," said Pete.

Atlas waved goodbye and smiled, then stepped out the back-door and onto the back deck. *One hundred. Ninety-seven. Ninety-four. Ninety-one. Eighty-eight. Eighty-five. Eighty-two.* After another few seconds, he was looking up at his parents from Gaia's primary port. He waved again and sealed the hatch.

Thirty seconds later, there was an extremely bright flash of light, and the spaceship was gone. The tree with the treehouse rocked softly, though the neighbors' trees were still.

Mena grabbed Pete's arm and squeezed harshly. "Merry Christmas."

"Merry Christmas," said Pete.

AUTHOR'S NOTE

This book arose from a moment of personal despair wrought by a stinging sense of failure.

After the birth of my oldest, I had decided to leave my job teaching high school Spanish for a new role in the private sector. The transition involved a nearly 50% raise. It also meant I was proving to myself that a liberal arts student had more job avenues available than (just) teaching.

Two weeks into the new job, nearly 80% of the company was laid off, including me. I spent the next several months looking for a new position without success. I'd stepped out of my comfort zone and fallen on my face.

Six months later, while changing a diaper, a song played on the stereo. The song was titled after the son of the composer. I looked at my son, tears forming in my eyes, and said, "I wish I could make something like that for you."

Immediately, a thought came to my head: "You can. That's what you went to school for."

That evening, after my family went to bed, I wrote the first chapter of this book. I thought about it, and decided to keep writing.

I wrote this for my son. Now I have two. This book is for them, but I hope others also enjoy it.

ACKNOWLEDGMENTS

I am eternally indebted to my wife, Kate, for always believing in me and especially for her honest critiques. Likewise, I am grateful for the candid and thoughtful feedback supplied by my sister, Natalie. My supremely talented brother, Eric, shot the photo on the next page.

The examples of love and support set by both my parents and in-laws established a high standard that I aspire to meet for my own children.

An equal measure of thanks to all those I've ever loved or hung out with, learned from or taught, argued or cried with, competed against or trained alongside, enjoyed their music or studied their books, and with whom I've shared a laugh or meal.

Most especially, I am grateful for the experiences I've had as a stay-at-home/work-from-home dad for Atlas and Ajax. No one makes me want to leave the world a better place more than you two.

ABOUT THE AUTHOR

 Over the years, D. B. Greenhalgh has pursued qualifications in Literature (BA), Creative Writing (MFA), Partnership (BFF, Mr.), Fatherhood (HRO), Drumming (ROQ), and Fitness (CF-L1, WL, Gym), all of which he accomplished with varying degrees of aptitude.

Prior to his children's birth, he taught Spanish, English, Creative Writing, Music, and Technology classes at the Arkansas Arts Academy for eight years.

He lives in Florida with his wife, two sons, and two dogs where they enjoy working out in the garage, reading in the library, playing drums, and building LEGO.

dbgreenhalgh.com

facebook.com/dbgreenhalgh

twitter.com/dbgreenhalgh

instagram.com/dbgreenhalgh